LINDA LAEL MILLER

THE McKETTRICK LEGEND

HQN™

ISBN-13: 978-0-373-77623-8

THE MCKETTRICK LEGEND

Copyright © 2010 by Harlequin Books S.A.

The publisher acknowledges the copyright holder of the individual works as follows:

SIERRA'S HOMECOMING
Copyright © 2006 by Linda Lael Miller

THE MCKETTRICK WAY
Copyright © 2007 by Linda Lael Miller

Recycling programs for this product may not exist in your area.

This is a work of fiction. Names, characters, places and incidents are either the product of the author's imagination or are used fictitiously, and any resemblance to actual persons, living or dead, business establishments, events or locales is entirely coincidental.

This edition published by arrangement with Harlequin Books S.A.

For questions and comments about the quality of this book please contact us at Customer_eCare@Harlequin.ca.

® and TM are trademarks of the publisher. Trademarks indicated with ® are registered in the United States Patent and Trademark Office, the Canadian Trade Marks Office and in other countries.

www.HQNBooks.com

Printed in U.S.A.

CONTENTS

SIERRA'S HOMECOMING

To Little Angels Everywhere

CHAPTER ONE

Present Day

"STAY IN THE CAR," Sierra McKettrick told her seven-year-old son, Liam.

He fixed her with an owlish gaze, peering through the lenses of his horn-rimmed glasses. "I want to see the graves, too," he told her, and put a mittened hand to the passenger-side door handle to make his point.

"Another time," she answered firmly. Part of her knew it was irrational to think a visit to the cemetery could provoke an asthma attack, but when it came to Liam's health, she was taking no chances.

A brief stare-down ensued, and Sierra prevailed, but barely.

"It's not fair," Liam said, yet he sounded resigned. He didn't normally give up so easily, but they'd just driven almost nonstop all the way from Florida to northern Arizona, and he was tired.

"Welcome to the real world," Sierra replied. She set the emergency brake, left the engine running with the heat on High, and got out of the ancient station wagon she'd bought on credit years before.

Standing ankle-deep in a patch of ragged snow, she took in her surroundings. Ordinary people were buried in churchyards and public cemeteries when they died, she reflected, feeling peevish. The McKettricks were a law unto themselves, living *or* dead. They weren't content with a mere plot, like other families. Oh, no. They had to have a place all their own, with a view.

And what a view it was.

Shoving her hands into the pockets of her cloth coat, which was nearly as decrepit as her car, Sierra turned to survey the Triple M Ranch, sprawling in every direction, well beyond the range of her vision. Red mesas and buttes, draped in a fine lacing of snow. Copses of majestic white oaks, growing at intervals along a wide and shining stream. Expanses of pastureland, and even the occasional cactus, a stranger to the high country, a misplaced wayfarer, there by mistake.

Like her.

A flash of resentment rose suddenly within Sierra, and a moment or two passed before she recognized the emotion for what it was: not her own opinion, but that of her late father, Hank Breslin.

When it came to the McKettricks, Sierra *had* no opinions that she could honestly claim, because she didn't know these people, except by reputation.

She'd taken their name for one reason and one reason only—because that was part of the deal. Liam needed health care, and she couldn't provide it. Eve McKettrick—Sierra's biological mother—had set up a medical trust fund for her grandson, but there were strings attached.

With the McKettricks, she heard her father say, as surely as if he were standing there beside her, *there are always strings attached.*

"Be quiet," Sierra said, out loud. She was grateful for Eve's help, and if she had to take the McKettrick name and live on the Triple M Ranch for a year to meet the conditions, so be it. It wasn't as if she had anyplace better to go.

Resolutely she approached the cemetery entrance, walked under the ornate metal archway forming the word "McKettrick" in graceful cursive.

A life-size bronze statue of a man on horseback, broad-shouldered and imposing, with a bandanna at his throat and a six-gun riding on his hip, took center stage.

Angus McKettrick, the patriarch. The founder of the Triple M, and the dynasty. Sierra knew little about him, but as she looked up into that hard, determined face, shaped by the rigors of life in the nineteenth century, she felt a kinship.

Ruthless old bastard, said the voice of Hank Breslin. *That's where McKettricks get their arrogance. From him.*

"Be quiet," Sierra repeated, thrusting her hands deeper into her coat pockets. She stood in silence for a long moment, listening to the rattle-throated hum of the station wagon's engine, the lonely cry of a nearby bird, the thrum of blood in her ears. A piney scent spiced the air.

Sierra turned, saw the marble angels marking the graves of Angus McKettrick's wives—Georgia, mother of Rafe, Kade and Jeb. Concepcion, mother of Kate.

Look for Holt and Lorelei, Eve had told her, the last time they'd spoken over the telephone. *That's our part of the family.*

Sierra caught sight of other bronze statues, smaller than Angus's but no less impressive in their detail. They were works of art, museum pieces, and if they hadn't been solidly anchored in cement, they probably would have been stolen. It said something about the McKettrick legend, she supposed, that there had been no vandalism in this lonely, wind-blown place.

Jeb McKettrick, the youngest of the brothers, was represented by a cowboy with his six-gun drawn; his wife,

Chloe, by a slender woman in pioneer dress, shading her eyes with one hand and smiling. Their children, grandchildren, great- and a few great-great-grandchildren surrounded them, their costly headstones laid out in neat rows, like the streets of a western town.

Next was Kade McKettrick, easy in his skin, wearing a six-shooter, like his brother, but with an open book in his hand. His wife, Mandy, wore trousers, a loose-fitting shirt, boots and a hat, and held a shotgun. Like Chloe, she was smiling. Judging by the number of other graves around theirs, these two had also been prolific parents.

The statue of Rafe McKettrick revealed a big, powerfully built man with a stubborn set to his jaw. His bride, Emmeline, stood close against his side; their arms were linked and she rested her head against the outside of his upper arm.

Sierra smiled. Again, their progeny was plentiful.

The last statue brought up an unexpected surge of emotion in Sierra. Here, then, was Holt, half brother to Rafe, Kade and Jeb, and to Kate. In his long trail coat, he looked both handsome and tough. A pair of very detailed ammunition belts criss-crossed his chest, and the badge pinned to his wide lapel read Texas Ranger.

Sierra stared into those bronze eyes and, once again, felt something stir deep inside her. I came from this man, she thought. We've got the same DNA.

Liam gave a jarring blast of the car horn, impatient to get to the ranch house that would be their home for the next twelve months.

Sierra waved in acknowledgment but moved on to the statue of Lorelei. She was mounted on a mule, long, lace-trimmed skirts spilling on either side of her impossibly small waist, face shadowed, not by a sunbonnet but by a man's hat. Her spirited gaze rested lovingly on her husband, Holt.

Liam laid on the horn.

Fearing he might decide to take the wheel and drive to the ranch house on his own, Sierra turned reluctantly from the markers and followed a path littered with pine needles and the dead leaves of the six towering white oaks that shared the space, heading back to the car.

Back to her son.

"Are all the McKettricks *dead?*" Liam asked, when Sierra settled into the driver's seat and fastened the belt.

"No," Sierra answered, waiting for some stray part of herself to finish meandering among those graves, making the acquaintance of ancestors, and catch up. "*We're* McKettricks, and we're not dead. Neither is your grandmother, or Meg." She knew there were cousins, too, descended from Rafe, Kade and Jeb, but it was too big a subject to explain to a seven-year-old boy. Besides, she was still trying to square them all away in her own mind.

"I thought my name was Liam *Breslin,*" the little boy said practically.

It should have been Liam Douglas, Sierra thought, remembering her first and only lover. As always, when Liam's father, Adam, came to mind, she felt a pang, a complicated mixture of passion, sorrow and helpless fury. She and Adam had never been married, so she'd given Liam her maiden name.

"We're McKettricks now," Sierra said with a sigh. "You'll understand when you're older."

She backed the car out carefully, keenly aware of the steep descent on all sides, and made the wide turn that would take them back on to the network of dirt roads bisecting the Triple M.

"I can understand *now,*" Liam asserted, having duly

pondered the matter in his solemn way. "After all, I'm *gifted*."

"You may be gifted," Sierra replied, concentrating on her driving, "but you're still seven."

"Do I get to be a cowboy and ride bucking broncs and stuff like that?"

Sierra suppressed a shudder. "No," she said.

"That bites," Liam answered, folding his arms and settling deeper into the heavy nylon coat she'd bought him on the road, when they'd reached the first of the cold-weather states. "What's the good of living on a ranch if you can't be a cowboy?"

CHAPTER TWO

THE ELDERLY STATION WAGON banged into the yard, bald tires crunching half-thawed gravel, and came to an obstreperous stop. Travis Reid paused behind the horse trailer hitched to Jesse McKettrick's mud-splattered black truck, pushed his hat to the back of his head with one leather-gloved finger and grinned, waiting for something to fall off the rig. Nothing did, which just went to prove that the age of miracles was not past.

Jesse appeared at the back of the trailer, leading old Baldy by his halter rope. "Who's that?" he asked, squinting in the wintry late afternoon sunshine.

Travis spared him no more than a glance. "A long-lost relative of yours, unless I miss my guess," he said easily.

The station wagon belched some smoke and died. Travis figured it for a permanent condition. He looked on with interest as a good-looking woman climbed out from behind the wheel, looked the old car over, and gave the driver's-side door a good kick with her right foot.

She was a McKettrick, all right. Of the female persuasion, too.

Jesse left Baldy standing to jump down from the bed of the trailer and lower the ramp to the ground. "Meg's half sister?" he asked. "The one who grew up in Mexico with her crazy, drunken father?"

"Reckon so," Travis said. He and Meg communicated regularly, most often by email, and she'd filled him in on

Sierra as far as she could. Nobody in the family knew her very well, including her mother, Eve, so the information was sparse. She had a seven-year-old son—now getting out of the car—and she'd been serving cocktails in Florida for the last few years, and that was about all Travis knew about her. As Meg's caretaker and resident horse trainer, not to mention her friend, Travis had stocked the cupboards and refrigerator, made sure the temperamental furnace was working and none of the plumbing had frozen, and started up Meg's Blazer every day, just to make sure it was running.

From the looks of that station wagon, it was a good thing he'd followed the boss-lady's orders.

"You gonna help me with this horse," Jesse asked testily, "or just stand there gawking?"

Travis chuckled. "Right now," he said, "I'm all for gawking."

Sierra McKettrick was tall and slender, with short, gleaming brown hair the color of a good chestnut horse. Her eyes were huge and probably blue, though she was still a stride or two too far away for him to tell.

Jesse swore and stomped back up the ramp, making plenty of noise as he did so. Like most of the McKettricks, Jesse was used to getting his way, and while he was a known womanizer, he'd evidently dismissed Sierra out of hand. After all, she was a blood relative—no sense driving his herd into *that* canyon.

Travis took a step toward the woman and the boy, who was staring at him with his mouth open.

"Is this Meg's house?" Sierra asked.

"Yes," Travis said, putting out his hand, pulling it back to remove his work gloves, and offering it again. "Travis Reid," he told her.

"Sierra Bres—McKettrick," she replied. Her grip was

firm. And her eyes were definitely blue. The kind of blue that pierces something in a man's middle. She smiled, but tentatively. Somewhere along the line, she'd learned to be sparing with her smiles. "This is my son, Liam."

"Howdy," Liam said, squaring his small shoulders.

Travis grinned. "Howdy," he replied. Meg had said the boy had health problems, but he looked pretty sound to Travis.

"That sure is an ugly horse," Liam announced, pointing towards the trailer.

Travis turned. Baldy stood spraddle-footed, midway down the ramp, a miserable gray specimen of a critter with pink eyes and liver-colored splotches all over his mangy hide.

"Sure is," Travis agreed, and glowered at Jesse for palming the animal off on him. It was like him to pull off a dramatic last-minute rescue, then leave the functional aspects of the problem to somebody else.

Jesse flashed a grin, and for a moment, Travis felt territorial, wanted to set himself between Sierra and her boy, the pair of them, and one of his oldest friends. He felt off balance, somehow, as though he'd been ambushed. What the hell was *that* all about?

"Is that a buckin' bronc?" Liam asked, venturing a step toward Baldy.

Sierra reached out quickly, caught hold of the fur-trimmed hood on the kid's coat and yanked him back. Cold sunlight glinted off the kid's glasses, making his eyes invisible.

Jesse laughed. "Back in the day," he said, "Baldy was a rodeo horse. Cowboys quivered in their boots when they drew him to ride. Now, as you can see, he's a little past his prime."

"And you would be—?" Sierra asked, with a touch of

coolness to her tone. Maybe she was the one woman out of a thousand who could see Jesse McKettrick for what he was—a good-natured case of very bad news.

"Your cousin Jesse."

Sierra sized him up, took in his battered jeans, work shirt, sheepskin coat and very expensive boots. "Descended from…?"

The McKettricks talked like that. Every one of them could trace their lineage back to old Angus, by a variety of paths, and while there would be hell to pay if anybody riled them as a bunch, they mostly kept to their own branch of the family tree.

"Jeb," Jesse said.

Sierra nodded.

Liam's attention remained fixed on the horse. "Can I ride him?"

"Sure," Jesse replied.

"No way," said Sierra, at exactly the same moment.

Travis felt sorry for the kid, and it must have shown in his face, because Sierra's gaze narrowed on him.

"We've had a long trip," she said. "I guess we'll just go inside."

"Make yourselves at home," Travis said, gesturing toward the house. "Don't worry about your bags. Jesse and I'll carry them in for you."

She considered, probably wondering if she'd be obligated in any way if she agreed, then nodded. Catching Liam by the hood of his coat again, she got him turned from the horse and hustled him toward the front door.

"Too bad we're kin," Jesse said, following Sierra with his eyes.

"Too bad," Travis agreed mildly, though privately he didn't believe it was such a bad thing at all.

* * *

The house was a long, sprawling structure, with two stories and a wraparound porch. Sierra's most immediate impression was of substance and practicality, rather than elegance, and she felt a subtle interior shift, as if she'd been a long time lost in a strange, winding street, thick with fog, and suddenly found herself standing at her own front door.

"Those guys are *real cowboys*," Liam said, once they were inside.

Sierra nodded distractedly, taking in the pegged wood floors, gleaming with the patina of venerable age, the double doors and steep staircase on the right, the high ceilings, the antique grandfather clock ticking ponderously beside the door. She peeked into a spacious living room, probably called a parlor when the house was new, and admired the enormous natural-rock fireplace, with its raised hearth and wood-nook. Worn but colorful rugs gave some relief to the otherwise uncompromisingly masculine decor of leather couches and chairs and tables of rough-hewn pine, as did the piano set in an alcove of floor-to-ceiling windows.

An odd nostalgia overtook Sierra; she'd never set foot on the Triple M before that day, let alone entered the home of Holt and Lorelei McKettrick, but she might have, if her dad hadn't snatched her the day Eve filed for divorce, and carried her off to San Miguel de Allende to share his expatriate lifestyle. She might have spent summers here, as Meg had, picking blackberries, wading in mountain streams, riding horses. Instead, she'd run barefoot through the streets of San Miguel, with no more memory of her mother than a faint scent of expensive perfume, sometimes encountered among the waves of tourists who frequented the markets, shops and restaurants of her home town.

Liam tugged at the sleeve of her coat. "Mom?"

She snapped out of her reverie, looked down at him, and smiled. "You hungry, bud?"

Liam nodded solemnly, but brightened when the door bumped open and Travis came in, lugging two suitcases.

Travis cleared his throat, as though embarrassed. "Plenty of grub in the kitchen," he said. "Shall I put this stuff upstairs?"

"Yes," Sierra said. "Thanks." At least that way she'd know which rooms were hers and Liam's without having to ask. She might have been concerned, sharing the place with Travis, but Meg had told her he lived in a trailer out by the barn. What Meg hadn't mentioned was that her resident caretaker was in his early thirties, not his sixties, as Sierra had imagined, and too attractive for comfort, with his lean frame, blue-green eyes and dark-blond hair in need of a trim.

She blushed as these thoughts filled her mind, and shuffled Liam quickly toward the kitchen.

It was a large room, with the same plank floors she'd seen in the front of the house and modern appliances, strangely juxtaposed with the black, chrome-trimmed wood cookstove occupying the far-left-hand corner. The table was long and rustic, with benches on either side and a chair at each end.

"Tables like that are a tradition with the McKettricks," a male voice said from just behind her.

Sierra jumped, startled, and turned to see Jesse in the doorway.

"Sorry," he said. He was handsome, Sierra thought. His coloring was similar to Travis's, and so was his build, and yet the two men didn't resemble each other at all.

"No problem," Sierra said.

Liam wrenched open the refrigerator. "Bologna!" he yelled triumphantly.

"Whoopee," Sierra replied, with a dryness that was lost on her son. "If there's bologna, there must be white bread, too."

"Jesse!" Travis's voice, from the direction of the front door. "Get out here and give me a hand!"

Jesse grinned, nodded affably to Sierra and vanished.

Sierra took off her coat, hung it from a peg next to the back door, and gestured for Liam to remove his, too. He complied, then went straight back to the bologna. He found a loaf of bread in a colorful polka-dot bag and started to build a sandwich.

Watching him, Sierra felt a faint brush of sorrow against the back of her heart. Liam was good at doing things on his own; he'd had a lot of practice, with her working the night shift at the club and sleeping days. Old Mrs. Davis from the apartment across the hall had been a conscientious babysitter, but hardly a mother figure.

She put coffee on to brew, once Liam was settled on a bench at the table. He'd chosen the side against the wall, so he could watch her moving about the kitchen.

"Cool place," he observed, between bites, "but it's haunted."

Sierra took a can of soup from a shelf, opened it and dumped the contents into a saucepan, placing it on the modern gas stove before answering. Liam was an imaginative child, often saying surprising things. Rather than responding instantly, Sierra usually tried to let a couple of beats pass before she answered.

"What makes you say that?"

"Don't know," Liam said, chewing. They'd had a drive-through breakfast, but that had been hours ago, and he was obviously starving.

Another jab of guilt struck Sierra, keener than the one before. "Come on," she prodded. "You must have had a reason." Of course he'd had a reason, she thought. They'd just been to a graveyard, so it was natural that death would be on his mind. She should have waited, made the pilgrimage on her own, instead of dragging Liam along.

Liam looked thoughtful. "The air sort of…buzzes," he said. "Can I make another sandwich?"

"Only if you promise to have some of this soup first."

"Deal," Liam said.

An old china cabinet stood against a far wall, near the cookstove, and Sierra approached it, even though she didn't intend to use any of the dishes inside. Priceless antiques, every one.

Her family had eaten off those dishes. Generations of them.

Her gaze caught on a teapot, sturdy looking and, at the same time, exquisite. Spellbound, she opened the glass doors of the cabinet and reached inside to touch the piece, ever so lightly, with just the tips of her fingers.

"Soup's boiling over," Liam said mildly.

Sierra gasped, turned on her heel and rushed back to the modern stove to push the saucepan off the flame.

"Mom," Liam interjected.

"What?"

"Chill out. It's only soup."

The inside door swung open, and Travis stuck his head in. "Stuff's upstairs," he said. "Anything else you need?"

Sierra stared at him for a long moment, as though he'd spoken in an alien language. "Uh, no," she said finally. "Thanks." Pause. "Would you like some lunch?"

"No, thanks," he said. "Gotta see to that damn horse."

With that, he ducked out again.

"How come I can't ride the horse?" Liam asked.

Sierra sighed, setting a bowl of soup in front of him. "Because you don't know how."

Liam's sigh echoed her own, and if they'd been talking about anything but the endangerment of life and limb, it would have been funny.

"How am I supposed to *learn* how if you won't let me try? You're being overprotective. You could scar my psyche. I might develop psychological problems."

"There are times," Sierra confessed, sitting down across from him with her own bowl of soup, "when I wish you weren't quite so smart."

Liam waggled his eyebrows at her. "I got it from you."

"Not," Sierra said. Liam had her eyes, her thick, fine hair, and her dogged persistence, but his remarkable IQ came from his father.

Don't think about Adam, she told herself.

Travis Reid sidled into her mind.

Even worse.

Liam consumed his soup, along with a second sandwich, and went off to explore the rest of the house while Sierra lingered thoughtfully over her coffee.

The telephone rang.

Sierra got up to fetch the cordless receiver and pressed Talk with her thumb. "Hello?"

"You're there!" Meg trilled.

Sierra noticed that she'd left the china cabinet doors open and went in that direction, intending to close them. "Yes," she said. Meg had been kind to her, in a long-distance sort of way, but Sierra had only been two when she'd last seen her half sister, and that made them strangers.

"How do you like it? The ranch house, I mean?"

"I haven't seen much of it," Sierra answered. "Liam and I just got here, and then we had lunch…." Her hand went, of its own accord, to the teapot, and she imagined she felt just the faintest charge when she touched it. "Lots of antiques around here," she said, thinking aloud.

"Don't be afraid to use them," Meg replied. "Family tradition."

Sierra withdrew her hand from the teapot, shut the doors. "Family tradition?"

"McKettrick rules," Meg said, with a smile in her voice. "Things are meant to be used, no matter how old they are."

Sierra frowned, uneasy. "But if they get broken—"

"They get broken," Meg finished for her. "Have you met Travis yet?"

"Yes," Sierra said. "And he's not at all what I expected."

Meg laughed. "What did you expect?"

"Some gimpy old guy, I guess," Sierra admitted, warming to the friendliness in her sister's voice. "You said he took care of the place and lived in a trailer by the barn, so I thought—" She broke off, feeling foolish.

"He's cute and he's single," Meg said.

"Even the teapot?" Sierra mused.

"Huh?"

Sierra put a hand to her forehead. Sighed. "Sorry. I guess I missed a segue there. There's a teapot in the china cabinet in the kitchen—I was just wondering if I could—"

"I know the one," Meg answered, with a soft fondness in her voice. "It was Lorelei's. She got it for a wedding present."

Lorelei. The matriarch of the family. Sierra took a step backward.

"*Use* it," Meg said, as if she'd seen Sierra's reflexive retreat.

Sierra shook her head. "I couldn't. I had no idea it was that old. If I dropped it—"

"Sierra," Meg said, "it's not china. It's cast iron, with an enamel overlay."

"Oh."

"Kind of like the McKettrick women, Mom always says."
Meg went on. "Smooth on the outside, tough as iron on the
inside."

Mom. Sierra closed her eyes against all the conflicting
emotions the word brought up in her, but it didn't help.

"We'll give you time to settle in," Meg said gently,
when Sierra was too choked up to speak. "Then Mom and
I will probably pop in for a visit. If that's okay with you,
of course."

Both Meg and Eve lived in San Antonio, Texas, where
they helped run McKettrickCo, a multinational corporation
with interests in everything from software to communication satellites, so they wouldn't be "popping in" without a
little notice.

Sierra swallowed hard. "It's your house," she said.

"And yours," Meg pointed out, very quietly.

After that, Meg made Sierra promise to call if she needed
anything. They said goodbye, and the call ended.

Sierra went back to the china cabinet for the teapot.

Liam clattered down the back stairs. "I *told* you this
place was haunted!" he crowed, his small face shining with
delight.

The teapot was heavy—definitely cast iron—but Sierra
was careful as she set it on the counter, just the same. "What
on earth are you talking about?"

"I just saw a kid," Liam announced. "Upstairs, in my
room!"

"You're imagining things."

Liam shook his head. "I *saw* him!"

Sierra approached her son, laid her hand to his forehead.
"No fever," she mused, worried.

"Mom," Liam protested, pulling back. "I'm not sick—
and I'm not delusional, either."

Delusional. How many seven-year-olds used that word? Sierra sighed and cupped Liam's eager face in both hands. "Listen. It's fine to have imaginary friends, but—"

"He's *not* imaginary."

"Okay," Sierra responded, with another sigh. It was possible, she supposed, that a neighbor child had wandered in before they arrived, but that seemed unlikely, given that the only other houses on the ranch were miles away. "Let's investigate."

Together they climbed the back stairs, and Sierra got her first look at the upper story. The corridor was wide, with the same serviceable board floors. The light fixtures, though old-fashioned, were electric, but most of the light came from the large arched window at the far end of the hallway. Six doors stood open, an indication that Liam had visited each room in turn after leaving the kitchen the first time.

He led her into the middle one, on the left side.

No one was there.

Sierra let out her breath, admiring the room. It was spacious, perfect quarters for a boy. Two bay windows overlooked the barn area, where Baldy, the singularly unattractive horse, stood stalwartly in the middle of the corral, looking as though he intended to break loose at any second and do some serious bucking. Travis was beside Baldy, stroking the animal's neck as he eased the halter off over its head.

A quivery sensation tickled the pit of Sierra's stomach.

"*Mom,*" Liam said. "He was here. He had on short pants and funny shoes and suspenders."

Sierra turned to look at her son, feeling fretful again. Liam stood near the other window, examining an antique telescope, balanced atop a shining brass tripod. "I believe you," she said.

"You don't," Liam argued, jutting out his chin. "You're *humoring* me."

Sierra sat down on the side of the bed positioned between the windows. Like the dressers, it was scarred with age, but made of sturdy wood. The headboard was simply but intricately carved, and a faded quilt provided color. "Maybe I am, a little," she admitted, because there was no fooling Liam. He had an uncanny knack for seeing through anything but the stark truth. "I don't know what to think, that's all."

"Don't you believe in ghosts?"

I don't believe in much of anything, Sierra thought sadly. "I believe in you," she said, patting the mattress beside her. "Come and sit down."

Reluctantly, he sat. Stiffened when she slipped an arm around his shoulders. "If you think I'm going to take a nap," he said, "you're dead wrong."

The word *dead* tiptoed up Sierra's spine to dance lightly at her nape. "Everything's going to be all right, you know," she said gently.

"I like this room," Liam confided, and the hopeful uncertainty in his manner made Sierra's heart ache. They'd always lived in apartments or cheap motel rooms. Had Liam been secretly yearning to call a house like this one home? To settle down somewhere and live like a normal kid?

"Me, too," Sierra said. "It has friendly vibes."

"Is that supposed to be like a closet?" Liam asked, indicating the huge pine armoire taking up most of one wall.

Sierra nodded. "It's called a wardrobe."

"Maybe it's like the one in that story. Maybe the back of it opens into another world. There could be a lion and a witch in there." From the smile on Liam's face, the concept intrigued rather than troubled him.

She ruffled his hair. "Maybe," she agreed.

His attention shifted back to the telescope. "I wish I could look through that and see Andromeda," he said. "Did you know that the whole galaxy is on a collision course with the Milky Way? All hell's going to break loose when it gets here, too."

Sierra shuddered at the thought. Most parents worried that their kids played too many video games. With Liam, the concern was the Discovery and Science Channels, not to mention programs like *Nova*. He thought about things like Earth losing its magnetic field and had nightmares about creatures swimming in dark oceans under the ice covering one of Jupiter's moons. Or was it Saturn?

"Don't get excited, Mom," he said, with an understanding smile. "It's going to be something like five billion years before it happens."

"Before what happens?" Sierra asked, blinking.

"The *collision*," he said tolerantly.

"Right," Sierra said.

Liam yawned. "Maybe I *will* take a nap." He studied her. "Just don't get the idea it's going to be a regular thing."

She mussed his hair again, kissed the top of his head. "I'm clear on that," she said, standing and reaching for the crocheted afghan lying neatly folded at the foot of the bed.

Liam kicked off his shoes and stretched out on top of the blue chenille bedspread, yawning again. He set his glasses on the night stand with care.

She covered him, resisted the temptation to kiss his forehead, and headed for the door. When she looked back from the threshold, Liam was already asleep.

1919

Hannah McKettrick heard her son's laughter before she rode around the side of the house, toward the barn, a week's worth of mail bulging in the saddlebags draped across the mule's neck. The snow was deep, with a hard crust, and the January wind was brisk.

Her jaw tightened when she saw her boy out in the cold, wearing a thin jacket and no hat. He and Doss, her brother-in-law, were building what appeared to be a snow fort, their breath making white plumes in the frigid air.

Something in Hannah gave a painful wrench at the sight of Doss; his resemblance to Gabe, his brother and her late husband, invariably startled her, even though they lived under the same roof and she should have been used to him by then.

She nudged the mule with the heels of her boots, but Seesaw-Two didn't pick up his pace. He just plodded along.

"What are you doing out here?" Hannah called.

Both Tobias and Doss fell silent, turning to gaze guiltily in her direction.

The breath plumes dissipated.

Tobias set his feet and pushed back his narrow shoulders. He was only eight, but since Gabe's coffin had arrived by train one warm day last summer, draped in an American flag and with Doss for an escort, her boy had taken on the mien of a man.

"We're just making a fort, Ma," he said.

Hannah blinked back sudden, stinging tears. A soldier, Gabe had died of influenza in an army infirmary, without ever seeing the battleground. Tobias thought in military terms, and Doss encouraged him, a fact Hannah did not appreciate.

"It's cold out here," she said. "You'll catch your death."

Doss shifted, pushed his battered hat to the back of his head. His face hardened, like the ice on the pond back of the orchard where the fruit trees stood, bare-limbed and stoic, waiting for spring.

"Go inside," Hannah told her son.

Tobias hesitated, then obeyed.

Doss remained, watching her.

The kitchen door slammed eloquently.

"You've got no business putting thoughts like that in his head," Doss said, in a quiet voice. He took old Seesaw's reins and held him while she dismounted, careful to keep her woolen skirts from riding up.

"That's a fine bit of hypocrisy, coming from you," Hannah replied. "Tobias had pneumonia last fall. We nearly lost him. He's fragile, and you know it, and as soon as I turn my back, you have him outside, building a snow fort!"

Doss reached for the saddlebags, and so did Hannah. There was a brief tug-of-war before she let go. "He's a kid," Doss said. "If you had your way, he'd never do anything but look through that telescope and play checkers!"

Hannah felt as warm as if she were standing close to a hot stove, instead of Doss McKettrick. Their breaths melded between them. "I fully *intend* to have my way," she said. "Tobias is my son, and I will not have you telling me how to raise him!"

Doss slapped the saddlebags over one shoulder and stepped back, his hazel eyes narrowed. "He's my nephew—my brother's boy—and I'll be damned if I'll let you turn him into a sickly little whelp hitched to your apron strings!"

Hannah stiffened. "You've said quite enough," she told him tersely.

He leaned in, so his nose was almost touching hers. "I haven't said *the half* of it, Mrs. McKettrick."

Hannah sidestepped him, marching for the house, but the snow came almost to her knees and made it hard to storm off in high dudgeon. Her breath trailed over her right shoulder, along with her words. "Supper's in an hour," she said, without turning around. "But maybe you'd rather eat in the bunkhouse."

Doss's chuckle riled her, just as it was no doubt meant to do. "Old Charlie's a sight easier to get along with than you are, but he can't hold a candle to you when it comes to home cooking. Anyhow, he's been gone for a month, in case you haven't noticed."

She felt a flush rise up her neck, even though she was shivering inside Gabe's old woolen work coat. His scent was fading from the fabric, and she wished she knew a way to hold on to it.

"Suit yourself," she retorted.

Tobias shoved a chunk of wood into the cookstove as she entered the house, sending sparks snapping up the gleaming black chimney before he shut the door with a clang.

"We were only building a fort," he grumbled.

Hannah was stilled by the sight of him, just as if somebody had thrown a lasso around her middle and pulled it tight. "I could make biscuits and sausage gravy," she offered quietly.

Tobias ignored the olive branch. "You rode down to the road to meet the mail wagon," he said, without meeting her eyes. "Did I get any letters?" With his hands shoved into the pockets of his trousers and his brownish-blond hair shining in the wintry sunlight flowing in through the windows, he looked the way Gabe must have, at his age.

"One from your grandpa," Hannah said. Methodically, she hung her hat on the usual peg, pulled off her knitted mittens and stuffed them into the pockets of Gabe's coat. She took that off last, always hating to part with it.

"Which grandpa?" Tobias lingered by the stove, warming his hands, still refusing to glance her way.

Hannah's family lived in Missoula, Montana, in a big

house on a tree-lined residential street. She missed them sorely, and it hurt a little, knowing Tobias was hoping it was Holt who'd written to him, not her father.

"The McKettrick one," she said.

"Good," Tobias answered.

The back door opened, and Doss came in, still carrying the saddlebags. Usually he stopped outside to kick the snow off his boots so the floors wouldn't get muddy, but today he was in an obstinate mood.

Hannah went to the stove and ladled hot water out of the reservoir into a basin, so she could wash up before starting supper.

"Catch," Doss said cheerfully.

She looked back, saw the saddlebags, burdened with mail, fly through the air. Tobias caught them ably with a grin.

When was the last time he'd smiled at her that way?

The boy plundered anxiously through the bags, brought out the fat envelope postmarked San Antonio, Texas. Her in-laws, Holt and Lorelei McKettrick, owned a ranch outside that distant city, and though the Triple M was still home to them, they'd been spending a lot of time away since the beginning of the war. Hannah barely knew them, and neither did Tobias, for that matter, but they'd kept up a lively correspondence, the three of them, ever since he'd learned to read, and the letters had been arriving on a weekly basis since Gabe died.

Gabe's folks had come back for the funeral, of course, and in the intervening months Hannah had been secretly afraid. Holt and Lorelei saw their lost son in Tobias, the same as she did, and they'd offered to take him back to Texas with them when they left. She hadn't had to refuse— Tobias had done that for her, but he'd clearly been torn. A part of him had *wanted* to leave.

Hannah's heart had wedged itself up into her throat and stayed there until Gabe's mother and father were gone. Whenever a letter arrived, she felt anxious again.

She glanced at Doss, now shrugging out of his coat. He'd gone away to the army with Gabe, fallen sick with influenza himself, recovered and stayed on at the ranch after he brought his brother's body home for burial. Though no one had come right out and said so, Hannah knew Doss had remained on the Triple M, instead of joining the folks in Texas, mainly to look after Tobias.

Maybe the McKettricks thought she'd hightail it home to Montana, once she got over the shock of losing Gabe, and they'd lose track of the boy.

Now Tobias stood poring over the letter, devouring every word with his eyes, getting to the last page and starting all over again at the beginning.

Deliberately Hannah diverted her attention, and that was when she saw the teapot, sitting on the counter. She looked toward the china cabinet, across the room. She hadn't touched the piece, knowing it was special to Lorelei, and she couldn't credit that Doss or Tobias would have taken it from its place, either. They'd been playing in the snow while she was gone to fetch the mail, not throwing a tea party.

"Did one of you get this out?" she asked casually, getting a good grip on the pot before carrying it back to the cabinet. It was made of metal, but the pretty enamel coating could have been chipped, and Hannah wasn't about to take the risk.

Tobias barely glanced her way before shaking his head. He was still intent on the letter from Texas.

Doss looked more closely, his gaze rising curiously from the teapot to Hannah's face. "Nope," he said at last, and busied himself emptying the contents of the coffeepot down the sink before pumping in water for a fresh batch.

Hannah closed the doors of the china cabinet, frowning.

"Odd," she said, very softly.

CHAPTER THREE

Present Day

SIERRA DESCENDED THE REAR STAIRCASE into the kitchen, being extra quiet so she wouldn't wake Liam up. He hadn't had an asthma attack in almost a month, but he needed his rest.

Intending to brew herself some tea and spend a few quiet minutes restoring her equilibrium, she chose a mug from one of the cupboards, located a box of orange pekoe, and reached for the heirloom teapot.

It was gone.

She glanced toward the china cabinet and saw Lorelei's teapot sitting behind the glass.

Jesse or Travis must have come inside while she was upstairs, she reasoned, and put it away.

But that seemed unlikely. Men, especially cowboys, didn't usually fuss with teapots, did they? Not that she knew that much about men in general or cowboys in particular.

She'd seen Travis earlier, from Liam's bedroom window, working with the horse, and she was sure he hadn't been back in the house after carrying in the bags.

"Jesse?" she called softly, half-afraid he might jump out at her from somewhere.

No answer.

She moved to the front of the house, peered between the lace curtains in the parlor. Jesse's truck was gone, leaving deep tracks in the patchy mud and snow, rapidly filling with gossamer white flakes.

Bemused, Sierra returned to the kitchen, grabbed her coat and went out the back door, shoving her hands into her pockets and ducking her head against the thickening snowfall and the icy wind that accompanied it. Nothing in her life had prepared her for high-country weather; she'd been raised in Mexico, moved to San Diego after her father died and spent the last several years living in Florida. She supposed it would be a while before she adjusted to the change in climate, but if there was one thing she'd learned to do, on the long journey from then to now, it was adapt.

The doors of the big, weathered-board barn stood open, and Sierra stepped inside, shivering. It was warmer there, but she could still see her breath.

"Mr. Reid?"

"Travis" came the taciturn answer from a nearby stall. "I don't answer to much of anything else."

Sierra crossed the sawdust floor and saw Travis on the other side of the door, grooming poor old Baldy with long, gentle strokes of a brush. He gave her a sidelong glance and grinned slightly.

"Settling in okay?" he asked.

"I guess," she said, leaning on the stall door to watch him work. There was something soothing about the way he attended to that horse, almost as though he were touching her own skin….

Perish the thought.

He straightened. A quiver went through Baldy's body. "Something wrong?" Travis asked.

"No," Sierra said quickly, attempting a smile. "I was just wondering…"

"What?" Travis went back to brushing again, though he was still watching Sierra, and the horse gave a contented little snort of pleasure.

Suddenly the whole subject of the teapot seemed silly. How could she ask if he or Jesse had moved it? And, so what if they had? Jesse was a McKettrick, born and raised, and the things in that house were as much a part of his heritage as hers. Travis was clearly a trusted family friend—if not more.

Sierra found that possibility unaccountably disturbing. Meg had said he was single and free, but she obviously trusted Travis implicitly, which might mean there was a deeper level to their relationship.

"I was just wondering…if you ever drink tea," Sierra hedged lamely.

Travis chuckled. "Not often, unless it's the electric variety," he replied, and though he was smiling, the expression in his eyes was one of puzzlement. He was probably asking himself what kind of nut case Meg and Eve had saddled him with. "Are you inviting me?"

Sierra blushed, even more self-conscious than before. "Well…yes. Yes, I guess so."

"I'd rather have coffee," Travis said, "if that's all right with you."

"I'll put a pot on," Sierra answered, foolishly relieved. She should have walked away, but she seemed fixed to the spot, as though someone had smeared the soles of her shoes with superglue.

Travis finished brushing down the horse, ran a gloved hand along the animal's neck and waited politely for Sierra to move, so he could open the stall door and step out.

"What's really going on here, Ms. McKettrick?" he asked, when they were facing each other in the wide aisle, Baldy's stall door securely latched. Along the aisle, other horses nickered, probably wanting Travis's attention for themselves.

"Sierra," she said. She tried to sound friendly, but it was forced.

"Sierra, then. Somehow I don't think you came out here to ask me to a tea party or a coffee klatch."

She huffed out a breath and pushed her hands deeper into her coat pockets. "Okay," she admitted. "I wanted to know if you or Jesse had been inside the house since you brought the baggage in."

"No," Travis answered readily.

"It would certainly be all right if you had, of course—"

Travis took a light grip on Sierra's elbow and steered her toward the barn doors. He closed and fastened them once they were outside.

"Jesse got in his truck and left, first thing," he said. "I've been with Baldy for the last half an hour. Why?"

Sierra wished she'd never begun this conversation. Never left the warmth of the kitchen for the cold and the questions in Travis's eyes. She'd done both those things, though, and now she would have to explain. "I took a teapot out of the china cabinet," she said, "and set it on the counter. I went up to Liam's room, to help him settle in for a nap, and when I came downstairs—"

A startling grin broke over Travis's features like a flash of summer sunlight over a crystal-clear pond. "What?" he prompted. He moved to Sierra's other side, shielding her from the bitter wind, increasing his pace, and therefore hers, as they approached the house.

"It was in the cabinet again. I would swear I put it on the counter."

"Weird," Travis said, kicking the snow off his boots at the base of the back steps.

Sierra stepped inside, shivering, took off her coat and hung it up.

Travis followed, closed the door, pulled off his gloves and stuffed them into the pockets of his coat before hanging it beside Sierra's, along with his hat. "Must have been Liam," he said.

"He's asleep," Sierra replied. The coffee she'd made earlier was still hot, so she filled two mugs, casting an uneasy glance toward the china cabinet as she did so. Liam couldn't have gotten downstairs without her seeing him, and even if he had, he wouldn't have been able to reach the high shelf in the china closet without dragging a chair over. She would have heard the scraping sound and, anyway, Liam being Liam, he wouldn't have put the chair back where he found it. There would have been evidence.

Travis accepted the cup Sierra offered with a nod of thanks, took a sip. "You must have put it away yourself, then," he said reasonably. "And then forgotten."

Sierra sat down in the chair closest to the wood-burning cookstove, suddenly yearning for a fire, while Travis made himself comfortable nearby, on the bench facing the wall.

"I know I didn't," she said, biting her lower lip.

Travis concentrated on his coffee for some moments before turning his gaze back to her face. "It's a strange house," he said.

Sierra blinked.

Cool place, Liam had said, right after they arrived, *but it's haunted.*

"What do you mean, 'It's a strange house'?" she asked. She made no attempt to keep the skepticism out of her voice.

"Meg's going to kill me for this," Travis said.

"I beg your pardon?"

"She doesn't want you scared off."

Sierra frowned, waiting.

"It's a good place," Travis said, taking the homey kitchen in with a fond glance. Clearly, he'd spent a lot of time there. "Odd things happen sometimes, though."

Sierra heard Liam's voice again. *I saw a kid, upstairs in my room.*

She shook off the memory. "Impossible," she muttered.

"If you say so," Travis replied affably.

"What *kind* of 'odd things' happen in this house?"

Travis smiled, and Sierra had the sense that she was being handled, skillfully managed, in the same way as the horse. "Once in a while, you'll hear the piano playing by itself. Or you walk into a room, and you get the feeling you passed somebody on the threshold, even though you're alone."

Sierra shivered again, but this time it had nothing to do with the icy January weather. The kitchen was snug and warm, even without the cookstove lit. "I would appreciate it," she said, "if you wouldn't talk that kind of nonsense in front of Liam. He's…impressionable."

Travis raised an eyebrow.

Suddenly, strangely, Sierra wanted to tell him what Liam had said about seeing another little boy in his room, but she couldn't quite bring herself to do it. She wouldn't have Travis Reid—or anybody else, for that matter—thinking Liam was…different. He got enough of that from other kids, being so smart, and his asthma set him apart, too.

"I must have moved the teapot myself," Sierra said, at last, "and forgotten. Just as you said."

Travis looked unconvinced. "Right," he agreed.

1919

Tobias carried the letter to the table, where Doss sat comfortably in the chair everyone thought of as Holt's. "They bought three hundred head of cattle," the boy told his uncle excitedly, handing over the sheaf of pages. "Drove them all the way from Mexico to San Antonio, too."

Doss smiled. "Is that right?" he mused. His hazel eyes warmed in the light of a kerosene lantern as he read. The place had electricity now, but Hannah tried to save on it where she could. The last bill had come to over a dollar, for a mere two months of service, and she'd been horrified at the expense.

Standing at the stove, she turned back to her work, stood a little straighter, punched down the biscuit dough with sharp jabs of the wooden spoon. Apparently, it hadn't occurred to Tobias that *she* might like to see that infernal letter. She was a McKettrick, too, after all, if only by marriage.

"I guess Ma and Pa liked that buffalo you carved for them," Doss observed, when he'd finished and set the pages aside. Hannah just happened to see, since she'd had to pass right by that end of the table to fetch a pound of ground sausage from the icebox. "Says here it was the best Christmas present they ever got."

Tobias nodded, beaming with pride. He'd worked all fall on that buffalo, even in his sick bed, whittling it from a chunk of firewood Doss had cut for him special. "I reckon I'll make them a bear for next year," he said. Not a word about carving something for *her* parents, Hannah noted, even though they'd sent him a bicycle and a toy fire engine back in December. The McKettricks, of course, had arranged for a spotted pony to be brought up from the main ranch house on Christmas morning, all decked out in a brand-new saddle and bridle, and though Tobias had dutifully written his Montana grandparents to thank them for their gifts, he'd never played with the engine. Just set it on a shelf in his room and forgotten all about it. The bicycle wouldn't be much use before spring, that was true, but he'd shown no more interest in it once the pony had arrived.

"Wash your hands for supper, Tobias McKettrick," Hannah said.

"Supper isn't ready," he protested.

"Do as your mother says," Doss told him quietly.

He obeyed immediately, which should have pleased Hannah, but it didn't.

Doss, meanwhile, opened the saddle bags, took out the usual assortment of letters, periodicals and small parcels, which Hannah had already looked through before the mail wagon rounded the bend in the road. She'd been both disappointed and relieved when there was nothing with her name on it. Once, in the last part of October, when the fiery leaves of the oak trees were falling in puddles around their trunks like the folds of a discarded garment, she'd gotten a letter from Gabe. He'd been dead almost four months by then, and her heart had fairly stopped at the sight of his handwriting on that envelope.

For a brief, dizzying moment, she'd thought there'd been a mistake. That Gabe hadn't died of the influenza at all, but some stranger instead. Mix-ups like that happened during and after a war, and she hadn't seen the body, since the coffin was nailed shut.

She'd stood there beside the road, with that letter in her hand, weeping and trembling so hard that a good quarter of an hour must have passed before she broke the seal and took out the thick fold of vellum pages inside. She'd come to her practical senses by then, but seeing the date at the top of the first page still made her bellow aloud to the empty countryside: March 17, 1918.

Gabe had still been well when he wrote that letter. He'd been looking forward to coming home. It was about time they added to their family, he'd said, and got cattle running on their part of the Triple M again.

She'd dropped to her knees, right there on the hard-packed dirt, too stricken to stand. The mule had wandered home, and presently Doss had come looking for her. Found her still clutching that letter to her chest, her throat so raw with sorrow that she couldn't speak.

He'd lifted her into his arms, Doss had, without saying a word. Set her on his horse, swung up behind her and taken her home.

"Hannah?"

She blinked, came back to the kitchen and the biscuit batter, the package of sausage in her hands.

Doss was standing beside her, smelling of snow and pine trees and man. He touched her arm.

"Are you all right?" he asked.

She swallowed, nodded.

It was a lie, of course. Hannah hadn't been all right since the day Gabe went away to war. Like as not, she would never be all right again.

"You sit down," Doss said. "I'll attend to supper."

She sat, because the strength had gone out of her knees, and looked around blankly. "Where's Tobias?"

Doss washed his hands, opened the sausage packet, and dumped the contents into the big cast iron skillet waiting on the stove. "Upstairs," he answered.

Tobias had left the room without her knowing?

"Oh," she said, unnerved. Was she losing her mind? Had her sorrow pushed her not only to absent-minded distraction, but beyond the boundaries of ordinary sanity as well?

She considered the mysterious movement of her mother-in-law's teapot.

Adeptly, Doss rolled out the biscuit dough, cut it into circles with the rim of a glass. Lorelei McKettrick had taught her boys to cook, sew on their own buttons and make up their beds in the morning. You could say *that* for her, and a lot of other things, too.

Doss poured Hannah a mug of coffee, brought it to her. Started to rest a hand on her shoulder, then thought better of it and pulled back. "I know it's hard," he said.

Hannah couldn't look at him. Her eyes burned with tears she didn't want him to see, though she reckoned he knew they were there anyhow. "There are days," she said, in a whisper, "when I don't think I can go another step. But I have to, because of Tobias."

Doss crouched next to Hannah's chair, took both her hands in his own and looked up into her face. "There's been a hundred times," he said, "when I wished it was me in that grave up there on the hill, instead of Gabe. I'd give anything to take his place, so he could be here with you and the boy."

A sense of loss cut into Hannah's spirit like the blade of a new ax, swung hard. "You mustn't think things like that," she said, when she caught her breath. She pulled her hands free, laid them on either side of his earnest, handsome face, then quickly withdrew them. "You *mustn't*, Doss. It isn't right."

Just then Tobias clattered down the back stairs.

Doss flushed and got to his feet.

Hannah turned away, pretended to have an interest in the mail, most of which was for Holt and Lorelei, and would have to be forwarded to San Antonio.

"What's the matter, Ma?" Tobias spoke worriedly into the awkward silence. "Don't you feel good?"

She'd hoped the boy hadn't seen Doss sitting on his haunches beside her chair, but obviously he had.

"I'm fine," she said briskly. "I just had a splinter in my finger, that's all. I got it putting wood in the fire, and Doss took it out for me."

Tobias looked from her to his uncle and back again.

"Is that why you're making supper?" he asked Doss.

Doss hesitated. Like Gabe, he'd been raised to abhor any kind of lie, even an innocent one, designed to soothe a boy who'd lost his father and feared, in the depths of his dreams, losing his mother, too.

"I'm making supper," he said evenly, "because I can."

Hannah closed her eyes, opened them again.

"Set the table, please," Doss told Tobias.

Tobias hurried to the cabinet for plates and silver-ware.

Hannah met Doss's gaze across the dimly lit room.

A charge seemed to pass between them, like before, when Hannah had come back from getting the mail and found Tobias outside, in the teeth of a high-country winter, building a snow fort.

"It's too damn dark in this house," Doss said. He walked to the middle of the room, reached up, and pulled the beaded metal cord on the overhead light. The bare bulb glowed so brightly it made Hannah blink, but she didn't object.

Something in Doss's face prevented her from it.

Present Day

Travis had long since finished his coffee and left the house by the time Liam got up from his nap and came downstairs, tousle-haired and puffy-eyed from sleep.

"That boy was in my room again," he said. "He was sit-ting at the desk, writing a letter. Can I watch TV? There's a nice HD setup in that room next to the front door. A computer, too, with a big, flat-screen monitor."

Sierra knew about the fancy electronics, since she'd explored the house after Travis left. "You can watch TV for an hour," she said. "Hands off the computer, though. It doesn't belong to us."

Liam's shoulders slumped slightly. "I *know* how to use a computer, Mom," he said. "We had them at school."

Between rent, food and medical bills, Sierra had never been able to scrape together the money for a PC of their own. She'd used the one in the office of the bar she worked in, back in Florida. That was how Meg had first contacted her. "We'll get one," she said, "as soon as I find another job."

"My mailbox is probably full," Liam replied, unappeased. "All the kids in the Geek Program were going to write to me."

Sierra, in the midst of putting a package of frozen chicken breasts into the microwave to thaw, felt as though she'd been poked with a sharp stick. "Don't call it the Geek Program, please," she said.

Liam shrugged one shoulder. "Everybody else does."

"Go watch TV."

He went.

A rap sounded at the back door, and Sierra peered through the glass, since it was dark out, to see Travis standing on the back porch.

"Come in," she called, and headed for the sink to wash her hands.

Travis entered, carrying a fragrant bag of take-out food in one hand. The collar of his coat was raised against the cold, his hat brim pulled low over his eyes.

"Fried chicken," he said, lifting the bag as evidence.

Sierra paused, shut off the faucet, dried her hands. The

timer on the microwave dinged. "I was about to cook," she said.

Travis grinned. "Good thing I got to you in time," he answered. "If you're anything like your sister, you shouldn't be allowed to get near a stove."

If you're anything like your sister.

The words saddened Sierra, settled bleak and heavy over her heart. She didn't know whether she was like her sister or not; until Meg had emailed her a smiling picture a few weeks ago, she wouldn't have recognized her on the street.

"Did I say something wrong?" Travis asked.

"No," Sierra said quickly. "It was—thoughtful of you to bring the chicken."

Liam must have heard Travis's voice, because he came pounding into the room, all smiles.

"Hey, Travis," he said.

"Hey, cowpoke," Travis replied.

"The computer's making a dinging noise," Liam reported.

Travis smiled, set the bag of chicken on the counter but made no move to take off his hat and coat. "Meg's got it set to do that, so she'll remember to check her email when she's here," he said.

"Mom won't let me log on," Liam told him.

Travis glanced at Sierra, turned to Liam again. "Rules are rules, cowpoke," he said.

"Rules bite," Liam said.

"Ninety-five percent of the time," Travis agreed.

Liam recovered quickly. "Are you going to stay and eat with us?"

Travis shook his head. "I'd like that a lot, but I'm expected somewhere else for supper," he answered.

Liam looked sorely disappointed.

Sierra wondered where that "somewhere else" was, and with whom Travis would be sharing a meal, and was irritated with herself. It was none of her business, and besides, she didn't care what he did or who he did it with anyway. Not the least little bit.

"Maybe another time," Travis said.

Liam sighed and retreated to the study and his allotted hour of television.

"You shouldn't have," Sierra said, indicating their supper with a nod.

"It's your first night here," Travis answered, opening the door to leave. "Seemed like the neighborly thing to do."

"Thank you," Sierra said, but he'd already closed the door between them.

Travis started up his truck, just in case Sierra was listening for the engine, drove it around behind the barn and parked. After stopping to check on Baldy and the three other horses in his care, he shrugged down into the collar of his coat and slogged to his trailer.

The quarters were close, smaller than the closet off his master bedroom at home in Flagstaff, but he didn't need much space. He had a bed, kitchen facilities, a bathroom and a place for his laptop. It was enough.

More than Brody was ever going to have.

He took off his hat and coat and tossed them on to the built-in, padded bench that passed for a couch. He tried not to think about Brody, and in the daytime, he stayed busy enough to succeed. At night, it was another matter. There just wasn't enough to do after dark, especially out here in the boonies, once he'd nuked a frozen dinner and watched the news.

He thought about Sierra and the boy, in there in the big house, eating the chicken and fixings he'd picked up in the deli at the one and only supermarket in Indian Rock. He'd never intended to join them, since they'd just arrived and were settling in, but he could picture himself sitting down at that long table in the kitchen, just the same.

He rooted through his refrigerator, something he had to crouch to do, and chose between Salisbury steak, Salisbury steak and Salisbury steak.

While the sectioned plastic plate was whirling round and round in the lilliputian microwave that came with the trailer, he made coffee and remembered his last visit from Rance McKettrick. Widowed, Rance lived alone in the house *his* legendary ancestor, Rafe, had built for his wife, Emmeline, and their children, back in the 1880s. He had two daughters, whom he largely ignored.

"This place is just a fancy coffin," Rance had observed, in his blunt way, when he'd stepped into the trailer. "Brody's the one that's dead, Trav, not you."

Travis rubbed his eyes with a thumb and forefinger. Brody was dead, all right. No getting around that. Seventeen, with everything to live for, and he'd blown himself up in the back room of a slum house in Phoenix, making meth.

He looked into the window over the sink, saw his own reflection.

Turned away.

His cell phone rang, and he considered letting voice mail pick up, but couldn't make himself do it. If he'd answered the night Brody called...

He fished the thing out, snapped it open and said, "Reid."

"Whatever happened to 'hello'?" Meg asked.

The bell on the microwave rang, and Travis reached in to retrieve his supper, burned his hand and cursed.

She laughed. "Better and better."

"I'm not in the mood for banter, Meg," he replied, turning on the water with his free hand and then switching to shove his scorched fingers into the flow.

"You never are," she said.

"The horses are fine."

"I know. You would have called me if they weren't."

"Then what do you want?"

"My, my, we *are* testy tonight. I called, you big grouch, to ask about my sister and my nephew. Are they okay? How do they look? Sierra is so private, she's almost standoffish."

"You can say that again."

"Thank you, but in the interest of brevity, I won't."

"Since when do you give a damn about brevity?" Travis inquired, but he was grinning by then.

Once again Meg laughed. Once again Travis wished he'd been able to fall in love with her. They'd tried, the two of them, to get something going, on more than one occasion. Meg wanted a baby, and he wanted not to be alone, so it made sense. The trouble was, it hadn't worked.

There was no chemistry.

There was no passion.

They were never going to be anything more than what they were—the best of friends. He was mostly resigned to that, but in lonely moments, he ached for things to be different.

"Tell me about my sister," Meg insisted.

"She's pretty," Travis said. *Real* pretty, added a voice in his mind. "She's proud, and overprotective as hell of the kid."

"Liam has asthma," Meg said quietly. "According to Sierra, he nearly died of it a couple of times."

Travis forgot his burned fingers, his Salisbury steak and his private sorrow. *"What?"*

Meg let out a long breath. "That's the only reason Sierra's willing to have anything to do with Mom and me. Mom put her on the company health plan and arranged for Liam to see a specialist in Flagstaff on a regular basis. In return, Sierra had to agree to spend a year on the ranch."

Travis stood still, absorbing it all. "Why here?" he asked. "Why not with you and Eve in San Antonio?"

"Mom and I would love that," Meg said, "but Sierra needs...distance. Time to get used to us."

"Time to get used to two McKettrick women. So we're talking, say, the year 2050, give or take a decade?"

"Very funny. Sierra *is* a McKettrick woman, remember? She's up to the challenge."

"She is definitely a McKettrick," Travis agreed ruefully. And very definitely a woman. "How did you find her?"

"Mom tracked her and Hank down when Sierra was little," Meg answered.

Travis dropped on to the edge of his bed, which was unmade. The sheets were getting musty, and every night, the pizza crumbs rubbed his hide raw. One of these days he was going to haul off and change them.

"'Tracked her down'?"

"Yes," Meg said, with a sigh. "I guess I didn't tell you about that part."

"I guess you didn't." Travis had known about the kidnapping, how Sierra's father had taken off with her the day the divorce papers were served, and that the two of them had ended up in Mexico. "Eve knew, and she still didn't lift a finger to get her own daughter back?"

"Mom had her reasons," Meg answered, withdrawing a little.

"Oh, well, then," Travis retorted, "that clears everything up. What *reason* could she possibly have?"

"It's not my place to say, Trav," Meg told him sadly.

"Mom and Sierra have to work it all through first, and it might be a while before Sierra's ready to listen."

Travis sighed, shoved a hand through his hair. "You're right," he conceded.

Meg brightened again, but there was a brittleness about her that revealed more than she probably wanted Travis to know, close as they were. "So," she said, "what would you say Mom's chances are? Of reconnecting with Sierra, I mean?"

"The truth?"

"The truth," Meg said, without enthusiasm.

"Zero to zip. Sierra's been pleasant enough to me, but she's as stubborn as any McKettrick that ever drew breath, and that's saying something."

"Gee, thanks."

"You said you wanted the truth."

"How can you be so sure Mom won't be able to get through to her?"

"It's just a hunch," Travis said.

Meg was quiet. Travis was famous for his hunches. Too bad he hadn't paid attention to the one that said his little brother was in big trouble, and that Travis ought to drop everything and look for Brody until he found him.

"Look, maybe I'm wrong," he added.

"What's your real impression of Sierra, Travis?"

He took his time answering. "She's independent to a fault. She's built a wall around herself and the kid, and she's not about to let anybody get too close. She's jumpy, too. If it wasn't for Liam, and the fact that she probably doesn't have two nickels to rub together, she definitely wouldn't be on the Triple M."

"Damn," Meg said. "We knew she was poor, but—"

"Her car gave out in the driveway as soon as she pulled

in. I took a peek under the hood, and believe me, the best mechanic on the planet couldn't resurrect that heap."

"She can drive my Blazer."

"That might take some convincing on your part. This is not a woman who wants to be obliged. It's probably all she can do not to grab the kid and hop on the next bus to nowhere."

"This is depressing," Meg said.

Travis got up off the bed, peeled back the plastic covering his dinner, and poked warily at the faux meat with the tip of one finger. Talk about depressing.

"Hey," he said. "Look on the bright side. She's here, isn't she? She's on the Triple M. It's a start."

"Take care of her, Travis."

"As if she'd go along with that."

"Do it for me."

"Oh, please."

Meg paused, took aim and scored a bull's-eye. "Then do it for Liam."

CHAPTER FOUR

1919

DOSS LEFT THE HOUSE AFTER supper, ostensibly to look in on the livestock one last time before heading upstairs to bed, leaving the dishwashing to Tobias and Hannah. He stood still in the dooryard, raising the collar of his coat against the wicked cold. Stars speckled the dark, wintry sky.

In those moments he missed Gabe with a piercing intensity that might have bent him double, if he wasn't McKettrick proud. That was what his mother called the quality, anyhow. In the privacy of his own mind, Doss named it stubbornness.

Thinking of his ma made his pa come to mind, too. He missed them almost as sorely as he did Gabe. His uncles, Rafe and Kade and Jeb, along with their wives, were all down south, around Phoenix, where the weather was more hospitable to their aging bones. Their sons, to a man, were still in the army, even though the war was over, waiting to be mustered out. Their daughters had all married, every one of them keeping the McKettrick name, and lived in places as far-flung as Boston, New York and San Francisco.

There was hardly a McKettrick left on the place, save himself and Hannah and Tobias. It deepened Doss's loneliness, knowing that. He wished everybody would just come back home, where they belonged, but it would have been easier to herd wild barn cats than that bunch.

Doss looked back toward the house. Saw the lantern glowing at the kitchen window. Smiled.

The moment he'd gone outside, Hannah must have switched off the bulb. She worried about running short of things, he'd noticed, even though she'd come from a prosperous family, and certainly married into one.

His throat tightened. He knew she'd been different before he brought Gabe home in a pine box, but then, they all had. Gabe's going left a hole in the fabric of what it meant to be a McKettrick, and not a tidy one, stitched at the edges. Rather, it was a jagged tear, and judging by the raw newness of his own grief, Doss had little hope of it ever mending.

Time heals, his mother had told him after they'd laid Gabe in the ground up there on the hill, with his Grandpa Angus and those that had passed after him, but she'd had tears in her eyes as she said it. As for his pa, well, he'd stood a long time by the grave. Stood there until Rafe and Kade and Jeb brought him away.

Doss thrust out a sigh, remembering. "Gabe," he said, under his breath, "Hannah says it's wrong of me, but I still wish it had been me instead of you."

He'd have given anything for an answer, but wherever Gabe was, he was busy doing other things. Maybe they had fishing holes up there in the sky, or cattle to round up and drive to market.

"Take care of Hannah and my boy," Gabe had told him, in that army infirmary, when they both knew there would be no turning the illness around. "Promise me, Doss."

Doss had swallowed hard and made that promise, but it was a hard one to keep. Hannah didn't seem to want taking care of, and every morning when Doss woke up, he was afraid this would be the day she'd decide to go back to her own people, up in Montana, and stay gone for good.

The back door opened, startling Doss out of his musings. He hesitated for a moment, then tramped in the direction of the barn, trying to look like a man bent on a purpose.

Hannah caught up, bundled into a shawl and carrying a lighted lantern in one hand.

"I think I'm going mad," she blurted out.

Doss stopped, looked down at her in puzzled concern. "It's the grief, Hannah," he told her gruffly. "It will pass."

"You don't believe that any more than I do," Hannah challenged, catching up with herself. The snow was deep and getting deeper, and the wind bit straight through to the marrow.

Doss moved to the windward side, to be a buffer for her. "I've got to believe it," he said. "Feeling this bad forever doesn't bear thinking about."

"I put the teapot away," Hannah said, her breath coming in puffs of white, "I *know* I put it away. But I must have gotten it out again, without knowing or remembering, and that scares me, Doss. That really scares me."

They reached the barn. Doss took the lantern from her and hauled open one of the big doors one-handed. It wasn't easy, since the snow had drifted, even in the short time since he'd left off feeding and watering the horses and the milk cow and that cussed mule Seesaw. The critter was a son of Doss's mother's mule, who'd borne the same name, and he was a son of something else, too.

"Maybe you're a mite forgetful these days," Doss said, once he'd gotten her inside, out of the cold. The familiar smells and sounds of the darkened barn were a solace

to him—he came there often, even when he didn't have
work to do, which was seldom. On a ranch, there was
always work to do—wood to chop, harnesses to mend,
animals to look after. "That doesn't mean you're not sane,
Hannah."

Don't say it, he pleaded silently. Don't say you might
as well take Tobias and head for Montana.

It was a selfish thought, Doss knew. In Montana,
Hannah could live a city life again. No riding a mule five
miles to fetch the mail. No breaking the ice on the water
troughs on winter mornings, so the cattle and horses
could drink. No feeding chickens and dressing like a
man.

If Hannah left the Triple M, Doss didn't know what he'd
do. First and foremost, he'd have to break his promise to
Gabe, by default if not directly, but there was more to it
than that. A lot more.

"There's something else, too," Hannah confided.

To keep himself busy, Doss went from stall to stall,
looking in on sleepy horses, each one confounded and
blinking in the light of his lantern. He was giving Hannah
space, enough distance to get out whatever it was she
wanted to say.

"What?" he asked, when she didn't speak again right
away.

"Tobias. He just told me—he told me—"

Doss looked back, saw Hannah standing in the moonlit
doorway, rimmed in silver, with one hand pressed to her
mouth.

He went back to her. Set the lantern aside and took her
by the shoulders. "What did he tell you, Hannah?"

"Doss, he's seeing things."

He tensed on the inside. Would have shoved a hand
through his hair in agitation if he hadn't been wearing a

hat and his ears weren't bound to freeze if he took it off. "What kind of things?"

"A boy." She took hold of his arm, and her grip was strong for such a small woman. It did curious things to him, feeling her fingers on him, even through the combined thickness of his coat and shirt. "Doss, Tobias says he saw a boy in his room."

Doss looked around. There was nothing but bleak, frozen land for miles around. "That's impossible," he said.

"You've got to talk to him."

"Oh, I'll talk to him, all right." Doss started for the house, so fixed on getting to Tobias that he forgot all about keeping Hannah sheltered from the wind. She had to lift her skirts to keep pace with him.

Present Day

"Tell me about the boy you saw in your room," Sierra said, when they'd eaten their fill of fried chicken, macaroni salad, mashed potatoes with gravy, and corn on the cob.

Liam's gaze was clear as he regarded her from his side of the long table. "He's a ghost," he replied, and waited, visibly expecting the statement to be refuted.

"Maybe an imaginary playmate?" Sierra ventured. Liam was a lonely little boy; their lifestyle had seen to that. After her father had died, drunk himself to death in a back-street cantina in San Miguel, the two of them had wandered like gypsies. San Diego. North Carolina, Georgia, and finally Florida.

"There's nothing imaginary about him," Liam said staunchly. "He wears funny clothes, like those kids on those old-time shows on TV. He's a *ghost,* Mom. Face it."

"Liam—"

"You never believe anything I tell you!"

"I believe *everything* you tell me," Sierra insisted evenly. "But you've got to admit, this is a stretch." Again she thought of the teapot. Again she pushed the recollection aside.

"I never lie, Mom."

She moved to pat his hand, but he pulled back. The set of his jaw was stubborn, and his gaze drilled into her, full of challenge. She tried again. "I know you don't lie, Liam. But you're in a strange new place and you miss your friends and—"

"And you won't even let me see if they sent me emails!" he cried.

Sierra sighed, rested her elbows on the tabletop and rubbed her temples with the fingertips of both hands. "Okay," she relented. "You can log on to the internet. Just be careful, because that computer is expensive, and we can't afford to replace it."

Suddenly Liam's face was alight. "I won't break it," he promised, with exuberance.

Sierra wondered if he'd just scammed her, if the whole boy-in-the-bedroom thing was a trick to get what he wanted.

In the next instant she was ashamed. Liam was direct to a fault. He *believed* he'd seen another child in his empty bedroom. She'd call his new doctor in Flagstaff in the morning, talk to the woman, see what a qualified professional made of the whole thing. She offered a silent prayer that her car would start, too, because the doctor was going to want to see Liam, pronto.

Meanwhile, Liam got to his feet and scrambled out of the room.

Sierra cleared away the supper mess, then followed him,

as casually as she could, to the room at the front of the house.

He was already online.

"Just what I thought!" he crowed. "My mailbox is *bulging*."

The TV was still on, a narrator dolefully describing the effects of a second ice age, due any minute. Run for the hills. Sierra shut it off.

"Hey," Liam objected. "I was listening to that."

Sierra approached the computer. "You're only seven," she said. "You shouldn't be worrying about the fate of the planet."

"Somebody's got to," Liam replied, without looking at her. "*Your* generation is doing a lousy job." He was staring, as if mesmerized, into the computer screen. Its bluish-gray light flickered on the lenses of his glasses, making his eyes disappear. "Look! The whole Geek Group wrote to me!"

"I asked you not to—"

"Okay," Liam sighed, without looking at her. "The brilliant children in the gifted program are engaging in communication."

"That's better," Sierra said, sparing a smile.

"You've got a few emails waiting yourself," Liam announced. He was already replying to the cybermissives, his small fingers ranging deftly over the keyboard. He'd skipped the hunt-and-peck method entirely, as had all the other kids in his class. Using a computer came naturally to Liam, almost as if he'd been born knowing how, and she knew this was a common phenomenon, which gave her some comfort.

"I'll read them later," Sierra answered. She didn't have that many friends, so most of her messages were probably sales pitches of the penis-enlargement variety. How had she gotten on that kind of list? It wasn't as if she visited porn sites or ordered battery-operated boyfriends online.

"They get to watch a real rocket launch!" Liam cried, without a trace of envy. *"Wow!"*

"Wow indeed," Sierra said, looking around the room. According to Meg, it had originally been a study. Old books lined the walls on sturdy shelves, and there was a natural rock fireplace, too, with a fire already laid.

Sierra found a match on the mantelpiece, struck it and lit the blaze.

A chime sounded from the computer.

"Aunt Meg just IM'd you," Liam said.

Where had he gotten this "Aunt Meg" thing? He'd never even met the woman in person, let alone established a relationship with her. "'IM'd'?" she asked.

"Instant Messaged," Liam translated. "Guess you'd better check it out. Just make it quick, because I've still got a *pile* of mail to answer."

Smiling again, Sierra took the chair Liam so reluctantly surrendered and read the message from Meg.

Travis tells me your car died. Use my Blazer. The keys are in the sugar bowl beside the teapot.

Sierra's pride kicked in. Thanks, she replied, at a fraction of Liam's typing speed, but I probably won't need it. My car is just... She paused. Her car was just what? Old? tired, she finished, inspired.

The Blazer won't run when I come back if somebody doesn't charge up the battery. It's been sitting too long, Meg responded quickly. She must have been as fast with a keyboard as Liam.

Is Travis going to report on everything I do? Sierra

wrote. She made so many mistakes, she had to retype the message before hitting Send, and that galled her.

Yes, Meg wrote. Because I plan to nag every last detail out of him.

Sierra sighed. It won't be that interesting, she answered, taking her time so she wouldn't have to revise. She was out of practice, and if she hoped to land anything better than a waitressing job in Indian Rock, she'd better polish her computer skills.

Meg sent a smiley face, followed by, Good night, Sis. (I've always wanted to say that.)

Sierra bit her lower lip. Good night, she tapped out, and rose from the chair with a glance at the clock on the mantel above the now-snapping fire.

Why had she lit it? She was exhausted, and now she would either have to throw water on the flames or wait until they died down. The first method, of course, would make a terrible mess, so that was out.

"Hurry up and finish what you're doing," she told Liam, who had plopped in the chair again the moment Sierra got out of it. "Half an hour till bedtime."

"I had a *nap*," Liam reminded her, typing simultaneously.

"Finish," Sierra repeated. With that, she left the study, climbed the stairs and went into Liam's room to get his favorite pajamas from one of the suitcases. She meant to put them in the clothes dryer for a few minutes, warm them up.

Something drew her to the window, though. She looked down, saw that the lights were on in Travis's trailer and his truck was parked nearby. Evidently, he hadn't stayed long in town, or wherever he'd gone.

Why did it please her so much, knowing that?

1919

Hannah stood in the doorway of Tobias's room, watching her boy sleep. He looked so peaceful, lying there, but she knew he had bad dreams sometimes. Just the night before, in the wee small hours, he'd crawled into bed beside her, snuggled as close as his little-boy pride would allow, and whispered earnestly that she oughtn't die anytime soon.

She'd been so choked up, she could barely speak.

Now she wanted to wake him, hold him tight in her arms, protect him from whatever it was in his mind that made him see little boys that weren't there.

He was lonely, that was all. He needed to be around other children. Way out here, he went to a one-room school, when it wasn't closed on account of snow, with only seven other pupils, all of whom were older than he was.

Maybe she *should* take him home to Montana. He had cousins there. They'd live in town, too, where there were shops and a library and even a moving-picture theater. He could ride his bicycle, come spring, and play baseball with other boys.

Hannah's throat ached. Gabe had wanted his son raised here, on the Triple M. Wanted him to grow up the way he had, rough-and-tumble, riding horses, rounding up stray cattle, part of the land. Of course, Gabe hadn't expected to die young—he'd meant to come home, so he and Hannah could fill that big house with children. Tobias would have had plenty of company then.

A tear slipped down Hannah's cheek, and she swatted it away. Straightened her spine.

Gabe was gone, and there weren't going to be any more children.

She heard Doss climbing the stairs, and wanted to

move out of the doorway. He thought she was too fussy, always hovering over Tobias. Always trying to protect him.

How could a man understand what it meant to bear and nurture a child?

Hannah closed her eyes and stayed where she was.

Doss stopped behind her, uncertain. She could feel that, along with the heat and sturdy substance of his body.

"Leave the child to sleep, Hannah," he said quietly.

She nodded, closed Tobias's door gently and turned to face Doss there in the darkened hallway. He carried a book under one arm and an unlit lantern in his other hand.

"It's because he's lonesome," she said.

Doss clearly knew she was referring to Tobias's hallucination. "Kids make up playmates," he told her. "And being lonesome is a part of life. It's a valley a person has to go through, not something to run away from."

No McKettrick ever ran from anything. Doss didn't have to say it, and neither did she. But she *wasn't* a McKettrick, not by blood. Oh, she still wrote the word, whenever she had to sign something, but she'd stopped owning the name the day they put Gabe in the ground.

She wasn't sure why. He'd been so proud of it, like all the rest of them were.

"Do you ever wish you could live someplace else?" Hannah heard herself say.

"No," Doss said, so quickly and with such gravity that Hannah almost believed he'd been reading her mind. "I belong right here."

"But the others—your uncles and cousins—they didn't stay...."

"Ask any one of them where home is," Doss answered, "and they'll tell you it's the Triple M."

Hannah started to speak, then held her tongue. Nodded. "Good night, Doss," she said.

He inclined his head and went on to his own room, shut himself away.

Hannah stood alone in the dark for a long time.

She'd been so happy on the Triple M when Gabe was alive, and even after he'd gone into the army, because she'd never once doubted that he'd return. Come walking up the path with a duffel bag over one shoulder, whistling. She'd rehearsed that day a thousand times in her mind—pictured herself running to meet him, throwing herself into his arms.

It was never going to happen.

Without him, she might as well have been alone on the barren landscape of the moon.

Her eyes filled.

She walked slowly to the end of the hall, into the room where Gabe had brought her on their wedding night. He'd been conceived and born in the big bed there, just as Tobias had. As so many other babes would have been, if only Gabe had lived.

Hannah didn't undress after she closed the door behind her. She didn't let her hair down and brush it, like usual, or wash her face at the basin on the bureau.

Instead, she sat down in Lorelei's rocking chair and waited. Just waited.

For what, she did not know.

Present Day

After Liam had gone to bed, Sierra went back downstairs to the computer and scanned her email. When she spotted Allie Douglas-Fletcher's return address, she wished she'd waited until morning. She was always stronger in the mornings.

Allie was Adam's twin sister. Liam's aunt. After Adam was murdered, while on assignment in South America, Allie had been inconsolable, and she'd developed an unhealthy fixation for her brother's child.

After taking a deep breath and releasing it slowly, Sierra opened the message. Typically, there was no preamble. Allie got right to the point.

The guest house is ready for you and Liam. You know Adam would want his son to grow up right here in San Diego, Sierra. Tim and I can give Liam everything—a real home, a family, an education, the very best medical care. We're willing to make a place for you, too, obviously. If you won't come home, at least tell us you arrived safely in Arizona.

Sierra sat, wooden, staring at the stark plea on the screen. Although Allie and Adam had been raised in relative poverty, both of them had done well in life. Adam had been a photojournalist for a major magazine; he and Sierra had met when he did a piece on San Miguel.

Allie ran her own fund-raising firm, and her husband was a neurosurgeon. They had everything—except what they wanted most. Children.

You can't have Liam, Sierra cried, in the silence of her heart. *He's mine.*

She flexed her fingers, sighed, and hit Reply. Allie was a good person, just as Adam had been, for all that he'd told Sierra a lie that shook the foundations of the universe. Adam's sister sincerely believed she and the doctor could do a better job of raising Liam than Sierra could, and maybe they were right. They had money. They had social status.

Tears burned in Sierra's eyes.

Liam is well. We're safe on the Triple M, and for the time being, we're staying put.

It was all she could bring herself to say.

She hit Send and logged off the computer.

The fire was still flourishing on the hearth. She got up, crossed the room, pushed the screen aside to jab at the burning wood with a poker. It only made the flames burn more vigorously.

She kicked off her shoes, curled up in the big leather chair and pulled a knitted afghan around her to wait for the fire to die down.

The old clock on the mantel tick-tocked, the sound loud and steady and almost hypnotic.

Sierra yawned. Closed her eyes. Opened them again.

She thought about turning the TV back on, just for the sound of human voices, but dismissed the idea. She was so tired, she was going to need all her energy just to go upstairs and tumble into bed. There was none to spare for fiddling with the television set.

Again, she closed her eyes.

Again, she opened them.

She wondered if the lights were still on in Travis's trailer.

Closed her eyes.

Was dragged down into a heavy, fitful sleep.

She knew right away that she was dreaming, and yet it was so real.

She heard the clock ticking.

She felt the warmth of the fire.

But she was standing in the ranch house kitchen, and it was different, in subtle ways, from the room she knew.

She was different.

Her eyes were shut, and yet she could see clearly.

A bare light bulb dangled overhead, giving off a dim but determined glow.

She looked down at herself, the dream-Sierra, and felt a wrench of surprise.

She was wearing a long woolen skirt. Her hands were smaller—chapped and work worn—someone else's hands.

"I'm dreaming," she insisted to herself, but it didn't help.

She stared around the kitchen. The teapot sat on the counter.

"Now what's that doing there?" asked this other Sierra. "I know I put it away. I know for sure I did."

Sierra struggled to wake up. It was too intense, this dream. She was in some other woman's body, not her own. It was sinewy and strong, this body. She felt the heartbeat, the breath going in and out. Felt the weight of long hair, pinned to the back of her head in a loose chignon.

"Wake up," she said.

But she couldn't.

She stood very still, staring at the teapot.

Emotions stormed within her, a loneliness so wretched and sharp that she thought she'd burst from the inside and shatter. Longing for a man who'd gone away and was never coming home, an unspeakable sorrow. Love for a child, so profound that it might have been mourning.

And something else. A forbidden wanting that had nothing to do with the man who'd left her.

Sierra woke herself then, by force of will, only to find her face wet with another woman's tears.

She must have been asleep for a while, she realized. The flames on the hearth had become embers. The room was chilly.

She shivered, tugged the afghan tighter around her, and

got out of the chair. She went to the window, looked out. Travis's trailer was dark.

"It was just a dream," she told herself out loud.

So why was her heart breaking?

She made her way into the kitchen, navigating the dark hallway as best she could, since she didn't know where the light switches were. When she reached her destination, she walked to the middle of the room, where she'd stood in the dream, and suppressed an urge to reach up for the metal-beaded cord she knew wasn't there.

What she needed, she decided, was a good cup of tea.

She found a switch beside the back door and flipped it.

Reality returned in a comforting spill of light.

She found an electric kettle, filled it at the sink and plugged it in to boil. Earlier she'd been too weary to get out of that chair in the study and turn on the TV. Now she knew it would be pointless to try to sleep.

Might as well do this up right, she thought.

She went to the china cabinet, got the teapot out, set it on the table. Added tea leaves and located a little strainer in one of the drawers. The kettle boiled.

She was sitting quietly, sipping tea and watching fat snowflakes drift past the porch light outside the back door, when Liam came down the back stairway in his pajamas. Blinking, he rubbed his eyes.

"Is it morning?" he asked.

"No," Sierra said gently. "Go back to bed."

"Can I have some tea?"

"No, again," Sierra answered, but she didn't protest when Liam took a seat on the bench, close to her chair. "But if there's cocoa, I'll make you some."

"There is," Liam said. He looked incredibly young, and

so very vulnerable, without his glasses. "I saw it in the pantry. It's the instant kind."

With a smile, Sierra got out of the chair, walked into the pantry and brought out the cocoa, along with a bag of semihard marshmallows. Thanks to Travis's preparations for their arrival, there was milk in the refrigerator and, using the microwave, she had Liam's hot chocolate ready in no time.

"I like it here," he told her. "It's better than any place we've ever lived."

Sierra's heart squeezed. "You really think so? Why?"

Liam took a sip of hot chocolate and acquired a liquid mustache. One small shoulder rose and fell in a characteristic shrug. "It feels like a real home," he said. "Lots of people have lived here. And they were all McKettricks, like us."

Sierra was stung, but she hid it behind another smile. "Wherever we live," she said carefully, "is a real home, because we're together."

Liam's expression was benignly skeptical, even tolerant. "We never had so much room before. We never had a barn with horses in it. And we never had *ghosts*." He whispered the last word, and gave a little shiver of pure joy.

Sierra was looking for a way to approach the ghost subject again when the faint, delicate sound of piano music reached her ears.

CHAPTER FIVE

"DO YOU HEAR THAT?" she asked Liam.

His brow furrowed as he shifted on the bench and took another sip of his cocoa. "Hear what?"

The tune continued, flowing softly, forlornly, from the front room.

"Nothing," Sierra lied.

Liam peered at her, perplexed and suspicious.

"Finish your chocolate," she prompted. "It's late."

The music stopped, and she felt relief and a paradoxical sorrow, reminiscent of the all-too-vivid dream she'd had earlier while dozing in the big chair in the study.

"What was it, Mom?" Liam pressed.

"I thought I heard a piano," she admitted, because she knew her son wouldn't let the subject drop until she told him the truth.

Liam smiled, pleased. "This house is so cool," he said. "I told the Geek—the kids—that it's haunted. Aunt Allie, too."

Sierra, in the process of lifting her cup to her mouth, set it down again, shakily. "When did you talk to Allie?" she asked.

"She sent me an email," he replied, "and I answered."

"Great," Sierra said.

"Would my dad really want me to grow up in San Diego?" Liam asked seriously. The idea had, of course, come from Allie. While Sierra wasn't without sympathy for the woman, she felt violated. Allie had no business trying to entice Liam behind her back.

"Your dad would want you to grow up with me," Sierra said firmly, and she knew that was true, for all that Adam had betrayed her.

"Aunt Allie says my cousins would like me," Liam confided.

Liam's "cousins" were actually half sisters, but Sierra wasn't ready to spring that on him, and she hoped Allie wouldn't do it, either. Although Adam had told Sierra he was divorced when they met, and she'd fallen immediately and helplessly in love with him, she'd learned six months later, when she was carrying his child, that he was still living with his wife when he wasn't on the road. It had been Allie, earnest, meddling Allie, who traveled to San Miguel, found Sierra and told her the truth.

Sierra would never forget the family photos Allie showed her that day—snapshots of Adam with his arm around his smiling wife, Dee. The two little girls in matching dresses posed with them, their eyes wide with innocence and trust.

"Forget him, kiddo," Hank had said airily, when Sierra went to him, in tears, with the whole shameful story. "It ain't gonna fly."

She'd written Adam immediately, but her letter came back, tattered from forwarding, and no one answered at any of the telephone numbers he'd given her.

She'd given birth to Liam eight weeks later, at home, attended by Hank's long-time mistress, Magdalena. Three days after that, Hank brought her an American newspaper, tossed it into her lap without a word.

She'd paged through it slowly, possessed of a quiet, escalating dread, and come across the account of Adam Douglas's death on page four. He'd been shot to death, according to the article, on the outskirts of Caracas, after infiltrating a drug cartel to take pictures for an exposé he'd been writing.

"Mom?" Liam snapped his fingers under Sierra's nose. "Are you hearing the music again?"

Sierra blinked. Shook her head.

"Do you think my cousins would like me?"

She reached out, her hand trembling only slightly, and ruffled his hair. "I think *anybody* would like you," she said. When he was older, she would tell him about Adam's other family, but it was still too soon. She took his empty cup, carried it to the sink. "Now, go upstairs, brush your teeth again and hit the sack."

"Aren't you going to bed?" Liam asked practically.

Sierra sighed. "Yes," she said, resigned. She didn't think she'd sleep, but she knew Liam would wonder if she stayed up all night, prowling around the house. "You go ahead. I'm just going to make sure the front door is locked."

Liam nodded and obeyed without protest.

Sierra considered marking the occasion on the calendar.

She went straight to the front room, and the piano, the moment Liam had gone upstairs. The keyboard cover was down, the bench neatly in place. She switched on a lamp and inspected the smooth, highly polished wood for fingerprints. Nothing.

She touched the cover, and her fingers left distinct smudges.

No one had touched the piano that night, unless they'd been wearing gloves.

Frowning, Sierra checked the lock on the front door.

Fastened.

She inspected the windows—all locked—and even the floor. It was snowing hard, and anybody who'd come in out of that storm would have left some trace, no matter how careful they were—a puddle somewhere, a bit of mud.

Again, there was nothing.

Finally she went upstairs, found a nightgown, bathed and got ready for bed. Since Travis had left her bags in the room adjoining Liam's, she opened the connecting door a crack and crawled between sheets worn smooth by time.

She was asleep in an instant.

1919

Hannah closed the cover over the piano keys, stacked the sheet music neatly and got to her feet. She'd played as softly as she could, pouring her sadness and her yearning into the music, and when she returned to the upstairs corridor, she saw light under Doss's door.

She paused, wondering what he'd do if she went in, took off her clothes and crawled into bed beside him.

Not that she would, of course, because she'd loved her husband and it wouldn't be fitting, but there were times when her very soul ached within her, she wanted so badly to be touched and held, and this was one of them.

She swallowed, mortified by her own wanton thoughts.

Doss would send her away angrily.

He'd remind her that she was his brother's widow—if he ever spoke to her again at all.

For all that, she took a single, silent step toward the door.

"Ma?"

Tobias spoke from behind her. She hadn't heard him get out of bed, come to the threshold of his room.

Thanking heaven she was still fully dressed, she turned to face him.

"What is it?" she asked gently. "Did you have another bad dream?"

Tobias shook his head. His gaze slipped past Hannah to Doss's door, then back to her face, solemn and worried. "I wish I had a pa," he said.

Hannah's heart seized. She approached, pulled the boy close, and he allowed it. During the day, he would have balked. "So do I," she replied, bending to kiss the top of his head. "I wish your pa was here. Wish it so much it hurts."

Tobias pulled back, looked up at her. "But Pa's dead," he said. "Maybe you and Doss could get hitched. Then he wouldn't be my uncle any more, would he? He'd be my pa."

"Tobias," Hannah said very softly, praying Doss hadn't overheard somehow. "That wouldn't be right."

"Why not?" Tobias asked.

She crouched, looked up into her son's face. One day, he'd be handsome and square-jawed, like the rest of the McKettrick men. For now he was still a little boy, his features childishly innocent. "I was your pa's wife. I'll love him for the rest of my days."

"That might be a long time," Tobias said, with a measure of dubiousness, as well as hope. He dropped his voice to a whisper. "I don't want Doss to marry somebody else, Ma," he said. "All the women in Indian Rock are sweet on him, and one of these days he might take a notion to get himself a wife."

"Tobias," Hannah reasoned, "you must put this foolishness out of your head. If Doss chooses to take a bride, that's certainly his right. But it won't be me he marries. It's too hard to explain right now, but Doss was your pa's brother. I couldn't—"

"You'd marry some man in Montana, though, wouldn't you?" Tobias demanded, suddenly angry, and this time, he made no effort to keep his voice down. "Some stranger who wears a suit to work!"

"Tobias!"

"I *won't* go to Montana, do you hear me? I won't leave the Triple M unless Doss goes, too!"

Hannah reddened with embarrassment and anger—Doss had surely heard—and rose to her full height. "Tobias McKettrick," she said sternly, "you go to bed this instant, and don't you *ever* talk to me like that again!"

Tobias's chin jutted out, in the McKettrick way, and his eyes flashed. "You go anyplace you want to," he told her, turning on one bare heel to flee into his room, "but I'm not going with you!" With that, he slammed the door in her face.

Hannah took a step toward it, even reached for the knob.

But in the end she couldn't face her son.

"Hannah."

Doss.

She stiffened but didn't turn. Doss would see too much if she did. Guess too much.

He caught hold of her arm, brought her gently around.

She whispered his name, despondent.

He took her hand, led her to the opposite end of the hall, opened the last door on the right, the one where she kept her sewing machine.

"What are you—?"

Doss stepped over the threshold first, turned, and drew her in behind him. Reached around her to shut the door.

She leaned against the panel. It was hard at her back.

"Doss," she said.

He cupped her face in his hands, bent his head, and kissed her, full on the mouth.

A sweet shock went through her. She knew she ought to break away, knew he wouldn't force himself on her if she uttered the slightest protest, but she couldn't say a word. Her body came alive as he pressed himself against her. His weight was hard and warm and blessedly real.

Doss reached behind her head, pulled the pins from her hair, let it fall around her shoulders, to her waist. He groaned, buried his face in it, burrowed through to take her earlobe between his lips and nibble on it.

Hannah gasped with guilty pleasure. Her knees went weak, and Doss held her upright with the lower part of his body.

She moaned softly.

"We can't," she whispered.

"We'd damn well better," Doss answered, "before we both go crazy."

"What if Tobias…?"

Doss leaned back, opened the buttons on her bodice, put his hands inside, under her camisole, to take the weight of her breasts. Chafed the nipples lightly with the sides of his thumbs.

"He won't hear," he said.

He bent to find a nipple, take it into his mouth. Suckled in the same nibbling, teasing way he'd tasted her earlobe.

Hannah plunged her fingers into his hair, groaned and tilted her head back, already surrendering. Already lost.

She tried to bring Gabe's face to her mind, hoping the image would give her the strength to stop—*stop*—before it was too late, but it wouldn't come.

Doss made free with her breasts, tonguing them until she was in a frenzy.

She sank against the door, barely able to breathe.

And then he knelt.

Hannah trembled. Even though the room was cold, perspiration broke out all over her body. She made a slight whimpering sound when Doss lifted her skirts, went under them and pulled down her drawers.

She felt him part her private place with his fingers, felt his tongue touch her, like fire. Sobbed his name, under her breath.

He took her full in his mouth, hungrily.

Her hips moved frantically, seeking him, and her knees buckled.

He braced her securely against the door, put her legs over his shoulders, first one, and then the other, and through all that, he drew on her.

She writhed against him, one hand pressed to her mouth so that the guttural cries pounding at the back of her throat wouldn't get out.

He suckled.

She felt a surge of heat, radiating from her center into every part of her, then stiffened in a spasm of release so violent that she was afraid she would splinter into pieces.

"Doss," she pleaded, because she knew it was going to happen again, and again.

And it did.

When it was over, he ducked out from under the hem of her skirt and held her as she sagged, spent, to her knees. They were facing each other, her breasts bared to him, her body still quivering with an ebbing tide of passion.

"We can stop here," he said quietly.

She shook her head. They'd gone past the place of turning back.

Doss opened his trousers, reached under her skirt and petticoat to take hold of her hips. Lifted her onto him.

She slid along his length, letting him fill her, exalting in the size and heat and slick hardness of him. She gave a loud moan, and he covered her mouth with his, kissed her senseless, even as he raised and lowered her, raised and lowered her. The friction was slow and exquisite. Hannah dug her fingers into his shoulders and rode him shamelessly until satisfaction overtook her again, convulsed her, like some giant fist, and didn't let go until she was limp with exhaustion.

Only when she wept with relief did Doss finish. She felt him erupt inside her, swallowed his groans as he gave himself up to her.

He brushed away her tears with his thumbs, still inside her, and looked deep into her eyes. "It's all right, Hannah," he said gruffly. "Please, don't cry."

He didn't understand.

She wasn't weeping for shame, though that would surely come, but for the most poignant of joys.

"No," she said softly. She plunged her fingers into his hair, kissed him boldly, fervently. "It's not that. I feel…"

He was growing hard within her again.

"Oh," she groaned.

He played with her nipples. And got harder still.

"Doss," she gasped. *"Doss—"*

Present Day

Sierra awakened with a start, sounding from the depths of a dream so erotic that she'd been on the verge of climax. The light dazzled her, and the muffled silence seemed to fill not only her bedroom, but the world beyond it.

She lay still for a long time, recovering. Listening to her own quick, shallow breathing. Waiting for her heartbeat to slow down.

Liam peeked through the doorway linking her room to his.

"Mom?"

"Come in," Sierra said.

He bounded across the threshold. "It snowed!" he whooped, heading straight for the window. "I mean, it *really* snowed!"

Sierra smiled, sat up in bed and put her feet on the floor.

A jolt of cold went through her.

"It's *freezing* in here!"

Liam turned from the window to grin at her. "Travis says the furnace is out."

"Travis?"

"He's downstairs," Liam said. "He'll get it going."

A dusty-smelling whoosh rose from the nearest heat vent, as if to illustrate the point.

"What's he doing here?" Sierra asked, scrambling through her suitcases for a bathrobe. All she had was a thin nylon thing, and when she saw it, she knew it would be worse than nothing, so she pulled the quilt off the bed and wrapped herself in that instead.

"Don't be a grump," Liam replied. "Travis is doing us a *favor,* Mom. We'd probably be icicles by now if it wasn't for him. Did you know that old stove downstairs *works?* Travis built a fire in it, and he put the coffee on, too. He said to tell you it will be ready in a couple of minutes and we're snowed in."

"Snowed in?"

"Keep up, Mom," Liam chirped. "There was a *blizzard* last night. That's why Travis came to make sure we were all right. I heard him knock, and I let him in."

Sierra joined Liam at the window and drew in her breath.

The whiteness of all that snow practically blinded her, but it was beautiful, too, in an apocalyptic way. She'd never seen anything like it before and, for a long moment, she was spellbound. Then her sensible side kicked in.

"Thank God the power didn't go out," she said, easing a little closer to the vent, which was spewing deliciously warm air.

"It *did,*" Liam informed her happily. "Travis got the generator started right away. We don't have lights or anything, but he said the furnace is all that matters."

She frowned. "How could he have made coffee?"

"On the *cookstove,* Mom," Liam said, with a roll of his eyes.

For the first time Sierra noticed that Liam was fully dressed.

He headed for the door. "I'd better go help Travis bring in the wood," he said. "Get some *clothes* on, will you?"

Five minutes later Sierra joined Travis and Liam in the kitchen, which was blessedly warm. Her jeans would do well enough, but she'd had to raid Meg's room for socks and a thick sweatshirt, because her tank tops weren't going to cut it.

"Are we *stranded* here?" she demanded, watching as Travis poured coffee from a blue enamel pot that looked like it came from a stash of camping gear.

He grinned. "Depends on how you look at it," he said. "Liam and I, we see it as an adventure."

"Some adventure," Sierra grumbled, but she took the coffee he offered and gave a grateful nod of thanks.

Travis chuckled. "Don't worry," he said. "You'll adjust."

Sierra hastened over to stand closer to the cookstove. "Does this happen often?"

"Only in winter," Travis quipped.

"Hilarious," she drawled.

Liam laughed uproariously.

"You are *enjoying* this," she accused, tousling her son's hair.

"It's *great!*" Liam cried. "Snow! Wait till the Geeks hear about this!"

"Liam," Sierra said.

He gave Travis a long-suffering look. "She hates it when I say 'geek,'" he explained.

Travis picked up his own mug of coffee, took a sip, his eyes full of laughter. Then he headed toward the door, put the cup on the counter and reclaimed his coat down from the peg.

"You're *leaving?*" Liam asked, horrified.

"Gotta see to the horses," Travis said, putting on his hat.

"Can I go with you?" Liam pleaded, and he sounded so desperately hopeful that Sierra swallowed the "no" that instantly sprang from her vocal cords.

"Your coat isn't warm enough," she said.

"Meg's got an old one around here someplace," Travis said carefully. "Hall closet, I think."

Liam dashed off to get it.

"I'll take care of him, Sierra," Travis told her quietly, when the boy was gone.

"You'd better," Sierra answered.

1919

Hannah knew by the profound silence, even before she opened her eyes, that it had been snowing all night. Lying alone in the big bed she'd shared with Gabe, she burrowed deeper into the covers and groaned.

She was sore.

She was satisfied.

She was a trollop.

A tramp.

She'd practically thrown herself at Doss the night before. She'd let him do things to her that no one else besides Gabe had ever done.

And now it was morning and she'd come to her senses and she would have to face him.

For all that, she felt strangely light, too.

Almost giddy.

Hannah pulled the covers up over her head and giggled.

Giggled.

She tried to be stern with herself.

This was *serious*.

Downstairs the stove lids rattled.

Doss was building a fire in the cookstove, the way he did every morning. He would put the coffee on to boil, then go out to the barn to attend to the livestock. When he got back, she'd be making breakfast, and they'd talk about how cold it was, and whether he ought to bring in extra wood from the shed, in case there was more snow on the way.

It would be an ordinary ranch morning.

Except that she'd behaved like a tart the night before.

Hannah tossed back the covers and got up. She wasn't one to avoid facing things, no matter how awkward they were. She and Doss had lost their heads and made love. That was that.

It wouldn't happen again.

They'd just go on, as if nothing had happened.

The water in the pitcher on the bureau was too cold to wash in.

Hannah decided she would heat some for a bath, after

the breakfast dishes were done. She'd send Tobias to the study to work at his school lessons, and Doss to the barn.

She dressed hastily, brushed her hair and wound it into the customary chignon at the back of her head. Just before she opened the bedroom door to step out into the new day, the pit of her stomach quivered. She drew a deep breath, squared her shoulders and turned the knob resolutely.

Doss had not left for the barn, as she'd expected. He was still in the kitchen, and when she came down the back stairs and froze on the bottom step, he looked at her, reddened and looked away.

Tobias was by the back door, pulling on his heaviest coat. "Doss and me are fixing to ride down to the bend and look in on the widow Jessup," he told Hannah matter-of-factly, and he sounded like a grown man, fit to make such decisions on his own. "Could be her pump's frozen, and we're not sure she has enough firewood."

Out of the corner of her eye, Hannah saw Doss watching her.

"Go out and see to the cow," Doss told Tobias. "Make sure there's no ice on her trough."

It was an excuse to speak to her alone, Hannah knew, and she was unnerved. She resisted an urge to touch her hair with both hands or smooth her skirts.

Tobias banged out the back door, whistling.

"He's not strong enough to ride to the Jessups' place in this weather," Hannah said. "It's four miles if it's a stone's throw, and you'll have to cross the creek."

"Hannah," Doss said firmly, grimly. "The boy will be fine."

She felt her own color rise then, remembering all they'd done together, on the spare room floor, herself and this man. She swallowed and lifted her chin a notch, so he wouldn't think she was ashamed.

"About last night—" Doss began. He looked distraught.

Hannah waited, blushing furiously now. Wishing the floor would open, so she could fall right through to China and never be seen or heard from again.

Doss shoved a hand through his hair. "I'm sorry," he said.

Hannah hadn't expected anything except shame, but she was stung by it, just the same. "We'll just pretend—" She had to stop, clear her throat, blink a couple of times. "We'll just pretend it didn't happen."

His jaw tightened. "Hannah, it *did* happen, and pretending won't change that."

She intertwined her fingers, clasped them so tightly that the knuckles ached. Looked down at the floor. "What else can we do, Doss?" she asked, almost in a whisper.

"Suppose there's a child?"

Hannah hadn't once thought of that possibility, though it seemed painfully obvious in the bright, rational light of day. She drew in a sharp breath and put a hand to her throat.

How would they explain such a thing to Tobias? To the McKettricks and the people of Indian Rock?

"I'd have to go to Montana," she said, after a long time. "To my folks."

"Not with my baby growing inside you, you wouldn't," Doss replied, so sharply that Hannah's gaze shot back to his face.

"Doss, the scandal—"

"To hell with the scandal!"

Hannah reached out, pulled back Holt's chair at

the table and sank into it. "Maybe I'm not. Surely just once—"

"Maybe you are," Doss insisted.

Hannah's eyes smarted. She'd wanted more children, but not like this. Not out of wedlock, and by her late husband's brother. Folks would call her a hussy, with considerable justification, and they'd make Tobias's life a plain misery, too. They'd point and whisper, and the other kids would tease.

"What are we going to do, then?" she asked.

He crossed the room, sat astraddle the long bench next to the table, so close she could feel the warmth of his body, glowing like the fresh fire blazing inside the cookstove.

His very proximity made her remember things better forgotten.

"There's only one thing we can do, Hannah. We'll get married."

She gaped at him. *"Married?"*

"It's the only decent thing to do."

The word *decent* stabbed at Hannah. She was a proud person, and she'd always lived a respectable life. Until the night before. "We don't love each other," she said, her voice small. "And anyway, I might not be—expecting."

"I'm not taking the chance," Doss told her. "As soon as the trail clears a little, we're going into Indian Rock and get married."

"I have some say in this," Hannah pointed out.

Outside, on the back porch, Tobias thumped his boots against the step, to shake off the snow.

"Do you?" Doss asked.

CHAPTER SIX

Present Day

WHILE TRAVIS AND LIAM WERE in the barn, Sierra inspected the wood-burning stove. She found a skillet, set it on top, took bacon and eggs from the refrigerator, which was ominously dark and silent, and laid strips of the bacon in the pan. When the meat began to sizzle, she felt a little thrill of accomplishment.

She was actually *cooking* on a stove that dated from the nineteenth century. Briefly, she felt connected with all the McKettrick women who had gone before her.

When the electricity came on, with a startling revving sound, she was almost sorry. Keeping an eye on breakfast, she switched on the small countertop TV to catch the morning news.

The entire northern part of Arizona had been inundated in the blizzard, and thousands were without power. She watched as images of people skiing to work flashed across the screen.

The telephone rang, and she held the portable receiver between her shoulder and ear to answer. "Hello?"

"It's Eve," a gracious voice replied. "Is that you, Sierra?"

Sierra went utterly still. Travis and Liam tramped in from outside, laughing about something. They both fell silent at the sight of her, and neither one moved after Travis pushed the door shut.

"Hello?" Eve prompted. "Sierra, are you there?"

"I'm…I'm here," Sierra said.

Travis took off his coat and hat, crossed the room and elbowed her away from the stove. "Go," he told her, cocking a thumb toward the center of the house. "Liam and I will see to the grub."

She nodded, grateful, and hurried out of the warm kitchen. The dining room was frigid.

"Is this a bad time to talk?" Eve asked. She sounded uncertain, even a little shy.

"No—" Sierra answered hastily, finally gaining the study. She closed the door and sat in the big leather chair she'd occupied the night before, waiting for the fire to go out. Now she could see her breath, and she wished the blaze was still burning. "No, it's fine."

Eve let out a long breath. "I see on the Weather Channel that you've been hit with quite a storm up there," she said.

Sierra nodded, remembered that her mother—this woman she didn't know—couldn't see her. "Yes," she replied. "We have power again, thanks to Travis. He got the generator running right away, so the furnace would work and—"

She swallowed the rush of too-cheerful words. She'd been blathering.

"Poor Travis," Eve said.

"Poor Travis?" Sierra echoed. "Why?"

"Didn't he tell you? Didn't Meg?"

"No," Sierra said. "Nobody told me anything."

There was a long pause, then Eve sighed. "I'm probably speaking out of turn," she said, "but we've all been a little worried about Travis. He's like a member of the family, you know. His younger brother, Brody, died in an explosion a few months ago. It really threw Travis. He walked away from the company and just about everyone he knew. Meg had to talk fast to get him to come and stay on the ranch."

Sierra was very glad she'd brought the phone out of the kitchen. "I didn't know," she said.

"I've already said more than I should have," Eve told her ruefully. "And anyway, I called to see how you and Liam are doing. I know you're not used to cold weather, and when I saw the storm report, I had to call."

"We're okay," Sierra said. Had she known the woman better, she might have confided her worries about Liam— how he claimed he'd seen a ghost in his room. She still planned to call his new doctor, but driving to Flagstaff for an appointment would be out of the question, considering the state of the roads.

"I hear some hesitation in your voice," Eve said. She was treading lightly, Sierra could tell, and she would be a hard person to fool. Eve ran McKettrickCo, and hundreds of people answered to her.

Sierra gave a nervous laugh, more hysteria than amusement. "Liam claims the house is haunted," she admitted.

"Oh, that," Eve answered, and she actually sounded relieved.

"'Oh, that'?" Sierra challenged, sitting up straighter.

"They're harmless," Eve said. "The ghosts, I mean. If that's what they are."

"You know about the ghosts?"

Eve laughed. "Of course I do. I grew up in that house. But I'm not sure *ghosts* is the right word. To me, it always felt more like sharing the place than its being haunted. I got the sense that they—the other people—were as alive as I was. That they'd have been just as surprised, had we ever come face-to-face."

Sierra's mind spun. She squeezed the bridge of her nose between a thumb and forefinger. The piano notes she'd heard the night before tinkled sadly in her memory. "You're not saying you actually *believe*—"

"I'm saying I've had experiences," Eve told her. "I've never seen anyone. Just had a strong sense of someone else being present. And, of course, there was the famous disappearing teapot."

Sierra sank against the back of the chair, both relieved and confounded. Had she told Meg about the teapot? She couldn't recall. Perhaps Travis had mentioned it—called Eve to report that her daughter was a little loony?

"Sierra?" Eve asked.

"I'm still here."

"I would get the teapot out," Eve recounted, "and leave the room to do something else. When I came back, it was in the china cabinet again. The same thing used to happen to my mother, and my grandmother, too. They thought it was Lorelei."

"How could that be?"

"Who knows?" Eve asked, patently unconcerned. "Life is mysterious."

It certainly is, Sierra thought. Little girls get separated from their mothers, and no one even comes looking for them.

"I'd like to come and see you," Eve went on, "as soon as the weather clears. Would that be all right, Sierra? If I spent a few days at the ranch? So we could talk in person?"

Sierra's heart rose into her throat and swelled there. "It's your house," she said, but she wanted to throw down the phone, snatch Liam, jump into the car and speed away before she had to face this woman.

"I won't come if you're not ready," Eve said gently.

I may never be ready, Sierra thought. "I guess I am," she murmured.

"Good," Eve replied. "Then I'll be there as soon as the jet can land. Barring another snowstorm, that should be tomorrow or the next day."

The jet? "Should we pick you up somewhere?"

"I'll have a car meet me," Eve said. "Do you need anything, Sierra?"

I could have used a mother when I was growing up. And when I had Liam and Dad acted as though nothing had changed—well, you would have come in handy then, too, Mom. "I'm fine," she answered.

"I'll call again before I leave here," Eve promised. Then, after another tentative pause and a brief goodbye, she rang off.

Sierra sat a long time in that chair, still holding the phone, and might not have moved at all if Liam hadn't come to tell her breakfast was on the table.

1919

It was a cold, seemingly endless ride to the Jessup place, and hard going all the way. More than once Doss glanced anxiously at his nephew, bundled to his eyeballs and jostling patiently alongside Doss's mount on the mule, and wished he'd listened to Hannah and left the boy at home.

More than once, he attempted to broach the subject that was uppermost in his mind—he'd been up half the night wrestling with it—but he couldn't seem to get a proper handle on the matter at all.

I mean to marry your ma.

That was the straightforward truth, a simple thing to say.

But Tobias was bound to ask why. Maybe he'd even raise an objection. He'd loved his pa, and he might just put his old uncle Doss right square in his place.

"You ever think about livin' in town?" Tobias asked, catching him by surprise.

Doss took a moment to change directions in his mind. "Sometimes," he answered, when he was sure it was what he really meant. "Especially in the wintertime."

"It's no warmer there than it is here," Tobias reasoned. Whatever he was getting at, it wasn't coming through in his tone or his manner.

"No," Doss agreed. "But there are other folks around. A man could get his mail at the post office every day, instead of waiting a week for it to come by wagon, and take a meal in a restaurant now and again. And I'll admit that library is an enticement, small as it is." He thought fondly of the books lining the study walls back at the ranch house. He'd read all of them, at one time or another, and most several times. He'd borrowed from his uncle Kade's collection, and his ma sent him a regular supply from Texas. Just the same, he couldn't get enough of the damn things.

"Ma's been talking about heading back to Montana," Tobias blurted, but he didn't look at Doss when he spoke. Just kept his eyes on the close-clipped mane of that old mule. "If she tries to make me go, I'll run away."

Doss swallowed. He knew Hannah thought about moving in with the homefolks, of course, but hearing it said out loud made him feel as if he'd not only been thrown from his horse, but stomped on, too. "Where would you go?" he asked, when he thought he could get the words out easy. He wasn't entirely successful. "If you ran off, I mean?"

Tobias turned in the saddle to look him full in the face. "I'd hide up in the hills somewhere," he said, with the conviction of innocence. "Maybe that canyon where Kade and Mandy faced down those outlaws."

Doss suppressed a smile. He'd grown up on that story himself, and to this day, he wondered how much of it was fact and how much was legend. Mandy was a sharpshooter, and she'd given Annie Oakley a run for her money, in her time. Kade had been the town marshal, with an office in Indian Rock back then, so maybe it had happened just the way his pa and uncles related it.

"Mighty cold up there," he told the boy mildly. "Just a cave for shelter, and where would you get food?"

Tobias's shoulders slumped a little, under all that wool Hannah had swaddled him in. If the kid took a spill from the mule, he'd probably bounce. "I could hunt," he said. "Pa taught me how to shoot."

"McKettricks," Doss replied, "don't run away."

Tobias scowled at him. "They don't live in *Missoula,* either."

Doss chuckled, in spite of the heavy feeling that had settled over his heart after he and Hannah had made love and stayed there ever since. Gabe was dead, but it still felt as if he'd betrayed him. "They live in all sorts of places," Doss said. "You know that."

"I won't go, anyhow," Tobias said.

Doss cleared his throat. "Maybe you won't have to."

That got the boy's full attention. His eyes were full of questions.

"I wonder what you'd say if I married your ma."

Tobias looked as though he'd swallowed a lantern with the wick burning. "I'd like that," he said. "I'd like that a *lot!*"

Too bad Hannah wasn't as keen on the prospect as

her son. "I thought you might not care for the idea," Doss confessed. "My being your pa's brother and all."

"Pa would be glad," Tobias said. "I know he would."

Secretly, Doss knew it, too. Gabe had been a practical man, and he'd have wanted all of them to get on with their lives.

Doss's eyes smarted something fierce, all of a sudden, and he had to pull his hat brim down. Look away for a few moments.

Take care of Hannah and my boy, Gabe had said. *Promise me, Doss.*

"Did Ma say she'd hitch up with you?" Tobias asked, frowning so that his face crinkled comically. "Last night I said she ought to, and she said it wouldn't be right."

Doss stood in the stirrups to stretch his legs. "Things can change," he said cautiously. "Even in a night."

"Do you love my ma?"

It was a hard question to answer, at least aloud. He'd loved Hannah from the day Gabe had brought her home as his bride. Loved her fiercely, hopelessly and honorably, from a proper distance. Gabe had guessed it right away, though. Waited until the two of them were alone in the barn, slapped Doss on the shoulder and said, *Don't you be ashamed, little brother. It's easy to love my Hannah.*

"Of course I do," Doss said. "She's family."

Tobias made a face. "I don't mean like that."

Doss's belly tightened. The boy was only eight, and he couldn't possibly know what had gone on last night in the spare room.

Could he?

"How *do* you mean, then?"

"Pa used to kiss Ma all the time. He used to swat her on the bustle, too, when he thought nobody was looking. It always made her laugh, and stand real close to him, with her arms around his neck."

Doss might have gripped the saddle horn with both hands, because of the pain, if he'd been riding alone. It wasn't the reminder of how much Hannah and Gabe had loved each other that seared him, though. It was the loss of his brother, the way of things then, and it all being over for good.

"I'll treat your mother right, Tobias," he said, after more hat-brim pulling and more looking away.

"You sound pretty sure she'll say yes," the boy commented.

"She already has," Doss replied.

Present Day

More snow began to fall at mid-morning and, worried that the power would go off again, and stay off this time, Sierra gathered her and Liam's dirty laundry and threw a load into the washing machine. She'd telephoned Liam's doctor in Flagstaff, from the study, while he and Travis were filling the dishwasher, but she hadn't mentioned the hallucinations. She'd heard the piano music herself, after all, and then Eve had made such experiences seem almost normal.

Sierra didn't know precisely what was happening, and she was still unsettled by Liam's claims of seeing a boy in old-time clothes, but she wasn't ready to bring up the subject with an outsider, whether that outsider had a medical degree or not.

Dr. O'Meara had reviewed Liam's records, since they'd been expressed to her from the clinic in Florida, and she wanted to make sure he had an inhaler on hand. She'd promised to call in a prescription to the pharmacy in Indian Rock, and they'd made an appointment for the following Monday afternoon.

Now Liam was in the study, watching TV, and Travis was outside splitting wood for the stove and the fireplaces. If the power went off again, she'd need firewood for cooking. The generator kept the furnace running, along with a few of the lights, but it burned a lot of gas and there was always the possibility that it would break down or freeze up.

Travis came in with an armload just as she was starting to prepare lunch.

Watching him, Sierra thought about what Eve had said on the phone earlier. Travis's younger brother had died horribly, and very recently. He'd left his job, Travis had, and come to the ranch to live in a trailer and look after horses.

He didn't look like a man carrying a burden, but appearances were deceiving. Nobody knew that better than Sierra did.

"What kind of work did you do, before you came here?" she asked, and then wished she hadn't brought the subject up at all. Travis's face closed instantly, and his eyes went blank.

"Nothing special," he said.

She nodded. "I was a cocktail waitress," she told him, because she felt she ought to offer him something after asking what was evidently an intrusive question.

Standing there, beside the antique cookstove and the wood box, in his leather coat and cowboy hat, Travis looked as though he'd stepped through a time warp, out of an earlier century.

"I know," he said. "Meg told me."

"Of course she did." Sierra poured canned soup into a saucepan, stirred it industriously and blushed.

Travis didn't say anything more for a long time. Then, "I was a lawyer for McKettrickCo," he told her.

Sierra stole a sidelong glance at him. He looked tense, standing there holding his hat in one hand. "Impressive," she said.

"Not so much," he countered. "It's a tradition in my family, being a lawyer, I mean. At least, with everyone but my brother, Brody. He became a meth addict instead, and blew himself to kingdom-come brewing up a batch. Go figure."

Sierra turned to face Travis. Noticed that his jaw was hard and his eyes even harder. He was angry, in pain, or both.

"I'm so sorry," she said.

"Yeah," Travis replied tersely. "Me, too."

He started for the door.

"Stay for lunch?" Sierra asked.

"Another time," he answered, and then he was gone.

1919

It was near sunset when Doss and Tobias rode in from the Jessup place, and by then Hannah was fit to be tied. She'd paced for most of the afternoon, after it started to snow again, fretting over all the things that could go wrong along the way.

The horse or the mule could have gone lame or fallen through the ice crossing the creek.

There could have been an avalanche. Just last year, a whole mountainside of snow had come crashing down on to the roof of a cabin and crushed it to the ground, with a family inside.

Wolves prowled the countryside, too, bold with the desperation of their hunger. They killed cattle and sometimes people.

Doss hadn't even taken his rifle.

When Hannah heard the horses, she ran to the window, wiped the fog from the glass with her apron hem. She watched as they dismounted and led their mounts into the barn.

She'd baked pies that day to keep from going crazy, and the kitchen was redolent with the aroma. She smoothed her skirts, patted her hair and turned away so she wouldn't be caught looking if Doss or Tobias happened to glance toward the house.

Almost an hour passed before they came inside—they'd done the barn chores—and Hannah had the table set, the lamps lighted and the coffee made. She wanted to fuss over Tobias, check his ears and fingers for frostbite and his forehead for fever, but she wouldn't let herself do it.

Doss wasn't deceived by her smiling restraint, she could see that, but Tobias looked downright relieved, as though he'd expected her to pounce the minute he came through the door.

"How did you find Widow Jessup?" she asked.

"She was right where we left her last time," Doss said with a slight grin.

Hannah gave him a look.

"She was fresh out of firewood," Tobias expounded importantly, unwrapping himself, layer by layer, until he stood in just his trousers and shirt, with melted snow pooling around his feet. "It's a good thing we went down there. She'd have froze for sure."

Doss looked tired, but his eyes twinkled. "For sure," he confirmed. "She got Tobias here by the ears and kissed him all over his face, she was so grateful that he'd saved her."

Tobias let out a yelp of mortification and took a swing at Doss, who sidestepped him easily.

"Stop your roughhousing and wash up for supper,"

Hannah said, but it did her heart good to see it. Gabe used to come in from the barn, toss Tobias over one shoulder and carry him around the kitchen like a sack of grain. The boy had howled with laughter and pummeled Gabe's chest with his small fists in mock resistance. She'd missed the ordinary things like that more than anything except being held in Gabe's arms.

She served chicken and dumplings, in her best Blue Willow dishes, with apple pie for dessert.

Tobias ate with a fresh-air, long-ride appetite and nearly fell asleep in his chair once his stomach was filled.

Doss got up, hoisted him into his arms and carried him, head bobbing, toward the stairs.

Hannah's throat went raw, watching them go.

She poured a second cup of coffee for Doss, had it waiting when he came back a few minutes later.

"Did you put Tobias in his nightshirt and cover him with the spare quilt?" she asked, when Doss appeared at the bottom of the steps. "He mustn't take a chill—"

"I took off his shoes and threw him in like he was," Doss interrupted. That twinkle was still in his eyes, but there was a certain wariness there, too. "I made sure he was warm, so stop fretting."

Hannah had put the dishes in a basin of hot water to soak, and she lingered at the table, sipping tea brewed in Lorelei's pot.

Doss sat down in his father's chair, cupped his hands around his own mug of steaming coffee. "I spoke to Tobias about our getting married," he said bluntly. "And he's in favor of it."

Heat pounded in Hannah's cheeks, spawned by indignation and something else that she didn't dare think about. "Doss McKettrick," she whispered in reproach, "you shouldn't have done that. I'm his mother and it was my place to—"

"It's done, Hannah," Doss said. "Let it go at that."

Hannah huffed out a breath. "Don't you tell me what's done and ought to be let go," she protested. "I won't take orders from you now or after we're married."

He grinned. "Maybe you won't," he said. "But that doesn't mean I won't give them."

She laughed, surprising herself so much that she slapped a hand over her mouth to stifle the sound. That gesture, in turn, brought back recollections of the night before, when Doss had made love to her, and she'd wanted to cry out with the pleasure of it.

She blushed so hard her face burned, and this time it was Doss who laughed.

"I figure we're in for another blizzard," he said. "Might be spring before we can get to town and stand up in front of a preacher. I hope you're not looking like a watermelon smuggler before then."

Hannah opened her mouth, closed it again.

Doss's eyes danced as he took another sip of his coffee.

"That was an insufferably *forward* thing to say!" Hannah accused.

"You're a fine one to talk about being forward," Doss observed, and repeated back something she'd said at that very height of her passion.

"That's *enough,* Mr. McKettrick."

Doss set his cup down, pushed back his chair and stood. "I'm going out to the barn to look in on the stock again. Maybe you ought to come along. Make the job go faster, if you lent a hand."

Hannah squirmed on the bench.

Doss crossed the room, took his coat and hat down from the pegs by the door. "Way out there, a person could holler if they wanted to. Be nobody to hear."

Hannah did some more squirming.

"Fresh hay to lie in, too," Doss went on. "Nice and soft,

and if a man were to spread a couple of horse blankets over it—"

Heat surged through Hannah, brought her to an aching simmer. She sputtered something and waved him away.

Doss chuckled, opened the door and went out, whistling merrily under his breath.

Hannah waited. If Doss McKettrick thought he was going to have his way with her—in the *barn,* of all places—well, he was just...

She got up, went to the stove and banked the fire with a poker.

He was just *right,* that was what he was.

She chose her biggest shawl, wrapped herself in it, and hurried after him.

Present Day

As soon as Sierra put supper on the table that night, the power went off again. While she scrambled for candles, Liam rushed to the nearest window.

"Travis's trailer's dark," he said. "He'll get *hypothermia* out there."

Sierra sighed. "I'll bet he comes back to see to the furnace, just like he did this morning. We'll ask him to have supper with us."

"I see him!" Liam cried gleefully. "He's coming out of the barn, with a lantern!" He raced for the door, and before Sierra could stop him, he was outside, with no coat on, galloping through the deepening snow and shouting Travis's name.

Sierra pulled on her own coat, grabbed Liam's and hurried after him.

Travis was already herding him toward the house.

"Mom made meat loaf, and she says you can have some," Liam was saying, as he tramped breathlessly along.

Sierra wrapped his coat around him, and would have scolded him, if her gaze hadn't collided unexpectedly with Travis's.

Travis shook his head.

She swallowed all that she'd been about to say and hustled her son into the house.

"I'll start the generator," Travis said.

Sierra nodded hastily and shut the door.

"Liam McKettrick," she burst out, "what were you thinking, going out in that cold without a coat?"

In the candlelight, she saw Liam's lower lip wobble. "Travis said it isn't the cowboy way. He was about to put his coat on me when you came."

"*What* isn't the 'cowboy way'?" she asked, chafing his icy hands between hers and praying he wouldn't have an asthma attack or come down with pneumonia.

"Not wearing a coat," Liam replied, downcast. "A cowboy is always prepared for any kind of weather, and he never rushes off half-cocked, without his gear."

Sierra relaxed a little, stifled a smile. "Travis is right," she said.

Liam brightened. "Do cowboys eat meat loaf?"

"I'm pretty sure they do," Sierra answered.

The furnace came on, and she silently blessed Travis Reid for being there.

He let himself into the kitchen a few minutes later. By then Sierra had set another place at the table and lit several more candles. They all sat down at the same time, and there was something so natural about their gathering that way that Sierra's throat caught.

"I hope you're hungry," she said, feeling awkward.

"I'm starved," Travis replied.

"Cowboys eat meat loaf, right?" Liam inquired.

Travis grinned. "This one does," he said.

"This one does, too," Liam announced.

Sierra laughed, but tears came to her eyes at the same time. She was glad of the relative darkness, hoping no one would notice.

"Once," Liam said, scooping a helping of meat loaf onto his plate, his gaze adoring as he focused on Travis, "I saw this show on the Science Channel. They found a cave man, in a block of ice. He was, like *fourteen thousand* years old! I betcha they could take some of his DNA and clone him if they wanted to." He stopped for a quick breath. "And he was all blue, too. That's what you'll look like, if you sleep in that trailer tonight."

"You're not a kid," Travis teased. "You're a forty-year-old wearing a pygmy suit."

"I'm *really* smart," Liam went on. "So you ought to listen to me."

Travis looked at Sierra, and their eyes caught, with an almost audible click and held.

"The generator's low on gas," Travis said. "So we have two choices. We can get in my truck and hope there are some empty motel rooms at the Lamplight Inn, or we can build up the fire in that cookstove and camp out in the kitchen."

Liam had no trouble at all making the choice. "Camp out!" he whooped, waving his fork in the air. "Camp out!"

"You can't be serious," Sierra said to Travis.

"Oh, I'm serious, all right," he answered.

"Lamplight Inn," Sierra voted.

"Roads are bad," Travis replied. "*Real* bad."

"Once on TV, I saw a thing about these people who froze to death right in their car," Liam put in.

"Be quiet," Sierra told him.

"Happens all the time," Travis said.

Which was how the three of them ended up bundled in sleeping bags, with couch and chair cushions for a make-shift mattress, lying side by side within the warm radius of the wood-burning stove.

CHAPTER SEVEN

1919

HANNAH AND DOSS RETURNED separately from the barn, by tacit agreement. Hannah, weak-kneed with residual pleasure and reeling with guilt, pumped water into a bucket to pour into the near-empty reservoir on the cookstove, then filled the two biggest kettles she had and set them on the stove to heat. She was adding wood to the fire when she heard Doss come in.

She blushed furiously, unable to meet his gaze, though she could feel it burning into her flesh, right through the clothes he'd sweet-talked her out of just an hour before, laying her down in the soft, surprisingly warm hay in an empty stall, kissing and caressing and nibbling at her until she'd begged him to take her.

Begged him.

She'd carried on something awful while he was at it, too.

"Look at me, Hannah," he said.

She glared at Doss, marched past him into the pantry and dragged out the big wash tub stored there under a high shelf. She set it in front of the stove with an eloquent *clang.*

"Hannah," Doss repeated.

"Go upstairs," she told him, flustered. "Leave me to my bath."

"You can't wash away what we did," he said.

She whirled on him that time, hands on her hips, fiery with temper. "Get out," she ordered, keeping her voice down in case Tobias was still awake or even listening at the top of the stairs. "I need my privacy."

Doss raised both hands to shoulder height, palms out, but his words were juxtaposed to the gesture. "If we're going to talk about what you need, Hannah, it's not a bath. It's a lot more of what we just did in the barn."

"Tobias might hear you!" Hannah whispered, outraged. If the broom hadn't been on the back porch, she'd have grabbed it up and whacked him silly with it.

"He wouldn't know what we were talking about even if he did," Doss argued mildly, lowering his hands. He approached, plucked a piece of straw from Hannah's hair and tickled her under the chin with it.

She felt as though she'd been electrified, and slapped his hand away.

He laughed, a low, masculine sound, leaned in and nibbled at her lower lip. "Good night, Hannah," he said.

A hot shiver of renewed need went through her. How could that be? He'd satisfied her that night, and the one before. Both times he'd taken her to heights she hadn't even reached with Gabe.

The difference was, she'd been Gabe's wife, in the eyes of God and man, and she'd *loved* him. She not only wasn't married to Doss, she didn't love him. She just *wanted* him, that was all, and the realization galled her.

"You've turned me into a hussy," she said.

Doss chuckled, shook his head. "If you say so, Hannah," he answered, "it must be true."

With that, he kissed her forehead, turned and left the kitchen.

She listened to the sound of his boot heels on the stairs,

heard his progress along the second-floor hallway, even knew when he opened Tobias's door to look in on the boy before retiring to his own room. Only when she'd heard his door close did Hannah let out her breath.

When the water in the kettles was scalding hot, Hannah poured it into the tub, sneaked upstairs for a towel, a bar of soap and a nightgown. By the time she'd put out all the lanterns in the kitchen and stripped off her clothes, her bathwater had cooled to a temperature that made her sigh when she stepped into it.

She soaked for a few minutes, and then scrubbed with a vengeance.

It turned out that Doss had been right.

She tried but she couldn't wash away the things he'd made her feel.

A tear slipped down her cheek as she dried herself off, then donned her nightgown. She dragged the tub to the back door and on to the step, drained it over one side and dashed back in, covered with gooseflesh from the chill.

"I'm sorry, Gabe," she said, very quietly, huddling by the stove. "I'm sorry."

Present Day

Travis was building up the fire when Sierra opened her eyes the next morning. "Stay in your sleeping bag," he told her. "It's colder than a meat locker in here."

Liam, lying between them throughout the night, was still asleep, but his breathing was a shallow rattle. Sierra sat bolt-upright, watchful, holding her own breath. Not feeling the external chill at all, except as a vague biting sensation.

Liam opened his eyes, blinked. "Mom," he said. "I can't—"

Breathe, Sierra finished the sentence for him, replayed it in her mind.

Mom, I can't breathe.

She bounded out of the sleeping bag, scrambled for her purse, which was lying on the counter and rummaged for Liam's inhaler.

He began to wheeze, and when Sierra turned to rush back to him, she saw a look of panic in his eyes.

"Take it easy, Liam," she said, as she handed him the inhaler.

He grasped it in both hands, all too familiar with the routine, and pressed the tube to his mouth and nose.

Travis watched grimly.

Sierra dropped on to her knees next to her boy, put an arm loosely around his shoulders. *Let it work,* she prayed silently. *Please let it work!*

Liam lowered the inhaler and stared apologetically up into Sierra's eyes. He could barely get enough wind to speak. He was, in essence, choking. "It's—I think it's broken, Mom—"

"I'll warm up the truck," Travis said, and banged out of the house.

Desperate, Sierra took the inhaler, shook it and shoved it back into Liam's hands. It *wasn't* empty—she wouldn't have taken a chance like that—but it must have been clogged or somehow defective. "Try again," she urged, barely avoiding panic herself.

Outside, Travis's truck roared audibly to life. He gunned the motor a couple of times.

Liam struggled to take in the medication, but the inhaler simply wasn't working.

Travis returned, picked Liam up in his arms, sleeping bag and all, and headed for the door again. Sierra, frightened as she was, had to hurry to catch up, snatching her coat from the peg and her purse from the counter on the way out.

The snow had stopped, but there must have been two feet of it on the ground. Travis shifted the truck into four-wheel drive and the tires grabbed for purchase, finally caught.

"Take it easy, buddy," he told Liam, who was on Sierra's lap, the seat belt fastened around both of them. "Take it real easy."

Liam nodded solemnly. He was drawing in shallow gasps of air now, but not enough. *Not enough.* His lips were turning blue.

Sierra held him tight, but not too tight. Rested her chin on top of his head and prayed.

The roads hadn't been plowed—in fact, except for sloping drifts on either side, Sierra wouldn't have known where they were. Still, the truck rolled over them as easily as if they were bare.

What if we'd been alone, Liam and me? Sierra thought frantically. Her old station wagon, a snow-covered hulk in the driveway in front of the house, probably wouldn't have started, and even if it had by some miracle, the chances were good that they'd have ended up in the ditch somewhere along the way to safety.

"It's going to be okay," she heard Travis say, and she'd thought he was talking to Liam. When she glanced at him, though, she knew he'd meant the words for her.

She kept her voice even. "Is there a hospital in Indian Rock?" She and Liam had passed through the town the day they arrived, but she didn't remember seeing anything but houses, a diner or two, a drugstore, several bars and a gas station. She'd been too busy trying to follow the hand-drawn map Meg had scanned and sent to her by email—the McKettricks' private cemetery was marked with an X, and the ranch house an uneven square with lines for a roof.

"A clinic," Travis said. He looked down at Liam again, then turned his gaze back to the road. The set of his jaw was hard, and he pulled his cell phone from the pocket of his coat and handed it to Sierra.

She dialed 411 and asked to be connected.

When a voice answered, Sierra explained the situation as calmly as she could, keeping it low-key for Liam's sake. They'd been through at least a dozen similar episodes during his short life, and it never got easier. Each time, Sierra was hysterical, though she didn't dare let that show. Liam was taking his cues from her. If she lost it, he would, too, and the results could be disastrous.

The clinic receptionist seemed blessedly unruffled. "We'll be ready when you get here," she said.

Sierra thanked the woman and ended the call, set the phone on the seat.

By the time they arrived at the town's only medical facility, Liam was struggling to remain conscious. Travis pulled up in front, gave the horn a hard blast and was around to Sierra's side with the door open before she managed to get the seat belt unbuckled.

Two medical assistants, accompanied by a gray-haired doctor, met them with a gurney. Liam was whisked away. Sierra tried to follow, but Travis and one of the nurses stopped her.

Her first instinct was to fight.

"My son needs me!" She'd meant it for a scream, but it came out as more of a whimper.

"We'll need your name and that of the patient," a clerk informed her, advancing with a clipboard. "And of course there's the matter of insurance—"

Travis glared the woman into retreat. "Her *name*," he said, "is McKettrick."

"Oh," the clerk said, and ducked behind her desk.

Sierra needed something, anything, to do, or she was going to rip apart every room in that place until she found

Liam, gathered him into her arms. "My purse," she said. "I must have left it in the truck—"

"I'll get it," Travis said, but first he steered her toward a chair in the waiting area and sat her down.

Tears of frustration and stark terror filled her eyes. What was happening to Liam? Was he breathing? Were they forcing the hated tube down into his bronchial passage even at that moment?

Travis cupped her face between his hands, for just a moment, and his palms felt cold and rough from ranch work.

The sensation triggered something in Sierra, but she was too distraught to know what it was.

"I'll be right back," he promised.

And he was.

Sierra snatched her bag from his hands, scrabbled through it to find her wallet. Found the insurance card Eve had sent by express the same day Sierra agreed to take the McKettrick name and spend a year on the Triple M, with Liam. She might have kissed that card, if Travis hadn't been watching.

The clerk nodded a little nervously when Sierra walked up to the desk and asked for the papers she needed to fill out.

Patient's Name. Well, that was easy enough. She scrawled Liam Bres—crossed out the last part, and wrote McKettrick instead.

Address? She had to consult Travis on that one. Everybody in Indian Rock knew where the Triple M was, she was sure, but the people in the insurance company's claims office might not.

Occupation? Child.

Damn it, Liam was a little boy, hardly more than a baby. Things like this shouldn't happen to him.

Sierra printed her own name, as guarantor. She bit her lip when asked about her job. Unemployed? She couldn't write that.

Travis, watching, took the clipboard and pen from her and inserted, Damn good mother.

The tears came again.

Travis got up, with the forms and the clipboard and the insurance card, inscribed with the magical name and carried them over to the waiting clerk.

He was halfway back to Sierra when the doctor reappeared.

"Hello, Travis," he said, but his gaze was on Sierra's face, and she couldn't read it, for all the practice she'd had.

"I'm Sierra McKettrick," she said. The name still felt like a garment that didn't quite fit, but if it would help Liam in any way, she would use it every chance she got. "My son—"

"He'll be fine," the doctor said kindly. His eyes were a faded blue, his features craggy and weathered. "Just the same, I think we ought to send him up to Flagstaff to the hospital, at least overnight. For observation, you understand. And because they've got a reliable power source up there."

"Is he awake?" Sierra asked anxiously.

"Partially sedated," replied the doctor, exchanging glances with Travis. "We had to perform an intubation."

Sierra knew how Liam hated tubes, and how frightened he probably was, sedated or not. "I have to see him," she said, prepared for an argument.

"Of course" was the immediate and very gentle answer.

Sierra felt Travis's hand close around hers. She clung, instead of pulling away, as she would have done with any other virtual stranger.

A few minutes later they were standing on either side of Liam's bed in one of the treatment rooms. His eyes widened with recognition when he saw Sierra, and he pointed, with one small finger, to the mouthpiece of his oxygen tube.

She nodded, blinking hard and trying to smile. Took his hand.

"You have to spend the night in the hospital in Flagstaff," she told him, "but don't be scared, okay? Because I'm going with you."

Liam relaxed visibly. Turned his eyes to Travis. Sierra's heart twisted at the hope she saw in her little boy's face.

"Me, too," Travis said hoarsely.

Liam nodded and drifted off to sleep.

The doctor had ordered an ambulance, and Sierra rode with Liam, while Travis followed in the truck.

There was more paperwork to do in Flagstaff, but Sierra was calmer now. She sat in a chair next to Liam's bed and filled in the lines.

Travis entered with two cups of vending-machine coffee, just as she was finishing.

"Thank you," Sierra said, and she wasn't just talking about the coffee.

"Wranglers like Liam and me," he replied, watching the boy with a kind of fretful affection, "we stick together when the going gets tough."

She accepted the paper cup Travis offered and set the ubiquitous clipboard aside to take a sip. Travis drew up a second chair.

"Does this happen a lot?" he asked, after a long and remarkably easy silence.

Sierra shook her head. "No, thank God. I don't know what we would have done without you, Travis."

"You would have coped," he said. "Like you've been

doing for a long time, if my guess is any good. Where's Liam's dad, Sierra?"

She swallowed hard, glanced at the boy to make sure he was sleeping. "He died a few days before Liam was born," she answered.

"You've been alone all this time?"

"No," Sierra said, stiffening a little on the inside, where it didn't show. Or, at least, she *hoped* it didn't. "I had Liam."

"You know that isn't what I meant," Travis said.

Sierra looked away, made herself look back. "I didn't want to—complicate things. By getting involved with someone, I mean. Liam and I have been just fine on our own."

Travis merely nodded, and drank more of his coffee.

"Don't you have to go back to the ranch and feed the horses or something?" Sierra asked.

"Eventually," Travis answered with a sigh. He glanced around the room again and gave the slightest shudder.

Sierra remembered his younger brother. The wounds must be raw. "I guess you probably hate hospitals," she said. "Because of—" the name came back to her in Eve's telephone voice "—Brody."

Travis shook his head. His eyes were bleak. "If he'd gotten this far—to a hospital, I mean—it would have meant there was hope."

Sierra moved to touch Travis's hand, but just before she made contact, his cell phone rang. He pulled it from the pocket of his western shirt, flipped open the case. "Travis Reid."

He listened. Raised his eyebrows. "Hello, Eve. I wouldn't have thought even *your* pilot could land in this kind of weather."

Sierra tensed.

Eve said something, and Travis responded. "I'll let Sierra explain," he said, and held out the phone to her.

Sierra swallowed, took it. "Hello, Eve," she said.

"Where are you?" her mother asked. "I'm at the ranch. It looks as if you've been sleeping in the kitchen—"

"We're in Flagstaff, in a hospital," Sierra told her. Only then did she realize that she and Travis were both wearing the clothes they'd slept in. That she hadn't combed her hair or even brushed her teeth.

All of a sudden she felt incredibly grubby.

Eve drew in an audible breath. "Oh, my *God*—Liam?"

"He had a pretty bad asthma attack," Sierra confirmed. "He's on a breathing machine, and he has to stay until tomorrow, but he's okay, Eve."

"I'll be up there as soon as I can. Which hospital?"

"Hold on," Sierra said. "There's really no need for you to come all this way, especially when the roads are so bad. I'm pretty sure we'll be home tomorrow—"

"Pretty sure?" Eve challenged.

"Well, he'll need his medication adjusted, and the inflammation in his bronchial tubes will have to go down."

"This sounds serious, Sierra. I think I should come. I could be there—"

"Please," Sierra interrupted. "Don't."

A thoughtful silence followed. "All right, then," Eve said finally, with a good grace Sierra truly appreciated. "I'll just settle in here and wait. The furnace is running and the lights are on. Tell Travis not to rush back—I can certainly feed the horses."

Sierra could only nod, so Travis took the phone back.

Evidently, a barrage of orders followed from Eve's end.

Travis grinned throughout. "Yes, ma'am," he said. "I will."

He ended the call.

"You will what?" Sierra inquired.

"Take care of you and Liam," Travis answered.

1919

That morning the world looked as though it had been carved from a huge block of pure white ice. Hannah marveled at the beauty of it, staring through the kitchen window, even as she longed with bittersweet poignancy for spring. For things to stir under the snowbound earth, to put out roots and break through the surface, green and growing.

"Ma?"

She turned, troubled by something she heard in Tobias's voice. He stood at the base of the stairs, still wearing his nightshirt and barefoot.

"I don't feel good," he said.

Hannah set aside her coffee with exaggerated care, even took time to wipe her hands on her apron before she approached him. Touched his forehead with the back of her hand.

"You're burning up," she whispered, stricken.

Doss, who had been rereading last week's newspaper at the table, his barn work done, slowly scraped back his chair.

"Shall I fetch the doc?" he asked.

Hannah turned, looked at him over one shoulder, and nodded. If you hadn't insisted on taking him with you to the widow Jessup's place, she thought—

But she would go no further.

This was not the time to place blame.

"You get back into bed," she told Tobias, briskly efficient and purely terrified. The bout of pneumonia that had nearly killed him during the fall had started like this. "I'll make you a mustard plaster to draw out the congestion, and your uncle Doss will go to town for Dr. Willaby. You'll be right as rain in no time at all."

Tobias looked doubtful. His face was flushed, and his nightshirt was soaked with perspiration, even though the kitchen was a little on the chilly side. The boy seemed dazed, almost as though he were walking in his sleep, and Hannah wondered if he'd taken in a word she'd said.

"I'll be back as soon as I can," Doss promised, already pulling on his coat and reaching for his hat. "There's whisky left from Christmas. It's in the pantry, behind that cracker tin," he added, pausing before opening the door. "Make him a hot drink with some honey. Pa used to brew up that concoction for us when we took sick, and it always helped."

Doss and Gabe, along with their adopted older brother, John Henry, had never suffered a serious illness in their lives, if you didn't count John Henry's deafness. What did they know about tending the sick?

Hannah nodded again, her mouth tight. She'd lost three sisters in childhood, two to diphtheria and one to scarlet fever; only she and her younger brother, David, had survived.

She was used to nursing the afflicted.

Doss hesitated a few moments on the threshold, as though there was something he wanted to say but couldn't put into words, then went out.

"You change into a dry nightshirt," Hannah told Tobias. His sheets were probably sweat-soaked, too, so she added, "And get into our bed."

Our bed.

Meaning Gabe's and hers.

And soon, after they were married, Doss would be sleeping in that bed, in Gabe's place.

She could not, would not, consider the implications of that.

Not now. Maybe not ever.

She was like the ranch woman she'd once read about in a Montana newspaper, making her way from the house to the barn and back in a blinding blizzard, with only a frozen rope to hold on to. If she let go, she'd be lost.

She had to attend to Tobias. That was her rope, and she'd follow it, hand over hand, thought over thought.

Hannah retrieved an old flannel shirt from the rag bag and cut two matching pieces, approximately twelve inches square. These would serve to protect Tobias's skin from the heat of the poultice, but like as not, he would still have blisters. She kept a mixture on hand for just such occasions, in a big jar with a wire seal. She dumped a big dollop of the stuff on to one of the bits of flannel, spread it like butter, and put the second cloth on top, her nose twitching at the pungent odors of mustard seed, pounded to a pulp, and camphor.

When she got upstairs, she found Tobias huddled in the middle of her bed, and his eyes grew big with recollection when he saw what she was carrying in her hands.

"No," he protested, but weakly. "No mustard plaster." He'd begun to shiver, and his teeth were chattering.

"Don't fuss, Tobias," Hannah said. "Your grandfather swears by them."

Tobias groaned. "My *Montana* grandfather," he replied. "My grandpa Holt wouldn't let *anybody* put one of those things on him!"

"Is that a fact?" Hannah asked mildly. "Well, next time you write to the almighty Holt McKettrick, you ask. I'll bet he'll say he wouldn't be without one when he's under the weather."

Tobias made a rude sound, blowing through his lips, but he rolled on to his back and allowed Hannah to open the top buttons of his nightshirt and put the poultice in place.

"Grandpa Holt," he said, bearing the affliction stalwartly, "would probably make me a whisky drink, just like he did for Pa and Uncle Doss."

Hannah sighed. Privately she thought there was a good deal of the roughneck in the McKettrick men, and while she wouldn't call any of them a drunk, they used liquor as a remedy for just about every ill, from snakebite to the grippe. They'd swabbed it on old Seesaw's gashes, when he tangled with a sow bear, and rubbed it into the gums of teething babies.

"What you're going to have, Tobias McKettrick, is oatmeal."

He made a face. "This burns," he complained, pointing to the mustard plaster.

Hannah bent and kissed his forehead. He didn't pull away, like he'd taken to doing of late, and she found that both reassuring and worrisome.

She glanced at the window, saw a scallop of icicles dangling from the eave. It might be many hours—even tomorrow—before Doss got back from Indian Rock with Dr. Willaby. The wait would be agony, but there was nothing to do but endure.

When Tobias closed his eyes and slept, Hannah left the room, descended the stairs and went into the pantry again. She moved the cracker tin aside, looked up at the bottle of whisky hidden behind it, gave a disdainful sniff, and took a canned chicken off the shelf instead. It was a treasure, that chicken—she'd been saving it for some celebration, so she wouldn't have to kill one of her laying hens—but it would make a fine, nourishing soup.

After gathering onions, rice and some of her spices—which she cherished as much as preserved meat, given how costly they were—Hannah commenced to make soup.

She was surprised when, only an hour after he'd ridden out, Doss returned with another man she recognized as one of the ranch hands down at Rafe's place. She frowned, watching from the window as Doss dismounted and left the newcomer to lead both horses inside.

That was odd. Doss hadn't been to Indian Rock yet; he couldn't have covered the distance in such a short time. Why would he ask someone to put up his horse?

Puzzled, impatient and a little angry, Hannah was waiting at the door when Doss came in.

"Bundle the boy up warm," he said, without any preamble at all. "Willie's going to stay here and look after the horses and the place. Once I've hitched the draft horses to the sleigh, we'll go overland to Indian Rock."

Hannah stared at him, confounded. "You're suggesting that we take Tobias all the way to Indian Rock?"

"I'm not 'suggesting' anything, Hannah," Doss interposed. "I met Seth Baker down by the main house, when I was about to cross the stream, and he hailed me, wanted to know where I was headed. I told him I was off to fetch Doc Willaby, because Tobias was feeling poorly. Seth said Willaby was down with the gout, but his nephew happened to be there, and he's a doctor, too. He's looking after the doc's practice, in town, so he wouldn't be inclined to come all the way out here."

Hannah's throat clenched, and she put a hand to it. "A ride like that could be the end of Tobias," she said.

Doss shook his head. "We can't just sit here," he countered, grim-jawed. "Get the boy ready or I'll do it myself."

"May I remind you that Tobias is *my* son?"

"He's a McKettrick," Doss replied flatly, as though that were the end of it—and for him, it probably was.

CHAPTER EIGHT

Present Day

TRAVIS WAITED UNTIL SIERRA HAD DRIFTED off into a fitful sleep in her chair next to Liam's hospital bed. Then he got a blanket from a nurse, covered Sierra with it and left.

A few minutes later, he was behind the wheel of his truck.

The roads were sheer ice, and the sky looked gray, burdened with fresh snow. After consulting the GPS panel on his dashboard, he found the nearest Wal-Mart, parked as close to the store as he could and went inside.

Shopping was something Travis endured, and this was no exception. He took a cart and wheeled it around, choosing the things Sierra and Liam would need if this hitch in Flagstaff turned out to be longer than expected. He'd spent the night at his own place, a few miles from the hospital, showered and changed there.

When he got back from his expedition—a January Santa Claus burdened down with bulging blue plastic bags—he made his way to Liam's room.

Sierra was awake, blinking and befuddled, and so was Liam. A huge teddy bear, holding a helium balloon in one paw, sat on the bedside table. The writing on the balloon said Get Well Soon in big red letters.

"Eve?" Travis asked, indicating the bear with a nod of his head.

Sierra took in the bags he was carrying. "Eve," she confirmed. "What have you got there?"

Travis grinned, though he felt tired all of a sudden, as though ten cups of coffee wouldn't keep him awake. Maybe it was the warmth of the hospital, after being out in the cold.

"A little something for everybody," he said.

Liam was sitting up, and the breathing tube had been removed. His words came out as a sore-throated croak, but he smiled just the same, and Travis felt a pinch deep inside. The kid was so small and so brave. "Even me?"

"Especially you," Travis said. He handed the boy one of the bags, watched as he pulled out a portable DVD player, still in its box, and the episodes of *Nova* he'd picked up to go with it.

"Wow," Liam said, his voice so raw that it made Travis's throat ache in sympathy. "I've always wanted one of these."

Sierra looked worried. "It's way too expensive," she said. "We can't accept it."

Liam hugged the box close against his little chest, obstinately possessive. Everything about him said, I'm not giving this up.

Travis ignored Sierra's statement and tossed her another of the bags, this one fat and light. "Take a shower," he told her. "You look like somebody who just went through a harrowing medical emergency."

She opened her mouth, closed it again. Peeked inside the bag. He'd bought her a sweatsuit, guessing at the sizes, along with toothpaste, a brush, soap and a comb.

She swallowed visibly. "Thanks."

He nodded.

While Sierra was in Liam's bathroom, showering, Travis helped the boy get the DVD player out of the box, plugged in and running.

"Mom might not let me keep it," Liam said sadly.

"I'm betting she will," Travis assured him.

Liam was engrossed in an episode about killer bees when Sierra came out of the bathroom, looking scrubbed and cautiously hopeful in her dark-blue sweats. Her hair was still wet from washing, and the comb had left distinct ridges, which Travis found peculiarly poignant.

Complex emotions fell into line after that one, striking him with the impact of a runaway boxcar, but he didn't dare explore any of them right away. He'd need to be alone to do that, in his truck or with a horse. For now, he was too close to Sierra to think straight.

She glanced at Liam, softened noticeably as she saw how much he was enjoying Travis's gift. His small hands clasped the machine on either side, as though he feared someone would wrench it away.

Something similar to Travis's thoughts must have gone through her mind, because he saw a change in her face. It was a sort of resignation, and it made him want to take her in his arms—though he wasn't about to do that.

"I could use something to eat," he said.

"Me, too," Sierra admitted. She tapped Liam on the shoulder, and he barely looked away from the screen, where bees were swarming. Music from the speakers portended certain disaster. "You'll be all right here alone for a while, if Travis and I go down to the cafeteria?"

The boy nodded distractedly, refocused his eyes on the bees.

Sierra smiled with a tiny, forlorn twitch of her lips.

They were well away from Liam's room, and waiting for an elevator, when she finally spoke.

"I'm grateful for what you did for Liam and me," she said, "but you shouldn't have given him something that cost so much."

"I won't miss the money, Sierra," Travis responded. "He's been through a lot, and he needed something else to think about besides breathing tubes, medical tests and shots."

She gave a brief, almost clipped nod.

That McKettrick pride, Travis thought. It was something to behold.

The elevator came, and the doors opened with a cheerful chiming sound. They stepped inside, and Travis pushed the button for the lower level. Hospital cafeterias always seemed to be in the bowels of the building, like the morgues.

Downstairs, they went through the grub line with trays, and chose the least offensive-looking items from the stock array of greasy green beans, mock meat loaf, brown gravy and the like.

Sierra chose a corner table, and they sat down, facing each other. She looked like a freshly showered angel from some celestial soccer team in the athletic clothes he'd provided, and Travis wondered if she had any idea how beautiful she was.

"I'm surprised Eve hasn't shown up," he said, to get the conversation started.

Sierra's cheeks pinkened a little, and she avoided his gaze. Poked at the faux meat loaf with a water-spotted fork.

"I don't know what I'm going to say to her," she said. "Beyond 'thank you,' I mean."

"How about, 'hello'?" Travis joked.

Sierra didn't look amused. Just nervous, like a rat cornered by a barn cat.

He reached across the table, closed his hand briefly over

hers. "Look, Sierra, this doesn't have to be hard. Eve will probably do most of the talking, at least in the beginning, and she'll feed you your lines."

She smiled again. Another tentative flicker, there and gone.

They ate in silence for a while.

"It's not as if I hate her," Sierra said, out of the blue. "Eve, I mean."

Travis waited, knowing they were on uneven ground. Sierra was as skittish as a spring fawn, and he didn't want to speak at the wrong time and send her bolting for the emotional underbrush.

"I don't know her," Sierra went on. "My own mother. I saw her picture on the McKettrickCo website, but she told me it didn't look a thing like her."

Still, Travis waited.

"What's she like?" Sierra asked, almost plaintively. "Really?"

"Eve is a beautiful woman," Travis said. *Like you,* he added silently. "She's smart, and when it comes to negotiating a business deal, she's as tough as they come. She's remarkable, Sierra. Give her a chance."

Sierra's lower lip wobbled, ever so slightly. Her blue, blue eyes were limpid with feelings Travis could only guess at. He wanted to dive into them, like a swimmer, and explore the vast inner landscape he sensed within her.

"You know what happened, don't you?" she asked, very softly. "Back when my mother and father were divorced."

"Some of it," Travis said, cautious, like a man touching a tender bruise.

"Dad took me to Mexico when I was two," she said, "right after someone from Eve's lawyer's office served the papers."

Travis nodded. "Meg told me that much."

"As little as I was, I remembered what she smelled like, what it felt like when she held me, the sound of her voice." A spasm of pain flinched in Sierra's eyes. "No matter how I tried, I could never recall her face. Dad made sure there weren't any pictures, and—"

He ached for her. The soupy mashed potatoes went pulpy in his mouth, and they went down like so much barbed wire when he swallowed. "What kind of man would—"

He caught himself.

None of your business, Trav.

To his surprise she smiled again, and warmth rose in her eyes. "Dad was never a model father, more like a buddy. But he took good care of me. I grew up with the kind of freedom most kids never know—running the streets of San Miguel in my bare feet. I knew all the vendors in the marketplace, and writers and artists gathered at our *casita* almost every night. Dad's mistress, Magdalena, home-schooled me. I attracted stray dogs wherever I went, and Dad always let me keep them."

"Not a traumatic childhood," Travis observed, still careful.

She shook her head. "Not at all. But I missed my mother desperately, just the same. For a while, I thought she'd come for me. That one day a car would pull up in front of the *casita*, and there she'd be, smiling, with her arms open. Then when there was no sign of her, and no letters came— well, I decided she must be dead. It was only after I got old enough to surf the internet that I found her."

"You didn't call or write?"

"It was a shock, realizing she was alive—that if I could find her, she could have found me. And she didn't. With the resources she must have had—"

Travis felt a sting of anger on Sierra's behalf. Pushed away his tray. "I used to work for Eve," he said. "And I've known her for most of my life. I can't imagine why she wouldn't have gone in with an army, once she knew where you were."

Sierra bit her lower lip again, so hard Travis almost expected it to bleed. Her eyes glistened with tears she was probably too proud to shed, at least for herself. She'd wept plenty for Liam, he suspected, alone and in secret. It paralyzed him when a woman cried, and yet in that moment he'd have rewritten history if he could have. He'd have been there, in the thick of Sierra's sorrows, whatever they were, to put his arms around her, promise that everything would be all right and move heaven and earth to make it so.

But the plain truth was, he hadn't been.

"I'd better get back to Liam," she said.

He nodded.

They carried their trays to the dropping-off place, went upstairs again, entered Liam's room.

He was asleep, with the DVD player still running on his lap.

Travis went to speak to one of the nurses, a woman he knew from college, and when he came back, he found Sierra stretched out beside her son, dead to the world.

He sighed, watching the pair of them.

He'd kept himself apart, even before Brody died, busy with his career. Dated lots of women and steered clear of anything heavy.

Now, without warning, the whole equation had shifted, and there was a good chance he was in big trouble.

1919

The air was so cold it bit through the bearskin throws and Hannah's many layers of wool to her flesh. She could see her breath billowing out in front of her, blue white, like Doss's. Like Tobias's.

Her boy looked feverishly gleeful, nestled between her and Doss, as the sleigh moved over an icy trail, drawn by the big draft horses, Cain and Abel. The animals usually languished in the barn all winter; in the spring, they pulled plows in the hayfields, in the fall, harvest wagons. Summers, they grazed. They seemed spry and vigorous to Hannah, gladly surprised to be working.

Where other horses or even mules might have floundered in the deep, crusted snow, the sons of Adam, as Gabe liked to call them, pranced along as easily as they would over dry ground.

Doss held the reins in his gloved hands, hunkered down into the collar of his sheepskin-lined coat, his earlobes red under the brim of his hat. Once in a while he glanced Hannah's way, but mostly when he spared a look, it was for Tobias.

"You warm enough?" he'd asked.

And each time Tobias would nod. If his blood had been frozen in his veins, he'd have nodded, Hannah knew that, even if Doss didn't. He idolized his uncle, always had.

Would he forget Gabe entirely, once she and Doss were married?

Everything within Hannah rankled at the thought.

Why hadn't she left for Montana before it was too late?

Now she was about to tie herself, for good, to a man she lusted after but would never love.

Of course she could still go home to her folks—she knew they'd welcome her and Tobias—but suppose she *was* carrying Doss's child? Once her pregnancy became apparent, they'd know she'd behaved shamefully. The whole world would know.

How could she bear that?

No. She would go ahead and marry Doss, and let sharing her bed with him be her private consolation. She'd find a way to endure the rest, like his trying to give her orders all the time and maybe yearning after other women because he'd taken a wife out of honor, not choice.

She'd be his cross to bear, and he would be hers.

There was a perverse kind of justice in that.

They reached the outskirts of Indian Rock in the late afternoon, with the sun about to go down. Doss drove straight to Dr. Willaby's big house on Third Street, secured the horses and reached into the sleigh for Tobias before Hannah got herself unwrapped enough to get out of the sleigh.

Doc Willaby's daughter, Constance, met them at the door. She was a beautiful young woman, and she'd pursued Gabe right up to the day he'd put a gold band on Hannah's finger. Now, from the way she looked at Doss, she was ready to settle for his younger brother.

The thought stirred Hannah to fury, though she'd have buttered, baked and eaten both her shoes before admitting it.

"We have need of a doctor," Doss said to Constance, holding Tobias's bundled form in both arms.

"Come in," Constance said. She had bright-auburn hair and very green eyes, and her shape, though slender, was voluptuous. What, Hannah wondered, did Doss think when he looked at her? "Papa's ill," the other woman went on, "but my cousin is here, and he'll see to the boy."

Hannah put aside whatever it was she'd felt, seeing Constance, for relief. Tobias would be looked after by a real doctor. He'd be all right now, and nothing else mattered but that.

She would darn Doss McKettrick's socks for the rest of

her life. She would cook his meals and trim his hair and wash his back. She would take him water and sandwiches in summer, when he was herding cattle or working in the hayfields. She'd bite her tongue, when he galled her, which would surely be often, and let him win at cards on winter nights.

The one thing she would never do was love him—her heart would always belong to Gabe—but no one on earth, save the two of them, was ever going to know the plain, regrettable truth.

"It's a bad cold," the younger doctor said, after carefully examining Tobias in a room set aside for the purpose. He was a very slender man, almost delicate, with dark hair and sideburns. He wore a good suit and carried a gold watch, which he consulted often. He was a city dweller, Hannah reflected, used to schedules. "I'd recommend taking a room at the hotel for a few days, though, because he shouldn't be exposed to this weather."

Doss took out his wallet, like it was his place to pay the doctor bills, and Hannah stepped in front of him. She was Tobias's mother, and she was still responsible for costs such as these.

"That'll be one dollar," the doctor said, glancing from Hannah's face, which felt pink with conviction and cold, to Doss's.

Hannah shoved the money into his hand.

"Give the boy whisky," the physician added, folding the dollar bill and tucking it into the pocket of his fine tailored coat. "Mixed with honey and lemon juice, if the hotel dining room's got any such thing on hand."

Doss, to his credit, did not give Hannah a triumphant look at this official prescription for a remedy he'd already suggested and she'd disdained, but she elbowed him in the ribs anyway, just as if he had.

They checked into the Arizona Hotel, which, like many

of the businesses in Indian Rock, was McKettrick owned. Rafe's mother-in-law, Becky Lewis, had run the place for years, with the help of her daughter, Emmeline. Now it was in the hands of a manager, a Mr. Thomas Crenshaw, hired out of Phoenix.

Doss was greeted like a visiting potentate when he walked in, once again carrying Tobias. A clerk was dispatched to take the sleigh and horses to the livery stable, and they were shown, the three of them, to the best rooms in the place.

The quarters were joined by a door in between, and Hannah would have preferred to be across the hall from Doss instead, but she made no comment. While Mr. Crenshaw hadn't gone quite so far as to put them all in the same room, it was clearly his assumption, and probably that of the rest of Indian Rock, too, that she and Doss were intimate. She could imagine how the reasoning went: Doss and his brother's widow shared a house, after all, way out in the country, and heaven only knew what they were up to, with only the boy around. He'd be easy to fool, being only eight years old.

Hannah went bright red as these thoughts moved through her mind.

Doss dismissed the manager and put Tobias on the nearest bed.

"I'll go downstairs and fetch that whisky concoction," he said, when it was just the three of them.

Tobias had never stayed in a hotel and, sick as he was, he was caught up in the experience. He nestled down in the bearskins, cupped his hands behind his head and gazed smiling up at the ceiling.

"Do as you please," Hannah told Doss, removing her heavy cloak and bonnet and laying them aside.

He sighed. "While we're in town, we'd best get married," he said.

"Yes," Hannah agreed acerbically. "And let's not forget to place an order at the feed-and-grain, buy groceries, pay the light bill and renew our subscription to the newspaper."

Doss gave a ragged chuckle and shook his head. "Guess I'd better dose you up with whisky, too," he replied. "Maybe that way you'll be able to stand the honeymoon."

Hannah's temper flared, but before she could respond, Doss was out the door, closing it smartly behind him.

"I like this place," Tobias said.

"Good," Hannah answered irritably, pulling off her gloves.

"What's a honeymoon," Tobias asked, "and how come you need whisky to stand it?"

Hannah pretended she hadn't heard the question.

She'd packed hastily before leaving the house, things for Tobias and for herself, but nothing for a wedding and certainly nothing for a wedding *night*. If the valises had been brought upstairs, she'd have something to do, shaking out garments, hanging them in the wardrobes, but as it was, her choices were limited. She could either pace or fuss over Tobias.

She paced, because Tobias would not endure fussing.

Doss returned with their bags, followed by a woman from the kitchen carrying two steaming mugs on a tray. She set the works down on a table, accepted a gratuity from Doss, stole a boldly speculative look at Hannah and bustled out.

"Drink up," Doss said cheerfully, handing one mug to Hannah and carrying the other to Tobias, who sat up eagerly to accept it.

Hannah sniffed the whisky mixture, took a tentative sip and was surprised at how good the stuff tasted. "Where's yours?" she asked, turning to Doss.

"I'm not the one dreading tonight," he answered.

Hannah's hands trembled. She set the mug down, beckoned for Doss to follow, and swept into the adjoining room. "What do you mean, *tonight?*" she whispered, though of course she knew.

Doss closed the door, examined the bed from a distance and proceeded to walk over to it and press hard on the mattress several times, evidently testing the springs.

Hannah's temper surged again, but she was speechless this time.

"Good to know the bed won't creak," Doss observed.

She found her voice, but it came out as a sputter. "Doss McKettrick—"

He ran his eyes over her, which left a trail of sensation, just as surely as if he'd stripped her naked and caressed her with his hands. "The preacher will be here in an hour," he said. "He'll marry us downstairs, in the office behind the reception desk. If Tobias is well enough to attend, he can. If not, we'll tell him about it later."

Hannah was appalled. "You made arrangements like that without consulting me first?"

"I thought we'd said all there was to say."

"Maybe I wanted time to get used to the idea. Did you ever think of that?"

"Maybe you'll *never* get used to the idea," Doss reasoned, sitting now, on the edge of the bed he clearly intended to share with her that very night. He stood, stretched in a way that could only have been called risqué. "I'm going out for a while," he announced.

"Out where?" Hannah asked, and then hated herself for caring.

He stepped in close—too close.

She tried to retreat and found she couldn't move.

Doss hooked a finger under her chin and made her look at him. "To buy a wedding band, among other things," he said. She felt his breath on her lips, and it made them tingle. "I'll send a wire to my folks and one to yours, too, if you want."

Hannah swallowed. Shook her head. "I'll write to Mama and Papa myself, when it's over," she said.

Sad amusement moved in Doss's eyes. "Suit yourself," he said.

And then he left her standing there.

She heard him speak quietly to Tobias, then the opening and closing of a door. After a few moments she returned to the next room.

Tobias had finished his medicinal whisky, and his eyelids were drooping. Hannah tucked the covers in around him and kissed his forehead. Whatever else was happening, he seemed to be out of danger. She clung to that blessing and tried not to dwell on her own fate.

He yawned. "Will Uncle Doss be my pa, once you and him are married?" he asked drowsily.

"No," Hannah said, her voice firm. "He'll still be your uncle." Tobias looked so disheartened that she added, "And your stepfather, of course."

"So he'll be *sort of* my father?"

"Sort of," Hannah agreed, relenting.

"I guess we won't be going to Montana now," Tobias mumbled, settling into his pillow.

"Maybe in the spring," Hannah said.

"You go," Tobias replied, barely awake now. "I'll stay here with Uncle Pa."

It wounded Hannah that Tobias preferred Doss's company to hers and that of her family, but the boy was ill and she wasn't going to argue with him. "Go to sleep, Tobias," she told him.

As if he'd needed her permission, the little boy lapsed into slumber.

Hannah sat watching him sleep for a long time. Then,

seeing snow drift past the windows in the glow of a gas streetlamp, she stood and went to stand with her hands resting on the wide sill, looking out.

It was dark by then, and the general store, the only place in Indian Rock where a wedding band could be found, had probably been closed for an hour. All Doss would have to do was rap on the door, though, and they'd open the place to him. Same as the telegraph office, or any other establishment in town.

After all, he was a McKettrick.

A tear slipped down her cheek.

She was a bride, and she should be happier.

Instead she felt as if she was betraying Gabe's memory. Letting down her folks, too, because they'd hoped she'd come home and eventually marry a local man, though they hadn't actually come out and said that last part. Now, because she'd been foolish enough, needy enough, to lie with Doss, not once but twice, she'd have to stay on the Triple M until she died of old age.

A tear slipped down her cheek, and she wiped it away quickly with the back of one hand.

"You made your bed, Hannah McKettrick," she told her reflection in the cold, night-darkened glass of the window, "and now you'll just have to lie in it."

By the time Doss returned, she'd washed her face, taken her hair down for a vigorous brushing and pinned it back up again. She'd put on a fresh dress, a prim but practical gray wool, and pinched some color into her cheeks.

He had on a brand-new suit of clothes, as fancy as the ones the doctor's nephew wore, and he'd gotten a haircut and a shave, too.

She was strangely touched by these things.

"I'd have bought you a dress for the wedding," he told her, staring at her as though he'd never seen her before, "but I didn't know what would fit, and whether you'd think it proper to wear white."

She smiled, feeling a tender sort of sorrow. "This dress will do just fine," she said.

"You look beautiful," Doss told her.

Hannah blushed. It was nonsense, of course—she probably looked more like a schoolmarm than anything else in her stern gray frock with the black buttons coming up to her throat—but she liked hearing the words. Had almost forgotten how they sounded, with Gabe gone.

Doss took her hand, and there was an uncharacteristic shyness in the gesture that made her wonder if he was as frightened and reluctant as she was.

"You don't have to go through with this, Doss," she said.

He ran his lips lightly over her knuckles before letting her hand go. "It's the right thing to do," he answered.

She swallowed, nodded.

"I guess the preacher must be here."

Doss nodded. "Downstairs, waiting. Shall we wake Tobias?"

Hannah shook her head. "Better to let him sleep."

"I'll fetch a maid to watch over him while we're gone," Doss said.

Now it was Hannah who nodded.

He left her again, and this time she felt it as a tearing-away, sharp and prickly. He came back with a plump, older woman clad in a black uniform and an apron, and then he took Hannah's hand once more and led her out of the room, down the stairs and into the office where she would become Mrs. McKettrick, for the second time.

At least, she thought philosophically, she wouldn't have to get used to a new name.

CHAPTER NINE

Present Day

THE WEATHER HADN'T IMPROVED, Sierra noted, standing at the window of Liam's hospital room the next morning. Orderlies had wheeled in a second bed the night before, and she'd slept in a paper gown. Now she was back in the sweats Travis had bought for her, rested and restored.

Dr. O'Meara had already been in to introduce herself, check on Liam's progress and do a work-up of her own, and she'd signed the release papers, too. Sierra liked and trusted the woman, though she was younger than expected, no more than thirty-five years old, with delicate features, very long brown hair held back by a barrette and a trim figure.

Armed with a prescription, Sierra was ready to take her son and leave.

Ready to face Eve, and all the emotional spade work involved.

Or not.

Just as she turned from the window, Travis entered the room, wearing slacks and a blue pullover sweater that accentuated the color of his eyes. He'd said he owned a house in Flagstaff, and Sierra knew he'd gone there to spend the night.

There was so much she *didn't* know about his life, and

this was unsettling, although she didn't have the time or energy to pursue it at the moment.

"Travis!" Liam crowed, as though he hadn't expected to see his friend ever again. "I get to go home today!"

The word *home* caught in Sierra's heart like a fish hook. The ranch house on the Triple M was Eve's home, and it was Meg's, but it didn't belong to her and Liam. They were temporary guests, and it had troubled Sierra all along to think Liam might become attached to the place and be hurt when they left.

Travis approached the bed, grinned and ruffled Liam's hair. "That's great," he said. "According to reports, the power is back on, the pantry is bulging, and your grandmother is waiting to meet you."

Sierra felt a wrench at the reminder. So much for thinking she was prepared to deal with Eve McKettrick.

Liam inspected Travis speculatively. "You don't look like a cowboy today," he declared.

Travis laughed. "Neither do you," he countered.

"Yeah, but I *never* do," Liam said, discouraged.

"We'll have to do something about that one of these days soon."

Sierra bristled. She and Liam were committed to staying on the ranch for a year, that was the bargain. Twelve months. The time would surely pass quickly, and she didn't want her son putting down roots only to be torn from that hallowed McKettrick ground.

"Liam looks fine the way he is," she said.

Travis gave her a long, thoughtful look. "True enough," he said mildly. "My buddy Liam is one handsome cowpoke. In fact, he looks a lot like Jesse did, at his age."

Another connection to the storied McKettrick clan. Uncomfortable, Sierra averted her eyes. She'd already gathered

Liam's things, but now she rearranged them busily, just for something to do.

Half an hour later, the three of them were in Travis's truck, headed back to the ranch. Liam, buckled in between Travis and Sierra, promptly fell asleep, but his hands were locked around his DVD player. Mentally Sierra clutched the new inhaler, prescribed by Dr. O'Meara, purchased at the hospital pharmacy and tucked away in her bag, just as anxiously.

She had been silent for most of the ride, gazing out at the winter landscape as it whipped past the passenger window.

Travis said little or nothing, concentrating on navigating the icy roads, but Sierra was fully aware of his presence just the same, and in a way that disturbed her. He'd been a rock since Liam's asthma attack, and she was grateful but she couldn't afford to become dependent on him, emotionally or in any other way, and she didn't want her son to, either.

Trouble was, it might be too late for Liam. He adored Travis Reid, and there was no telling what fantasies he'd cooked up in that high-powered little brain of his. He and Travis riding the range, probably. Wearing baseball mitts and playing catch. Going fishing in some pristine mountain lake.

All the things a boy did with a dad.

"Sierra?"

She didn't dare look at Travis, for fear he might see the vulnerability she was feeling. All her nerves seemed to be on the outside of her skin, and they were doing the jingle-bell rock. "What?"

"I was just wondering what you were thinking."

She couldn't tell him, of course. He'd think she was attracted to him, and she wasn't.

Much.

So she lied. "All about Eve," she said.

He chuckled at the flimsy joke, but Sierra gave him points for recognizing an obscure reference to an old movie. Maybe they had a thing or two in common after all.

"I imagine the lady's on pins and needles herself, right about now. She wants to see you and Liam more than anything, I'd guess, but it won't be easy for her."

"I don't *want* it to be easy for her," Sierra answered.

Travis hesitated only a beat or two. "Maybe she has good reasons for what she did."

Sierra's silence was eloquent.

"Give her a chance, Sierra."

She glanced at him. "I'm doing that," she said. "I drove all the way here from Florida. I agreed to stay on the Triple M for a full year."

"Would you have done it if it weren't for the insurance?"

Damn it. He *was* a lawyer. "Probably not," she admitted.

"You'd do just about anything for Liam."

"Not 'just about,'" Sierra said. "*Anything* covers it."

"What about yourself? What would you do for Sierra?"

"Are we going to talk about me in the third person?"

"Stop hedging. I understand your devotion to Liam. I'd just like to know what you'd be doing right now if you didn't have a child, especially one with medical problems."

Sierra glanced at Liam, making sure he was asleep. "Don't talk about him as though he were somehow…deficient."

"I'm not. He's a great kid, and he'll grow up to be an exceptional man. And I'm still waiting to hear what your dreams are for yourself."

She gave a desultory little chuckle. "Nothing spectacular. I'd like to survive."

"Not much of a life. Not for you and not for Liam."

Sierra squirmed. "Maybe I've forgotten how to dream," she said.

"And that doesn't concern you?"

"Up until now, it hasn't been a factor."

"That's unfortunate. Liam will pattern his attitudes after yours. Is that what you want for him? Just survival?"

"Are you channeling some disincarnate life coach?" Sierra demanded.

Travis laughed, low and quiet. "Not me," he said.

"You're just playing the cowboy version of Dr. Phil, then?"

"Okay, Sierra," Travis conceded. "I'll back off. For now."

"What are *your* dreams, hotshot?" Sierra retorted, too nettled to let the subject alone. "You have a law degree, but you train horses and shovel out stalls for a living."

This time there was no laughter. Travis's glance was utterly serious, and the pain Sierra saw in it made her ashamed of the way she'd spoken to him.

"I guess I had that coming," he said quietly. "And here's my answer. I'd like to be able to dream again. *That's* my dream."

"I'm sorry," Sierra told him, after a few moments had passed. The man had lost his brother in a very tragic way. He was probably doing the best he could, like almost everybody else. "I didn't mean to be unkind. I was just feeling—"

"Cornered?"

"That's a good word for it."

"You must have been burned pretty badly," Travis observed. "And not just by Eve." He looked down at Liam. "Maybe by this little guy's dad?"

"Maybe," Sierra said.

After that, conversation fell by the wayside again, but Sierra did plenty of thinking.

When they arrived at the ranch, all the lights in the house seemed to be on, even though it was barely noon. A glowing tangle of color loomed in the parlor window, and Sierra squinted, sure she must be seeing things.

Travis followed her gaze and chuckled. "Uh-oh," he said. "Looks as if Christmas sneaked back in while we weren't around."

Liam's eyes popped open at the magic word. "Christmas?"

Sierra smiled, in spite of the knot of worry lying heavily in the pit of her stomach. What was Eve up to?

Travis pulled up close to the back door, and Sierra braced herself as it sprang open. There was Eve McKettrick, standing on the top step, a tall, slender woman, breathtakingly attractive in expensive slacks and a blue silk blouse.

"Is *that* my grandma?" Liam asked. "She looks like a movie star!"

She *did* look like a movie star, a young Maureen O'Hara. And Sierra was suddenly, stunningly aware that she'd seen this woman before, in San Miguel, not once, but several times. She'd been a periodic guest at one of the better B&Bs when Sierra was small, and they'd had ice cream together at a sidewalk café near the *casita*, several times.

For a moment Sierra forgot how to breathe.

The Lady. She'd always called Eve "the Lady," and she'd secretly believed she was an angel. But it had been years since she'd given the memory conscious house room.

Now it all came flooding back, in a breathtaking rush.

Travis shut off the truck and opened the door to get out. "Sierra?" he prompted, when she didn't move.

"Hello!" Liam yelled, delighted, from his place next to Sierra. "My name is Liam and I'm seven!"

Eve smiled, and her vivid green eyes glistened with emotion. "My name is Eve," she said quietly, "and I'm fifty-three. Come here and give me a hug."

Sierra finally came unstuck, opened the passenger-side door and climbed down, planting her feet in the crusty snow. Liam scrambled past her so quickly that he generated a slight breeze.

Eve leaned down to gather her grandson in her arms. She kissed the top of his head and met Sierra's gaze again as she straightened.

"I'll see to the horses," Travis said.

"Don't go," Sierra blurted, before she could stop herself.

Eve steered Liam into the kitchen, watching with interest as Travis rounded the front end of the truck and stood close to Sierra.

"You'll be all right," he told her.

She bit her lower lip, feeling like a fool. It was still all she could do not to grab one of his hands with both of hers and cling like some crazy codependent girlfriend about to be hustled out of town on the last bus of the day.

So long. It's been real.

For a few long moments she and Travis just stared into each other's eyes. He was determined; she was scared. And something *else* was happening, too, something a lot harder to define.

Finally Travis broke the impasse by turning and striding off toward the barn.

Sierra drew a deep breath and marched toward the open

door of the kitchen and the woman who waited on the threshold.

"There's a surprise in the living room," Eve said to Liam, once they were all inside and she'd shut the door against the unrelenting cold.

He raced to investigate.

"You're the Lady," Sierra said, stricken.

"The Lady?" Eve echoed, but Sierra could see by the expression in her mother's eyes that it was mere rhetoric.

"The one I used to see in San Miguel."

"Yes," Eve said. "Sit down, Sierra. I'll make tea, and we'll chat."

"Wow!" Liam yelled, from the living room. "Mom, there *is* a Christmas tree in here, with *major* presents under it!"

"Oh, Lord," Sierra said, and sank on to one of the benches at the table.

"They're *all* for me!" Liam whooped.

Sierra watched her mother take Lorelei's teapot from the cabinet, spoon tea leaves into it, fill and plug in the electric kettle. "Christmas presents?" she asked.

Eve smiled a little guiltily. "I had seven years of grand-mothering to make up for," she said. "Cut me a break, will you?"

Sierra would have tallied the numbers differently, but there was no point in saying so. "I thought you were an angel," she confessed. "In San Miguel, I mean."

Eve busied herself with the tea-brewing process, steal-ing the occasional hungry glance at Sierra. "You've cer-tainly grown up to be a beautiful woman," she said. Finally she stopped her puttering, clasped her hands together and practically gobbled Sierra up with her eyes. "It's...it's so wonderful to see you."

Sierra didn't answer.

Liam pounded in from the living room. "Can I open my presents?"

"If it's all right with your mother," Eve said.

Sierra sighed. "Go ahead. And calm down, please. You just got out of the hospital, remember? Overexcitement and asthma do not mix."

Liam gave a shout of delight and thundered off again, ignoring her admonition completely.

The electric kettle whistled, and Eve poured the contents into the antique teapot, and brought it to the table. She selected two cups and saucers from the priceless collection and carried those over, too. Then, at last, looking as nervous as Sierra felt, Eve sat down in the chair at the end of the table.

"How's Liam?" she asked.

"He's fine," Sierra answered. "But he's just getting over a crisis, as you know, so he's going to bed as soon as he finishes opening his presents." The bear and the balloon were in the back of Travis's truck, under the heavy plastic cover, and she imagined her mother ordering them for a grandson she'd never seen.

"So many things to say," Eve fretted, "and I haven't the first idea where to start."

Suddenly Sierra was tired. And *not* so suddenly she was overwhelmed. "Why didn't you tell me who you were— when we met in San Miguel?"

Eve poured tea, warmed beautifully manicured and bejeweled hands around a translucent china cup. "Nothing like cutting to the chase," she said, with rueful appreciation.

"Nothing like it," Sierra agreed implacably.

"If I'd told you who I was, you would have told Hank, and he might have taken you and disappeared again. It took me almost five years to find you the first time, so I wasn't about to let that happen."

Sierra absorbed her mother's words quietly. She *had* mentioned "the Lady" to her father, at least after the first encounter, but if he'd suspected anything, he'd probably dismissed the accounts as flights of a child's imagination. Besides, elegant tourists were common in San Miguel, and they were generous to local children.

"If I'd been in that situation—if it were Liam who'd been snatched away and I'd found him—I'd have taken him home with me."

Eve's eyes filled with tears, but she blinked them back. "Would you?" she challenged softly. "Even if he seemed happy and healthy, and you knew he didn't remember you? Would you simply kidnap him—tear him away from everyone and everything he knew? Without thought for any of the psychological repercussions?"

Sierra blinked. She *would* have been terrified if Eve had stolen her back from Hank, whisked her out of the country in some clandestine way. And she would have had to do exactly that, because even though Sierra's father seemed benignly disinterested most of the time, word would have gotten back to him quickly, had Eve tried to spirit her away. He would have called out the *federales,* as well as the municipal authorities, many of whom were his friends, and Eve would probably *still* be languishing in a Mexican jail.

And she'd had another daughter to consider, as well as a home and a business.

"I've been grown up for quite some time," Sierra pointed out, after long reflection. "What stopped you from contacting me after Dad died and Liam and I came to the States?"

Eve looked down into her cup.

Liam burst into the room, making both women start.

"Look, Mom!" he cried, clutching an expensive telescope in both arms, already attached to its tripod. "I'll be able to see all the way back to the Big Bang with this thing!"

"You're getting too excited," Sierra reiterated, sparing a glance for Eve before rising from her chair. "You'd better go and lie down for a while."

Liam balked, of course. He was seven, faced with unexpected largesse. "But I haven't even opened half my presents!"

"Later," Sierra said. She got up, put a hand on her son's shoulder and steered him toward the back stairs.

He protested all the way, clutching Eve's telescope in the same way he had Travis's DVD player. The stuff *she'd* given him for Christmas, all bought on sale with her tips from the bar, paled by comparison to this bounty, and even though she was glad for him, she also felt a deep slash of resentment.

"Look at it this way," she said a few minutes later, tucking him into bed in a fresh pair of pajamas, the telescope positioned in front of the window, beside the antique one that had been there when they arrived. "You've still got a lot of loot downstairs. Rest awhile, and you can tear into it again."

"Do you promise?" Liam asked suspiciously. "You won't make my grandma take it all back to the store or something?"

"When have I ever lied to you?"

"When you said there was a Santa Claus."

Sierra sighed. "Okay. Name one other time."

"You said we didn't have any family. We've got Grandma and Aunt Meg."

"I give up," Sierra said, spreading her hands. "I'm a shameless prevaricator."

Liam grinned. "If that boy comes back, I'm going to show him *my* telescope!"

A tiny chill moved down Sierra's spine. "Liam," she insisted, "there *is* no boy."

"That's what *you* think," Liam replied, and he looked damnably smug as he settled back into his pillows. "This is his room. This is his bed, and that's his old telescope."

Sierra took off the boy's shoes, tucked him under the faded quilt and sat with him until he drifted off to sleep.

And even then she didn't move, because she didn't want to go downstairs again and hear more well-rehearsed reasons why her mother had abandoned her when she was smaller than Liam.

1919

Hannah couldn't help comparing her second wedding to her first, at least in the privacy of her mind. She and Gabe had been married in the summer, in the side yard at the main ranch house. Gabe's grandfather, Angus, had been alive then and, as head of the McKettrick clan, he'd issued a decree to that effect. There had been a big cake and a band and long improvised tables burdened with food. There had been guests and gifts and dancing.

After the celebration, Gabe had driven her to town in a surrey, and they'd stayed right here at the Arizona Hotel, caught the next day's train out of Indian Rock. Traveled all the way to San Francisco for a honeymoon. Tobias had been conceived during that magical time, and the box of photographs commemorating the trip was one of Hannah's most treasured possessions.

Now she found herself standing in the cramped and cluttered office behind the reception desk, a widow about to become a bride. Only, this time there was no cake, no honeymoon trip to look forward to, and certainly no music and dancing.

Those things wouldn't have mattered, Hannah was

certain, if she'd loved Doss and known he loved her. It wasn't the modesty of the ceremony that troubled her, but the coldly practical reasons behind it.

While the preacher droned the sacred words, with Mr. Crenshaw and one of the maids for witnesses, Hannah stole the occasional sidelong glance at her groom.

Doss looked stalwart, determined and impossibly handsome.

What will become of us? Hannah wondered, in silent and stoic despair. She'd pasted a wobbly smile on her face, because she wouldn't have the preacher gossiping afterward, saying she'd looked like a deer with one foot stuck in a railroad track, and the train about to come clackety-clacking round the bend at full throttle.

Oh, no. If she did what she really wanted to do, which was either run or break down and cry, that self-righteous old coot would spread the news from one end of the state to the other, and what a time folks would have with *that*.

A weeping bride.

A grimly resigned groom.

The talk wouldn't die down for years.

So Hannah endured.

She repeated her vows, when she was prompted, and kept her chin high, her backbone straight and her eyes bone dry. The ordeal was almost over when suddenly the office door banged open and Doss's uncle Jeb strolled in. He was still handsome, though well into middle age, and he grinned as he took in the not-so-happy couple.

"Thought I'd missed it," he said.

Doss laughed, evidently pleased to set eyes on another blood-McKettrick.

The minister cleared his throat, not entirely approving of the interruption, it would seem.

"I now pronounce you man and wife," he said quickly.

"Kiss your bride," Jeb prompted, watching his nephew closely.

Hannah blushed.

Doss kissed her, and she wondered if he'd have remembered to do it at all, if his uncle hadn't provided a verbal nudge.

"No flowers?" Jeb asked, after Doss had paid the preacher and the man had gone. He looked around the office. "No guests?"

"It was a hasty decision," Doss explained.

Hannah blushed again.

"Oh," Jeb said. He shook Doss's hand, whacked him once on the shoulder and then turned to Hannah, gently kissing her cheek. "Be happy, Hannah," he whispered, close to her ear. "Gabe would want that."

Tears brimmed in Hannah's eyes, and this after she'd held up so well, made such an effort to play the happy bride. Did her true feelings show? Or was Jeb McKettrick just perceptive?

She nodded, unable to speak.

"I thought you were down in Phoenix," Doss said to his uncle. If he'd noticed Hannah's tears, he was keeping the observation to himself.

"I came up here to take care of some business at the Cattleman's Bank," Jeb explained. "Arrived on the afternoon train. It's a long ride out to the ranch, and the meeting ran long, so I decided to spend the night here at the hotel and head back to Phoenix tomorrow. I was sitting in the dining room, taking my supper, when somebody mentioned that the two of you were shut up in here with a preacher." He glanced at Hannah again, and she saw concern flash briefly in his eyes. "I decided to invite myself to the festivities.

Of course when I tell Chloe about it, she'll say I ought to learn a few manners. After all this time, my wife still hasn't given up on grinding off my rough edges."

Doss slipped an arm around Hannah's waist. "We're glad you came," he told Jeb. "Aren't we, Hannah?"

She didn't answer right away, and he had the gall to pinch her lightly under her ribs, through the fabric of her sadly practical gray dress.

"Yes," she said.

"Where's Tobias?" Jeb asked. "Chloe'll skin me if I don't bring back a detailed report. That woman likes to know everything about everybody. How much the boy's grown, how he's doing with his lessons, and all that."

"He's down with a cold," Doss said. "That's why we brought him to town. So he could see the doctor."

"And you just decided to get married while you were here?"

Doss colored up.

Hannah was stricken to silence again.

Jeb smiled. "The boy's here in the hotel, then?"

Hannah nodded, still mute.

Jeb's gaze shifted to Doss. "Why don't you go up there and see if he's agreeable to a visit from his old Uncle Jeb?" he said.

Doss hesitated, then nodded and left the room.

"I'm going to ask Doss the same thing I'm about to ask you," Jeb said, the moment they were alone with the door closed. "What's going on here?"

Hannah swallowed painfully. "Well, it just seemed sensible for us to get married."

"Sensible?"

"Both of us living out there on the ranch, I mean. You know how folks…speculate about things like that."

"I know, all right," Jeb answered. "Chloe and I stirred up plenty of talk in our day. I guess I just figured if there'd been a wedding in the offing, the family would have heard something about it before now."

"Doss wired his folks, and I was going to write to mine—"

"You're both adults and it's your business what you do," Jeb said. "Do you love Doss, Hannah?"

She fell back on something she'd said to Tobias, out at the ranch, when he'd asked a similar question. "He's family," she replied.

"He's also a man. A young one, with his whole life ahead of him. He deserves a wife who's glad to *be* his wife."

Hannah lifted her chin. "A few minutes ago you told me Gabe would want this. Doss and me married, I mean. And you're probably right. So I did it as much for him as anybody."

"There's only one person you ought to please in a situation like this, Hannah, and that's yourself."

"Tobias needs Doss."

"I don't doubt that's true. Losing Gabe was hard on everybody in this family, but it was worse for you and Tobias. The question on my mind right now is, do *you* need Doss, Hannah?"

Hannah needed her new husband, all right, but not in a way she was going to discuss with his uncle—or anyone else on the face of the earth, for that matter. "I'll see that he's happy, if that's what you're worried about," she said, and felt her cheeks burn again, fearing she'd revealed exactly what she'd been so determined to keep secret.

"He'll be happy," Jeb said, with such remarkable certainty that Hannah wondered if he knew something she didn't. "Will you?"

"I'll learn to be," she answered.

Jeb placed his hands on her shoulders, squeezed lightly and kissed her forehead. Then, without another word, he went out, leaving Hannah standing there alone, full of confusion and sorrow.

She was waiting in the lobby when Doss came downstairs, some minutes later, looking shy as a schoolboy. Evidently, Jeb had already spoken to him and was with Tobias now.

Doss tried to smile but fell a little short. Now that they were actually married, he apparently didn't know what to say, and neither did Hannah. They were making the best of things, both of them, and it shouldn't have been that way.

"I guess we ought to have some supper," Doss said. "Tobias has already eaten. The maid went down to the kitchen and brought him up a meal while we were—"

Hannah looked down at her feet. "You deserve somebody who loves you," she said softly, miserable with shame.

Doss put a finger under her chin and raised her head, so he could look into her eyes. "I don't know if your mind and heart love me, Hannah McKettrick," he said solemnly, with no trace of arrogance, "but your body does. And maybe it will teach the rest of you to feel the same way."

She took a gentle hold on the lapels of his new suit, bought just for the wedding. "Gabe would want this," she said. "Our being married, I mean."

Doss swallowed. "I loved my brother," he told her gravely, "but I don't want to talk about him. Not tonight."

Hannah wept inside, even though her eyes were dry. "All right," she agreed.

He led her into the dining room, and they both ordered fried chicken dinners. It was an occasion, to eat a restaurant meal, almost as unusual, in Hannah's life, as getting married. She was starved, after a long and hectic day, and yet the food tasted like sawdust from the first bite.

Jeb appeared, just as they were trying to choke down dessert. Chocolate cake, normally Hannah's favorite, with powdered sugar icing.

"Tobias," Jeb announced, "is spending the night in the room next to mine. I've already made arrangements for the maid to stay with him."

Hannah laid down her fork, relieved not to have to pretend to eat any longer. It was almost as hard as pretending to be happy, and she didn't think she could manage both.

"I guess that's all right," she allowed.

Doss looked down at his plate. He hadn't eaten much more than Hannah had, though, like her, he'd made a good show of it. Making illicit love on the ranch was one thing, she realized, and being married was quite another. Was he as nervous about the night to come as she was?

Jeb congratulated them both and left.

Their plates were cleared away.

Doss paid the bill.

And then there was nothing to do but go upstairs and get on with their wedding night.

CHAPTER TEN

TOBIAS'S BED WAS EMPTY, and his things had been removed. Hannah glanced nervously at Doss, now her husband, and put a hand to her throat.

He sighed and loosened his string tie, then unbuttoned his collar. If there had been whisky in that hotel room, Hannah was sure he would have poured himself a double and downed it in a gulp. She felt moved to touch his arm, soothe him somehow, but the urge died aborning. Instead she stood rigid upon the soles of her practical high-button shoes, and wished she'd put her foot down while there was still time, called the whole idea of getting married for the damn fool notion that it was, stopped the wedding and let the gossips say what they would.

She was miserable.

Doss was miserable.

What in the world had possessed them?

"We could get an annulment," she said shakily.

Doss's gaze sliced to her, sharp enough to leave the thick air quivering in its wake. "Oh, I'd say we were past that," he retorted coldly. "Wouldn't you?"

Hannah's cheeks burned as smartly as if they'd been chapped by the bitter wind even then rattling at the windows and seeping in as a draft. "I only meant that we haven't…well…*consummated* the marriage, and—"

He narrowed his eyes. "I remember it a little differently," he said.

Damn him, Hannah thought fiercely. He'd been so

all-fired set on going through with the ceremony—
it had been *his* idea to exchange vows, not hers—and
now he was acting as though he'd been wooed, enticed,
trapped.

"I will thank you to remember *this,* Doss McKettrick—I
didn't seduce you. *You* seduced *me!*"

He hooked a finger in his tie and jerked at it. Took an
angry step toward her and glared down into her face. "You
could have said no at any time, Hannah," he reminded
her, making a deliberate effort to keep his voice down.
"My recollection is that you didn't. In fact, you—"

"Stop," Hannah blurted. "If you're any kind of gentleman, you won't throw that in my face! I was—we were
both—*lonely,* Doss. We lost our heads, that's all. We could
find the preacher, tell him it was a mistake, ask him to tear
up the license—"

"You might as well stand in the middle of Main Street,
ring a cowbell to draw a crowd, and tell the whole damn
town what we did as do that!" Doss seethed. "And what's
going to happen in six months or so, when your belly is
out to here with my baby?"

Hannah's back teeth clamped together so hard that she
had to will them apart. "What makes you so sure there
is a baby?" she demanded. "Gabe and I wanted more
children after Tobias, but nothing happened."

Doss opened his mouth, closed it again forcefully.
Whatever he'd been about to say, he'd clearly thought
better of it. All of a sudden Hannah wanted to reach down
his throat and *haul* the words out of him like a bucket
from a deep well, even though she knew she'd be just as
furious to hear them spoken as she was right then, left to
wonder.

For what seemed to Hannah like a very long time, the
two of them just stood there, practically nose to nose,
glowering at each other.

Hannah broke first, shattered against that McKettrick stubbornness the way a storm-tossed ship might shatter on a rocky shore. With a cry of sheer frustration, she turned on one heel, strode into the next room and slammed the door hard behind her.

There was no key to turn the lock, and nothing to brace under the knob to keep Doss from coming after her. So Hannah paced, arms folded, until some of her fury was spent.

Her gaze fell on her nightgown, spread by some thoughtful soul—probably the maid who had looked after Tobias while she and Doss were downstairs ruining their lives—across the foot of the bed.

Resignation settled over Hannah, heavy and cold as a wagonload of wet burlap sacks.

I might as well get this over with, she thought, trying to ignore the unbecoming shiver of excitement she felt at the prospect of being alone with Doss, bared to him, surrendering and, at the same time, conquering.

Resolutely she took off her clothes, donned the nightgown and unpinned her hair.

And waited.

Where was Doss?

She sat down on the edge of the mattress, twiddling her thumbs.

He didn't arrive.

She got up and paced.

Still no Doss.

She was damned if she'd open the door and invite him in after the way he'd acted, but the waiting was almost unbearable.

Finally Hannah sneaked across the room, bent and peered through the keyhole. Her view was limited, and while she couldn't actually see Doss, that didn't mean he wasn't there. If he'd left, she would have heard him—wouldn't she?

She paced again, briskly this time, muttering under her breath.

The room was growing cold, and not just because there was no fire to light. She marched over to the radiator, under the window, and cranked on the handle until she heard a comforting hiss. Something caught her eye, through the night-darkened glass, as she straightened, and she wiped a peephole in the steam with the sleeve of her nightgown. Squinted.

Was that Doss, standing in the spill of light flowing over the swinging doors of the Blue Garter Saloon down at the corner? His shape and stance were certainly familiar, but the clothes were wrong—or were they? Doss had worn a suit to the wedding, and this man was dressed for the open range.

Hannah stared harder, and barely noticed when the tip of her nose touched the icy glass. Then the man struck a match against the saloon wall, and lit a cheroot, and she saw his face clearly in the flare of orange light.

It *was* Doss, and he was looking in her direction, too. He'd seen her, watching him from the hotel room window like some woebegone heroine in a melodrama.

No. It couldn't be him.

They had a lot to settle, it was true, but this was their *wedding night.*

Hannah clenched her fists and turned from the window for a few moments, struggling to regain her composure as well as her dignity. By now everyone in Indian Rock knew about the hurry-up wedding, knew they ought to be honeymooning, she and Doss, even if they hadn't gotten any further than the Arizona Hotel. If Doss passed the evening in the Blue Garter Saloon, tonight of all nights—

She whirled, fumbling to pull up the sash, meaning to call out to him, though God only knew what she'd say. But before she could open the window, he turned his back on her and went right through those saloon doors. Hannah watched helplessly as they swung on their hinges and closed behind him.

Present Day

Sierra stood with her hands on her hips, studying the January Christmas tree. The lights shimmered and the colors blurred as she took in the mountain of gifts still to be unwrapped, the wads of bright paper, the expensive loot Liam had already opened.

Sweaters. A leather coat, reminiscent of Travis's. Cowboy boots and a hat. A set of toy pistols. Why, there was more stuff there than she'd been able to give Liam in all seven years of his life, let alone for one Christmas.

Eve had done it all, of course. The decorating, anyway. She might have brought the presents with her from Texas, after sending some office minion out to ransack the high-end stores.

Did it mean she genuinely cared, Sierra wondered, or was she merely trying to buy some form of absolution?

Sierra sensed Eve's presence almost immediately, but it was a few moments before she could look her in the eye.

"The pistols might have been an error in judgment," Eve conceded quietly, poised in the doorway as though unsure whether to bolt or stay and face the music. "I should have asked."

"The whole thing is an error in judgment," Sierra responded, her insides stretched so taut that they seemed to hum. "It's too much." She turned, at last, and faced her mother. "You had no right."

"Liam is my grandson," Eve pointed out, and the very rationality of her words snapped hard around Sierra's heart, like some giant rubber band, yanked to its limits and then let go.

"You had no right!" Sierra repeated, in a furious undertone.

To her credit, Eve didn't flinch. "What are you so afraid of, Sierra? That he'll like me?"

Sierra swayed a little, suddenly light-headed. "Don't you understand? I can't give Liam things like this. I don't want him getting used to this way of life—it will be too hard on him later, when we have to leave it all behind."

"What way of life?" Eve persisted. Her attitude wasn't confrontational, but it was obvious that she intended to stand her ground. It was all so easy for her, with her money and her power. She could make grand gestures, but Sierra would be the one picking up the pieces when she and Liam made a hard—and inevitable—landing in the real world.

"The *McKettrick* way of life!" Sierra burst out. "This big house, the land, the money—"

"Sierra, you *are* a McKettrick, and so is Liam."

Sierra closed her eyes for a moment, struggling to regain her composure. "I agreed to come here for one reason and one reason only," she finally said, with hard-won moderation, "because my son needs medical attention, and I can't afford to provide it. But the agreement was for one year—*one year,* Eve—and we won't be here a single day after that condition is met!"

"And after that one year is up, you think I'm just going to forget that I have a second daughter and a grandson? Whether you're still too blasted stubborn to accept my help or not?"

"I don't *need* your help, Eve!"

"Don't you?"

Sierra shook her head, more in an effort to clear her mind than to deny Eve's meaning, found a chair and sank slowly into it. "I appreciate what you're doing," she said, after a few slow, deep breaths. "I really do. But if you expect anything beyond what we agreed to, there's a problem."

Eve moved to the fireplace, took a long match from the mantel and lit the newspaper and kindling already stacked in the grate. She waited until the flames caught, crackling merrily, then added more wood from the basket next to the hearth. "What did Hank tell you about me, Sierra?" she asked quietly, turning back to study Sierra's face. "Did he tell you I was dead? Or did he say I didn't want you?"

"He didn't have to say you didn't want me. That was perfectly obvious."

"Was it?" Eve dusted off a place on the raised hearth and sat down, folding her hands loosely in her lap. "I want to know what he told you, Sierra. After all these years, after all he took from me, I think I have the right to ask."

"He never said you didn't want me. He said you didn't want *him*."

"Well, that was certainly true enough."

Sierra swallowed. "I guess I was five or six before I noticed that other little girls had mothers, not just fathers. I started asking a lot of questions, and I guess he got tired of it. He said there'd been an accident, that you'd been badly hurt and you'd probably have to go to heaven."

Eve lowered her head then, wiped furtively at her cheek with the back of one hand. "Who would have thought Hank Breslin would say *two* true things out of three in the same lifetime?"

Sierra slid to the edge of her chair, eager and tense at the same time.

Don't get sucked in, she heard Hank say, as clearly as

if he'd been standing in the room, taking part in the conversation.

"There *was* an accident?" Sierra asked on a breath, mentally shushing her father. Just asking the question meant a part of her hadn't believed Hank, but this, like so many other things, would have to be considered later, when she was alone. And calm.

Eve nodded.

"What kind of accident?"

Eve visibly collected herself, sitting up a little straighter. Her eyes seemed focused on a past Sierra hadn't been a part of. "I was having lunch at an outdoor café in San Antonio— with my lawyer, as it happens. We'd found you after two years of searching, or at least the investigators we'd hired had, and I'd seen you with my own eyes, in San Miguel. Spoken to you. I wanted to contact Hank, work out some kind of arrangement—"

A peculiar, buzzing sensation dimmed Sierra's hearing.

"Your father had to be handled very carefully. I knew that. It would have been like Hank to take you deeper into Mexico—even into South America—if he'd gotten spooked, and he'd have been a lot more careful to disappear for good the second time."

Sierra waited, willing her head to clear, listening with everything in her. "The accident?" she prompted, very softly.

"A car jumped the curb, crashed through the stucco wall between the tables and the street. We were sitting just on the other side. My lawyer—his name was Jim Furman and he had a wife and five children—was killed instantly. I was in traction for weeks, and it took me another year and a half just to walk again."

The incident sounded like something from a soap opera,

and yet Sierra knew it was true. Her stomach churned as horrific images, complete with a soundtrack of crashes and screams, flashed through her mind.

"By the time I recovered," Eve went on, after a few long moments of silence, "I knew it was too late, that I'd have to wait until you were older, when you could make choices for yourself. You were happy and healthy and very bright. You were still so young. I couldn't just waltz into your life and say, 'Hello, I'm your mother.' I was still afraid of what Hank might do, and I was struggling to rebuild my life after the accident. Meg was spending most of her time with nannies as it was, and I had to turn the company over to the board of directors because I couldn't seem to focus my mind on anything. With all that going on, how could I take you away from the only home you knew, only to turn around and leave you in the care of strangers?"

Sierra sat quietly, drawing careful, measured breaths, taking it all in. "Okay," she said, finally. "I can buy all that. But there's still a pretty big gap between then and six weeks ago, when you finally contacted me."

Eve was silent.

So I was right, Sierra thought bitterly. There's more.

"I was ashamed," Eve said.

"Ashamed?"

Silence.

"Eve?"

"After the accident," Eve went on, her voice pitched so low that Sierra had to lean forward to hear, "I took a lot of pain pills. They became less and less effective, while the pain seemed to get worse, so I started washing them down with alcohol."

Sierra's mouth dropped open. "Meg never mentioned—"

"Of course she wouldn't," Eve said. "It was my place to

tell you and, besides, you don't just email something like that to somebody. What was she supposed to say? 'Oh, by the way, Mother is a pill-freak and a drunk'?"

"My God," Sierra whispered.

"I was intermittently clean and sober," Eve went on. "But I always fell off the wagon eventually. If Rance hadn't stepped in after I took control of the company again, God bless him, I probably would have run McKettrickCo into the ground."

"Rance?"

"Your cousin."

Sierra struggled to hit a lighter note, because they both needed that. "Which branch of the family tree was *he* hatched in?"

Eve smiled weakly, but with a kind of gratitude that pinched Sierra's heart in one of the tenderest places. "Rance is descended from Rafe and Emmeline," she answered. "Rafe was old Angus's son."

"It took you all this time to get your life back together?" Sierra asked tentatively, after yet another lengthy silence had run its course.

"No," Eve said. Color stained her cheeks. "No, I've been on the straight-and-narrow for ten years or so. I said it before, Sierra—I was ashamed. So much time had gone by, and I didn't know what to say. Where to start. It became a vicious cycle. The longer I put it off, the harder it was to take the risk."

"But you finally tracked me down again. What changed?"

"I didn't have to track you down. I always knew where you were." Eve sighed, and her shoulders stooped a little. "I found out about Liam's asthma, and I couldn't wait any longer." She paused, straightened her back again. "Fair is fair, Sierra. I've answered the hard questions, though I realize there will be more. Now, it's your turn. Why did you spend your life moving from place to place, serving cocktails, instead of putting down roots somewhere and making something of your life?"

Sierra considered her past and felt something sink within her. She'd taken a few night courses, here and there. She'd used her fluent Spanish with customers and volunteered, when she could, at some of Liam's schools. But she'd never had roots or any direction except "away."

"There's nothing wrong with serving cocktails," she said, trying not to sound defensive and not quite succeeding.

"Of course there isn't," Eve readily agreed. "But why didn't you go to college?"

Sierra smiled ruefully. "There are only twenty-four hours in a day, Eve. I had a child to support."

Eve nodded reflectively. And waited.

Sierra waited, too.

"That doesn't explain all the moving from place to place," Eve said at last.

"I wish I had a ready answer," Sierra said, after considerable searching. "I guess I just always had this low-grade anxiety, like I was trying to outrun something."

Eve took that in silently.

"Why did you divorce my father?" Sierra asked. She hadn't seen the question coming, but she knew it had been fermenting in the back of her mind for a long time. Whenever it arose, she pushed it down, told herself it didn't matter, but this was a time for truth, however painful it might be.

"Hank," Eve replied carefully, "was one of those men who believe they're entitled to call the shots, by virtue of possessing a penis. He quit his job a month after we were married—he sold condominiums—planning to become a golf pro at the country club. He never actually got around to applying, of course, and it would have been quite a trick to get hired anyway, since there wasn't an opening and he didn't know a nine-iron from a putter."

Sierra moistened her lips, uncomfortable.

"He was an emotional lightweight," Eve went on, quietly relentless. "But you knew that, didn't you, Sierra?"

She *had* known, but admitting it aloud was beyond her. She did manage a stiff nod, though.

"How did he earn a living?" Eve asked. "Even in Mexico, there's rent to pay, and food costs money."

Sierra blushed. Hank had tended bar at the corner cantina on occasion, and played a lot of backroom poker. The house they'd lived in belonged to Magdalena. "He just seemed to…coast," she said.

"But you had clothes, shoes. Medical care. Birthday cakes. Toys at Christmas?"

Sierra nodded. Her childhood had been marked by two things—a vague, pervasive loneliness, and a bohemian kind of freedom. At last, realization struck. "*You* were sending him money somehow."

"I was sending *you* money, through Hank's sister, from the day he took you away. Nell, your aunt, was pretty clever. She always cashed the check, then wired it to Hank, through various places—sometimes a bank, sometimes the courtesy desk in a supermarket, sometimes a convenience store. Eventually my investigators picked up the trail, but it wasn't so easy in those days, before computers."

Sierra flashed on a series of memories—her dad walking away from one of the many *cambio* outlets in San Miguel, where tourists cashed traveler's checks and exchanged their own currency for *pesos*. She'd been very small, but she'd seen him folding a wad of bills and tucking it into his pocket, and she'd wondered. Now she felt a stab of shame on his behalf, recalling his small, secret smile.

Eve was right. Hank Breslin had felt *entitled* to that money, and while he'd always made sure Sierra had the necessities, he'd never been overly generous. In fact, it had been Magdalena not Hank, who had provided extras. Sweet, plump, spice-scented Magdalena of the patient smile and manner.

Sierra's emotions must have been clearly visible in her face. Eve rose, came over to her and laid a hand on her shoulder. Then, without another word, she turned and left the room.

Sierra had loved her father, for all his shortcomings, and seeing him in this light destroyed a lot of fantasies. Even worse, she knew that Adam, Liam's father, had been a younger version of Hank. Oh, he'd had a career. But she'd been an amusement to him and nothing more. He'd been willing to sell her out, sell out his own wife and daughters, for a good time. Like Hank, he'd felt entitled to whatever pleasures happened to be available, and to hell with all the people who got hurt in the process.

For a moment she hated Adam, hated Hank, hated all men.

She'd been attracted to Travis Reid.

Now she took an internal step back, and an enormous *no!* boiled up from her depths, spewing like a geyser and then freezing solid at its height.

CHAPTER ELEVEN

1919

DOSS RETURNED TO THE ROOM well after midnight, smelling of cigar smoke and whisky. Hannah lay absolutely still, playing possum, watching through her lashes as he shed his hat and coat and kicked off his boots. Maybe he knew she was awake, and maybe he was fooled. She wasn't about to give herself away by speaking to him and, besides, she didn't trust herself not to tear into him like a shrew. Once the first word tumbled out of her mouth, others would follow, like a raging horde with swords and cudgels.

On the other hand, if he had the pure audacity to think, for one blessed moment, that he was going to enjoy his husbandly privileges, she'd come up out of that bed like a tigress, claws bared and slashing.

She breathed slowly, deeply and regularly, making her body soft.

Doss moved to the bureau, filled the china wash basin from the pitcher provided, and washed. She waited, in delicious dread, for him to undress, since he obviously intended to sleep in that room, in that bed, with her.

To her surprise, relief and complete annoyance, he remained fully clothed, sat down on the edge of the bed, and stretched out on top of the covers.

"I know you're not asleep," he said.

Hannah bit down hard on her lower lip. Though her eyes were shut tight, tears squeezed beneath her lids. Gabe would never have done such a thing to her, never have gone out on their wedding night to smoke and drink whisky and carouse with bad companions. Never have subjected her to such a public humiliation.

A sob shook her body. "I *hate* you, Doss McKettrick," she said.

He sighed, sounding resigned. If he'd apologized, if he'd put his arm around her and held her close, she would have felt better, in spite of it all, but he didn't. He kept to his own side of the bed, a weight atop the blankets, within touching distance and yet as remote from Hannah as Indian Rock was from the Eastern Seaboard.

"We'll have to make the best of things," he told her.

She rolled on to her side, with her back to him. "No, we won't," she whispered snappishly, "because as soon as Tobias is well enough, he and I are getting on the train and leaving for good."

"If it's a comfort to you," Doss replied, "then you just go ahead and think that. The truth of the matter is, you're my wife now, and as long as there's a chance you're carrying my baby, you're not going anywhere."

"I hate you," Hannah repeated.

"So you said," Doss answered, with a long-suffering sigh.

"I'll leave if I want to."

"I'll bring you back. And believe me, Hannah, I can keep up the game as long as you can."

"Then you mean to keep me prisoner." Hannah spoke into the darkness, and it seemed like a shadow, cast by her very soul, that gloom, rather than mere night, with the moon following its ancient course and the stars in their right places. It was, in that moment, as if the sun would never rise again.

"I won't lock you in the cellar, if that's what you mean," Doss told her. "I won't mistreat you or force my attentions on you, and I'll be civil as long as you are. But until I know whether you're pregnant or not, you're staying right here."

Hannah huddled deeper into the covers, feeling small, and wiped away a tear with the edge of the sheet. "I hope I'm not," she whispered. "I hope I'm not carrying your baby."

Even as she said the words, though, she knew they were the frayed and tattered weavings of a lie. She longed for another child, a girl this time, yearned to feel a life growing and stirring under her heart. She just didn't want Doss McKettrick to be the father, that was all.

She cried quietly, lying there next to Doss. Cried till her pillow was wet. She'd have bet money she wouldn't sleep a wink, but at some point she succumbed.

The next thing she knew, it was morning.

Doss's side of the bed was empty, and fat, lazy flakes of snow drifted past the window. The room was cold, but she could hear voices in the next room and the clattering of silverware against dishes. The aroma of bacon teased her nose; her stomach clenched with hunger, and then she was nauseous.

"No," she said, in a whisper, sitting bolt-upright.

Yes, her body replied. She'd had the same reaction within ten days of Tobias's conception.

Tobias appeared in the doorway, with Doss standing just behind him.

"You want some breakfast, Ma?" the boy asked. He looked slightly feverish, but stronger, too, and he was wearing a new suit of clothes—black woolen trousers, a blue-and-white-plaid flannel shirt, even suspenders.

The whole picture turned hazy, and the mention of food, let alone the smell, sent bile scalding into the back of Hannah's throat. Avoiding Doss's gaze, she gulped and shook her head.

Doss laid a hand on Tobias's shoulder and gently steered him back into the other room. He pulled the door closed, too, and the instant he did, Hannah rolled out of bed, pulled the chamber-pot out from underneath, distractedly grateful that it was clean, and threw up until she collapsed onto the hooked rug, utterly spent.

She heard the door open again, heard Doss say her name, but she couldn't respond. She just lay there, on her side, wretched and empty, as though she'd lost her soul as well as the remains of her wedding supper.

Doss knelt, gathered her in his arms, and put her back into bed, covering her gently. He fetched a basin of tepid water from the other room, along with a washcloth, and cleaned her up. When that was done, he handed her a glass, and she rinsed her mouth, then spat into the basin.

"I'll get the doctor," he said.

She shook her head. "Don't," she answered, and the word came out raspy and raw. "I just need to rest."

Doss drew up a chair, sat beside the bed, keeping a silent vigil. Hannah wished he'd go away, and at the same time she dreaded his leave-taking with the whole echoing hollowness of her being.

A maid came in, replacing the fouled chamber pot, washing out the basin, taking the pitcher away and bringing it back full. Although she cast the occasional worried glance in Hannah's direction, the woman never said a word, and when she was gone, Doss remained.

He plumped the pillows behind Hannah's back and adjusted the radiator to warm the room.

"I thought I'd bundle Tobias up," Doss ventured, at some length, "and take him down to the general store.

Get him some things to play with, maybe a book to read."

Hannah was in a strange, dazed state, weak all over. "You see that he doesn't take a chill," she muttered. Common sense said Tobias ought to stay in, out of the weather, and if she'd been herself, she would have insisted on that. As things stood, she didn't have the strength, and anyway she knew the boy was desperate to get out, if only for a little while.

Doss stood, tucked the covers in around her. To look at them, Hannah thought, anybody would have thought they were a normal husband and wife, people who loved each other. "Can I bring you something back?"

"No," she said, and closed her eyes, drifting.

When she opened them again, Doss was back, with the chilly scent of fresh air surrounding him. She could hear Tobias in the next room, chatting with somebody.

"Feeling better?" Doss asked. He was holding a parcel in his hands, wrapped in brown paper and tied with string.

"Thirsty," Hannah murmured.

Doss nodded, set the package aside and brought her another glass of water, this time from the pitcher on the bureau.

She drank it down, waited, and was pathetically pleased when it didn't come right back up.

"You'd best have something to eat, if you can," Doss said.

Hannah nodded. Suddenly she was ravenous.

He left again, was gone so long that she wondered if he meant to hunt down the food, skin it, and cook it over a slow fire. Tobias wandered in, cheeks pink from the cold, eyes bright. "Uncle Jeb wants to buy me a sandwich," he told her. "Downstairs, in the restaurant. Is it all right if I go?"

Hannah smiled. "Sure it is," she said.

Tobias drew a step nearer, moving tentatively, as though approaching something fragile enough to fall over and break at the slightest touch. "Doss says you're not dying," he said.

"He's right," Hannah answered.

"Then what's the matter? You *never* stay in bed in the daytime."

Hannah extended her hand, and after hesitating Tobias took it. "I'm being lazy," she said, giving his fingers a squeeze.

He clung for a moment, then let go. His eyes were wide and worried. "I heard you being sick," he told her.

A door opened in the distance, and Hannah heard Doss and Jeb exchange quiet words, though she couldn't make them out. "I'll be fine by tomorrow," she promised. "You go and have that sandwich. It isn't every day you get to eat in a real restaurant."

Tobias relaxed visibly. He smiled, planted a kiss on her forehead and fled, nearly colliding with Doss in the doorway. Doss tightened his grip on the tray of food he was carrying. A teapot, with steam wisping from the spout. A bowl of something savory and fragrant.

Hannah's nose twitched, and her formerly rebellious stomach growled an audible welcome.

"Chicken and dumplings," Doss said, with a grin.

He set the tray carefully on Hannah's lap. Poured her a cup of tea and probably would have spoon-fed her, too, if she hadn't taken charge of the situation.

"Thank you," she said, trying to square this attentive man with the one who had left her alone on their wedding night to visit the Blue Garter Saloon.

"You're welcome," he replied. He sat down to watch her eat, and his gaze strayed once or twice to the package on the nightstand, still wrapped and mysterious.

Hannah did not assume it was for her, since she'd clearly refused Doss's earlier offer to bring her something from the mercantile, but she was curious, just the same. The shape was booklike, and before she'd married Gabe, she'd read so much her mother and father used to fret that her eyes might go bad. After she became a wife, she was too busy, and when Gabe went away to war, she found she couldn't concentrate on the printed word. Letters were all she'd been able to manage then.

She ate what she could and sipped her tea, hot and sweet and pale with milk, and Doss took the tray away, set it on the bureau. Jeb and Tobias had long since gone downstairs for their midday meal, and except for the sounds of wagons passing in the street below and the faint hiss of the radiator, the room was silent.

Doss cleared his throat and shifted uncomfortably in his chair. "Hannah, about last night—"

"Stop," Hannah said quickly, and with as much force as she could manage, given her curiously fragile state. The teacup rattled in its saucer, and Doss leaned forward to take it from her, set it next to the parcel. He looked resigned, and a little impatient.

Hannah leaned back on her pillows, fighting another spate of tears. She would have sworn she'd cried them all out the night before, after Doss came back from the Blue Garter and told her he wouldn't let her go home to Montana, but here they were, burning behind her eyes, threatening to spill over.

"I figure you know what this means, your being sick like this," Doss said presently, and in a tone that said he wouldn't be silenced before he'd finished his piece. "That's the only reason I didn't bring the doctor over here, first thing."

Hannah closed her eyes. Nodded.

"I know you'd rather it was Gabe sitting here," he went

on. "That he'd be the one who fathered that child, the one taking you home to the ranch, the one bringing Tobias up to be a man. But the plain fact of the matter is, it'll be me doing those things, Hannah, and you might as well make peace with that."

She didn't speak, because she couldn't. She tried to summon up Gabe's image in her mind, but it wouldn't come to her. All she saw was Doss, coming in after a night at the Blue Garter, taking off his coat and hat and boots, lying down beside her on the bed, keeping a careful distance.

He retrieved the parcel from the nightstand and laid it in her lap. She listened, despondent, as he left the room, closed the door quietly behind him.

She ought to refuse the package, throw it against the wall or into Doss's face when he came back. But some part of her wanted a gift, something frivolous and impractical, chosen purely to bring a smile to her face.

She barely remembered what it was like to smile, without thinking about it first, without deciding she ought to, because it was called for or expected.

Her hands trembled as she undid the string, wound it into a little ball to keep, turned back the brown paper, which she would carefully fold and save against some future need, to find that Doss had indeed given her a book. Her breath caught at the beauty of the green leather cover. The title, embossed in shining gold, seemed to sing beneath the tips of her fingers.

The Flowers of Western America, Native and Imported: An Illustrated Guide.

Hannah held the thick volume reverently, savoring the anticipation for a few moments before opening it to look at the title page, memorize the author's name, as well as that of the artist who'd done the original woodcuttings and metal etchings for the pictures.

When she couldn't bear to wait another moment, Hannah turned that page, expecting to read the table of contents. Instead, there was a note, written in Doss's strong, clear handwriting.

> On the occasion of our marriage, and
> because I know you long for spring, and your
> garden.
> Doss McKettrick
> January 17, 1919

An emotion Hannah could not recognize swelled in her throat, fairly cutting off her breath. She traced his name with her eyes and then with the tip of her index finger. Doss McKettrick. As if men by that name were common as thorns in a blackberry thicket, and any one of them might be her husband. As if he had to be sure she knew which one would give her a book and which had noticed how fiercely, how desperately she craved that first green stirring in the cold earth and in the bare-limbed branches of trees.

Did he know how she listened for the breaking of the ice on the pond far back in the woods behind the house? How she watched the frigid sky for the first brave birds, carrying back the merry little songs she pined for, in the secret regions of her heart, when the snow was just beginning to seep into the ground?

Hannah closed the book, held it against her chest.

Then she opened it again and carefully turned to the first illustration, a lovely colored woodcut of purple crocuses, blooming above a thin snowfall. She drank them in, surfeited herself on lilacs and climbing roses, sweet williams and peonies.

Doss had given her *flowers,* in the dead of winter. Just looking at the pictures, she could imagine their distinctive scents, the shape of their petals, the depth upon depth of their various colors—everything from the palest of whites to the fathomless purples and crimsons.

She gobbled them all greedily with her eyes, page after page of them, tumbled flower-drunk into sleep and dreamed of them. Dreamed of spring, of trout quickening in the creeks, of green grass and of fresh, warm breezes teasing her hair and tingling on her skin.

When she wakened, drowsy and confused, the room was lavender with twilight, and a rim of golden light edged the lower part of the door. She heard Doss and Tobias talking in the next room, knew by a series of decisive clicks that they were playing checkers. Tobias gave a shout of triumphant laughter, and the sound seemed so poignant to Hannah that tears thickened in her throat.

She got up, used the chamber pot, washed her hands at the basin. She rummaged for her flannel wrapper, pulled it on and crossed the cold wooden floor to the door.

Opened it.

Tobias and Doss both turned to look at her.

Tobias smiled, delighted.

Doss looked shy, as though they'd just met. He got up suddenly, came to her, took her arm. Escorted her to a chair.

"Don't fuss," she scolded, but it was after the fussing was through.

"I beat Uncle Doss *four* times!" Tobias crowed.

"Did you?" Hannah asked, deliberately widening her eyes.

Doss went over to the other bed, pulled the quilt off, made Hannah stand, wrapped her up like renderings in a sausage skin and sat her down again.

What am I to make of you, Doss McKettrick? she asked silently.

"I'll go down and order us some supper," Doss said.

"Has your uncle Jeb gone?" Hannah asked Tobias, when they were alone.

Tobias nodded, kneeling on the floor, stacking checker pieces into red and black towers that teetered on the wooden board. "He took the afternoon train back to Phoenix. Said to tell you he hoped you'd be feeling better soon."

"I wish I could have said goodbye," Hannah said, but it wasn't the complete truth. She'd not been eager to face Doss's uncle; he was half again too wise and, besides, he must have known that her new husband had spent much of their wedding night in a saloon, just to avoid her. He'd never have mentioned it, of course, but she'd have seen the knowledge in his eyes.

Would he tell his wife, Chloe, when he got home? Would she, in turn, tell Emmeline and Mandy and the other McKettrick women? Get them all feeling sorry for poor Hannah?

She'd know soon enough. Concerned letters would begin arriving, probably in the next batch of mail, full of wary congratulations and carefully worded questions. The Aunts, as both Gabe and Doss had always referred to them, were not gossips, so she needn't fear scandal from that quarter, but they would have plenty of private discussions among themselves, and they'd give Doss what for when they returned to the Triple M in the spring, settling into their houses on all parts of the ranch, throwing open windows and doors, planting gardens and entertaining a steady stream of children and grandchildren.

Hannah thought she would have welcomed even their curiosity, if it meant the long winter was over.

"Ma?"

Hannah realized she'd let her mind wander and turned her attention to Tobias, who was studying her closely and clearly had something of moment to say. "Yes, sweetheart?"

"Is Uncle Doss my pa, now that you and him are married?"

Hannah blinked. Took in a slow breath and took her time letting it out. "I told you before, Tobias. Doss is still your uncle. Your father will always be—your father."

Tobias's forehead creased as he frowned. "But Pa's *dead*," he said.

Hannah sighed. "Yes."

"Uncle Doss is *alive*."

"He certainly is."

"I want a pa. Somebody to take me fishin' and teach me how to shoot."

"Uncles can do those things." Hannah didn't want Tobias within a mile of a gun, but she didn't have the strength to fight that battle just then, so she let it go.

"It isn't the same," Tobias reasoned.

"Tobias, there are some things in this life a person has to accept. Your father is gone. Doss is your uncle, not your pa. You'll just have to make the best of that."

"The best would be if he was my pa instead of my uncle."

"Tobias."

"You said once that Uncle Doss would be my stepfather if you got married. Now, you're his wife. So if you leave off the 'step' part, that makes him my pa."

Hannah rubbed her temples with her fingertips.

Tobias beamed. Eight years old, and he could argue like a senior senator at a campaign picnic.

The door to the corridor opened, and Doss came in, followed by two maids carrying trays laden with food.

"Pa's back," Tobias said.

Hannah's gaze locked with Doss's. Something passed between them, silent and charged.

Hannah looked away first.

CHAPTER TWELVE

Present Day

"YOU NEED TIME TO ABSORB all this," Eve told Sierra the next morning at the breakfast table. Eve had made waffles for them all, and everyone had eaten with a hearty appetite. Now Liam was upstairs, dressing for his first visit to Indian Rock Elementary School—Sierra planned to register him but wasn't sure he was ready for a full day of class—and Travis had given the ranch house a wide berth ever since their return from Flagstaff the previous afternoon. "So I'm going to leave," Eve finished, gently decisive.

Sierra, who had spent a largely sleepless night, had mixed feelings about Eve's going away. On the one hand, there were so many things she wanted to know about her mother—things that had nothing to do with their long separation. What kind of books did she read? What places had she visited? Had she loved anyone before or after Hank Breslin? What made her laugh? Did she cry at sad movies, or was she a stone-realist, prone to saying, "It's only a story"?

On the other, Sierra craved solitude, to think and reflect and sort what she had learned into some kind of sensible order. She wanted to huddle up somewhere, with her arms around her knees and decide what she believed and what she didn't.

"Okay," she said.

"There is one thing I want to show you before I go," Eve said, rising from the kitchen table and crossing to the china cabinet to lean down and open one of the drawers. She brought out a large, square object, wrapped in soft blue flannel, and set it before Sierra, who had shoved her plate and coffee cup aside in the meantime and wiped her part of the tabletop clean with a checkered cloth napkin.

Sierra's heart raced a little and, at a nod from Eve, she folded back the flannel covering to reveal an old photo album.

"These are your people, Sierra," Eve said quietly. "Your ancestors. There are journals and other photographs in the attic, and they need cataloging. It would be a great favor to me if you would gather them and make sure they're properly preserved."

"I can do that," Sierra said. Her hand, resting on the album cover, trembled a little, with both anticipation and a certain reluctance to get involved. Biologically she had a connection with the faces and names between the battered leather covers of the book, but in terms of real life, she was just passing through. She couldn't afford to forget that.

Eve laid a hand on her shoulder. "Sorry about the Christmas tree," she said with a slight smile. "I was the one who put it up, and I should be the one to take it down, but the plane will be arriving in an hour, so there isn't time. The corresponding boxes are in the basement, at the bottom of the steps."

Sierra nodded a second time. Liam had finished opening his presents the night before, and the mess had been cleaned up. Putting away the tree, like sorting photos and journals, would be a bittersweet enterprise. She hadn't looked closely at the ornaments, but she supposed they were heirlooms, like so many other things in that house, each one with a meaning she could never fully understand.

So many McKettrick Christmases, and she hadn't been a part of any of them. With Hank the holiday had gone almost unnoticed, although there were always a few gifts. Sierra hadn't felt deprived at the time, because she hadn't known that other people made more of a fuss.

The McKettricks, most likely, made a lot of fuss, not just over Christmas, but other holidays, too. They'd probably kept happy secrets at Yuletide, sung carols around that haunted piano, toasted each other with eggnog poured into cut-glass cups that were older than any of them....

Enough, Sierra told herself sternly. That time is gone. You missed it. Get over wishing you hadn't.

Eve bent to kiss Sierra on top of the head, then went upstairs to the big master bedroom, to pack up her things.

Sierra cleared the table and loaded the dishwasher, but her gaze kept straying to the album. It was as though the people in the photographs, all long dead, were calling to her.

Get to know us.

We are part of you. We are part of Liam.

Sierra shook off the feeling as a nostalgic whim. She was as much a Breslin as a McKettrick, after all. She knew how to be Hank's daughter, but being Eve's was a whole new ball game. It was as though she had an entirely separate and unfamiliar identity, and that person was a stranger to her.

Liam bounded down the back stairs as she was rinsing out the coffee carafe, beaming at the prospect of starting school. He'd been thrilled to learn, through the research he and Sierra had done on Meg's computer, after last night's present-unwrapping frenzy, that there was no "Geek Program" at Indian Rock Elementary.

He wanted to be an "ordinary" kid.

Not sick.

Not gifted.

"Just regular" as he'd put it.

Sierra's heart ached with love and empathy. As a child, home taught by Magdalena, she'd yearned to go to a real school, but Hank had forbidden it.

Now she realized Hank had been hiding her, probably fearful that some visitor, expatriate parent or teacher might catch on to the fact that he'd snatched her, and look into the matter.

For a moment she indulged in a primitive anger so deep that it was visceral, causing her stomach to clench and her jaws to tighten.

"Grandma says we'd better take Meg's Blazer into town today, because ours is a heap, not to mention a veritable eyesore," Liam reported cheerfully. "When are we going to get a new car?"

"When I win the lottery or get a job," Sierra said, deliberately relaxing her shoulders, which had immediately tensed, and taking Liam's new "cowboy" coat, as he'd dubbed it, down from the peg. While she would have objected if she'd known Eve was out buying all those gifts, let alone wrapping them and putting them under a fully decorated Christmas tree, she was glad of this one. It was made of leather and lined with sheepskin, well beyond her budget, and it would definitely keep her little boy warm.

Just then Eve came back, bundled up for winter weather herself, and carrying a small, expensive suitcase in one hand. Her coat was full length and black, elegantly cut and probably cashmere.

"We're in the process of opening a branch office of McKettrickCo in Indian Rock," she announced, evidently unabashed that she'd been eavesdropping. "Keegan is heading it up, but I'm sure there will be a place for you in the organization if you want one. You do speak Spanish, don't you?"

"Keegan," Sierra mused mildly, letting the indirect job offer slide, along with the reference to her language skills, at least for the moment. "Another McKettrick cousin?"

"Descended from Kade and Mandy," Eve confirmed, smiling slightly and nodding toward the album. "It's all in the book."

"How are you getting back to the airstrip—or wherever your jet is landing?" Sierra asked, shrugging into her coat, which looked like something from the bottom of a grungy bin at a thrift store, compared to the ones Eve and Liam were decked out in.

"Travis is taking me in his truck," Eve said, setting her suitcase down by the door, heading to the china cabinet to pluck a set of keys from a sugar bowl, taking Sierra's hand, opening it and placing them on her palm. "Use the Blazer. That wreck of yours won't make it out of the driveway, if it starts at all."

Sierra hesitated a moment before closing her fingers around the keys. "Not to mention that it's a veritable eyesore," she said pointedly, but with a little smile.

"You said it," Eve replied brightly. "I didn't."

"Yes, you did," Liam countered. "Upstairs, you told me—"

Outside Travis honked the truck horn.

Eve touched her grandson's neatly groomed hair. "Give your old granny a hug," she said. "I'll be back in a few weeks, and if the weather is good, maybe you'd like to take a ride in the company jet."

Liam let out a whoop.

Sierra didn't get a chance to protest, because Travis rapped lightly, opened the back door and took up Eve's suitcase. He gave Sierra a nod for a greeting and grinned down at Liam.

"Hey, cowpoke," he said. "Lookin' good in that new gear."

Liam preened, showing off the coat. "I wanted to wear the hat, too," he replied, "but Mom said I might lose it at school."

"The world," Travis replied, with a longer glance at Sierra, "is full of hats."

"What's that supposed to mean?" Sierra asked, feeling defensive again.

Travis sighed. A look passed between him and Eve. Then he simply turned, without answering and headed for the truck.

Eve hugged Liam, then Sierra.

Moments later she and Travis were in the truck and barreling away.

Sierra found the door leading into the garage—cleverly hidden in back of the pantry, like the architectural after-thought it surely was—and assessed her sister's shining red Blazer. Liam strained to reach the button on the wall, and the garage door grumbled up on its rollers, letting in a shivery chill.

Her station wagon was parked outside, behind the SUV, and Sierra muttered as she started Meg's vehicle, after she and Liam were both buckled in, and maneuvered around the eyesore.

1919

Despite the bitter cold, Hannah sat well away from Doss as they drove home in the sleigh two days after the wedding, Tobias cosseted between them.

She was married.

Each time her thoughts drifted in that direction, she started inwardly, surprised all over again.

She was a wife—but she certainly didn't *feel* like one.

Doss remained silent for the greater part of the journey, his gloved hands gripping the reins with the ease of long practice. Hannah felt his gaze on her a couple of times, but when she looked in his direction, he was always watching the snow-packed trail ahead.

By the time they reached the ranch, Hannah sorely wished she could simply crawl into bed, pull the covers up over her head and remain there until something changed.

It was an indulgence ranch women were not afforded.

Doss drew the team and sleigh up close to the house, lifted a half-sleeping Tobias from the seat and carried him in. Hannah got down on her own, bringing her valise, the flower book tucked safely inside among her dirty clothes, and followed stalwartly.

The kitchen was frigidly cold.

Doss pulled the string on the lightbulb in the middle of the room as he passed, heading for the stairs with Tobias.

Hannah rose above an inclination to turn it right back off again. She set her valise down and made for the stove. By the time Doss returned, she had a fire going and lamps lighted. She'd fetch some eggs from the spring house, she decided, provided that Willie had gathered them during their absence, and make an omelet for their supper. Perhaps she'd fry up some of the sausage she'd preserved last fall, and make biscuits and gravy, too.

"I'll see to the team," Doss said.

"Where do you suppose Willie's got to?" Hannah asked. She'd seen no sign of the hired man when they were driving in, and she feared for her chickens, along with the livestock in the barn. Like many laborers, Willie was a drifter, and might have taken it into his head to kick off the traces and take to the road anywhere along the line.

"I saw him when we came in," Doss answered, opening the door to go out again. "Out by the bunkhouse, stacking firewood."

Hannah gave a sigh of relief. In the next moment, she wanted to tell Doss to stay inside where it was warm, that she'd have the coffee ready in a few minutes, but it would have been a waste of breath. He was a rancher, born and bred, and that meant he looked after the cattle and horses first and saw to his own comforts later, when the work was done.

"Supper will be on the table in half an hour," she said, as though she were a landlady in a boarding house and he a paying guest, planning the briefest of stays. "Willie's welcome to join us, if he wants."

Doss nodded, raised his coat collar around his ears and went out.

Sometime later, he returned alone. Hannah had already fetched the eggs from the spring house, and they were scrambled, cooked and waiting on a platter in the warming oven above the stove. The kitchen was snug, and the softer light of lanterns glowed, replacing the glare of the overhead bulb.

"Willie's gone on back to the main ranch house," he said. "But he thanks you kindly for the invite to supper."

Hannah wiped her hands on her apron and took plates from the china cabinet to set the table. That was when she noticed the album lying there, as though someone had been perusing it and intended to come back and look some more later.

She stopped in her tracks.

Doss, in the act of shedding his coat and hat, followed her gaze.

"What's the matter, Hannah?" he asked, with a quiet alertness in his voice.

"The album," she said.

"What about it?" Doss asked, passing her to approach the stove. He poured himself a cup of coffee and came to stand beside her.

"Willie wouldn't have gone through our things, would he?"

Doss shook his head. "Not likely it would even have occurred to him to do that," he said. "Judging by how cold it was in here when we got home, he probably didn't set foot in the house once he'd finished off that chicken soup you made before we left."

Hannah wrung her hands, took a step toward the table and then paused. "Do you...do you ever get the feeling we're not alone in this house?" she asked, almost whispering the words.

"No," Doss said, with conviction.

"It was bad enough when the teapot kept moving. Now, the album—"

"Hannah." He touched her arm. "You sound like Tobias, going on about seeing a boy in his room."

"Maybe," Hannah ventured to speculate, almost breathless with the effort of speaking the words aloud, "he's not imagining things. Maybe it wasn't the fever."

Doss cupped Hannah's elbow in one hand and steered her to the table, letting go only to pull back a chair. It was pure fancy, of course, but as Hannah sat down, it seemed to her that the album, fairly new and reverently cared for, was very old. The sensation lasted only a moment or so, but it was so powerful that it left her feeling weak.

"We've all been under a strain, Hannah," Doss reasoned. "One of us must have gotten the album out and forgotten about it."

She looked up into his face. "Did you?" she challenged softly.

He paused, shook his head.

"I know *I* didn't," she insisted.

"Tobias, then," Doss said.

"No," Hannah replied. "He was too sick."

Doss set his coffee on the table, sat astride the bench, facing her. "There's a simple explanation for this, Hannah. Somebody might have come up from one of the other places, let themselves in."

As close as the McKettricks were, they didn't go into each other's houses when no one was at home. If one of them had wanted to see the album, they'd have said so. Anyway, the aunts and uncles were all in Phoenix, their children grown and gone. The people who looked after their places wouldn't have considered snooping like this, even if they'd been interested, which seemed unlikely.

"The biscuits will burn if you don't take them out of the oven," Hannah said, staring at the album, almost expecting it to move on its own, float through the air like a spirit medium's trumpet at a séance.

Doss got up, crossed the room and rescued the biscuits. The sausage gravy was done, warming at the back of the stove, so he retrieved one of the plates Hannah had gotten out, filled it for her and brought it to the table.

"Tobias will be hungry," she said, thinking aloud.

"I'll see to him," Doss answered. "Eat."

Hannah moved the album out of the way and pulled

the plate toward her, resigned to taking her supper, even though she didn't want it. Doss brought her silverware, then filled another plate for Tobias and took it downstairs.

When he returned, he dished up his own meal and joined Hannah at the table. She was still staring at her scrambled eggs, sausage gravy and biscuits.

"Eat," he repeated.

She took up a fork. "There's someone here," she said. "Someone we can't see. Someone who moves the teapot and now the album, too."

"Let's assume, for a moment, that that's true," Doss ruminated, tucking into his food with an energy Hannah envied. "What do you plan to do about it?"

Hannah swallowed a bite of tasteless food. "I don't know," she answered, but it wasn't the complete truth. An idea was already brewing in her mind.

They finished their supper.

Hannah cleared the table, put the album back in its drawer in the china cabinet, and went upstairs to look in on Tobias while Doss washed the dishes.

Her son was sitting up in bed when she entered his room, his supper half-eaten and set aside on the bedside table. "The boy's not here," he said. "I wonder if he's gone away."

Hannah frowned. "What boy?" she asked, even though she knew.

"The one I see sometimes. With the funny clothes."

Hannah stroked her boy's hair. Sat down on the edge of his bed. "Does this boy ever speak to you? Does he have a name?"

Tobias shook his head. His eyes were large in his pale face. The trip back from Indian Rock had been hard on him, and Hannah was both worried about her son and determined not to let on.

"We mostly just look at each other. I reckon he's as surprised to see me as I am to see him."

"Next time he shows up, will you tell me?"

Tobias bit his lower lip, then nodded. "You believe me?"

"Of course I do, Tobias."

"Pa said he was imaginary. When we talked about it, I mean."

Hannah sighed. "Tobias, Doss is your uncle, not your pa."

Suddenly, Tobias's eyes glistened with unshed tears. "Why won't you let him be my pa?" he asked. "He's your husband, isn't he? If you can have a husband, why can't *I* have a pa?"

Had Tobias been older, Hannah thought, she might have explained that Doss wasn't a *real* husband, that theirs was a marriage of convenience, but he was still far too young to understand.

In point of fact, she didn't entirely understand the situation herself.

"A woman can have more than one husband," she said cautiously. "A boy has only one father. And your father was Gabriel Angus McKettrick. I don't want you to forget that."

"I *won't* forget," Tobias said. "You can wash my mouth out with soap, if you want to, but I'm still going to call Uncle Doss my pa. I've got enough uncles—Jeb and Kade and Rafe, and John Henry, too. What I need is a *pa*."

Hannah was too exhausted to argue, and she knew she wouldn't win anyhow. "So long as you promise me you will never forget who your real father is," she said. "And

I would appreciate it if you would include your uncle David—my brother—in that list of relations you just mentioned."

Tobias brightened and put out one small hand for a shake. "It's a deal," he agreed. "I like Uncle David. He can spit a long way."

"Go to sleep," Hannah told him with a smile, reaching to turn down the wick in the lantern next to his bed.

"I didn't wash my face or brush my teeth," he confessed, settling back on to his pillows.

"Just this once we'll pretend you did," she said.

The lamp went out.

She kissed his forehead, found it blessedly cool and tucked the covers in close around him. "Good night, Tobias," she said.

"Good night, Ma," Tobias replied with a yawn.

He was probably asleep before she reached the door.

She'd hoped Doss would have turned in by the time she went downstairs, so she wouldn't have to be alone with him in the intimacy of evening, but he was right there in the kitchen, with the bathtub set out in the middle of the floor and buckets and kettles of water heating on the stove.

"I just came down to say good night," she lied. Actually, she'd been planning to sit up awhile, pondering her plan. It wasn't much, but she was bound and determined to find out something about the strange goings-on in that house.

"You can have this bath if you want," Doss told her. "I can always take one later."

"You have it," Hannah said, even though she would have loved to soak the chill out of her bones in a tub of hot water. She wondered if he was planning to share her bed, but she'd have broken the ice on top of the horse trough and stripped bare for a dunking before asking him outright.

He simply nodded.

"Don't forget to bank the fire," she said.

He grinned. "I never do, Hannah," he reminded her.

She turned, blushing a little, and went back upstairs. Entering her room, the one she'd shared with Gabe, she exchanged her clothes for a nightgown. She took her hair down, brushed it, plaited it into a long braid, trying all the while not to imagine Doss right downstairs, naked as the day he was born, lounging in that tub in front of the stove.

Would he join her later?

He was her legal husband, and he had every right to sleep beside her. She, on the other hand, had every right to turn him away, wedding band or none.

Would she?

She honestly didn't know, and in the end, it didn't matter.

She put out her lamp, threw back the covers on her bed and stretched out, waiting and listening.

Presently she heard Doss climb the stairs, walk along the hallway and pass her room.

His door closed moments later.

Hannah told herself she was relieved, and then cried herself into a fitful sleep.

Present Day

The roads had been plowed, and Sierra was secretly proud of the way she handled the Blazer. She'd grown up in Mexico, after all, and spent the last few years in Florida, which precluded driving in snow. This was an accomplishment.

At the elementary school, she got Liam registered and watched as he rushed off to join his class before she could even suggest that he start slowly. His eagerness left her feeling a little bereft.

She shook that off. He had his inhaler. The school nurse had been apprised of his asthma. She had to let go.

She would be living on the Triple M for a year, per her agreement with Eve. Might as well drive around a bit, see what the town was like.

Thirty minutes later she'd seen it all.

The supermarket. The library. The Cattleman's Bank. Two cafés, three bars, a gas station. A dry cleaners, and the ubiquitous McDonald's. The Indian Rock Historical Society. A real estate firm. A few hundred houses, many of them old and, at the edge of town, a spanking-new office complex with the word McKettrickCo inlaid in colored stone over a gleaming set of automatic doors.

I'm sure there will be a place for you in the organization, if you want one, she heard Eve's voice say.

Slowing the Blazer, she studied the place, imagined herself going inside, in her jeans, sweatshirt and ratty coat, her hair combed in a slap-dash method, no mirror required. Face bare of makeup. "Hi, there," she would say to her cousin Keegan, who would no doubt be less than thrilled to see her but manage a polite greeting, anyway. "My name is Sierra and, what do you know? Turns out, I'm a McKettrick, just like you. Go figure. Oh, and by the way, my mother says you're to give me a job. Top-dollar salary and all the fringe benefits, if you don't mind."

She smiled ruefully at the thought. "Of course, all I know how to do is serve cocktails and speak Spanish," she might add. "No problem, I'm sure."

She pulled up in front of the Cattleman's Bank, patted her purse, which contained a few hundred dollars in traveler's checks, all the money she had in the world, and went in to open a checking account.

"You already have one, Ms. McKettrick," a perky young teller told her, after a few taps on her computer keyboard. The girl's eyes widened as she peered at the screen. "It's pretty substantial, too."

Sierra frowned, momentarily puzzled. "There must be some mistake. I've only been in town a few days, and I haven't—"

And then it struck her. Eve had been up to her tricks again.

The teller turned her pivoting monitor around so Sierra could read the facts for herself. The bottom line made her catch hold of the counter with both hands, lest she faint dead away.

Two million dollars?

"Of course you'll need to sign a signature card," the clerk said, still chipper. "Do you have two forms of personal identification?"

"I need to use your telephone," Sierra managed to say. The floor was still at an odd tilt, and her knuckles hurt where she gripped the edge of the counter.

The teller blinked. "You don't carry a cell phone?" she marveled, in a tone usually reserved for people who think they've been abducted by aliens and subjected to a lot of very painful and explicit medical procedures.

"No," Sierra said, trying not to hyperventilate, "I do not carry a cell phone."

"Over there," the teller said, pointing to a friendly looking nook marked off in brass letters as the Customer Comfort area.

Sierra made her way to the telephone, rummaged through

her purse for Eve's cell number and dialed. The operator came on and informed her the call was long distance, and there would be charges.

"Make it collect," Sierra snapped.

One ring. Two. Eve was probably still in flight, aboard the company jet, with her phone shut off. Sierra was about to give up when, after the third ring, her mother chimed, "Eve McKettrick."

"I have a bank account with two million dollars in it!" Sierra whispered into the receiver, bent around it like someone calling a 900 number during a church service.

"Yes, dear," Eve said sweetly. "I know."

"I will not accept—"

"Your trust fund?"

Sierra sucked in her breath. Almost choked on it. "My *trust fund?*"

"Yes," Eve answered. "You also have a share in McKettrickCo, of course."

Sierra swallowed, carefully this time. "I will not take your charity."

"Tell it to your grandfather," Eve responded, unruffled. "Of course, you'll need a clairvoyant to help, because he's been dead for fifteen years."

Sierra held the receiver away from her, stared at it, jammed it to her ear again. "My grandfather left me *two million* dollars?"

"Yes," Eve said. "We kept it safely tucked away in Switzerland, so your father wouldn't get his paws on it."

Sierra closed her eyes.

"Sweetheart?" her mother asked, sounding concerned now. "Are you still there?"

"Yes," Sierra breathed. She could have walked away from all that money. She really could have—if not for Liam.

"Why didn't you tell me about this, when you were at the house?"

"Because I knew you weren't ready to hear it, and I didn't want to waste precious time arguing."

Sierra swallowed. "How come you can talk on a cell phone in flight?"

Eve laughed. "Because I patch the number into the phone onboard the plane before takeoff," she answered. "I'm quite the technological whiz. Any more questions?"

"Yes. What am I supposed to do with two million dollars?"

CHAPTER THIRTEEN

1919

BY THE TIME HANNAH CAME downstairs, Doss had built up the fire, brewed the coffee and left for the barn, like he did every morning. She put on Gabe's old coat—there was nothing of his scent left in it now—and made a trip to the privy, then the chicken house. She was washing her hands in a basin of hot water when Doss came in from doing the chores.

"I guess I'll drive the sleigh down and look in on the widow Jessup again," he said. "This cold snap might outlast her firewood."

"You'll have a good, hot breakfast first," Hannah told him. "While I'm fixing it, why don't you get some preserves from the pantry and pack them up? Mrs. Jessup especially loves those cinnamon pears and pickled crab apples I put up for Christmas."

Doss nodded, a grin crooking one corner of his mouth in a way that made Hannah feel sweetly flustered. "How's Tobias today?"

"He's sleeping in," she said, cracking eggs into a bowl, keeping her gaze averted with some difficulty. "And don't think for a moment you're going to take him with you. It's too cold and he's worn-out from yesterday."

She'd thought Doss was in the pantry, but all of a

sudden his hands closed over her shoulders, startling her so that she stiffened.

He turned her around to face him. Looked straight into her eyes.

Her heart beat a little faster.

Was he about to kiss her?

Say something important?

She held her breath, hoping he would. Hoping he wouldn't.

"Before he went back to Phoenix, Uncle Jeb said we ought to help ourselves to some hams from the smoke-house down at Rafe and Emmeline's place," he said. "A side of bacon, too. That means I'll be gone a little longer than usual."

Hannah merely nodded.

They stood, the two of them facing each other for a long moment.

Then Doss let go of Hannah's shoulders, and she turned to whip the eggs and slice bread for toasting. He found a crate and filled it with provisions for the widow Jessup.

After he'd gone, Hannah carried a plate up to Tobias, who seemed content to stay in bed with one of his many picture books.

"I'm getting worried about that boy," Tobias told Hannah solemnly. "He ought to be back by now."

"I'm sure you'll see him again soon," Hannah said moderately. "Remember, you promised to let me know right away when you do."

He nodded, looking glum.

She kissed his forehead and went out, leaving the door open so she'd hear if he called for her. What he needed most right now was rest, and good food to build his strength. When Doss got back with the bacon and hams, she'd make up a special meal.

Downstairs Hannah tidied the kitchen, washed the dishes, dried them and put them away. When that was done, she built up the fire and went to the china cabinet to open the top drawer. The album was there, where it belonged, but a little shiver went up her spine at the sight of it, just the same.

She reached past it, found the small leather-bound remembrance book Lorelei and Holt had sent her for a Christmas present. The cover was a rich shade of blue, the pages edged in shiny gold.

She hadn't written a word in the journal, hadn't even opened it. She hadn't wanted to record her grief, hadn't wanted to make it real by writing it down in dark, formal letters.

Now she had something very different in mind. She carried the remembrance book to the table, and then went to the study for a bottle of ink and a pen. The room was chilly. She rarely went there, because it always brought back memories of Gabe, sitting at the desk, reading or pondering over a ledger.

It was especially empty that day; though, strangely, it was Doss's absence Hannah felt most keenly, not Gabe's. She collected the items she needed and hurried out again.

Back in the kitchen she found a rag to wipe the pen clean. When she was finished she opened the ink and turned to the first page.

She bit her lower lip, dipped the pen, summoned up all her resolve and began to write.

My name is Hannah McKettrick. Today's date is January 19, 1919...

Present Day

The first thing Sierra noticed when she got back to the house later that morning—with a load of groceries and a head spinning with possibilities now that she was rich—was that Travis wasn't around. The second thing was that the album Eve had brought out to show her was gone.

She'd left it on the kitchen table, and it had vanished.

She paused, holding her breath. Listening. Was there someone in the house?

No, it was empty. She didn't need to search the rooms, open closet doors, peer under beds, to know that.

Her practical side took over. She brought in the rest of the supermarket bags and put everything away. Put on a pot of coffee. Made a tuna salad sandwich and ate it.

Only when she'd rinsed the plate and put it in the dishwasher did she walk over to the china cabinet and open the top drawer, as Eve had done earlier that morning.

The album was back in its place.

Sierra frowned.

Invisible fingers played a riff on her spine, touching every vertebra.

She closed the drawer again.

She would look at the photographs later. Combine that with the job of cataloging the ones stored in the attic.

She brought the Christmas boxes up from the basement, carried them into the living room. Carefully and methodically removed and wrapped each ornament. Some were obviously expensive, others were the handiwork of generations of children.

By the time she'd put them all away and dismantled the silk tree, it was time to drive into town and pick Liam up at school. Backing the Blazer out of the garage, she almost ran over Travis, who had the hood up on the station wagon and was standing to one side, fiddling with one of its parts.

He leaped out of her path, grinning.

She slammed on the brakes, buzzed down the window on the passenger side. "You scared me," she said.

Travis laughed, leaning in. "*I* scared *you?*"

"I wasn't expecting you to be standing there."

"I wasn't expecting *you* to come shooting out of the garage at sixty-five miles an hour, either."

Sierra smiled. "Do you always argue about everything?"

"Sure," he said, with an affable shrug of his impressive shoulders. "Gotta stay sharp in case I ever want to practice law again. Where are you headed in such a hurry, anyway?"

"Liam's about to get out of school for the day."

"Right," Travis said, stepping back.

"Do you want to come along?"

Now what made her say *that?* She liked Travis Reid well enough, and certainly appreciated all he'd done to help, but he also made her poignantly uncomfortable.

He must have seen her thoughts playing out in her face. "Maybe another time," he said easily. "Eve told me you were going to take down the Christmas tree. It's a big sucker, so I'll lug it back to the basement if you want."

"That would be good. The coffee's on—help yourself."

Travis grinned. Nodded. Stepped back from the side of the Blazer with exaggerated haste.

As she drove away, Sierra wasn't thinking about her two-million-dollar trust fund, the vanishing teapot, the piano that played itself, teleporting photo album or even Liam.

She was thinking about the hired help.

* * *

Peering through his new telescope at the night sky, Liam felt that familiar shiver in the air. He knew, even before he turned around to look, that the boy would be there.

And he was. Lying in the bed, staring at Liam.

"What's your name?" the boy asked.

For a moment, Liam couldn't believe his ears. He wasn't scared, but his throat got tight, just the same. He'd planned on telling the boy all about his first day at the new school, and a lot of other things, too, as soon as he showed up, but now the words got stuck and wouldn't come out.

"Mine's Tobias."

"I'm Liam."

"That's an odd name."

Liam straightened his back. "Well, 'Tobias' is pretty weird, too," he countered.

Tobias tossed back the covers and got out of bed. He was wearing a funny flannel nightgown, more suited to a girl than a boy. It reached clear past his knees. "What's that?" he asked, pointing to Liam's telescope.

Liam patiently explained the obvious. "Wanna look? You can see all the way to Saturn with this thing."

Tobias peered through the viewer. "It's bouncing around. And it's *blue!*"

"Yep," Liam agreed. "How come you're wearing a nightie?"

Tobias looked up. His eyes flashed, and his cheeks got red. "This," he said, "is a night*shirt*."

"Whatever," Liam said.

Tobias gave him the eyeball. "Those are mighty peculiar duds," he announced.

"Thanks a lot," Liam said, but he wasn't mad. He figured "duds" must mean clothes. "Are you a ghost?"

"No," Tobias said. "I'm a boy. What are you?"

"A boy," Liam answered.

"What are you doing in my room?"

"This is *my* room. What are *you* doing here?"

Tobias grinned, poked a finger into Liam's chest, as though testing to see if it would go right through. "My ma told me to let her know first thing if I saw you again," he said.

Liam put out his own finger and found Tobias to be as solid as he was.

"Are you going to?" he asked.

"I don't know," Tobias said. He put his eye to the viewer again. "Is that *really* Saturn, or is this one of those moving-picture contraptions?"

1919

Hannah blew on the ink until it dried. Then she wiped the pen clean, sealed the ink bottle and closed the remembrance book.

Now that she'd written in it, she felt a little foolish, but what was done was done. She took the book back to the china cabinet and placed it carefully beneath the top cover of the family album.

She was just mounting the steps to go and check on Tobias when she realized he was talking to someone. She couldn't make out the words, just the conversational tone of his voice. He spoke with an eager lilt she hadn't heard in a long time.

She stood absolutely still, straining to listen.

"Ma!" he yelled suddenly.

She bolted up the stairs, along the hallway, into his room.

She found him lying comfortably in bed, wide awake,

his eyes shining with an almost feverish excitement. "I saw the boy," he said. "His name is Liam and he showed me Saturn."

"Liam," Hannah repeated stupidly, because anything else was quite beyond her.

"I said it was a strange name, Liam, I mean, and he said Tobias was a weird thing to be called, too."

Hannah opened her mouth, closed it again. Twisted the hem of her apron in both hands. Her knees felt as though they'd turned to liquid, and even though she'd asked Tobias to let her know straight away if he saw the boy again, she realized she hadn't been prepared to hear it. She wished Doss were there, even though he'd probably be a hindrance, rather than a help.

"Ma?" Tobias sounded worried, and his eyes were great in his face.

She hurried to his bed, sat down on the edge of the mattress, touched a hand to his forehead.

He squirmed away. "I'm not sick," he protested. "I saw *Saturn*. It's blue, and it really does have rings."

Hannah withdrew her hand, and it came to rest, fluttering, at the base of her throat.

"You don't believe me!" Tobias accused.

"I don't know *what* to believe," Hannah admitted softly. "But I know you're not lying, Tobias."

"I'm not seeing things, either!"

"I— It's just so strange."

Tobias subsided a little, falling back on to his pillows with a sigh. "He told me lots of stuff, Ma," he said, his voice small and uncertain.

Hannah took his hand, squeezed it. Tried to appear calm. "What 'stuff,' Tobias?" she managed, after a few slow, deep breaths.

"That Saturn has moons, just like the earth does. Only, it's got four, instead of just one. One of them is covered in ice, and it might even have an ocean underneath, full of critters with no eyes."

Hannah swallowed a slight, guttural cry of pure dismay. "What else?"

"People have boxes in their houses, and they can watch all kinds of stories on them. Folks act them out, like players on a stage."

Tears of pure panic burned in Hannah's eyes, but she blinked them back. "You must have been dreaming, Tobias," she said, fairly croaking the words, like a frog in a fable. "You fell asleep, and it only *seemed* real—"

"No," Tobias said flatly. "I saw Liam. I talked to him. He said it was 2007, where he lives. I told him he was full of sheep dip—that it was 1919, and I'd get the calendar to prove it. Then *he* said if I was eight years old in 1919, I was probably dead or in a nursing home someplace by 2007." He paused. "What's a nursing home, Ma? And how could I be two places at once? A kid here, and an old man somewhere else?"

Dizzy, Hannah gathered her boy in both arms and held him so tightly that he struggled.

"Let me *go,* Ma," he said. "You're fair smothering me!"

With a conscious effort, Hannah broke the embrace. Let her arms fall to her sides.

"What's happening to us?" she whispered.

"I need to use the chamber pot," Tobias announced.

Hannah stood slowly, like a sleepwalker. She moved out of that room, closed the door behind her and got as far as the top of the back stairs before her legs gave out and she had to sit down.

She was still there when Doss came in, back from his

travels to the smokehouse and the widow Jessup's place. As though he'd sensed her presence, he came to the foot of the steps, still in his coat and hat.

"Hannah? What's the matter? Is Tobias all right?"

"He's...yes."

Doss tossed his hat away, came up the steps, sat down next to Hannah and put an arm around her shoulders. She sagged against his side, even as she despised herself for the weakness. Turned her face into his cold-weather-and-leather-scented shoulder and wept with confusion and relief and a whole tangle of other emotions.

He held her until the worst of it had passed.

She sniffled and sat up straight. Even tried to smile. "How was the widow Jessup?" she asked.

Present Day

That night Sierra invited Travis to supper. Just marched right out to his trailer, knocked on the door and, the moment he opened it, blurted, "We're having spaghetti tonight. It's Liam's favorite. It would mean a lot to him if you came and ate with us."

Travis grinned. Evidently, he'd been changing clothes, because his shirt was half-unbuttoned. "If you're trying to make up for almost running over me backing out of the garage this afternoon, it's okay," he teased. "I'm still pretty fast on my feet."

Sierra was doing her level best not to admire what she could see of his chest, which was muscular. She wondered what it would be like to slide her hands inside that shirt, feel his skin against her palms and her splayed fingers.

Then she looked up into his eyes again, saw the knowing smile there and blushed. "It's more about thanking you for taking the Christmas tree downstairs," she fibbed.

"At your service," he said with a slight drawl.

Was that a double entendre?

Don't be silly, she told herself. Of course it wasn't.

"There's wine, too," she blurted out, and then blushed again. At this rate, Travis would think she'd already had a few nips.

"Everything but music," he quipped.

Afraid to say another word, she turned and hurried back toward the house, and she distinctly heard him chuckle before he closed the trailer door.

Liam was strangely quiet at supper. He usually gobbled spaghetti, but tonight he merely nibbled. He had a perfect opportunity to talk "cowboy" with Travis, or chatter on about his first day of school; instead, he asked to be excused so he could take a bath and get to bed early. At Sierra's nod, he murmured something and fled.

"He must be sick," Sierra fretted, about to go after him.

"Let him go," Travis counseled. "He's all right."

"But—"

"He's *all right,* Sierra." He refilled her wineglass, then his own.

They finished their meal, cleared the table together, loaded the dishwasher. When Sierra would have walked away, Travis caught hold of her arm and gently stopped her. Switched on the countertop radio with his free hand.

Soft, smoky music poured into the room.

The next thing she knew, Sierra was in Travis's arms, close against that chest she'd admired earlier at the door of his trailer, and they were slow dancing.

Why didn't she pull away?

Maybe it was the wine.

"Relax," he said. His breath was warm in her hair.

She giggled, more nervous than amused. What was the

matter with her? She was attracted to Travis, had been from the first, and he was clearly attracted to her. They were both adults. Why not enjoy a little slow dancing in a ranch-house kitchen?

Because slow dancing led to other things, especially when it was wine powered. She took a step back and felt the counter flush against her lower back. Travis naturally came with her, since they were holding hands and he had one arm around her waist.

Simple physics.

Then he kissed her.

Physics again—this time, not so simple.

"Yikes," she said, when their mouths parted.

He grinned. "Nobody's ever said that after I kissed them."

She felt the heat and substance of his body pressed against hers, right where it counted. If Liam hadn't been just upstairs, and likely to come back down at any moment, she might have wrapped her legs around Travis's waist and kissed him nuclear-style.

"It's going to happen, isn't it?" she heard herself whisper.

"Yep," Travis answered.

"But not tonight," Sierra said on a sigh.

"Probably not," Travis agreed, grinding his hips a little. His erection burned into her abdomen like a firebrand.

"When, then?"

He chuckled, gave her a slow, nibbling kiss. "Tomorrow morning," he said. "After you drop Liam off at school."

"Isn't that…a little…soon?"

"Not soon enough," Travis answered. He cupped a hand around her breast, and even through the fabric of her shirt and bra, her nipple hardened against the chafing motion of his thumb. "Not nearly soon enough."

After Travis had gone, Sierra felt like an idiot.

She looked in on Liam, who was sound asleep, and then took a cool shower. It didn't help.

She would come to her senses by morning, she told herself, as she stood at her bedroom window, gazing down at the lights burning in Travis's trailer.

She'd get a good night's sleep. That was all she needed.

She slept, as it happened, like the proverbial log, but she woke up thinking about Travis. About the way she'd felt when he kissed her, when he backed her up against the counter...

She made breakfast.

Took Liam to school.

Zoomed straight back to the ranch, even though she'd intended to drive around town for a while, giving herself a chance to cool down.

Instead, she was on autopilot.

But it wasn't as if she gave up easily. She raised every argument she could think of. It was *way* too soon. She didn't know Travis well enough to sleep with him.

She would regret this in the morning.

No, long *before* then.

The truth was, she'd denied herself so much, for so long, that she couldn't stand it any more.

She didn't even bother to park the Blazer in the garage. She shut it down between the house and Travis's trailer, up to the wheel wells in snow, jumped out, and double-timed it to his door.

Knocked.

Maybe he's not home, she thought desperately.

Let him be here.

Let him be in China.

His truck was parked in its usual place, next to the barn.

The trailer door creaked open.

He grinned down at her. "Hot damn," he said.

Sierra shoved her hands into her coat pockets. Wished she could dig her toes right into the ground somehow and hold out against the elemental forces that were driving her.

Travis stepped back. "Come in," he said.

So much for the toehold. She was inside in a single bound.

He leaned around her to pull the door shut.

"This is crazy," she said.

He began unbuttoning her coat. Slipped it back off her shoulders. Bent his head to taste her earlobe and brush the length of her neck with his lips.

She groaned.

"Talk some sense into me," she pleaded. "Say this is stupid and we shouldn't do it."

He laughed. "You're kidding, right?"

"It's wrong."

"Think of it as therapy."

She trembled as he tossed her coat aside. "For whom? You or me?"

He opened her blouse, undid the catch at the front of her bra, caught her breasts in his hands when they sprang free.

"Oh, I think we'll both benefit," he said.

Sierra groaned again. He sat her down on the side of his bed, crouched to pull off her snow boots, peel off her socks. Then he stood her up again, and undressed her, garment by garment. Blouse...bra...jeans...and, finally, her lacy underpants.

He suckled at her breasts, somehow managing to shed

his own clothes in the process; Sierra was too dazed, and too aroused, to consider the mechanics of it.

He laid her down on the bed, gently. Eased two pillows under her bottom. Knelt between her legs.

"Oh, God," she whimpered. "You're not going to—?"

Travis kissed his way from her mouth to her neck.

"I sure am," he mumbled, before pausing to enjoy one of her breasts, then the other.

He kept moving downward, stroking the tender flesh on the insides of her thighs. He plumped up the pillows, raising her higher.

Sierra moaned.

He parted the nest of moist curls at the junction of her thighs. Breathed on her. Touched her lightly with the tip of his tongue.

She arched her back and gave a low, throaty cry of need.

"I thought so," Travis said, almost idly.

"You—thought—what?" Sierra demanded.

"That you needed this as much as I do." He took her full into his mouth.

She welcomed him with a sob and an upward thrust of her hips.

He slid his hands under her buttocks and lifted her higher still.

She was about to explode, and she fought it. It wasn't as though she had orgasms every day. She wanted this experience to *last*.

He drove her straight over the edge.

She convulsed with the power of her release—once— twice—three times.

It was over.

But it wasn't.

Before she had time to lament, he was taking her to a new level.

She came again, voluptuously, piercingly, her legs over his shoulders now. And before she could begin the breathless descent, he grasped the undersides of her knees and parted them, tongued her until she climaxed yet again. Only, this time she couldn't make a sound. She could only buckle in helpless waves of pleasure.

And still it wasn't over.

He waited until she'd opened her eyes. Until her breathing had evened out. After all of the frenzy, he waited until she nodded.

He entered her in a long, slow, deep stroke, supporting himself with his hands pressing into the narrow mattress on either side of her shoulders, gazing intently down into her face. Taking in every response.

She began the climb again. Rasped his name. Clutched at his shoulders.

He didn't increase his pace.

She pumped, growing more and more frantic as the delicious friction increased, degree by degree, toward certain meltdown.

The wave crashed over her like a tsunami, and when she stopped flailing and shouting in surrender—and only then—she saw him close his eyes. His neck corded, like a stallion's, as he threw back his head and let himself go.

His powerful body flexed, and flexed again, every muscle taut, and Sierra almost wept as she watched his control give way.

Afterward he lowered himself to lie beside her, wrapping her close in his arms. Kissed her temple, where the hair was moist with perspiration. Stroked her breasts and her belly.

She listened as his breathing slowed.

"You're not going to fall asleep, are you?" she asked.

He laughed. "No," he said. He rolled on to his back, pulling her with him, so that she lay sprawled on top of him. Caressed her back, her shoulders, her buttocks.

She nestled in. Buried her face in his neck. Popped her head up again, suddenly alarmed. "Did you use…?"

"Yes," he said.

She snuggled up again. "That was…great," she confessed, and giggled.

He shifted beneath her. She felt some fumbling.

"We can't possibly do that again," she said.

"Wanna bet?" He eased her upright, set her knees on either side of his hips.

Felt him move inside her, sleek and hard.

A violent tremor went through her, left her shuddering.

He cupped her breasts in his hands, drew her forward far enough to suck her breasts. All the while, he was raising and lowering her along his length. She took him deeper.

And then deeper still.

And then the universe dissolved into shimmering particles and rained down on them both like atoms of fire.

CHAPTER FOURTEEN

SIERRA SLEPT, SNUGGLED AGAINST TRAVIS'S SIDE, one arm draped across his chest, one shapely leg flung over his thighs.

Travis pulled the quilt up over them both, so she wouldn't get cold, and considered his situation.

He'd been to bed with a lot of women in his time.

He knew how to give and receive pleasure.

He said goodbye as easily as hello.

But this was different.

Different feeling. Different woman.

He'd been a dead man up until now, and this trailer had been his coffin.

Rance had sure been right about that.

Sierra McKettrick, who had probably expected no more from this encounter than he had—a roll in the hay, some much-needed satisfaction, a break in the monotony—had resurrected him. Probably inadvertently, but the effect was the same.

"Shit," he whispered. He'd *needed* that all-pervasive numbness and the insulation it provided. Needed *not* to feel.

Sierra had awakened everything inside him, and it hurt, to the center of his soul, like frost-bitten flesh thawing too fast.

She stirred against him, uttered a soft, hmmm sound, but didn't awaken.

He held her a little closer and thought about Brody. His little brother. Brody would never make love to a woman like Sierra. He'd never watch the moon rise over a mountain creek, the water purple in the twilight, or choke up at the sight of a ragged band of wild horses racing across a clearing for no other reason than that they had legs to run on. He'd never throw a stick for a faithful old dog to fetch, watch Fourth-of-July fireworks with a kid perched on his shoulders or eat pancakes swimming in syrup in a roadside café while hokey music played on the jukebox.

There were so many things Brody would never do.

Travis's throat went raw, and his eyes stung.

The loss yawned inside him, a black hole, an abyss.

He'd thought losing his brother would be the hardest thing he'd ever had to do, but now he knew it wasn't. Dying inside was easy—it was having the guts to *live* that was hard.

He shifted.

Sierra sighed, raised her head, looked straight into his face.

It was too much to hope, he figured, that she wouldn't notice the tear that had just trickled out of the corner of his eye to streak toward his ear.

If she saw, she had the good grace not to comment, and the depth of his gratitude for that simple blessing was downright pathetic, by his reckoning.

"What time is it?" she asked, looking anxious and womanly.

Real womanly.

He stretched, groped for his watch on the little shelf above the bed. "Twelve-thirty," he answered gruffly. He wanted to say a whole lot more, but he wasn't sure what it was. He'd have to say it all to himself first, and make sense of it, before he could tell it to anyone else.

Especially Sierra.

Not that he loved her or anything. It was too early for that.

But he sure as hell felt *something,* and he wished he didn't.

"You okay?" she asked, raising herself on to one elbow and studying his face a lot more intently than he would have liked.

"Fine," he lied.

"This doesn't have to change anything," Sierra reasoned, hurrying her words a little—pushing them along, like rambunctious cattle toward a narrow chute. Was she trying to convince him, or herself?

"Right," he said.

She pulled away, sat on the backs of her thighs, the quilt pulled up to her chin. "I'd better—get back to the house."

He nodded.

She nodded.

Neither of them moved.

"What just happened here?" Sierra asked, after a long time had passed, with the two of them just staring at each other.

Whatever had happened, it had been a lot more than the obvious. He was sure of that, if nothing else.

"I'll be damned if I know," Travis said.

"Me, neither," Sierra said. Then she bent and kissed his forehead, before scrambling out of bed.

He sat up, watched as she gathered her scattered clothes and shimmied into them. He wished he smoked, because lighting a cigarette would have given him something to do. Something to distract him from the rawness of what he felt and his frustration at not being able to wrestle it down and give it a name.

"I guess you must think I do things like this all the

time," she said. Maybe he wasn't alone in being confused. The idea stirred a forlorn hope within him. "And I don't. I *don't* sleep with men I barely know, and I don't—"

He smiled. "I believe you, Sierra," he said. He did, too. Anybody who came with the kind of sensual abandon she had, on a regular basis, would be superhuman, dead of exhaustion or both.

Actually, he admired her stamina, and her uncommon passion.

And she was up, moving around, dressing. He wasn't entirely sure he could stand.

She sat on the side of the bed, keeping a careful if subtle distance, to pull on her socks and boots. "Travis?" she said without looking at him. He saw a pink glow along the edge of her cheek, and thought of a summer dawn, rimming a mountain peak.

"What?"

"It was good. What we did was good. Okay?"

He swallowed. Reached out and squeezed her hand briefly before letting it go. "Yeah," he agreed. "It was good."

She left then, and Travis felt her absence like a vacuum.

He cupped his hands behind his head, lay back and began making a list in his mind.

All the things he had to do before he left the Triple M for good.

She'd made a damn fool of herself.

Sierra let herself into the house, closed the door behind her and leaned back against it.

What had she been thinking, throwing herself at Travis that way? She'd been like a woman possessed—and a *stupid* woman, at that.

Sierra McKettrick, the sexual sophisticate.

Right.

Sierra McKettrick, who had been intimate with exactly two men in her life—one of whom had fathered her child, lied to her and left her behind, apparently without a second thought.

What if Travis hadn't been telling the truth when he said he used protection?

What if she was pregnant again?

"Get a grip," she told herself out loud. Travis had clearly had a lot of experience in these matters, unlike her. Furthermore he was a lawyer. He might not have given a damn whether *she* was protected or not, but he surely would have covered his *own* backside, if only to avoid a potential paternity suit.

She stood still, breathing like a woman in the early stages of labor, until she'd regained some semblance of composure. She had to pull herself together. In a couple of hours she'd be picking Liam up at school.

He'd want to tell her all about his class. The other kids. The teachers.

There would be supper to fix and homework to oversee.

She was a *mother,* for God's sake, not some bimbo in a soap opera, sneaking off to have prenoon monkey sex in a trailer with a virtual stranger.

She straightened.

Her own voice echoed in her mind.

It was good. What we did was good. Okay?

And it *had* been good, just not in the noble sense of the word.

Sierra went slowly upstairs, took a long, hot shower, dressed in fresh jeans and a white cotton blouse. Borrowed one of Meg's cardigans, to complete the "Mom" look.

By the time she was finished, she still had more than an hour until she had to leave for town.

Her gaze strayed to the china cabinet.

She would look at the pictures in the album. Get a frame of reference for all those McKettricks that had gone before. Try to imagine herself as one of them, a link in the biological chain.

She heard Travis's truck start up, resisted an urge to go to the window and watch him drive away. There was too much danger that she would morph into a desperate housewife, smile sweetly and wave.

Not gonna happen.

Keeping her thoughts and actions briskly businesslike, she retrieved the album, carried it to the table, sat down and lifted the cover.

A small blue book was tucked inside, its corners curled with age.

A tremor of something went through Sierra like a wash of ice water, some premonition, some subconscious awareness straining to reach the surface.

She opened the smaller volume.

Focused on the beautifully scripted lines, penned in ink that had long since faded to an antique brown.

My name is Hannah McKettrick. Today's date is January 19, 1919.

I know you're here. I can sense it. You've moved the teapot, and the album in which I've placed this remembrance book.

Please don't harm my boy. His name is Tobias. He's eight years old.

He is everything to me.

Sierra caught her breath. There was more, but her shock was such that, for the next few moments, the remaining words might as well have been gibberish.

Was this woman, probably long dead, addressing her from another century?

Impossible.

But then, it was impossible for teapots and photograph albums to move by themselves, too. It was impossible for an ordinary piano to play itself, with no one touching the keys.

It was impossible for Liam to see a boy in his room.

Sierra swallowed, lowered her eyes to the journal again. The words had been written so very long ago, and yet they had the immediacy of an email.

How could this be happening?

She sucked in another breath. Read on.

I must be losing my mind. Doss says it's grief, over Gabe's dying. I don't even know why I'm writing this, except in the hope that you'll write something back. It's the only way I can think of to speak to you.

Sierra glanced at the clock. Only a few minutes had passed since she sat down at the table, but it seemed like so much longer.

She got out of her chair, found a pen in the junk drawer next to the sink. This was *crazy*. She was about to deface what might be an important family record. And yet there was something so plaintive in Hannah's plea that she couldn't ignore it.

My name is Sierra McKettrick, and it's January 20, 2007.

I have a son, too, and his name is Liam. He's seven, and he has asthma. He's the center of my life.

You have nothing to fear from me. I'm not a ghost, just an ordinary flesh-and-blood woman. A mother, like you.

The telephone rang, jolting Sierra out of the spell.

Conditioned to unexpected emergencies, because of Liam's illness, she hurried to answer, squinting at the caller ID.

"Indian Rock Elementary School."

The room swayed.

"This is Sierra McKettrick," she said. "Is my son all right?"

The voice on the other end of the line was blessedly calm. "Liam is just a little sick at his stomach, that's all," the woman said. "The school nurse thinks he ought to come home. He'll probably be fine in the morning."

"I'll be right there," Sierra answered, and hung up without saying goodbye.

Liam is safe, she told herself, but she felt panicky, just the same.

She deliberately closed Hannah McKettrick's journal, put it back inside the album. Placed the album inside the drawer.

Then she raced around the kitchen, frantically searching for the Blazer keys, before remembering that she'd left them in the ignition earlier, when she'd come back from town. She'd been so focused on having an illicit tryst with Travis Reid....

She grabbed her coat, dashed out the door, jumped into the SUV.

The roads were icy, and by the time Sierra sped into Indian Rock, huge flakes of snow were tumbling from a grim gray sky. She forced herself to slow down, but when she reached the school parking lot, she almost forgot to shut off the motor in her haste to get inside, find her son.

Liam lay on a cot in the nurse's office, alarmingly pale. Someone had laid a cloth over his forehead, presumably cool, but he was all by himself.

How could these people have left him alone?

"Mom," he said. "My stomach hurts. I think I'm gonna hurl again."

She went to him. He rolled on to his side and vomited onto her shoes.

"I'm sorry!" he wailed.

She stroked his sweat-dampened hair. "It's all right, Liam. Everything is going to be all right."

He threw up again.

Sierra snatched a handful of paper towels from the wall dispenser, wet them down at the sink and washed his face.

"My coat!" he lamented. "I don't want to leave my cowboy coat—"

"Don't worry about your coat," Sierra said, wondering distractedly how she could possibly be the same woman who'd spent half the morning naked in Travis's bed.

The nurse, a tall blond woman with kindly blue eyes, stepped into the room, carrying Liam's coat and backpack. Silently she laid the things aside in a chair and came to assist in the cleanup effort.

Sierra went to get the coat.

"No!" Liam cried out, as she approached him with it. "What if I puke on it?"

"Sweetheart, it's cold outside, and we can always have it cleaned—"

The nurse caught her eye. Shook her head. "Let's just bundle Liam up in a couple of blankets. I'll help you get him to the car. This coat is important to him—*so* important that, sick as he was, he insisted I go and get it for him."

Sierra bit her lip. She and the nurse wrapped Liam in the blankets, and Sierra lifted him into her arms. He was getting so big. One day soon, she probably wouldn't be able to carry him any more.

The main doors whooshed open when Sierra reached them.

"Oh, great," Liam moaned. "Everybody's looking. Everybody knows I *ralphed*."

Sierra hadn't noticed the children filling the corridor. The dismissal bell must have rung, but she hadn't heard it.

"It's okay, Liam," she said.

He shook his head. "No, it *isn't!* My *mom* is carrying me out of the school in a bunch of *blankets,* like a *baby!* I'll never live this down!"

Sierra and the nurse exchanged glances.

The nurse smiled and shifted Liam's coat and backpack so she could pat his shoulder. "When you get back to school," she said, "you come to my office and I'll tell you *plenty* of stories about things that have happened in this school over the years. You're not the first person to throw up here, Liam McKettrick, and you won't be the last, either."

Liam lifted his head, apparently heartened. "Really?"

The nurse rolled her eyes expressively. "If you only *knew*," she said, in a conspiratorial tone, opening the Blazer door on the passenger side, so Sierra could set Liam on the seat and buckle him in. "I wouldn't name names, of course, but I've seen kids do a lot worse than vomit."

Sierra shut the door, turned to face the nurse.

"Thanks," she said. Liam peered through the window, his face a greenish, bespectacled moon, his hair sticking out in spikes. "You have a unique way of comforting an embarrassed kid, but it seems to be effective."

The nurse smiled, put out her hand. "My name is Susan Yarnia," she said. "If you need anything, you call me, either here at the school or at home. My husband's name is Joe, and we're in the book."

Sierra nodded. Took the coat and backpack and put them into the rig, after ferreting for Liam's inhaler, just in case he needed it on the way home. "Do you think I should take him to the clinic?" she asked in a whisper, after she'd closed the door again.

"That's up to you, of course," Susan said. "There's been a flu bug going around, and my guess is Liam caught it. If I were you, I'd just take him home, put him to bed and make a bit of a fuss over him. See that he drinks a lot of liquids, and if you can get him to swallow a few spoonfuls of chicken soup, so much the better."

Sierra nodded, thanked the woman again and rounded the Blazer to get behind the wheel.

"What if I spew in Aunt Meg's car?" Liam asked.

"I'll clean it up," Sierra answered.

"This whole thing is *mortifying*. When I tell Tobias—"

Tobias.

If Sierra hadn't been pulling out on to a slick road, she probably would have slammed on the brakes.

Please don't harm my boy, Hannah McKettrick had written, eighty-eight years ago, in her journal. *His name is Tobias. He's eight years old.*

"Who is Tobias?" Sierra asked moderately, but her palms were so wet on the steering wheel that she feared her grip wouldn't hold if she had to make a sudden turn.

"The. Boy. In. My. Room," Liam said very carefully, as

though English were not even Sierra's *second* language, let alone her first. "I told you I saw him."

"Yeah," Sierra replied, her stomach clenching so hard that she wasn't sure *she* wouldn't be the next one to throw up, "but you didn't mention having a conversation with him."

Liam turned away from her, rested his forehead against the passenger-side window, probably because it was cool. "I thought you'd freak," he said. "Or send me off to some bug farm."

Sierra drove past the clinic where she and Travis had taken Liam the day of his asthma attack. It was all she could do not to pull in and demand that he be put on life support, or air-lifted to Stanford.

It's stomach flu, she insisted to herself, and kept driving by sheer force of will.

"When have I ever threatened to send you *anywhere,* let alone to a 'bug farm'?"

"There's always a first time," Liam reasoned.

"You were sick last night," Sierra realized aloud. "That's why you were so quiet at supper."

"I was quiet at supper because I figured Tobias would be there when I went upstairs."

"Were you scared?"

Liam flung her a scornful look. "No," he said. And then his cheeks puffed out, and he made a strangling sound.

Sierra pulled to the side of the road, got out of the SUV and barely got around to open the door before he decorated her shoes again.

This is your real life, she thought pragmatically.

Not the two million dollars.

Not great sex in a cowboy's bed.

It's a seven-year-old boy, barfing on your shoes.

The reflections were strangely comforting, given the circumstances.

When Liam was through, she wiped off her boots with handfuls of snow, got back into the Blazer and drove to the nearest gas station, where she bought him a bottle of Gatorade so he could rinse out his mouth, spit gloriously onto the pavement, and hopefully retain enough electrolytes to keep from dehydrating.

Twilight was already gathering by the time she pulled into the garage at the ranch house, having noticed, in spite of herself, that Travis was back from wherever he'd gone, and the lights were glowing golden in the windows of his trailer.

Not that it mattered.

In fact, she wasn't the least bit relieved when he walked into the garage before she could shut the door or even turn off the engine.

Liam unsnapped his seat belt and lowered his window. "I *horked* all over the schoolhouse," he told Travis gleefully. "People will probably talk about it for *years*."

"Excellent," Travis said with admiration. His eyes danced under the brim of his hat as he looked at Sierra over Liam's head, then returned his full attention to the little boy. "Need some help getting inside? One cowpoke to another?"

"Sure," Liam replied staunchly. "Not that I couldn't make it on my own or anything."

Travis chuckled. "Maybe you ought to carry *me*, then." His gaze snagged Sierra's again. "It happens that I'm feeling a little weak in the knees myself."

Sierra's face heated. She switched off the ignition.

Liam giggled, and the sound was restorative. "You're too big to carry, Travis," he said, with such affection that

Sierra's throat tightened again, and she honestly thought she'd cry.

Fortunately, Travis wasn't looking at her. He gathered Liam into his arms, blankets and all, and carried him inside. Sierra followed with her son's things, scrambling to get her emotions under control.

"It's *arctic* in here," Liam said.

"You're right," Travis agreed easily. He set Liam in the chair where Sierra had sat writing in the diary of a woman who was probably buried somewhere among all those bronze statues in the family cemetery, and approached the old stove. "Nothing like a good wood fire to warm a place up."

"Drink your Gatorade," Sierra told Liam, because she felt she had to say something, and that was all that came to mind.

"Can we sleep down here again?" Liam asked. "Like we did when the blizzard came and the furnace went out?"

"No," Sierra answered, much too quickly.

Travis gave her a sidelong glance and a grin, then stuffed some crumpled newspaper and kindling into the belly of the wood stove, and lit the fire. Sierra shivered, hugging herself, while he adjusted the damper.

"Is something wrong with the furnace again?" she asked.

"Probably," Travis answered.

She was oddly grateful that he hadn't called her on asking a stupid question. But then, he wouldn't. Not in front of her son. She knew that much about Travis Reid, at least. Along with the fact that he was one hell of a lover.

Don't even think about that, Sierra scolded herself. But it was like deciding not to imagine a pink elephant skating on a pond and wearing a tutu.

"I think we should all sleep right here," Liam persisted.

Travis chuckled, more, Sierra suspected, at her discomfort than at Liam's campaign for another kitchen campout. "If a man's got a bed," Travis said, "he ought to use it."

Sierra's cheeks stung. "Was that necessary?" she whispered furiously, after approaching the wood box to grab up a few chunks of pine. If she was going to live in this house for a year, she'd better learn to work the stove.

"No," Travis whispered back, "but it was fun."

"Will you *stop?*"

Another grin. He seemed to have an infinite supply of those, and all of them were saucy. "Nope."

"What are you guys whispering about?" Liam asked suspiciously. "Are you keeping secrets?"

Travis took the wood from Sierra's hands, stuffed it into the stove. She tried to look away but she couldn't. "No secrets," he said.

Sierra bit her lower lip.

The kitchen began to warm up, but she couldn't be certain it was because of the fire in the cookstove.

Travis left them to go downstairs and attend to the furnace.

"I wish he was my dad," Liam said.

Sierra blinked back more tears. Lifted her chin. "Well, he's not, sweetie," she said gently, and with a slight quaver in her voice. "Best let it go at that, okay?"

Liam looked so sad that Sierra wanted to take him on to her lap and rock him the way she had when he was younger and a lot more amenable to motherly affection. "Okay," he agreed.

She crossed to him, ruffled his hair, which was already mussed. "Think you could eat something?" she asked. "Maybe some chicken noodle soup?"

"Yuck," he answered. "And I *still* think we should sleep in the kitchen, because it's cold and I'm sick and I might catch pneumonia or something up there in my room."

The mention of Liam's room made Sierra think of Hannah again and Tobias. She went to the china cabinet, opened the drawer, raised the cover on the photo album. The journal was still there, and she looked inside.

Hannah's words.

Her words.

Nothing more.

Did she expect an answer? More lines of faded ink, entered beneath her own ballpoint scrawl?

A tingle of anticipation went through her as she closed the journal, then the album, then the drawer, and straightened.

Yes.

Oh, yes.

She *did* expect an answer.

The furnace made that familiar whooshing sound.

Liam muttered something that might have been a swear word.

Sierra pretended not to notice.

Travis came back up the basement stairs, dusting his hands together. Another job well done.

"It's still going to be *really* cold upstairs," Liam asserted.

"You're probably right," Travis agreed.

Sierra gave him an eloquent look.

Travis was undaunted. He just grinned another insufferable, three-alarm grin. "I'll make you a bed on the floor," he said, and though he was looking at Sierra, he was talking to Liam. Hopefully. "Just until it gets warm upstairs."

Liam yelped with delighted triumph, punching the air

with one fist. Then, just as quickly, he sobered. "What about you and Mom?"

"I reckon we'll just tough it out," Travis drawled. With that, he went about carrying in a couple of sofa cushions to lay on the floor, not too close to the stove but close enough for warmth.

Sierra fetched a pillow and fresh blankets.

Liam stretched out on the makeshift bed like an Egyptian king traveling by barge. Sighed happily.

"Are you staying for supper, Travis?" he asked.

"Am I invited?" Travis asked, looking at Sierra.

She sighed. "Yes," she said.

Liam let out another yippee.

Sierra made grilled cheese sandwiches and heated canned spaghetti, but by the time she served the feast, Liam was sound asleep.

Travis, seated on the bench, his sleeves still rolled up from washing in the bathroom down the hall, nodded toward him.

"If I were you," he said, "I'd start checking out law schools. That kid is probably going to be on the Supreme Court before he's thirty."

CHAPTER FIFTEEN

1919

HANNAH'S HANDS TREMBLED slightly as she raised the cover of the family album and reached for the remembrance book tucked inside. She held her breath as she opened it.

Only her own words were there, alone and stark.

She was a practical woman, and she knew she should not have expected anything else. Spirits, if there was such a thing, did not take up pens and write in remembrance books. And yet she was stricken with a profound disappointment, the likes of which she'd never experienced before. She'd suffered plenty in her life, seeing three sisters perish as a girl and, as a woman grown, losing Gabe, knowing none of the brave dreams they'd talked about with such hope and faith would ever come true.

No more stolen kisses.

No more secret laughter.

No more cattle grazing on a thousand hills.

And certainly no more babies, born squalling in their room upstairs.

Hannah told herself, I will not cry, I have cried enough. I have emptied myself of tears.

So why do they keep coming?

"Hannah?"

She started, looked up to see Doss standing at the foot

of the stairs. He'd been working in the barn, the last she knew, doing the morning chores. Chopping extra wood because there was another storm coming. It bothered her that she hadn't heard him come in.

"Tobias is worse," he said.

Alarm swelled into Hannah's throat, cutting off her wind.

She started for the stairs, but when she would have passed Doss, he stopped her.

"I'm going to town for the doc," he told her.

"I'll just wrap Tobias up warm and we'll—"

Doss's grip tightened on her shoulders. Only then did she realize he hadn't merely stepped into her path, he was touching her. "No, Hannah," he said. "The boy's too sick for that."

"Suppose the doctor won't come?"

"He'll come," Doss said. "You go to Tobias. Don't let the fire go out, no matter what. I'll be back as soon as I can."

Hannah nodded, bursting to get to her son, but somehow wanting to cling to Doss, too. Tell him not to go, that they'd manage some way but he oughtn't to leave, because something truly terrible might happen if he did.

"Go to him," Doss told her, letting go of her shoulders.

She felt as though he'd been holding her up. Swayed a little to catch her balance. Then, on impulse, she stood on tiptoe and kissed him right on the mouth. "You be careful, Doss McKettrick," she said. "You come back to us, safe and sound."

He looked deeply into her eyes for a moment, as though he could see secrets she kept even from herself, then nodded and made for the door. The last Hannah saw of him, just before she dashed up the rear stairs, he was putting on his coat and hat.

Tobias lay fitful in his bed, his nightshirt soaked with perspiration, like the sheets. His teeth chattered, and his lips were blue, but his flesh burned to the touch.

Hannah could not afford to let panic prevail.

She had mothering to do, and however inadequate and fearful she felt, there was no one but her to do it.

She pushed up her sleeves, added more pins to her hair so it wouldn't tumble down and get in her way, and headed downstairs to heat water.

Heedful of Doss's warning not to let the fire die, she added wood from the generous supply he'd brought in earlier without her noticing. She pumped water into every bucket and kettle she owned, and put them on the stove to heat. Then she dragged the bathtub out of the pantry and set it in the middle of the floor.

The instructions seemed to come from somewhere inside her. She didn't plan what to do, or take the time to debate one intuition against another. It was as if some stronger, smarter, better Hannah had stepped to the fore, and pushed the timid and uncertain one aside.

This Hannah knew what to do. The regular one stood in the background, wringing her hands and counseling hysteria.

Tobias was practically delirious when Hannah roused him from his bed, an hour later when the tub was full of hot water, and half carried, half led him downstairs.

In the kitchen she stripped him and put him into the bath. Scrubbed him down, all the while talking quietly, confidently, without ever stopping to think up the words she'd say next.

"You'll be fine, Tobias. Come spring, you'll be able to ride your pony through the fields and swim in the pond. We'll get you that dog you've been wanting—you can pick him out yourself—and he can sleep right in your room, too. On the foot of your bed, if you want. You can call your uncle Doss 'Pa' from now on, and there'll be a brand-new baby in this house at harvest time—think of it, Tobias. A little brother or sister. You can choose the name—"

Tobias shuddered, chilled even in water that would be too hot to stand any other time.

Hannah dried him with towels, put him in a clean night-shirt, got him back upstairs again. Settled him into her own bed while she hastened to put fresh sheets and blankets on his.

All that morning, and all that afternoon, she tended her boy, touching a cold cloth to his forehead. Holding his hands. Telling him that his pa had gone to town for the doctor, and he needn't worry because he was going to be just fine.

They were *all* going to be just fine.

Tobias had occasional moments of lucidity. "Liam's sick, too," he said once. "I want to be with Liam."

Another time, he asked, "Where's Pa? Is Pa all right?"

Hannah had bitten her lower lip and reassured him gently. "Yes, sweetheart, your pa's just fine."

The day wore on, into evening.

And Doss hadn't returned.

Hannah put more wood on the fire, donned Gabe's coat and made her way out to the barn, through ever-deepening snow, to feed the livestock, because there was no one else to do it.

The wind bit through to Hannah's bones as she worked. Made them ache, then go numb.

Where was Doss?

The other Hannah, the fretful one pushed into the background, kept calling out that question, as if from the bottom of a well.

Where...where...where?

It was completely dark by the time she'd finished, and as she left the barn, she heard the faint rumble of thunder. Rare in a snowstorm, like lightning, but Hannah had seen that, too, there in the high country of Arizona, and in Montana, as well. A staggering sense of foreboding descended upon her, and it had nothing to do with Tobias being sick.

Hannah returned to the house, switched on the kitchen bulb before even taking off Gabe's coat, thinking somehow the light might draw Doss back to her and Tobias, through the storm. Even in daylight, and even for a man as tough and as skilled as Doss, navigating the most familiar trails would be difficult in weather like that, if not impossible. In the dark, it was plain treacherous.

"Ma?" Tobias called. "Ma, are you down there?"

It heartened her, the strength she heard in his voice, but her joy was tempered by worry. Doss should have been home by then. Unless—*please, God, let it be so*—he'd decided to stay in town.

"Yes," she called back, as cheerfully as she could. "I'm here, and I'm about to fix you some supper."

"Come up, Ma. Right now. That boy's here."

In the process of shedding the coat she'd worn to feed the livestock and the chickens and milk the cow, Hannah let the garment drop, forgotten, to the floor. She took the stairs two at a time and burst into Tobias's room.

With no lamp burning, it was stone dark. She made out the outline of Tobias's bed and him lying there.

"He's here, Ma," Tobias said, in a delighted whisper, as though speaking too loudly might cause his invisible friend to disappear. "Liam's here."

Hannah hurried to the bedside.

"I don't see him," she said.

Just then the sky itself seemed to part, with a great,

tearing roar so horrendous Hannah put her hands to her ears. The floor trembled beneath her feet, and the windowpanes rattled. Light quivered in the room—she knew it was snow lightning, but it was otherworldly, just the same—and for one single, incredulous moment, she saw not Tobias lying in that bed, but another little boy. And she saw the woman standing on the other side of the bed, too. Staring at her. Looking every bit as surprised as Hannah herself.

Within half a heartbeat, the whole incident was over.

"Did you see them?" Tobias asked desperately, grasping at her hand. Clinging. "Ma, *did you see them?*"

"Yes," Hannah whispered. She dropped to her knees next to Tobias's bed, unable to stand for another instant. Tobias had said "them." He'd seen the woman, too, then, as well as the boy. "Dear God, yes."

"She was wearing *trousers,* Ma," Tobias marveled.

Hannah raised herself from the floor to perch tremulously on the side of Tobias's bed. Fumbled for the matches and lit the lamp on the stand.

"Tell me what else you saw, Tobias," she said. Her hands were shaking so badly that the lamp chimney rattled when she set it back in place.

"She had short hair. Brown, I think. And she saw *us,* Ma, just as sure as we saw her!"

Hannah nodded numbly.

"What does it mean, Ma?" Tobias asked.

"I wish I knew," Hannah said.

Present Day

Sierra stood still at Liam's bedside, hugging herself and trembling, trying to understand what she'd just seen.

What the hell *had* she just seen?

Lightning.

A woman in an old-fashioned dress, standing on the opposite side of Liam's bed.

Hannah?

"What's wrong, Mom?" Liam asked sleepily. He'd protested a little, when she'd roused him from his slumbers in the kitchen and brought him up here to sleep in his own bed. Then he'd fallen into natural oblivion.

She couldn't catch her breath.

"Mom?" Liam prompted, sounding more awake now.

"We'll…we'll talk about it in the morning."

"Can I sleep with you?"

Sierra swallowed. Travis had gone back to his trailer several hours before. She'd sat downstairs in the study, with a low fire going, catching up on her email, checking in on Liam at regular intervals. Anything, she realized now, but open the family album and come face-to-face with a long line of McKettricks, every one of them a stranger.

The house seemed empty and, at the same time, too crowded for comfort.

"I'll sleep in here with you," she said. "How would that be?"

"Awesome," Liam said.

"Just let me change." Down the hall, she stripped to the skin, put on sweats and made for the bathroom, where she splashed her face with cool water and brushed her teeth.

Such ordinary things.

In the wake of what she'd just experienced, she wondered if anything would ever be "ordinary" again.

Liam was snoring softly when she got back to his room. She slipped into the narrow bed beside him, turned on to her side and stared into the darkness until at last she, too, fell asleep.

1919

While Doc Willaby's nephew was getting his medical gear together, Doss took the opportunity to slip into the church down on the corner. He hadn't set foot inside it since he and Gabe had come back from the army, him sitting ramrod straight on a train seat and Gabe lying in a pine box.

He'd had no truck with God after that.

Now they had some business to discuss.

Doss opened the door, which was always unlocked, lest some wayfarer seek to pray or to find salvation, and took off his hat. He walked down front, to the plain wooden table that served as an altar, and lit one of the beeswax candles with a match from his pocket.

"I'm here to talk about Tobias," he said.

God didn't answer.

Doss shifted uncomfortably on his feet. They were so cold from the long drive into town that he couldn't feel them. Cain and Abel had been fractious on the way, and he'd had all sorts of trouble with them. Once, they'd just stopped and refused to go any farther, and then, crossing the creek, the team had made it over just fine but the sleigh had fallen through. Sunk past the runners in the frigid water.

He'd still be back there, wet to the skin and frozen stiff as laundry left on a clothesline before a blizzard, if three of Rafe's ranch hands hadn't come along to help. They'd given him dry clothes, fetched from a nearby line shack, dosed him with whisky, hitched their lassos to the half-submerged sleigh and hauled it up on to the bank by horsepower.

He'd thanked the men kindly and sent them on their way, and then spent more precious time coaxing Cain and Abel to proceed. They'd been mightily reluctant to do that, and he'd finally had to threaten them with a switch to get them moving.

The whole day had gone like that, though the frustrations were at considerable variance, and by the time he'd pulled up in front of the doc's house, the worthless critters were so worn-out he knew they wouldn't make it back home. He'd sent to the livery stable for another rig and fresh horses.

Doss cleared his throat respectfully. "Hannah can't lose that boy," he went on. "You took Gabe, and if You don't mind my saying so, that was bad enough. I guess what I want to say is, if You've got to claim somebody else, then it ought to be me, not Tobias. He's only eight and he's got a lot of living yet to do. I don't know exactly what kind of outfit You're running up there, but if there are cattle, I'm a fair hand in a roundup. I can ride with the best of them, too. I'll make myself useful— You've got my word on that." He paused, swallowed. His face felt hot, and he knew he was acting like a damn fool, but he was desperate. "I reckon that's my side of the matter, so amen."

He blew out the candle—it wouldn't do for the church to take fire and burn to the ground—and turned to head back down the aisle.

Doc Willaby was standing just inside the door, leaning on his cane, because of that gouty foot of his, and dressed for a long, hard ride out to the Triple M.

"You ought to tell Hannah," the old man said.

"Tell her what?" Doss countered, abashed at being caught pouring out his heart like some repentant sinner at a revival.

"That you love her enough to die in place of her boy."

Doss heard a team and wagon clatter to a stop out front. "Nobody needs to know that besides God," he said, and slammed his hat back on his head. "What are you doing here, anyhow? Besides eavesdropping on a man's private conversation?"

The doc smiled. He was heavy-set, with a face like a full moon, a scruff of beard and keen little eyes that never seemed to miss much of anything. "I'm going out to your place with you. And we'd better be on our way, if that boy's as sick as you say he is."

"What about your nephew?"

"He'd never stand the trip," Doc said. "My bag's out on the step, and I'll thank you to help me up into the wagon so we can get started."

Doss felt a mixture of chagrin and relief. Doc Willaby was old as desert dirt, but he'd been tending McKettricks, and a lot of other folks, for as long as Doss could remember. His own health might be failing, but Doc knew his trade, all right.

"Come on, old man," Doss said. "And don't be fussing over hard conditions along the way. I've got neither the time nor the inclination to be coddling you."

Doc chuckled, though his eyes were serious. He slapped Doss on the shoulder. "Just like your grandfather," he said. "Tough as a boiled owl, with a heart the size of the whole state of Arizona and two others like it."

Getting the old coot into the box of the hired wagon was like trying to hoist a cow from a tar pit, but Doss managed it. He climbed up, took the reins in one hand and tossed a coin to the livery stable boy, shivering on the sidewalk, with the other. Cain and Abel would be spending the night in warm stalls, maybe longer, with all the hay they required and some grain to boot, and, cussed as they were, Doss was glad for them.

He and the doc were almost to the ranch house when the lightning struck, loud enough to shake snow off the branches of trees, throwing the dark countryside into clear relief.

The horses screamed and shied.

The wagon slid on the icy trail and plunged on to its side.

Doss heard the doc yell, felt himself being thrown sky high.

Just before he hit the ground, it came to him that God had taken him up on the bargain he'd offered back there in Indian Rock at the church. He was about to die, but Tobias would be spared.

Someone was pounding at the back door.

Hannah muttered a hasty word of reassurance to Tobias, who sat up in bed, wide-eyed, at the sound.

"That can't be Pa," he said. "He wouldn't knock. He'd just come inside—"

"Hush," Hannah told him. "You stay right there in that bed."

She hurried down the stairs and was shocked to see old Doc Willaby limping over the threshold. He looked a sight, his clothes wet and disheveled, his hair wild around his head, without his hat to contain it. His skin was gray with exertion, and he seemed nigh on to collapsing.

"There was an accident," he finally sputtered. "Down yonder, at the base of the hill. Doss is hurt."

Hannah steered the old man to a chair at the table. "Are you all right?" she asked breathlessly.

The doctor considered the question briefly, then nodded. "Don't mind about me, Hannah. It's Doss—I couldn't wake him—I had to turn the horses loose so they wouldn't kick each other to death."

She hurried into the pantry, moved the cracker tin aside and took down the bottle of Christmas whisky Doss kept there. She offered it to Doc Willaby, and he gulped down a couple of grateful swigs while she pulled on Gabe's coat and grabbed for a lantern.

"You'd better take this along, too," Doc said, and shoved the whisky bottle at her.

Hannah dropped it into her coat pocket. She didn't like leaving the old man *or* Tobias alone, but she had to get to Doss.

She raised her collar against the bitter wind and threw herself out the back door. Out in the barn, she tossed a halter on Seesaw and stood on a wheelbarrow to mount him. There was no time for saddles and bridles.

Holding the lamp high in one hand and clutching the halter rope with the other, Hannah rode out. She soon met two of the horses Doc had freed, and followed their trail backward, until the shape of an overturned wagon loomed in the snowy darkness.

"Doss!" she cried out. The name scraped at her throat, and she realized she must have called it over and over again, not just the once.

She found him sprawled facedown in the snow, at some distance from the wagon, and feared he'd smothered, if not broken every bone in his body. Scrambling off Seesaw's back, she plodded to where he lay, utterly still.

She knelt, setting the lantern aside, and turned him over.

"Doss," she whispered.

He didn't move.

Hannah put her cheek down close to his mouth. Felt his breath, his blessed breath, warm against her skin.

Tears of relief sprang to her eyes. She dashed them away quickly, lest they freeze in her lashes.

"Doss!" she repeated.

He opened his eyes.

"What are you doing here?" he asked, sounding befuddled.

"I've come looking for you, you damn fool," she answered.

"You're not dead, are you?"

"Of course I'm not dead," Hannah retorted, weeping freely. "And you're not either, which is God's own wonder, the way you must have been driving that wagon to get yourself into a fix like this. Can you move?"

Doss blinked. Hoisted himself on to his elbows. Felt around for his hat.

"Where's the doc?" His features tightened. "Tobias—"

"Tobias is fine," she said. "And Doc's up at the house, thawing out. It's a miracle he made it that far, with that foot of his."

A grin broke over Doss's face, and Hannah, filled with joy, could have slapped him for it. Didn't he know he'd nearly killed himself? Nearly fixed it so she'd have to bear and raise their baby all alone?

"I reckon Doc was right," Doss said. "I ought to tell you—"

"Tell me what?" Hannah fretted. "It's getting colder out here by the minute, and the wind's picking up, too. Can you get to your feet? Poor old Seesaw's going to have to carry us both home, but I think he can manage it."

"Hannah." Doss clasped both her shoulders in his hands, gave her just the slightest shake. "I love you."

Hannah blinked, stunned. "You're talking crazy, Doss. You're out of your head—"

"I love you," he said. He got to his feet, hauling Hannah with him. Knocked the lantern over in the process so it went out. "It started the day I met you."

She stared up at him.

"I don't know how you feel about me, Hannah. It would be a grand thing if you felt the same way I do, but if you don't, maybe you can learn."

"I don't have to learn," she heard herself say. "I came

out into this wretched snowstorm to find you, didn't I? After I suffered the tortures of the damned wondering what was keeping you. Of *course* I love you!"

He kissed her, an exultant kiss that warmed her to her toes.

"I'm going to be a real husband to you from now on," he told her. He made a stirrup of his hands, and Hannah stepped into them, landed astraddle Seesaw's broad, patient old back.

Doss swung up behind her, reached around to catch hold of the halter rope. "Let's go home," he said, close to her ear.

Hannah forgot all about the whisky in her coat pocket.

It was stone dark out, but the lights of the house were visible in the distance, even through the flurries of snow.

Anyway, Seesaw knew his way home, and he plodded patiently in that direction.

Present Day

The world was frozen solid when Sierra awakened the next morning, to find herself clinging to the edge of Liam's empty bed. Voices wafted up from downstairs, along with heat from the furnace and probably the wood stove, too.

She scrambled out of bed, finger combed her hair and hurried down the hallway.

Travis said something, and Liam laughed aloud. The sound affected Sierra like an injection of sunshine. Then a third voice chimed in, clearly female.

Sierra quickened her pace, her bare feet thumping on the stairs as she descended them.

Travis and Liam were seated at the table, reading the

comic strips in the newspaper. A slender blond woman wearing jeans and a pink thermal shirt with the sleeves pushed up stood by the counter, sipping coffee.

"Meg?" Sierra asked. She'd seen her sister's picture, but nothing had prepared her for the living woman. Her clear skin seemed to glow, and her smile was a force of nature.

"Hello, Sierra," she said. "I hope you don't mind my showing up unannounced, but I just couldn't wait any longer, so here I am."

Travis stood, put a hand on Liam's shoulder. Without a word, the two of them left the room, probably headed for the study.

"Everything Mom said was true," Meg told Sierra quietly. "You're beautiful, and so is Liam."

Sierra couldn't speak, at least for the moment, even though her mind was full of questions, all of them clamoring to be offered at once.

"Maybe you should sit down," Meg said. "You look as though you might faint dead away."

Sierra pulled back the chair at the head of the table and sank into it. "When...when did you get here?" she asked.

"Last night," Meg answered. She poured a fresh cup of coffee, brought it to Sierra. "I hope I'm not interrupting anything."

"Interrupting anything?"

Meg's enormous blue eyes took on a mischievous glint. She swung a leg over the bench and straddled it, as several generations of McKettricks must have done before her, facing Sierra.

"Something's going on between you and Travis," Meg said. "I can feel it."

Sierra wondered if she could carry off a lie and decided not to try. She and Meg had been apart since they were small children, but they were sisters, and there was a bond. Besides, she didn't want to start off on the wrong foot.

"The question is," she said carefully, "is anything going on between *you* and Travis."

"No," Meg answered, "more's the pity. We tried to fall in love. It just didn't happen."

"I'm not talking about falling in love."

Wasn't she? Travis had rocked her universe, and much as she would have liked to believe it was only physical, she knew it was more. She'd never felt anything like that with Adam, and she *had* been in love with him, however naively. However foolishly.

Meg grinned. "You mean sex? We didn't even get that far. Every time we tried to kiss, we ended up laughing too hard to do anything else."

Sierra marveled at the crazy relief she felt.

"Too bad he's leaving," Meg said. "Now we'll have to find somebody else to look after the horses, and it won't be easy."

The bottom fell out of Sierra's stomach.

"Travis is leaving?"

Meg set her coffee cup down with a thump and reached for Sierra's hand. "Oh, my God. You didn't know?"

"I didn't know," Sierra admitted.

Damned if she'd cry.

Who needed Travis Reid, anyway?

She had Liam. She had a family and a home and a two-million-dollar trust fund.

She'd gotten along without Travis, and his lovemaking, all her life. The man was entirely superfluous.

So why did she want to lay her head down on her arms and wail with sorrow?

CHAPTER SIXTEEN

1919

COME MORNING HANNAH made her way through the still, chilly dawn to the barn. Besides their own stock, four livery horses were there, gathered at the back of the barn, helping themselves to the haystack. Remnants of harness hung from their backs.

Hannah smiled, led each one into a stall, saw that they each got a bucket of water and some grain. She was milking old Earleen, the cow, when Doss joined her, stiff and bruised but otherwise none the worse for his trials, as far as Hannah could see.

They'd shared a bed the night before, but they'd both been too exhausted, after the rigors of the day and getting Doc Willaby settled comfortably in the spare room, to make love.

"You ought to go into the house, Hannah," Doss said, sounding both confounded and stern. "This work is mine to do."

"Fine," she said, still milking. There was a rhythm in the task that settled a person's thoughts. "You can gather the eggs and get some butter from the spring house. I reckon Doc will be in the grip of a powerful hunger when he wakes up. He'll want hotcakes and some of that bacon you brought from the smokehouse."

Doss moved along the middle of the barn, limping a little. Stopping to peer into each stall along the way. Hannah watched his progress out of the corner of her eye, smiling to herself.

"I meant what I said last night, Hannah," he said, when he finally reached her. "I love you. But if you really want to go back to your folks in Montana, I won't interfere. I know it's hard, living out here on this ranch."

Hannah's throat ached with love and hope. "It *is* hard, Doss McKettrick, and I wouldn't mind spending winters in town. But I'm not going to Montana unless you go, too."

He leaned against one of the beams supporting the barn roof, pondering her with an unreadable expression. "Gabe knew," he said.

She stopped milking. "Gabe knew what?"

"How I felt about you. From the very first time I saw you, I loved you. He guessed right away, without my saying a word. And do you know what he told me?"

"I can't imagine," Hannah said, very softly.

"That I oughtn't to feel bad, because you were easy to love."

Tears stung Hannah's eyes. "He was a good man."

"He was," Doss agreed gruffly, and gave a short nod. "He asked me to look after you and Tobias, before he died. Maybe he figured, even then, that you and I would end up together."

"It wouldn't surprise me," Hannah replied. Dear, dear Gabe. She'd loved him so, but he'd gone on, and he'd want her to carry on and be as happy as she could. Tobias, too.

"What I mean to say is," Doss went on, taking off his hat and turning it round and round in his hands by the brim, "I understand what he meant to you. You can say it, straight out, anytime. I won't be jealous."

Hannah stood up so fast she spooked Earleen, who kicked over the milk bucket, three-quarters of the way full now, steaming in the cold and rich with cream. She put her arms around Doss and didn't try to hide her tears.

"You're as good a man as Gabe ever was, Doss McKettrick," she said, "and I won't let you forget it."

He grinned down at her, wanly, but with that familiar spark in his eyes. "I'll build you a house in town, Hannah," he said. "We'll spend winters there, so you can see folks and Tobias can go to school without riding two miles through the snow. Would you like that?"

"Yes," Hannah said. "But I'd stay on this ranch forever, too, if it meant I could be with you."

Doss bent his head. Kissed her. His hands rested lightly on the sides of her waist, beneath the heavy fabric of Gabe's coat.

"You go inside and see to breakfast, Mrs. McKettrick. I'll finish up out here."

She swallowed, nodded. "I love you, Mr. McKettrick," she said.

His eyes danced mischievously. "Once we get Doc back to town," he replied, "I mean to bed you, good and proper."

Hannah blushed. Batted her lashes. "When is he leaving?"

Present Day

Travis was packing, loading things into his truck. Even whistling as he went about it. Meg got into her Blazer and drove off somewhere.

Sierra waited as long as she could bear to—she didn't know how she was going to explain this to Liam, who was sleeping off his flu bug—didn't know how to explain it herself.

She got out the album, for something to do, and set the remembrance book aside without opening it. Even after seeing Hannah and Tobias the night before, in Liam's room, she just didn't believe in magic any more.

So she took a seat at the table and lifted the cover of the album.

A cracked and yellowed photograph, done in sepia, filled most of the page. Angus McKettrick, the patriarch of the family, stared calmly up at her. He'd been handsome in his youth; she could see that. Though, in the picture his thick hair was white, his stern, square-jawed face etched with lines of sorrow as well as joy. His eyes were clear, intelligent and full of stubborn humor.

It was almost as though he'd known Sierra would be looking at the photo one day, searching for some part of herself in those craggy features, and crooked up one corner of his mouth in the faintest smile, just for her.

Be strong, he seemed to say. *Be a McKettrick.*

Sierra sat for a long time, silently communing with the image.

I don't know how to "be a McKettrick." What does that mean, anyway?

Angus's answer was in his eyes. Being a McKettrick meant claiming a piece of ground to stand on and putting your roots down deep into it. Holding on, no matter what came at you. It meant loving with passion and taking the rough spots with the smooth. It meant fighting for what you wanted, letting go when that was the best thing to do.

Sierra absorbed all that and turned to the next page.

A good-looking couple posed in the front yard of the

very house where Sierra sat, so many years later. A small boy and a girl in her teens stood proudly on either side of them, and underneath someone had written the names in carefully. Holt McKettrick. Lorelei McKettrick. John Henry McKettrick. Lizzie McKettrick.

They wore the name like a badge, all of them.

After that came more pictures of Holt and Lorelei together and separately. In one, they were each holding the hand of a laughing, golden-haired toddler.

Gabriel Angus McKettrick, stated a fading caption beneath.

On the facing page, Lorelei sat proud and straight in a chair, holding an infant. Young Gabriel, older now, stood with a hand on her thigh, his ankles crossed, with the toe of one old-fashioned shoe touching the floor. Holt flanked them all, one hand resting on Lorelei's shoulder. The baby, according to the inscription, was Doss Jacob McKettrick.

Sierra continued to turn pages, and moved through the lives of Gabe and Doss along with them, or so it seemed, catching a glimpse of them on important dates. Birthdays. School. Mounted on ponies. Fishing in a pond.

Sierra felt as though she were looking not at mere photographs, but through little sepia-stained windows into another time, a time as vivid and real as her own.

She watched Gabe and Doss McKettrick grow into young men, both of them blond, both of them handsome and sturdy.

At last she came to the wedding picture. Her gaze landed on Hannah, standing proudly beside Gabe. She was wearing a lovely white dress, holding a nosegay.

Hannah.

The woman with whom, in some inexplicable way, she shared this house. The woman she had seen in Liam's bedroom the night before, caring for her own sick child even as Sierra was caring for hers.

Sierra could go no further. Not then.

She closed the album carefully.

"Mom?"

She turned, looked around to see Liam standing at the foot of the stairs, in his flannel pajamas. His hair was rumpled, his glasses were askew, and he looked desperately worried.

"Hey, buddy," she said.

"Travis is putting stuff in his truck," he told her. "Like he's going away or something."

Sierra's heart broke into two pieces. She got up, went to him. "I guess he was just here temporarily, to look after your aunt Meg's horses."

Liam blinked. A tear slipped down his cheek. "He can't go," he said plaintively. "Who'll make the furnace work? Who'll get us to the clinic if I get sick?"

"I can do those things, Liam," Sierra said. She offered a weak smile, and Liam looked skeptical. "Okay, maybe not the furnace. But I know how to get a fire going in the wood stove. And I can handle the rest, too."

Liam's lower lip wobbled. "I thought...maybe—"

Sierra hugged him, hard. She wanted to cry herself, but not in front of Liam. Not when his heart was breaking, just like hers. One of them had to be strong, and she was elected.

She was an adult.

She was a McKettrick.

Before she could think of anything to say, the back door opened and suddenly Travis was there. He looked at her briefly, but then his gaze went straight to Liam's face.

"If you came to say goodbye," Liam blurted out, "then

don't! I don't care if you're leaving—*I don't care!*" With that, he turned and fled up the stairs.

"That went well," Travis said, taking off his hat and hanging it on the peg. He didn't take his coat off, though, which meant he really *was* going away. Sierra had known that—and, at the same time, she *hadn't* known it. Not until she was faced with the reality.

"He's attached to you," she said evenly. "But he'll be all right."

Travis studied her so closely that for a moment she thought he was going to refute her words. "I know this all seems pretty sudden," he began.

Sierra kept her distance, glad she wasn't standing too close to him. "It's your life, Travis. You've done a lot to help us, and we're grateful."

Upstairs, something crashed to the floor.

Sierra closed her eyes.

"I'd better go up and talk to him," Travis said.

"No," Sierra replied. "Leave him alone. Please."

Another crash.

She found Liam's backpack, unzipped it and took out the inhaler. "I've got to get him calmed down," she said quietly. "Thanks for…everything. And goodbye."

"Sierra…"

"Goodbye, Travis."

With that, she turned and went up the stairs.

Liam had destroyed his new telescope and his DVD player. He was standing in the middle of the wreckage, trembling with the helplessness of a child in a world run by adults, his face flushed and wet with tears.

Sierra picked up his shoes, made her way to him. "Put these on, buddy," she said gently, crouching to help. "You'll cut your feet if you don't."

"Is he—" Liam gulped down a sob "—gone?"

"I think so," Sierra said.

"Why?" Liam wailed, putting a hand on her shoulder to keep from falling while he jammed one foot into a shoe, then the other. "Why does he have to go?"

Sierra sighed. "I don't know, honey," she answered.

"Make him stay!"

"I can't, Liam."

"Yes, you can! You just don't want to! You don't *want* me to have a dad!"

"Liam, that is enough." Sierra stood, handed him the inhaler. "Breathe," she ordered.

He obeyed, puffing on the inhaler between intermittent, heartbreaking sobs. "Make him stay," he pleaded.

She squired him to the bed, pulled his shoes off again, tucked him in. "Liam," she said.

Outside, the truck door slammed. The engine started up.

And suddenly Sierra was moving.

She ran down the stairs, through the kitchen, and wrenched open the back door. Coatless, shivering, she dashed across the yard toward Travis's truck.

He was backing out, but when he saw her, he stopped. Rolled down the window.

She jumped on to the running board, her fingers curved around the glass. *"Wait,"* she said, and then she felt stupid because she didn't know what to say after that.

Travis eased the door open, and she was forced to step back down on to the ground. Unbuttoning his coat as he got out, he wrapped it around her. But he didn't say anything at all. He just stood there, staring at her.

She huddled inside his coat. It smelled like him, and she wished she could keep it forever. "I thought it meant something," she finally murmured. "When we made love, I mean. I thought it *meant something.*"

He cupped a gloved hand under her chin. "Believe me," he said gruffly, "it did."

"Then why are you leaving?"

"Because there didn't seem to be anything else to do. You were busy with Liam, and you'd made it pretty clear we had nothing to talk about."

"We have *plenty* to talk about, Travis Reid. I'm not some…some rodeo groupie you can just have sex with and forget!"

"You can say that again," Travis agreed, smiling a little. "Do you mind if we go inside to have this conversation? It's colder than a well-digger's ass out here, and I'm not wearing a coat."

Sierra turned on her heel and marched toward the house, and Travis followed.

She tried not to think about all the things that might mean.

Inside she gestured toward the table, took off Travis's coat and started a pot of coffee brewing, so she'd have a chance to think up something to say.

Travis stepped up behind her. Laid his hands on her shoulders.

"Sierra," he said. "Stop fiddling with the coffeemaker and talk to me."

She turned, looked up into his eyes. "It's not like I was expecting marriage or anything," she said, whispering. Liam was probably crouched at the top of the stairs by then, listening. "We're adults. We had…we're adults. But the least you could have done, after all that's gone on, was give us a little notice—"

"When Brody died," Travis said, "I died, too. I walked away from everything—my house, my job, everything. Then I met you, and when—" He paused, with a little smile, and glanced toward the stairs, evidently suspecting that

YOUR PARTICIPATION IS REQUESTED!

Dear Reader,

Since you are a lover of romance fiction – we would like to get to know you!

Inside you will find a short Reader's Survey. Sharing your answers with us will help our editorial staff understand who you are and what activities you enjoy.

To thank you for your participation, we would like to send you 2 books and 2 gifts – **ABSOLUTELY FREE!**

Enjoy your gifts with our appreciation,

Pam Powers

SEE INSIDE FOR READER'S SURVEY

YOUR READER'S SURVEY
"THANK YOU" FREE GIFTS INCLUDE:
▶ 2 Romance books
▶ 2 lovely surprise gifts

PLEASE FILL IN THE CIRCLES COMPLETELY TO RESPOND

1) What type of fiction books do you enjoy reading? (Check all that apply)
○ Suspense/Thrillers ○ Action/Adventure ○ Modern-day Romances
○ Historical Romance ○ Humour ○ Paranormal Romance

2) What attracted you most to the last fiction book you purchased on impulse?
○ The Title ○ The Cover ○ The Author ○ The Story

3) What is usually the greatest influencer when you <u>plan</u> to buy a book?
○ Advertising ○ Referral ○ Book Review

4) How often do you access the internet?
○ Daily ○ Weekly ○ Monthly ○ Rarely or never.

5) How many NEW paperback fiction novels have you purchased in the past 3 months?
○ 0 - 2   ○ 3 - 6   ○ 7 or more
FDH2   FDJE   FDJQ

YES! I have completed the Reader's Survey. Please send me the 2 FREE books and 2 FREE gifts (gifts are worth about $10) for which I qualify. I understand that I am under no obligation to purchase any books, as explained on the back of this card.

194/394 MDL

FIRST NAME   LAST NAME

ADDRESS

APT.#   CITY

STATE/PROV.   ZIP/POSTAL CODE

The Reader Service — Here's How It Works:

Liam was there, all ears, just as she did. "When we *were adults,* I knew the game was up. I had to get it together. Start living my life again."

Sierra blinked, speechless.

He touched his mouth to hers. It wasn't a kiss, and yet it affected Sierra that way. "It's too soon to say this," he said, "but I'm going to say it anyway. Something happened to me yesterday. Something I don't understand. All I know is, I can't live another day like a dead man walking. I called Eve and asked for my old job back, and I'll be working in Indian Rock, at McKettrickCo, with Keegan. In the meantime I've got to put my house on the market and make arrangements to store my stuff. But it won't be long before I'm at your door, with every intention of winning you over for good."

"What are you saying?"

Liam came shooting down the stairs, wheeling his arms. "Get a clue, Mom! He's in love with you!"

"That's right," Travis said. He gave Liam a look of mock sternness. "I *was* planning to break it to her gradually, though."

"You're in…?" Sierra sputtered.

"Love," Travis finished for her. "Just tell me this one thing. Do I have a chance with you?"

"Give him a *chance,* Mom!" Liam cried jubilantly. "That's not too much to ask, is it? All the man wants is a chance!"

Sierra laughed, even as tears filled her eyes, blurring her vision. "Liam, hush!" she said.

"What do you say, McKettrick?" Travis asked, taking hold of her shoulders again. "Do I get a chance?"

"Yes," she said. "Oh, yes."

"If you're going to work in town," Liam enthused, tugging at Travis's shirtsleeve by then, "you might as well just move in with us!"

Travis chuckled, released Sierra to lean down and scoop Liam up in one arm. "Whoa," he said. "I'm all for *that* plan, but I think your mother needs a little more time."

"You're not leaving?" Liam asked, so hopefully that Sierra's heartbeat quickened.

"I'm not leaving," Travis confirmed. "I've got some things to do in Flagstaff, then I'll be back."

"Will you live right here, on the ranch?" Liam demanded.

"Not right away, cowpoke," Travis answered. "This whole thing is real important. I don't want to get it wrong. Understand?"

Liam nodded solemnly.

"Good," Travis said. "Now, get on back upstairs, so I can kiss your mother without you ogling us."

"I broke my DVD player," Liam confessed, suddenly crestfallen. "On purpose, too." He paused, swallowed audibly. "Are you mad?"

"You're the one who'll have to do without a DVD player," Travis said reasonably. "Why would *I* be mad?"

"I'm sorry, Travis," Liam told him.

Travis set the boy back on his feet. "Apology accepted. While we're at it, *I'm* sorry, too. I should have talked to you—your mother, too—before I packed up my stuff. I guess I was just in too much of a hurry to get things rolling."

"I forgive you," Liam said.

Travis ruffled his hair. "Beat it," he replied.

Liam scampered toward the stairs and hopped up them as though he were on a pogo stick.

"Are you sure he's sick?" Travis asked.

Sierra laughed. "Kiss me, cowpoke," she said.

1919

Doc Willaby was with them for three full days, waiting for his bumps and bruises to heal and the weather to clear. He played endless games of checkers with Tobias, next to the kitchen stove, and Hannah and Doss tried hard to pretend they were sensible people. The truth was, they could barely keep their hands off each other.

"How come I have to move to the other end of the hall?" Tobias asked Doss, on the morning of the third endless day.

"You just do," Doss answered.

Early that afternoon, the sleigh came pulling into the yard, drawn by Cain and Abel and driven by Kody Jackson, from the livery stable. Two outriders completed the procession.

"Glory be," Doc said, peering out the window, along with Hannah. "They've come to fetch me back to Indian Rock." He looked down at Hannah and smiled wisely. "Now you and Doss can stop acting like a couple of old married folks and do what comes naturally."

Hannah blushed, but she couldn't help smiling in the process. "It's been good having you here, Doc," she said, and she meant it, too. "You saved Doss's life the other night, coming all that way to fetch me, in the shape you were in. I'll be grateful all my days."

He took her hand. Squeezed it. "He loves you, Hannah."

"I know," she said softly. "And I love him, too."

"That's all that counts, in the long run. Or the short one, for that matter. We each of us get a certain number of days to spend on this earth. Only the good Lord knows how many. Spend them loving that man of yours and that fine boy, and you'll have done the right thing."

Hannah stood on tiptoe. Kissed the doctor on the cheek. "Thank you," she said.

Doss came out of the barn to greet Kody and the other men.

They all went down the hill together to set the other wagon upright, leading the team along behind them. Doss put Cain and Abel away, while Kody drove the rig up alongside the house.

Doc was outside by then, ready to go, with his medical bag clutched in one hand and his cane in the other. He turned and waved at Hannah through the window, and she waved back, watching fondly as Doss and another man helped him up into the wagon box.

When Doss didn't come back in right away, Hannah busied herself making the kitchen presentable. Tobias was upstairs, resting in his new bedroom at the front of the house. Now that he'd adjusted to the change, he liked being able to see so clear across the valley from the gabled window, but what had really swayed him was the reminder that Doss and Gabe had shared that room when they were boys.

She swept the floor and put fresh coffee on to brew and even switched on the lightbulb instead of lighting lamps, as wintry afternoon shadows darkened the room.

Still, there was no sign of Doss, so she built up the fire in the stove, opened the drawer of the china cabinet, lifted the cover of the album and took out her remembrance book.

In the three busy days since she'd seen the other woman and her boy, up there in Tobias's bedroom, she'd thought often of the journal, and kept a close eye on the teapot, too.

Nothing extraordinary happened, but inside, in a quiet part of herself, Hannah was waiting. She carried the remembrance book over to the rocking chair drawn up close to the stove and sat down. Perhaps she'd begin making regular entries in that journal.

She'd write about her and Doss, and make notes as Tobias grew toward manhood. She'd record the dates the peonies bloomed, and tuck a photograph inside, now and then. Doss had promised her they'd build a house in Indian Rock, and pass the hard high-country winters there. She would capture the dimensions of the new place in these pages, and perhaps even make sketches. One day she'd take up a pen and write that the baby had come, safe and strong and well.

She was so caught up in the prospect of all the years ahead, just waiting to be lived and then set down on paper, that a few moments passed before she realized that another hand had written beneath her own short paragraphs.

My name is Sierra McKettrick, and today is January 20, 2007.

I have a son, too, and his name is Liam. He's seven, and he has asthma. He's the center of my life.

You have nothing to fear from me. I'm not a ghost, just an ordinary flesh-and-blood woman. A mother, like you.

Hannah stared at the words in disbelief.

Read them again, and then again.

It couldn't be.

But it was.

The woman she'd seen was a McKettrick, too, living far in the future. She had the proof right here—not that she meant to show it to just everybody. Some folks would say she'd written those words herself, of course, but Hannah knew she hadn't.

She touched the clear blue ink in wonder. It looked different, somehow, from the kind that came in a bottle.

The door opened, and Doss came in. He took off his coat and hat, hung them up neatly, like he always did.

Hannah held the remembrance book close against her chest. Should she let Doss see? Would he believe, as she did, that two different centuries had somehow managed to touch and blend, right here in this house?

Her heart fluttered in her breast.

"Hannah?" He sounded a little worried.

"Come and look at this, Doss," she said.

He came, crouched beside her chair, read the two entries in the journal, hers and Sierra's.

She watched his face, hopeful and afraid.

Doss raised his eyes to meet hers. "That," he said, "is the strangest thing I've ever run across."

"There's more," Hannah said. "I saw her, Doss. I saw this woman, and her little boy, the night of your accident."

He closed a hand over hers. "If you say so, Hannah," he told her quietly, "then I believe you."

"You do?"

He grinned. "Does that surprise you?"

"A little," she admitted. "When Tobias mentioned seeing the boy, you said it must be his imagination."

Doss handed back the book. "Life is strange," he said. "There's a mystery just about everywhere you look, when you think about it. Babies being born. Grass poking up through hard ground after a long winter. The way it makes me feel inside when you smile at me."

Hannah leaned, kissed his forehead. "Flatterer," she said.

"Is Tobias asleep?" he asked.

She blushed. "Yes."

He pulled her to her feet, set the remembrance book aside on the counter and kissed her.

"I think we've waited long enough, don't you?" he asked.

Hours later, hair askew, bundled in a wrapper, well and thoroughly loved, Hannah sneaked back downstairs. She gathered ink and a pen from the study and lit a lantern in the kitchen.

Then, smiling, she sat down to write.

Present Day

Travis lay sprawled on his stomach in Sierra's bed, sound asleep. She sat up beside him, stroked his bare back once with a gentle pass of her hand. In the three days since he'd moved out of the trailer, he'd been back several times, on one pretext or another. Finally Meg had packed some of her things and some of Liam's, and the two of them had gone to stay in town with friends of hers.

"You two really need some time alone," she'd said, with a wicked grin lighting her eyes.

Sierra smiled down at Travis. So far they'd made good use of that time alone. They'd talked a lot, in between bouts of lovemaking, and they still had plenty to say to each other—maybe enough to last a lifetime.

She switched on the lamp, took Hannah's remembrance

book from the bedside table, and opened it. Her eyes widened, and she drew in a breath.

Beneath her own entry, in the same stately, faded writing as before, Hannah had written:

It's nice to know there's another woman in the house, even if I can't see or hear you, most of the time. We must be family, since your name is McKettrick. Maybe you're descended from us, from Doss and me. I told my son, Tobias, that your name is Sierra. He said that was pretty, and he'd like the new baby to be called that, too, if it's a girl...

There was more, but Sierra couldn't read it, because her eyes were blurred with tears of amazement. She bounded out of bed, not caring if she awakened Travis, and hurried downstairs, switching on lights as she went. She had the album out and was flipping through the pages at the middle when he joined her, blinking and shirtless, with his jeans misbuttoned.

"What's going on?" he asked, yawning.

Sierra's heart thumped at the base of her throat.

She forced herself to slow down, turn the pages gently. And then she found what she was looking for—an old, old photograph of two children, smiling for the camera lens. The little boy she'd seen in Liam's room, with Hannah, holding a baby wearing a long, lacy gown.

Beneath the picture, Hannah had written Tobias's name and the baby's.

Sierra Elizabeth McKettrick.

Sierra put a hand to her mouth and gasped.

Travis drew closer. "Sierra—"

"Look at this," Sierra said, stabbing at the image with one finger. "What do you see?"

Travis frowned. "An old picture of two kids."

"Look at the baby's name."

"Sierra. You must have been named for her."

"I think *she* was named for *me*," Sierra said.

"How could *she* be named for *you*?"

"Sit down," Sierra told him. She reached for Hannah's remembrance book, offered it when he was seated. "Read this."

He read. Looked up at her with wide eyes. "You don't really think—"

"That I've been communicating with a woman who lived in this house in 1919, and probably for years after that? Yes, Travis, that is *exactly* what I think!"

"But, *how?*"

"You said it yourself, when I first got here. Strange things happen in this house."

"This is beyond strange. Are you going to tell anybody else about this?"

"Mother and Meg," Sierra said. "Liam, too, when he's a little older."

He reached for her hand, wove his fingers through hers, squeezed. "And me. You told *me*, Sierra."

"Well, *yeah*."

"You must trust me."

She grinned. "You're right," she said. "I must trust you a whole lot, Travis Reid."

"Can we go back to bed now?"

She closed the album and tucked Hannah's remembrance book carefully inside. "Race you!" she cried, and dashed for the stairs.

* * * * *

THE McKETTRICK WAY

In memory of my dad, Grady "Skip" Lael.
Happy trails, Cowboy.

CHAPTER ONE

BRAD O'BALLIVAN OPENED the driver's-side door of the waiting pickup truck, tossed his guitar case inside and turned to wave a farewell to the pilot and crew of the private jet he hoped never to ride in again.

A chilly fall wind slashed across the broad, lonesome clearing, rippling the fading grass, and he raised the collar of his denim jacket against it. Pulled his hat down a little lower over his eyes.

He was home.

Something inside him resonated to the Arizona high country, and more particularly to Stone Creek Ranch, like one prong of a perfectly balanced tuning fork. The sensation was peculiar to the place—he'd never felt it in his sprawling lakeside mansion outside Nashville, on the periphery of a town called Hendersonville, or at the villa in Mexico, or any of the other fancy digs where he'd hung his hat over the years since he'd turned his back on the spread—and so much more—to sing for his supper.

His grin was slightly ironic as he stood by the truck and watched the jet soar back into the sky. His retirement from the country music scene, at the age of thirty-five and the height of his success, had caused quite a media stir. He'd sold the jet and the big houses and most of what was in them, and given away the rest, except for the guitar and the clothes he was wearing. And he knew he'd never regret it.

He was through with that life. And once an O'Ballivan was through with something, that was the end of it.

The jet left a trail across the sky, faded to a silver spark, and disappeared.

Brad was about to climb into the truck and head for the ranch house, start coming to terms with things there, when he spotted a familiar battered gray Suburban jostling and gear-grinding its way over the rough road that had never really evolved beyond its beginnings as an old-time cattle trail.

He took off his hat, even though the wind nipped at the edges of his ears, and waited, partly eager, partly resigned.

The old Chevy came to a chortling stop a few inches from the toes of his boots, throwing up a cloud of red-brown dust, and his sister Olivia shut the big engine down and jumped out to round the hood and stride right up to him.

"You're back," Olivia said, sounding nonplussed. The eldest of Brad's three younger sisters, at twenty-nine, she'd never quite forgiven him for leaving home—much less getting famous. Practical to the bone, she was small, with short, glossy dark hair and eyes the color of a brand-new pair of jeans, and just as starchy. Olivia was low-woman-on-the-totem-pole at a thriving veterinary practice in the nearby town of Stone Creek, specializing in large animals, and Brad knew she spent most of her workdays in a barn someplace, or out on the range, with one arm shoved up where the sun didn't shine, turning a crossways calf or colt.

"I'm delighted to see you, too, Doc," Brad answered dryly.

With an exasperated little cry, Olivia sprang off the soles of her worn-out boots to throw her arms around his neck, knocking his hat clear off his head in the process. She hugged him tight, and when she drew back, there were tears on her dirt-smudged cheeks, and she sniffled self-consciously.

"If this is some kind of publicity stunt," Livie said, once she'd rallied a little, "I'm never going to forgive you." She bent to retrieve his hat, handed it over.

God, she was proud. She'd let him pay for her education, but returned every other check he or his accountant sent with the words *NO THANKS* scrawled across the front in thick black capitals.

Brad chuckled, threw the hat into the pickup, to rest on top of the guitar case. "It's no stunt," he replied. "I'm back for good. Ready to 'take hold and count for something,' as Big John used to say."

The mention of their late grandfather caused a poignant and not entirely comfortable silence to fall between them. Brad had been on a concert tour when the old man died of a massive coronary six months before, and he'd barely made it back to Stone Creek in time for the funeral. Worse, he'd had to leave again right after the services, in order to make a sold-out show in Chicago. The large infusions of cash he'd pumped into the home place over the years did little to assuage his guilt.

How much money is enough? How famous do you have to be? Big John had asked, in his kindly but irascible way, not once but a hundred times. *Come home, damn it. I need you. Your little sisters need you. And God knows, Stone Creek Ranch needs you.*

Shoving a hand through his light brown hair, in need of trimming as always, Brad thrust out a sigh and scanned the surrounding countryside. "That old stallion still running loose out here, or did the wolves and the barbed wire finally get him?" he asked, raw where the memories of his grandfather chafed against his mind, and in sore need of a distraction.

Livie probably wasn't fooled by the dodge, but she was gracious enough to grant Brad a little space to recover in, and he appreciated that. "We get a glimpse of Ransom every once in a while," she replied, and a little pucker of worry formed between her eyebrows. "Always off on the horizon somewhere, keeping his distance."

Brad laid a hand on his sister's shoulder. She'd been fascinated with the legendary wild stallion since she was little. First sighted in the late nineteenth century and called King's Ransom because that was what he was probably worth, the animal was black and shiny as wet ink, and so elusive that some people maintained he wasn't flesh and blood at all, but spirit, a myth believed for so long that thought itself had made him real. The less fanciful maintained that Ransom was one in a long succession of stallions, all descended from that first mysterious sire. Brad stood squarely in this camp, as Big John had, but he wasn't so sure Livie took the same rational view.

"They're trying to trap him," she said now, tears glistening in her eyes. "They want to pen him up. Get samples of his DNA. Turn him out to stud, so they can sell his babies."

"Who's trying to trap him, Liv?" Brad asked gently. It was cold, he was hungry, and setting foot in the old ranch house, without Big John there to greet him, was a thing to get past.

"Never mind," Livie said, bucking up a little. Setting her jaw. "You wouldn't be interested."

There was no point in arguing with Olivia O'Ballivan, DVM, when she got that look on her face. "Thanks for bringing my truck out here," Brad said. "And for coming to meet me."

"I didn't bring the truck," Livie replied. Some people would have taken the credit, but Liv was half again too stubborn to admit to a kindness she hadn't committed, let alone one she considered unwarranted. "Ashley and Melissa did that. They're probably at the ranch house right now, hanging streamers or putting up a Welcome Home, Brad banner or something. And I only came out here because I saw that jet and figured it was some damn movie star, buzzing the deer."

Brad had one leg inside the truck, ready to hoist himself into the driver's seat. "That's a problem around here?" he asked, with a wry half grin. "Movie stars buzzing deer in Lear jets?"

"It happens in Montana all the time," Livie insisted, plainly incensed. She felt just as strongly about snowmobiles and other off-road vehicles.

Brad reached down, touched the tip of her nose with one index finger. "This isn't Montana, shortstop," he pointed out. "See you at home?"

"Another time," Livie said, not giving an inch. "After all the hoopla dies down."

Inwardly, Brad groaned. He wasn't up for hoopla, or any kind of celebration Ashley and Melissa, their twin sisters, might have cooked up in honor of his return. Classic between-a-rock-and-a-hard-place stuff—he couldn't hurt their feelings, either.

"Tell me they're not planning a party," he pleaded.

Livie relented, but only slightly. One side of her mouth quirked up in a smile. "You're in luck, Mr. Multiple Grammy Winner. There's a McKettrick baby shower going on over in Indian Rock as we speak, and practically the whole county's there."

The name McKettrick unsettled Brad even more than the prospect of going home to banners, streamers and a collection of grinning neighbors, friends and sisters. "Not Meg," he muttered, and then blushed, since he hadn't intended to say the words out loud.

Livie's smile intensified, the way it did when she had a solid hand at gin rummy and was fixing to go out and stick him with a lot of aces and face cards. She shook her head. "Meg's back in Indian Rock for good, rumor has it, and she's still single," she assured him. "Her sister Sierra's the one having a baby."

In a belated and obviously fruitless attempt to hide his relief at this news, Brad shut the truck door between himself and Livie and, since the keys were waiting in the ignition, started up the rig.

Looking smug, Livie waved cheerily, climbed back into the Suburban and drove off, literally in a cloud of dust.

Brad sat waiting for it to settle.

The feelings took a little longer.

"Go haunt somebody else!" Meg McKettrick whispered to the ghost cowboy riding languidly in the passenger seat of her Blazer, as she drove past Sierra's new house, on the outskirts of Indian Rock, for at least the third time. Both sides of the road were jammed with cars, and if she didn't find a parking place soon, she'd be late for the baby shower. If not the actual *baby*. "Pick on Keegan—or Jesse—or Rance—*anybody* but me!"

"They don't need haunting," he said mildly. He looked nothing like the august, craggy-faced, white-haired figure in his portraits, grudgingly posed for late in his long and vigorous life. No, Angus McKettrick had come back in his prime, square-jaw handsome, broad shouldered, his hair thick and golden brown, his eyes intensely blue, at ease in the charm he'd passed down to generations of male descendents.

Still flustered, Meg found a gap between a Lexus and a minivan, wedged the Blazer into it, and turned off the ignition with a twist of one wrist. Tight-lipped, she jumped out of the rig, jerked open the back door, and reached for the festively wrapped package on the seat. "I've got news for you," she sputtered. "*I* don't need haunting, either!"

Angus, who looked to Meg as substantial and "real" as anybody she'd ever encountered, got out and stood on his side of the Blazer, stretching. "So you say," he answered, in a lazy drawl. "All of *them* are married, starting families of their own. Carrying on the McKettrick name."

"Thanks for the reminder," Meg bit out, in the terse undertone she reserved for arguments with her great-great-however-many-greats grandfather. Clutching the gift she'd bought for Travis and Sierra's baby, she shouldered both the back and driver's doors shut.

"In my day," Angus said easily, "you'd have been an old maid."

"Hello?" Meg replied, without moving her mouth. Over her long association with Angus McKettrick—which went back to her earliest childhood memories—she'd developed her own brand of ventriloquism, so other people, who couldn't see him, wouldn't think she was talking to herself. "This *isn't* 'your day.' It's mine. Twenty-first century, all the way. Women don't define themselves by whether they're married or not." She paused, sucked in a calming breath. "Here's an idea—why don't you wait in the car? Or, better yet, go ride some happy trail."

Angus kept pace with her as she crossed the road, clomping along in his perpetually muddy boots. As always, he wore a long, cape-shouldered canvas coat over a rough-spun shirt of butternut cotton and denim trousers that weren't quite jeans. The handle of his ever-present pistol, a long-barreled Colt .45, made a bulge behind his right coat pocket.

He wore a hat only when there was a threat of rain, and since the early October weather was mild, he was bareheaded that evening.

"It might be your testy nature that's the problem," Angus ruminated. "You're downright pricklish, that's what you are. A woman ought to have a little sass to her, to spice things up a mite. You've got more than your share, though, and it ain't becoming."

Meg ignored him, and the bad grammar he always affected when he wanted to impart folksy wisdom, as she tromped up the front steps, shuffling the bulky package in her arms to jab at the doorbell. *Here comes your nineteenth noncommittal yellow layette,* she thought, wishing she'd opted for the sterling baby rattles instead. If Sierra and Travis knew the sex of their unborn child, they weren't telling, which made shopping even more of a pain than normal.

The door swung open and Eve, Meg and Sierra's mother, stood frowning in the chasm. "It's about time you got here," she said, pulling Meg inside. Then, in a whisper, "Is he with you?"

"Of course he is," Meg answered, as her mother peered past her shoulder, searching in vain for Angus. "He never misses a family gathering."

Eve sniffed, straightened her elegant shoulders. "You're late," she said. "Sierra will be here any minute!"

"It's not as if she's going to be surprised, Mom," Meg said, setting the present atop a mountain of others of a suspiciously similar size and shape. "There must be a hundred cars parked out there."

Eve shut the door smartly and then, before Meg could shrug out of her navy blue peacoat, gripped her firmly by the shoulders. "You've lost weight," she accused. "And there are dark circles under your eyes. Aren't you sleeping well?"

"I'm fine," Meg insisted. And she *was* fine—for an old maid.

Angus, never one to be daunted by a little thing like a closed door, materialized just behind Eve, looked around at his assembled brood with pleased amazement. The place was jammed with McKettrick cousins, their wives and husbands, their growing families.

Something tightened in the pit of Meg's stomach.

"Nonsense," Eve said. "If you could have gotten away with it, you would have stayed home today, wandering around that old house in your pajamas, with no makeup on and your hair sticking out in every direction."

It was true, but beside the point. With Eve McKettrick for a mother, Meg couldn't get away with much of anything. "I'm here," she said. "Give me a break, will you?"

She pulled off her coat, handed it to Eve, and sidled into the nearest group, a small band of women. Meg, who had spent all her childhood summers in Indian Rock, didn't recognize any of them.

"It's all over the tabloids," remarked a tall, thin woman wearing a lot of jewelry. "Brad O'Ballivan is in rehab again."

Meg caught her breath at the name, and nearly dropped the cup of punch someone shoved into her hands.

"Nonsense," a second woman replied. "Last week those rags were reporting that he'd been abducted by aliens."

"He's handsome enough to have fans on other planets," observed a third, sighing wistfully.

Meg tried to ease out of the circle, but it had closed around her. She felt dizzy.

"My cousin Evelyn works at the post office over in Stone Creek," said yet another woman, with authority. "According to her, Brad's fan mail is being forwarded to the family ranch, just outside of town. He's not in rehab, and he's not on another planet. He's *home*. Evelyn says they'll have to build a second barn just to hold all those letters."

Meg smiled rigidly, but on the inside, she was scrambling for balance.

Suddenly, woman #1 focused on her. "You used to date Brad O'Ballivan, didn't you, Meg?"

"That—that was a long time ago," Meg said as graciously as she could, given that she was right in the middle of a panic attack. "We were just kids, and it was a summer thing—" Frantically, she calculated the distance between Indian Rock and Stone Creek—a mere forty miles. Not nearly far enough.

"I'm sure Meg has dated a lot of famous people," one of the other women said. "Working for McKettrickCo the way she did, flying all over the place in the company jet—"

"Brad wasn't famous when I knew him," Meg said lamely.

"You must miss your old life," someone else commented.

While it was true that Meg was having some trouble shifting from full throttle to a comparative standstill, since the family conglomerate had gone public a few months before, and her job as an executive vice president had gone with it, she *didn't* miss the meetings and the sixty-hour workweeks all that much. Money certainly wasn't a problem; she had a trust fund, as well as a personal investment portfolio thicker than the Los Angeles phone book.

A stir at the front door saved her from commenting.

Sierra came in, looking baffled.

"Surprise!" the crowd shouted as one.

The surprise is on me, Meg thought bleakly. *Brad O'Ballivan is back.*

* * *

Brad shoved the truck into gear and drove to the bottom of the hill, where the road forked. Turn left, and he'd be home in five minutes. Turn right, and he was headed for Indian Rock.

He had no damn business going to Indian Rock.

He had nothing to say to Meg McKettrick, and if he never set eyes on the woman again, it would be two weeks too soon.

He turned right.

He couldn't have said why.

He just drove.

At one point, needing noise, he switched on the truck radio, fiddled with the dial until he found a country-western station. A recording of his own voice filled the cab of the pickup, thundering from all the speakers.

He'd written that ballad for Meg.

He turned the dial to Off.

Almost simultaneously, his cell phone jangled in the pocket of his jacket; he considered ignoring it—there were a number of people he didn't want to talk to—but suppose it was one of his sisters calling? Suppose they needed help?

He flipped the phone open, not taking his eyes off the curvy mountain road to check the caller ID panel first. "O'Ballivan," he said.

"Have you come to your senses yet?" demanded his manager, Phil Meadowbrook. "Shall I tell you again just *how much* money those people in Vegas are offering? They're willing to build you your own *theater,* for God's sake. This is a three-year gig—"

"Phil?" Brad broke in.

"Say yes," Phil pleaded.

"I'm retired."

"You're thirty-five," Phil argued. "*Nobody* retires at thirty-five!"

"We've already had this conversation, Phil."

"Don't hang up!"

Brad, who'd been about to thumb the Off button, sighed.

"What the hell are you going to do in Stone Creek, Arizona?" Phil demanded. "Herd cattle? Sing to your horse? Think of the money, Brad. Think of the women, throwing their underwear at your feet—"

"I've been working real hard to repress that image," Brad said. "Thanks a lot for the reminder."

"Okay, forget the underwear," Phil shot back, without missing a beat. "But think of the money!"

"I've already got more of that than I need, Phil, and so do you, so spare me the riff where your grandchildren are homeless waifs picking through garbage behind the supermarket."

"I've used that one, huh?" Phil asked.

"Oh, yeah," Brad answered.

"What are you doing, right this moment?"

"I'm headed for the Dixie Dog Drive-In."

"The *what?*"

"Goodbye, Phil."

"What are you going to do at the Dixie-Whatever Drive-In that you couldn't do in Music City? Or Vegas?"

"You wouldn't understand," Brad said. "And I can't say I blame you, because I don't really understand it myself."

Back in the day, he and Meg used to meet at the Dixie Dog, by tacit agreement, when either of them had been away. It had been some kind of universe-thing, purely intuitive. He guessed he wanted to see if it still worked—and he'd be damned if he'd try to explain that to Phil.

"Look," Phil said, revving up for another sales pitch, "I

can't put these casino people off forever. You're riding high right now, but things are bound to cool off. I've got to tell them *something*—"

"Tell them 'thanks, but no thanks,'" Brad suggested. This time, he broke the connection.

Phil, being Phil, tried to call twice before he finally gave up.

Passing familiar landmarks, Brad told himself he ought to turn around. The old days were gone, things had ended badly between him and Meg anyhow, and she wasn't going to be at the Dixie Dog.

He kept driving.

He went by the Welcome To Indian Rock sign, and the Roadhouse, a popular beer-and-burger stop for truckers, tourists and locals, and was glad to see the place was still open. He slowed for Main Street, smiled as he passed Cora's Curl and Twirl, squinted at the bookshop next door. That was new.

He frowned. Things changed, places changed.

What if the Dixie Dog had closed down?

What if it was boarded up, with litter and sagebrush tumbling through a deserted parking lot?

And what the hell did it matter, anyhow?

Brad shoved a hand through his hair. Maybe Phil and everybody else was right—maybe he was crazy to turn down the Vegas deal. Maybe he *would* end up sitting in the barn, serenading a bunch of horses.

He rounded a bend, and there was the Dixie Dog, still open. Its big neon sign, a giant hot dog, was all lit up and going through its corny sequence—first it was covered in red squiggles of light, meant to suggest catsup, and then yellow, for mustard. There were a few cars lined up in the drive-through lane, a few more in the parking lot.

Brad pulled into one of the slots next to a speaker and rolled down the truck window.

"Welcome to the Dixie Dog Drive-In," a youthful female voice chirped over the bad wiring. "What can I get you today?"

Brad hadn't thought that far, but he was starved. He peered at the light-up menu box under the chunky metal speaker. Then the obvious choice struck him and he said, "I'll take a Dixie Dog," he said. "Hold the chili and onions."

"Coming right up" was the cheerful response. "Anything to drink?"

"Chocolate shake," he decided. "Extra thick."

His cell phone rang again.

He ignored it again.

The girl thanked him and roller-skated out with the order about five minutes later.

When she wheeled up to the driver's-side window, smiling, her eyes went wide with recognition, and she dropped the tray with a clatter.

Silently, Brad swore. Damn if he hadn't forgotten he was famous.

The girl, a skinny thing wearing too much eye makeup, immediately started to cry. "I'm sorry!" she sobbed, squatting to gather up the mess.

"It's okay," Brad answered quietly, leaning to look down at her, catching a glimpse of her plastic name tag. "It's okay, Mandy. No harm done."

"I'll get you another dog and a shake right away, Mr. O'Ballivan!"

"Mandy?"

She stared up at him pitifully, sniffling. Thanks to the copious tears, most of the goop on her eyes had slid south. "Yes?"

"When you go back inside, could you not mention seeing me?"

"But you're Brad O'Ballivan!"

"Yeah," he answered, suppressing a sigh. "I know."

She was standing up again by then, the tray of gathered debris clasped in both hands. She seemed to sway a little on her rollers. "Meeting you is just about the most important thing that's ever happened to me in my whole entire *life*. I don't know if I could keep it a secret even if I tried!"

Brad leaned his head against the back of the truck seat and closed his eyes. "Not forever, Mandy," he said. "Just long enough for me to eat a Dixie Dog in peace."

She rolled a little closer. "You wouldn't happen to have a picture you could autograph for me, would you?"

"Not with me," Brad answered. There were boxes of publicity pictures in storage, along with the requisite T-shirts, slick concert programs and other souvenirs commonly sold on the road. He never carried them, much to Phil's annoyance.

"You could sign this napkin, though," Mandy said. "It's only got a little chocolate on the corner."

Brad took the paper napkin, and her order pen, and scrawled his name. Handed both items back through the window.

"Now I can tell my grandchildren I spilled your lunch all over the pavement at the Dixie Dog Drive-In, and here's my proof." Mandy beamed, waggling the chocolate-stained napkin.

"Just imagine," Brad said. The slight irony in his tone was wasted on Mandy, which was probably a good thing.

"I won't tell anybody I saw you until you drive away," Mandy said with eager resolve. "I *think* I can last that long."

"That would be good," Brad told her.

She turned and whizzed back toward the side entrance to the Dixie Dog.

Brad waited, marveling that he hadn't considered incidents like this one before he'd decided to come back home. In retrospect, it seemed shortsighted, to say the least, but the truth was, he'd expected to be—Brad O'Ballivan.

Presently, Mandy skated back out again, and this time, she managed to hold on to the tray.

"I didn't tell a soul!" she whispered. "But Heather and Darlene *both* asked me why my mascara was all smeared." Efficiently, she hooked the tray onto the bottom edge of the window.

Brad extended payment, but Mandy shook her head.

"The boss said it's on the house, since I dumped your first order on the ground."

He smiled. "Okay, then. Thanks."

Mandy retreated, and Brad was just reaching for the food when a bright red Blazer whipped into the space beside his. The driver's-side door sprang open, crashing into the metal speaker, and somebody got out, in a hurry.

Something quickened inside Brad.

And in the next moment, Meg McKettrick was standing practically on his running board, her blue eyes blazing.

Brad grinned. "I guess you're not over me after all," he said.

CHAPTER TWO

AFTER SIERRA HAD OPENED all her shower presents, and cake and punch had been served, Meg had felt the old, familiar tug in the middle of her solar plexus and headed straight for the Dixie Dog Drive-In. Now that she was there, standing next to a truck and all but nose to nose with Brad O'Ballivan through the open window, she didn't know what to do—or say.

Angus poked her from behind, and she flinched.

"Speak up," her dead ancestor prodded.

"Stay out of this," she answered, without thinking.

Puzzlement showed in Brad's affably handsome face. "Huh?"

"Never mind," Meg said. She took a step back, straightened. "And I am *so* over you."

Brad grinned. "Damned if it didn't work," he marveled. He climbed out of the truck to stand facing Meg, ducking around the tray hooked to the door. His dark-blond hair was artfully rumpled, and his clothes were downright ordinary.

"*What* worked?" Meg demanded, even though she knew.

Laughter sparked in his blue-green eyes, along with considerable pain, and he didn't bother to comment.

"What are you doing here?" she asked.

Brad spread his hands. Hands that had once played Meg's

body as skillfully as any guitar. Oh, yes. Brad O'Ballivan knew how to set all the chords vibrating.

"Free country," he said. "Or has Indian Rock finally seceded from the Union with the ranch house on the Triple M for a capitol?"

Since she felt a strong urge to bolt for the Blazer and lay rubber getting out of the Dixie Dog's parking lot, Meg planted her feet and hoisted her chin. *McKettricks,* she reminded herself silently, *don't run.*

"I heard you were in rehab," she said, hoping to get under his hide.

"That's a nasty rumor," Brad replied cheerfully.

"How about the two ex-wives and that scandal with the actress?"

His grin, insouciant in the first place, merely widened. "Unfortunately, I can't deny the two ex-wives," he said. "As for the actress—well, it all depends on whether you believe her version or mine. Have you been following my career, Meg McKettrick?"

Meg reddened.

"Tell him the truth," Angus counseled. "You never forgot him."

"No," Meg said, addressing both Brad *and* Angus.

Brad looked unconvinced. He was probably just egotistical enough to think she logged onto his website regularly, bought all his CDs and read every tabloid article about him that she could get her hands on. Which she did, but that was *not* the point.

"You're still the best-looking woman I've ever laid eyes on," he said. "That hasn't changed, anyhow."

"I'm not a member of your fan club, O'Ballivan," Meg informed him. "So hold the insincere flattery, okay?"

One corner of his mouth tilted upward in a half grin, but his eyes were sad. He glanced back toward the truck, then met Meg's gaze again. "I don't flatter anybody," Brad said. Then he sighed. "I guess I'd better get back to Stone Creek."

Something in his tone piqued Meg's interest.

Who was she kidding?

Everything about him piqued her interest. As much as she didn't want that to be true, it was.

"I was sorry to hear about Big John's passing," she said. She almost touched his arm, but managed to catch herself just short of it. If she laid a hand on Brad O'Ballivan, who knew what would happen?

"Thanks," he replied.

A girl on roller skates wheeled out of the drive-in to collect the tray from the window edge of Brad's truck, her cheeks pink with carefully restrained excitement. "I might have said something to Heather and Darleen," the teenager confessed, after a curious glance at Meg. "About you being who you are and the autograph and everything."

Brad muttered something.

The girl skated away.

"I've gotta go," Brad told Meg, looking toward the drive-in. Numerous faces were pressed against the glass door; in another minute, there would probably be a stampede. "I don't suppose we could have dinner together or something? Maybe tomorrow night? There are—well, there are some things I'd like to say to you."

"Say yes," Angus told her.

"I don't think that would be a good idea," Meg said.

"A drink, then? There's a redneck bar in Stone Creek—"

"Don't be such a damned prig," Angus protested, nudging her again.

"I'm not a prig."

Brad frowned, threw another nervous look toward the

drive-in and all those grinning faces. "I never said you were," he replied.

"I wasn't—" Meg paused, bit her lower lip. *I wasn't talking to you. No, siree, I was talking to Angus McKettrick's ghost.* "Okay," she agreed, to cover her lapse. "I guess one drink couldn't do any harm."

Brad climbed into his truck. The door of the drive-in crashed open, and the adoring hordes poured out, screaming with delight.

"Go!" Meg told him.

"Six o'clock tomorrow night," Brad reminded her. He backed the truck out, made a narrow turn to avoid running over the approaching herd of admirers and peeled out of the lot.

Meg turned to the disappointed fans. "Brad O'Ballivan," she said diplomatically, "has left the building."

Nobody got the joke.

The sun was setting, red-gold shot through with purple, when Brad crested the last hill before home and looked down on Stone Creek Ranch for the first time since his grandfather's funeral. The creek coursed, silvery-blue, through the middle of the land. The barn and the main house, built by Sam O'Ballivan's own hands and shored up by every generation to follow, stood as sturdy and imposing as ever. Once, there had been two houses on the place, but the one belonging to Major John Blackstone, the original landowner, had been torn down long ago. Now a copse of oak trees stood where the major had lived, surrounding a few old graves.

Big John was buried there, by special dispensation from the Arizona state government.

A lump formed in Brad's throat. *You see that I'm laid to*

rest with the old-timers when the bell tolls, Big John had told him once. *Not in that cemetery in town.*

It had taken some doing, but Brad had made it happen.

He wanted to head straight for Big John's final resting place, pay his respects first thing, but there was a cluster of cars parked in front of the ranch house. His sisters were waiting to welcome him home.

Brad blinked a couple of times, rubbed his eyes with a thumb and forefinger, and headed for the house.

Time to face the proverbial music.

Meg drove slowly back to the Triple M, going the long way to pass the main ranch house, Angus's old stomping grounds, in the vain hope that he would decide to haunt it for a while, instead of her. A descendant of Angus's eldest son, Holt, and daughter-in-law Lorelei, Meg called their place home.

As they bumped across the creek bridge, Angus assessed the large log structure, added onto over the years, and well-maintained.

Though close, all the McKettricks were proud of their particular branch of the family tree. Keegan, who occupied the main house now, along with his wife, Molly, daughter, Devon, and young son, Lucas, could trace his lineage back to Kade, another of Angus's four sons.

Rance, along with his daughters, was Rafe's progeny. He and the girls and his bride, Emma, lived in the grandly rustic structure on the other side of the creek from Keegan's place.

Finally, there was Jesse. He was Jeb's descendant, and resided, when he wasn't off somewhere participating in a rodeo or a poker tournament, in the house Jeb had built for his wife, Chloe, high on a hill on the southwestern section of the ranch. Jesse was happily married to a hometown girl, the former Cheyenne Bridges, and like Keegan's Molly and Rance's Emma, Cheyenne was expecting a baby.

Everybody, it seemed to Meg, was expecting a baby.

Except her, of course.

She bit her lower lip.

"I bet if you got yourself pregnant by that singing cowboy," Angus observed, "he'd have the decency to make an honest woman out of you."

Angus had an uncanny ability to tap into Meg's wavelength; though he swore he couldn't read her mind, she wondered sometimes.

"Great idea," she scoffed. "And for your information, I *am* an honest woman."

Keegan was just coming out of the barn as Meg passed; he smiled and waved. She tooted the Blazer's horn in greeting.

"He sure looks like Kade," Angus said. "Jesse looks like Jeb, and Rance looks like Rafe." He sighed. "It sure makes me lonesome for my boys."

Meg felt a grudging sympathy for Angus. He'd ruined a lot of dates, being an almost constant companion, but she loved him. "Why can't you be where they are?" she asked softly. "Wherever that is."

"I've got to see to you," he answered. "You're the last holdout."

"I'd be all right, Angus," she said. She'd asked him about the afterlife, but all he'd ever been willing to say was that there was no such thing as dying, just a change of perspective. Time wasn't linear, he claimed, but simultaneous. The "whole ball of string," as he put it, was happening at once—past, present and future. Some of the experiences the women in her family, including herself and Sierra, had had up at Holt's house lent credence to the theory.

Sierra claimed that, before her marriage to Travis and

the subsequent move to the new semi-mansion in town, she and her young son, Liam, had shared the old house with a previous generation of McKettricks—Doss and Hannah and a little boy called Tobias. Sierra had offered journals and photograph albums as proof, and Meg had to admit, her half sister made a compelling case.

Still, and for all that she'd been keeping company with a benevolent ghost since she was little, Meg was a left-brain type.

When Angus didn't comment on her insistence that she'd get along fine if he went on to the great roundup in the sky, or whatever, Meg tried again. "Look," she said gently, "when I was little, and Sierra disappeared, and Mom was so frantic to find her that she couldn't take care of me, I really needed you. But I'm a grown woman now, Angus. I'm independent. I have a life."

Out of the corner of her eye, she saw Angus's jaw tighten. "That Hank Breslin," he said, "was no good for Eve. No better than *your* father was. Every time the right man came along, she was so busy cozying up to the *wrong* one that she didn't even notice what was right in front of her."

Hank Breslin was Sierra's father. He'd kidnapped Sierra, only two years old at the time, when Eve served him with divorce papers, and raised her in Mexico. For a variety of reasons, Eve hadn't reconnected with her lost daughter until recently. Meg's own father, about whom she knew little, had died in an accident a month before she was born. Nobody liked to talk about him—even his name was a mystery.

"And you think I'll make the same mistakes my mother did?" Meg said.

"Hell," Angus said, sparing her a reluctant grin, "right now, even a *mistake* would be progress."

"With all due respect," Meg replied, "having you around all the time is not exactly conducive to romance."

They started the long climb uphill, headed for the house that now belonged to her and Sierra. Meg had always loved that house—it had been a refuge for her, full of cousins. Looking back, she wondered why, given that Eve had rarely accompanied her on those summer visits, had instead left her daughter in the care of a succession of nannies and, later, aunts and uncles.

Sierra's kidnapping had been a traumatic event, for certain, but the problems Eve had subsequently developed because of it had left Meg relatively unmarked. She hadn't been lonely as a child, mainly because of Angus.

"I'll stay clear tomorrow night, when you go to Stone Creek for that drink," Angus said.

"You like Brad."

"Always did. Liked Travis, too. 'Course, I knew he was meant for your sister, that they'd meet up in time."

Meg and Sierra's husband, Travis, were old friends. They'd tried to get something going, convinced they were perfect for each other, but it hadn't worked. Now that Travis and Sierra were together, and ecstatically happy, Meg was glad.

"Don't get your hopes up," she said. "About Brad and me, I mean."

Angus didn't reply. He appeared to be deep in thought. Or maybe as he looked out at the surrounding countryside, he was remembering his youth, when he'd staked a claim to this land and held it with blood and sweat and sheer McKettrick stubbornness.

"You must have known the O'Ballivans," Meg reflected, musing. Like her own family, Brad's had been pioneers in this part of Arizona.

"I was older than dirt by the time Sam O'Ballivan brought his bride, Maddie, up from Haven. Might have seen them once or twice. But I knew Major Blackstone, all right."

Angus smiled at some memory. "He and I used to arm wrestle sometimes, in the card room back of Jolene Bell's Saloon, when we couldn't best each other at poker."

"Who won?" Meg asked, smiling slightly at the image.

"Same as the poker," Angus answered with a sigh. "We'd always come out about even. He'd win half the time, me the other half."

The house came in sight, the barn towering nearby. Angus's expression took on a wistful aspect.

"When you're here," Meg ventured, "can you see Doss and Hannah and Tobias? Talk to them?"

"No," Angus said flatly.

"Why not?" Meg persisted, even though she knew Angus didn't want to pursue the subject.

"Because they're not dead," he said. "They're just on the other side, like my boys."

"Well, I'm not dead, either," Meg said reasonably. She refrained from adding that she could have shown him their graves, up in the McKettrick cemetery. Shown him his own, for that matter. It would have been unkind, of course, but there was another reason for her reluctance, too. In some version of that cemetery, given what he'd told her about time, there was surely a headstone with *her* name on it.

"You wouldn't understand," Angus told her. He always said that, when she tried to find out how it was for him, where he went when he wasn't following her around.

"Try me," she said.

He vanished.

Resigned, Meg pulled up in front of the garage, added onto the original house sometime in the 1950s, and equipped with an automatic door opener, and pushed the button so she could drive in.

She half expected to find Angus sitting at the kitchen table when she went into the house, but he wasn't there.

What she needed, she decided, was a cup of tea.

She got Lorelei's teapot out of the built-in china cabinet and set it firmly on the counter. The piece was legendary in the family; it had a way of moving back to the cupboard of its own volition, from the table or the counter, and vice versa.

Meg filled the electric kettle at the sink and plugged it in to heat.

Tea was not going to cure what ailed her.

Brad O'Ballivan was back.

Compared to that, ghosts, the mysteries of time and space, and teleporting teapots seemed downright mundane.

And she'd agreed, like a fool, to meet him in Stone Creek for a drink. What had she been thinking?

Standing there in her kitchen, Meg leaned against the counter and folded her arms, waiting for the tea water to boil. Brad had hurt her so badly, she'd thought she'd never recover. For years after he'd dumped her to go to Nashville, she'd barely been able to come back to Indian Rock, and when she had, she'd driven straight to the Dixie Dog, against her will, sat in some rental car, and cried like an idiot.

There are some things I'd like to say to you, Brad had told her, that very day.

"What things?" she asked now, aloud.

The teakettle whistled.

She unplugged it, measured loose orange pekoe into Lorelei's pot and poured steaming water over it.

It was just a drink, Meg reminded herself. An innocent drink.

She should call Brad, cancel gracefully.

Or, better yet, she could just stand him up. Not show

up at all. Just as he'd done to her, way back when, when she'd loved him with all her heart and soul, when she'd believed he meant to make a place for her in his busy, exciting life.

Musing, Meg laid a hand to her lower abdomen.

She'd stopped believing in a lot of things when Brad O'Ballivan ditched her.

Maybe he wanted to apologize.

She gave a teary snort of laughter.

And maybe he really had fans on other planets.

A rap at the back door made her start. Angus? He never knocked—he just appeared. Usually at the most inconvenient possible time.

Meg went to the door, peered through the old, thick panes of greenish glass, saw Travis Reid looming on the other side. She wrestled with the lock and let him in.

"I'm here on reconnaissance," he announced, taking off his cowboy hat and hanging it on the peg next to the door. "Sierra's worried about you, and so is Eve."

Meg put a hand to her forehead. She'd left the baby shower abruptly to go meet Brad at the Dixie Dog Drive-In. "I'm sorry," she said, stepping back so Travis could come inside. "I'm all right, really. You shouldn't have come all the way out here—"

"Eve tried your cell—which is evidently off—and Sierra left three or four messages on voice mail," he said with a nod toward the kitchen telephone. "Consider yourself fortunate that I got here before they called out the National Guard."

Meg laughed, closed the door against the chilly October twilight, and watched as Travis took off his sheepskin-lined coat and hung it next to the hat. "I was just feeling a little—overwhelmed."

"Overwhelmed?" She'd been *possessed*.

Travis went to the telephone, punched in a sequence of numbers and waited. "Hi, honey," he said presently, when Sierra answered. "Meg's alive and well. No armed intruders. No bloody accident. She was just—overwhelmed."

"Tell her I'll call her later," Meg said. "Mom, too."

"She'll call you later," Travis repeated dutifully. "Eve, too." He listened again, promised to pick up a gallon of milk and a loaf of bread on the way home and hung up.

Knowing Travis wasn't fond of tea, Meg offered him a cup of instant coffee, instead.

He accepted, taking a seat at the table where generations of McKettricks, from Holt and Lorelei on down, had taken their meals. "What's really going on, Meg?" he asked quietly, watching her as she poured herself some tea and joined him.

"What makes you think anything is going on?"

"I know you. We tried to fall in love, remember?"

"Brad O'Ballivan's back," she said.

Travis nodded. "And this means—?"

"Nothing," Meg answered, much too quickly. "It means nothing. I just—"

Travis settled back in his chair, folded his arms, and waited.

"Okay, it was a shock," Meg admitted. She sat up a little straighter. "But you already knew."

"Jesse told me."

"And nobody thought to mention it to me?"

"I guess we assumed you'd talked to Brad."

"Why would I do that?"

"Because—" Travis paused, looked uncomfortable. "It's no secret that the two of you had a thing going, Meg. Indian Rock and Stone Creek are small places, forty miles apart. Things get around."

Meg's face burned. She'd thought, she'd truly believed,

that no one on earth knew Brad had broken her heart. She'd pretended it didn't matter that he'd left town so abruptly. Even laughed about it. Gone on to finish college, thrown herself into that first entry-level job at McKettrickCo. Dated other men, including the then-single Travis.

And she hadn't fooled anyone.

"Are you going to see him again?"

Meg pressed the tips of her fingers hard into her closed eyes. Nodded. Then shook her head from side to side.

Travis chuckled. "Make a decision, Meg," he said.

"We're supposed to have a drink together tomorrow night, at a cowboy bar in Stone Creek. I don't know why I said I'd meet him—after all this time, what do we have to say to each other?"

"'How've ya been?'" Travis suggested.

"I *know* how he's been—rich and famous, married twice, busy building a reputation that makes Jesse's look tame," she said. "I, on the other hand, have been a workaholic. Period."

"Aren't you being a little hard on yourself? Not to mention Brad?" A grin quirked the corner of Travis's mouth. "Comparing him to *Jesse?*"

Jesse had been a wild man, if a good-hearted, well-intentioned one, until he'd met up with Cheyenne Bridges. When he'd fallen, he'd fallen hard, and for the duration, the way bad boys so often do.

"Maybe Brad's changed," Travis said.

"Maybe not," Meg countered.

"Well, I guess you *could* leave town for a while. Stay out of his way." Travis was trying hard not to smile. "Volunteer for a space mission or something."

"I am *not* going to run," Meg said. "I've always wanted to live right here, on this ranch, in this house. Besides, I intend to be here when the baby comes."

Travis's face softened at the mention of the impending birth. Until Sierra came along, Meg hadn't thought he'd ever settle down. He'd had his share of demons to overcome, not the least of which was the tragic death of his younger brother. Travis had blamed himself for what happened to Brody. "Good," he said. "But what do you actually *do* here? You're used to the fast lane, Meg."

"I take care of the horses," she said.

"That takes, what—two hours a day? According to Eve, you spend most of your time in your pajamas. She thinks you're depressed."

"Well, I'm not," Meg said. "I'm just—catching up on my rest."

"Okay," Travis said, drawing out the word.

"I'm not drinking alone and I'm not watching soap operas," Meg said. "I'm vegging. It's a concept my mother doesn't understand."

"She loves you, Meg. She's worried. She's not the enemy."

"I wish she'd go back to Texas."

"Wish away. She's not going anywhere, with a grand-child coming."

At least Eve hadn't taken up residence on the ranch; that was some comfort. She lived in a small suite at the only hotel in Indian Rock, and kept herself busy shopping, day trading on her laptop and spoiling Liam.

Oh, yes. And nagging Meg.

Travis finished his coffee, carried his cup to the sink, rinsed it out. After hesitating for a few moments, he said, "It's this thing about seeing Angus's ghost. She thinks you're obsessed."

Meg made a soft, strangled sound of frustration.

"It's not that she doesn't believe you," Travis added.

"She just thinks I'm a little crazy."

"No," Travis said. "Nobody thinks that."

"But I should get a life, as the saying goes?"

"It would be a good idea, don't you think?"

"Go home. Your pregnant wife needs a gallon of milk and a loaf of bread."

Travis went to the door, put on his coat, took his hat from the hook. "What do *you* need, Meg? That's the question."

"Not Brad O'Ballivan, that's for sure."

Travis grinned again. Set his hat on his head and turned the doorknob. "Did I mention him?" he asked lightly.

Meg glared at him.

"See you," Travis said. And then he was gone.

"He puts me in mind of that O'Ballivan fella," Angus announced, nearly startling Meg out of her skin.

She turned to see him standing over by the china cabinet. Was it her imagination, or did he look a little older than he had that afternoon?

"Jesse looks like Jeb. Rance looks like Rafe. Keegan looks like Kade. You're seeing things, Angus."

"Have it your way," Angus said.

Like any McKettrick had ever said *that* and meant it.

"What's for supper?"

"What do you care? You never eat."

"Neither do you. You're starting to look like a bag of bones."

"If I were you, I wouldn't make comments about bones. Being dead and all, I mean."

"The problem with you young people is, you have no respect for your elders."

Meg sighed, got up from her chair at the table, stomped over to the refrigerator and selected a boxed dinner from the stack in the freezer. The box was coated with frost.

"I'm sorry," Meg said. "Is that a hint of silver I see at your temples?"

Self-consciously, Angus shifted his weight from one booted foot to the other. "If I'm going gray," he scowled, "it's on account of you. None of my boys ever gave me half as much trouble as you, or my Katie, either. And they were plum full of the dickens, all of them."

Meg's heart pinched. Katie was Angus's youngest child, and his only daughter. He rarely mentioned her, since she'd caused some kind of scandal by eloping on her wedding day—with someone other than the groom. Although she and Angus had eventually reconciled, he'd been on his deathbed at the time.

"I'm *all right,* Angus," she told him. "You can go. Really."

"You eat food that could be used to drive railroad spikes into hard ground. You don't have a husband. You rattle around in this old house like some—ghost. I'm not leaving until I know you'll be happy."

"I'm happy *now.*"

Angus walked over to her, the heels of his boots thumping on the plank floor, took the frozen dinner out of her hands, and carried it to the trash compactor. Dropped it inside.

"Damn fool contraption," he muttered.

"That was my supper," Meg objected.

"Cook something," Angus said. "Get out a skillet. Dump some lard into it. Fry up a chicken." He paused, regarded her darkly. "You *do* know how to cook, don't you?"

CHAPTER THREE

JOLENE'S, BUILT ON THE SITE of the old saloon and brothel where Angus McKettrick and Major John Blackstone used to arm wrestle, among other things, was dimly lit and practically empty. Meg paused on the threshold, letting her eyes adjust and wishing she'd listened to her instincts and cancelled; now there would be no turning back.

Brad was standing by the jukebox, the colored lights flashing across the planes of his face. Having heard the door open, he turned his head slightly to acknowledge her arrival with a nod and a wisp of a grin.

"Where is everybody?" she asked. Except for the bartender, she and Brad were alone.

"Staying clear," Brad said. "I promised a free concert in the high school gym if we could have Jolene's to ourselves for a couple of hours."

Meg nearly fled. If it hadn't been against the McKettrick code, as inherent to her being as her DNA, she would have given in to the urge and called it good judgment.

"Have a seat," Brad said, drawing back a chair at one of the tables. Nothing in the whole tavern matched, not even the bar stools, and every stick of furniture was scarred and scratched. Jolene's was a hangout for honky-tonk angels; the winged variety would surely have given the place a wide berth.

"What'll it be?" the bartender asked. He was a squat man, wearing a muscle shirt and a lot of tattoos. With his handlebar mustache, he might have been from Angus's era, instead of the present day.

Brad ordered a cola as Meg forced herself across the room to take the chair he offered.

Maybe, she thought, as she asked for an iced tea, the rumors were true, and Brad was fresh out of rehab.

The bartender served the drinks and quietly left the saloon, via a back door.

Brad, meanwhile, turned his own chair around and sat astraddle it, with his arms resting across the back. He wore jeans, a white shirt open at the throat and boots, and if he hadn't been so breathtakingly handsome, he'd have looked like any cowboy, in any number of scruffy little redneck bars scattered all over Arizona.

Meg eyed his drink, since doing that seemed slightly less dangerous than looking straight into his face, and when he chuckled, she felt her cheeks turn warm.

Pride made her meet his gaze. "What?" she asked, running damp palms along the thighs of her oldest pair of jeans. She'd made a point of *not* dressing up for the encounter—no perfume, and only a little mascara and lip gloss. War paint, Angus called it. Her favorite ghost had an opinion on everything, it seemed, but at least he'd honored his promise not to horn in on this interlude, or whatever it was, with Brad.

"Don't believe everything you read," Brad said easily, settling back in his chair. "Not about me, anyway."

"Who says I've been reading about you?"

"Come on, Meg. You expected me to drink Jack Daniel's straight from the bottle. That's hype—part of the bad-boy image. My manager cooked it up."

Meg huffed out a sigh. "You haven't been to rehab?"

He grinned. "Nope. Never trashed a hotel room, spent a

weekend in jail, or any of the rest of the stuff Phil wanted everybody to believe about me."

"Really?"

"Really." Brad pushed back his chair, returned to the jukebox, and dropped a few coins in the slot. An old Johnny Cash ballad poured softly into the otherwise silent bar.

Meg took a swig of her iced tea, in a vain effort to steady her nerves. She was no teetotaler, but when she drove, she didn't drink. Ever. Right about then, though, she wished she'd hired a car and driver so she could get sloshed enough to forget that being alone with Brad O'Ballivan was like having her most sensitive nerves bared to a cold wind.

He started in her direction, then stopped in the middle of the floor, which was strewn with sawdust and peanut shells. Held out a hand to her.

Meg went to him, just the way she'd gone to the Dixie Dog Drive-In the day before. Automatically.

He drew her into his arms, holding her close but easy, and they danced without moving their feet.

As the song ended, Brad propped his chin on top of Meg's head and sighed. "I've missed you," he said.

Meg came to her senses.

Finally.

She pulled back far enough to look up into his face.

"Don't go there," she warned.

"We can't just pretend the past didn't happen, Meg," he reasoned quietly.

"Yes, we can," she argued. "Millions of people do it, every day. It's called denial, and it has its place in the scheme of things."

"Still a McKettrick," Brad said, sorrow lurking behind the humor in his blue eyes. "If I said the moon was round, you'd call it square."

She poked at his chest with an index finger. "Still an

O'Ballivan," she accused. "Thinking you've got to explain the shape of the moon, as if I couldn't see it for myself."

The jukebox in Jolene's was an antique; it still played 45s, instead of CDs. Now a record flopped audibly onto the turntable, and the needle scratched its way into Willie Nelson's version of "Georgia."

Meg stiffened, wanting to pull away.

Brad's arms, resting loosely around her waist, tightened slightly.

Over the years, the McKettricks and the O'Ballivans, owning the two biggest ranches in the area, had been friendly rivals. The families were equally proud and equally stubborn—they'd had to be, to survive the ups and downs of raising cattle for more than a century. Even when they were close, Meg and Brad had always identified strongly with their heritages.

Meg swallowed. "Why did you come back?" she asked, without intending to speak at all.

"To settle some things," Brad answered. They were swaying to the music again, though the soles of their boots were still rooted to the floor. "And you're at the top of my list, Meg McKettrick."

"You're at the top of mine, too," Meg retorted. "But I don't think we're talking about the same kind of list."

He laughed. God, how she'd missed that sound. How she'd missed the heat and substance of him, and the sun-dried laundry smell of his skin and hair...

Stop, she told herself. She was acting like some smitten fan or something.

"You bought me an engagement ring," she blurted, without intending to do anything of the kind. "We were supposed to elope. And then you got on a bus and went to Nashville and married what's-her-name!"

"I was stupid," Brad said. "And scared."

"No," Meg replied, fighting back furious tears. "You were *ambitious*. And of course the bride's father owned a recording company—"

Brad closed his eyes for a moment. A muscle bunched in his cheek. "Valerie," he said miserably. "Her name was Valerie."

"Do you really think I give a damn what her name was?"

"Yeah," he answered. "I do."

"Well, you're wrong!"

"That must be why you look like you want to club me to the ground with the nearest blunt object."

"I got over you like that!" Meg told him, snapping her fingers. But a tear slipped down her cheek, spoiling the whole effect.

Brad brushed it away gently with the side of one thumb. "Meg," he said. "I'm so sorry."

"Oh, that changes everything!" Meg scoffed. She tried to move away from him again, but he still wouldn't let her go.

One corner of his mouth tilted up in a forlorn effort at a grin. "You'll feel a lot better if you forgive me." He curved the fingers of his right hand under her chin, lifted. "For old times' sake?" he cajoled. "For the nights when we went skinny-dipping in the pond behind your house on the Triple M? For the nights we—"

"No," Meg interrupted, fairly smothering as the memories wrapped themselves around her. "You don't deserve to be forgiven."

"You're right," Brad agreed. "I don't. But that's the thing about forgiveness. It's all about grace, isn't it? It's supposed to be undeserved."

"Great logic if you're on the *receiving* end!"

"I had my reasons, Meg."

"Yeah. You wanted bright lights and big money. Oh, and fast women."

Brad's jaw tightened, but his eyes were bleak. "I couldn't have married you, Meg."

"Pardon my confusion. You gave me an engagement ring and proposed!"

"I wasn't thinking." He looked away, faced her again with visible effort. "You had a trust fund. I had a mortgage and a pile of bills. I laid awake nights, sweating blood, thinking the bank would foreclose at any minute. I couldn't dump that in your lap."

Meg's mouth dropped open. She'd known the O'Ballivans weren't rich, at least, not like the McKettricks were, but she'd never imagined, even once, that Stone Creek Ranch was in danger of being lost.

"They wanted that land," Brad went on. "The bankers, I mean. They already had the plans drawn up for a housing development."

"I didn't know—I would have helped—"

"Sure," Brad said. "You'd have helped. And I'd never have been able to look you in the face again. I had one chance, Meg. Valerie's dad had heard my demo and he was willing to give me an audition. A fifteen-minute slot in his busy day. I tried to tell you—"

Meg closed her eyes for a moment, remembering. Brad had told her he wanted to postpone the wedding until after his trip to Nashville. He'd promised to come back for her. She'd been furious and hurt—and keeping a secret of her own—and they'd argued….

She swallowed painfully. "You didn't call. You didn't write—"

"When I got to Nashville, I had a used bus ticket and a guitar. If I'd called, it would have been collect, and I wasn't *about* to do that. I started half a dozen letters, but they all sounded like the lyrics to bad songs. I went to the library a couple of times, to send you an email, but beyond 'how are you?' I just flat-out didn't know what to say."

"So you just hooked up with Valerie?"

"It wasn't like that."

"I'm assuming she was a rich kid, just like me? I guess you didn't mind if *she* saved the old homestead with a chunk of her trust fund."

Brad's jawline tightened. "*I* saved the ranch," he said. "Most of the money from my first record contract went to paying down the mortgage, and it was still a struggle until I scored a major hit." He paused, obviously remembering the much leaner days before he could fill the biggest stadiums in the country with devoted fans, swaying to his music in the darkness, holding flickering lighters aloft in tribute. "I didn't love Valerie, and she didn't love me. She was a rich kid, all right. Spoiled and lonesome, neglected in the ways rich kids so often are, and she was in big trouble. She'd gotten herself pregnant by some married guy who wanted nothing to do with her. She figured her dad would kill her if he found out, and given his temper, I tended to agree. So I married her."

Meg made her way back to the table and sank into her chair. "There was…a baby?"

"She miscarried. We divorced amicably, after trying to make it work for a couple of years. She's married to a dentist now, and really happy. Four kids, at last count." Brad joined Meg at the table. "Do you want to hear about the second marriage?"

"I don't think I'm up to that," Meg said weakly.

Brad's hand closed over hers. "Me, either," he replied. He ducked his head, in a familiar way that tugged at Meg's heart, to catch her eye. "You all right?"

"Just a little shaken up, that's all."

"How about some supper?"

"They serve supper here? At Jolene's?"

Brad chuckled. "Down the road, at the Steakhouse. You can't miss it—it's right next to the sign that says Welcome To Stone Creek, Arizona, Home Of Brad O'Ballivan."

"Braggart," Meg said, grateful that the conversation had taken a lighter turn.

He grinned engagingly. "Stone Creek has always been the home of Brad O'Ballivan," he said. "It just seems to mean more now than it did when I left that first time."

"You'll be mobbed," Meg warned.

"The whole town could show up at the Steakhouse, and it wouldn't be enough to make a mob."

"Okay," Meg agreed. "But you're buying."

Brad laughed. "Fair enough," he said.

Then he got up from his chair and summoned the bartender, who'd evidently been cooling his heels in a storeroom or office.

The floor felt oddly spongy beneath Meg's feet, and she was light-headed enough to wonder if there'd been some alcohol in that iced tea after all.

The Steakhouse, unlike Jolene's, was jumping. People called out to Brad when he came in, and young girls pointed and giggled, but most of them had been at the welcome party Ashley and Melissa had thrown for him on the ranch the night before, so some of the novelty of his being back in town had worn off.

Meg drew some glances, though—all of them admiring, with varying degrees of curiosity mixed in. Even in jeans, boots and a plain woolen coat over a white blouse, she looked like what she was—a McKettrick with a trust fund and an impressive track record as a top-level executive. When McKettrickCo had gone public, Brad had been surprised when she didn't turn up immediately as the CEO of some corporation. Instead, she'd come home to hibernate on the Triple M, and he wondered why.

He wondered lots of things about Meg McKettrick.

With luck, he'd have a chance to find out everything he wanted to know.

Like whether she still laughed in her sleep and ate cereal with yogurt instead of milk and arched her back like a gymnast when she climaxed.

Since the Steakhouse was no place to think about Meg having one of her noisy orgasms, Brad tried to put the image out of his mind. It merely shifted to another part of his anatomy.

They were shown to a booth right away, and given menus and glasses of water with the obligatory slices of fresh lemon rafting on top of the ice.

Brad ordered a steak, Meg a Caesar salad.

The waitress went away, albeit reluctantly.

"Okay," Brad said, "it's my turn to ask questions. Why did you quit working after you left McKettrickCo?"

Meg smiled, but she looked a little flushed, and he could tell by her eyes that she was busy in there, sorting things and putting them in their proper places. "I didn't need the money. And I've always wanted to live full-time on the Triple M, like Jesse and Rance and Keegan. When I spent summers there, as a child, the only way I could deal with leaving in the fall to go back to school was to promise myself that one day I'd come home to stay."

"You love it that much?" Given his own attachment to Stone Creek Ranch, Brad could understand, but at the same time, the knowledge troubled him a little, too. "What do you do all day?"

Her mouth quirked in a way that made Brad want to kiss her. And do a few other things, too. "You sound like my mother," she said. "I take care of the horses, ride some-times—"

He nodded. Waited.

She didn't finish the sentence.

"You never married." He hadn't meant to say that. Hadn't meant to let on that he'd kept track of her all these years, mostly on the Internet, but through his sisters, too.

She shook her head. "Almost," she said. "Once. It didn't work out."

Brad leaned forward, intrigued and feeling pretty damn territorial, too. "Who was the unlucky guy? He must have been a real jackass."

"You," she replied sweetly, and then laughed at the expression on his face.

He started to speak, then gulped the words down, sure they'd come out sounding as stupid as the question he'd just asked.

"I've dated a lot of men," Meg said.

The orgasm image returned, but this time, he wasn't Meg's partner. It was some other guy bringing her to one of her long, exquisite, clawing, shouting, bucking climaxes, not him. He frowned.

"Maybe we shouldn't talk about my love life," she suggested.

"Maybe not," Brad agreed.

"Not that I exactly have one."

Brad felt immeasurably better. "That makes two of us."

Meg looked unconvinced. Even squirmed a little on the vinyl seat.

"What?" Brad prompted, enjoying the play of emotions on her face. He and Meg weren't on good terms—too soon for that—but it was a hopeful sign that she'd met him at Jolene's and then agreed to supper on top of it.

"I saw that article in *People* magazine. 'The Cowboy with the Most Notches on His Bedpost,' I think it was called?"

"I thought we weren't going to talk about our love lives. And would you mind keeping your voice down?"

"We agreed not to talk about *mine,* if I remember correctly, which, as I told you, is nonexistent. And to avoid the subject of your second wife—at least, for now."

"There have been women," Brad said. "But that bedpost thing was all Phil's idea. Publicity stuff."

The food arrived.

"Not that I care if you carve notches on your bedpost," Meg said decisively, once the waitress had left again.

"Right," Brad replied, serious on the outside, grinning on the inside.

"Where is this Phil person from, anyway?" Meg asked, mildly disgruntled, her fork poised in midair over her salad. "Seems to me he has a pretty skewed idea on the whole cowboy mystique. Rehab. Trashing hotel rooms. The notch thing."

"There's a 'cowboy mystique'?"

"You know there is. Honor, integrity, courage—those are the things being a cowboy is all about."

Brad sighed. Meg was a stickler for detail; good thing she hadn't gone to law school, like she'd once planned. She probably would have represented his second ex-wife in the divorce and stripped his stock portfolio clean. "I tried. Phil works freestyle, and he sure knew how to pack the concert halls."

Meg pointed the fork at him. "*You* packed the concert halls, Brad. You and your music."

"You like my music?" It was a shy question; he hadn't quite dared to ask if she liked *him* as well. He knew too well what the answer might be.

"It's…nice," she said.

Nice? Half a dozen Grammies and CMT awards, weeks at number one on every chart that mattered, and she thought his music was "nice"?

Whatever she thought, Brad finally concluded, that was all she was going to give up, and he had to be satisfied with it.

For now.

He started on the steak, but he hadn't eaten more than two bites when there was a fuss at the entrance to the restaurant and Livie came storming in, striding right to his table.

Sparing a nod for Meg, Brad's sister turned immediately to him. "He's hurt," she said. Her clothes were covered with straw and a few things that would have upset the health department, being that she was in a place where food was being served to the general public.

"Who's hurt?" Brad asked calmly, sliding out of the booth to stand.

"Ransom," she answered, near tears. "He got himself cut up in a tangle of rusty barbed wire. I'd spotted him with binoculars, but before I could get there to help, he'd torn free and headed for the hills. He's hurt bad, and I'm not going to be able to get to him in the Suburban—we need to saddle up and go after him."

"Liv," Brad said carefully, "it's dark out."

"He's *bleeding,* and probably weak. The wolves could take him down!" At the thought of that, Livie's eyes glistened with moisture. "If you won't help, I'll go by myself."

Distractedly, Brad pulled out his wallet and threw down the money for the dinner he and Meg hadn't gotten a chance to finish.

Meg was on her feet, the salad forgotten. "Count me in,

Olivia," she said. "That is, if you've got an extra horse and some gear. I could go back out to the Triple M for Banshee, but by the time I hitched up the trailer, loaded him and gathered the tack—"

"You can ride Cinnamon," Olivia told Meg, after sizing her up as to whether she'd be a help or a hindrance on the trail. "It'll be cold and dark up there in the high country," she added. "Could be a long, uncomfortable night."

"No room service?" Meg quipped.

Livie spared her a smile, but when she turned to Brad again, her blue eyes were full of obstinate challenge. "Are you going or not—cowboy?"

"Hell, yes, I'm going," Brad said. Riding a horse was a thing you never forgot how to do, but it had been a while since he'd been in the saddle, and that meant he'd be groaning-sore before this adventure was over. "What about the stock on the Triple M, Meg? Who's going to feed your horses, if this takes all night?"

"They're good till morning," Meg answered. "If I'm not back by then, I'll ask Jesse or Rance or Keegan to check on them."

Livie led the caravan in her Suburban, with Brad following in his truck, and Meg right behind, in the Blazer. He was worried about Ransom, and about Livie's obsession with the animal, but there was one bright spot in the whole thing.

He was going to get to spend the night with Meg McKettrick, albeit on the hard, half-frozen ground, and the least he could do, as a gentleman, was share his sleeping bag—and his body warmth.

"Right smart of you to go along," Angus commented, appearing in the passenger seat of Meg's rig. "There might be some hope for you yet."

Meg answered without moving her mouth, just in case Brad happened to glance into his rearview mirror and catch her talking to nobody. "I thought you were giving me some elbow room on this one," she said.

"Don't worry," Angus replied. "If you go to bed down with him or something like that, I'll skedaddle."

"I'm not going to 'bed down' with Brad O'Ballivan."

Angus sighed. Adjusted his sweat-stained cowboy hat. Since he usually didn't wear one, Meg read it as a sign bad weather was on its way. "Might be a good thing if you did. Only way to snag some men."

"I will not dignify that remark with a reply," Meg said, flooring the gas pedal to keep up with Brad, now that they were out on the open road, where the speed limit was higher. She'd never actually been to Stone Creek Ranch, but she knew where it was. Knew all about King's Ransom, too. Her cousin Jesse, practically a horse-whisperer, claimed the animal was nothing more than a legend, pieced together around a hundred campfires, over as many years, after all the lesser tales had been told.

Meg wanted to see for herself.

Wanted to help Olivia, whom she'd always liked but barely knew.

Spending the night on a mountain with Brad O'Ballivan didn't enter into the decision at all. Much.

"Is he real?" she asked. "The horse, I mean?"

Angus adjusted his hat again. "Sure he is," he said, his voice quiet, but gruff. Sometimes a look came into his eyes, a sort of hunger for the old days and the old ways.

"Is there anything you can do to help us find him?"

Angus shook his head. "You've got to do that yourselves, you and the singing cowboy and the girl."

"Olivia is not a girl. She's a grown woman and a veterinarian."

"She's a snippet," Angus said. "But there's fire in her. That O'Ballivan blood runs hot as coffee brewed on a cookstove in hell. She needs a man, though. The knot in *her* lasso is way too tight."

"I hope that reference wasn't sexual," Meg said stiffly, "because I do *not* need to be carrying on that type of conversation with my dead multi-great grandfather."

"It makes me feel old when you talk about me like I helped Moses carry the commandments down off the mountain," Angus complained. "I was young once, you know. Sired four strapping sons and a daughter by three different women—Ellie, Georgia and Concepcion. And I'm not dead, neither. Just...different."

Olivia had stopped suddenly for a gate up ahead, and Meg nearly rear-ended Brad before she got the Blazer reined in.

"Different as in dead," Meg said, watching through the windshield, in the glow of her headlights, as Brad got out of his truck and strode back to speak to her, leaving the driver's-side door gaping behind him.

He didn't look angry—just earnest.

"If you want to ride with me," he said when Meg had buzzed down her window, "fine. But if you're planning to drive this rig up into the bed of my truck, you might want to wait until I park it in a hole and lower the tailgate."

"Sorry," Meg said after making a face.

Brad shook his head and went back to his truck. By then, Olivia had the gate open, and he drove ahead onto an unpaved road winding upward between the juniper and Joshua trees clinging to the red dirt of the hillside.

"What was that about?" Meg mused, following Brad and Olivia's vehicles through the gap and not really addressing Angus, who answered, nonetheless.

"Guess he's prideful about the paint on that fancy jitney of his," he said. "Didn't want you denting up his buggy."

Meg didn't comment. Angus was full of the nineteenth-century equivalent of "woman driver" stories, and she didn't care to hear any of them.

They topped a rise, Olivia still in the lead, and dipped down into what was probably a broad valley, given what little Meg knew about the landscape on Stone Creek Ranch. Lights glimmered off to the right, revealing a good-size house and a barn.

Meg was about to ask if Angus had ever visited the ranch when he suddenly vanished.

She shut off the Blazer, got out and followed Brad and Olivia toward the barn. She wished it hadn't been so dark—it would have been interesting to see the place in the daylight.

Inside the barn, which was as big as any of the ones on the Triple M and boasted all the modern conveniences, Olivia and Brad were already saddling horses.

"That's Cinnamon over there," Olivia said with a nod to a tall chestnut in the stall across the wide breezeway from the one she was standing in, busily preparing a palomino to ride. "His gear's in the tack room, third saddle rack on the right."

Meg didn't hesitate, as she suspected Olivia had expected her to do, but found the tack room and Cinnamon's gear, and lugged it back to his stall. Brad and his sister were already mounted and waiting at the end of the breezeway when Meg led the gelding out, however.

"Need a boost?" Brad asked, in a teasing drawl, saddle leather creaking as he shifted to step down from the big paint he was riding and help Meg mount up.

Cinnamon was a big fella, taller by several hands than any of the horses in Meg's barn, but she'd been riding since she was in diapers, and she didn't need a boost from a "singing cowboy," as Angus described Brad.

"I can do it," she replied, straining to grip the saddle horn and get a foot into the high stirrup. It was going to be a stretch.

In the next instant, she felt two strong hands pushing on her backside, hoisting her easily onto Cinnamon's broad back.

Thanks, Angus, she said silently.

CHAPTER FOUR

IT WAS A PURELY CRAZY thing to do, setting out on horseback, in the dark, for the high plains and meadows and secret canyons of Stone Creek Ranch, in search of a legendary stallion determined not to be found. It had been way too long since she'd done anything like it, Meg reflected, as she rode behind Olivia and Brad, on the borrowed horse called Cinnamon.

Olivia had brought a few veterinary supplies along, packed in saddle bags, and while Meg was sure Ransom, wounded or not, would elude them, she couldn't help admiring the kind of commitment it took to set out on the journey anyway. Olivia O'Ballivan was a woman with a cause and for that, Meg envied her a little.

The moon was three-quarters full, and lit their way, but the trail grew steadily narrower as they climbed, and the mountainside was steep and rocky. One misstep on the part of a distracted horse and both animal and rider would plunge hundreds of feet into an abyss of shadow, to their very certain and very painful deaths.

When the trail widened into what appeared, in the thin wash of moonlight, to be a clearing, Meg let out her breath, sat a little less tensely in the saddle, loosened her grip on Cinnamon's reins. Brad drew up his own mount to wait for her, while Olivia and her horse shot forward, intent on their mission.

"Do you think we'll find him?" Meg asked. "Ransom, I mean?"

"No," Brad answered, unequivocally. "But Livie was bound to try. I came to look out for her."

Meg hadn't noticed the rifle in the scabbard fixed to Brad's saddle before, back at the O'Ballivan barn, but it stood out in sharp relief now, the polished wooden stock glowing in a silvery flash of moonlight. He must have seen her eyes widen; he patted the scabbard as he met her gaze.

"You're expecting to shoot something?" Meg ventured. She'd been around guns all her life—they were plentiful on the Triple M—but that didn't mean she liked them.

"Only if I have to," Brad said, casting a glance in the direction Olivia had gone. He nudged his horse into motion, and Cinnamon automatically kept pace, the two geldings moving at an easy trot.

"What would constitute having to?" Meg asked.

"Wolves," Brad answered.

Meg was familiar with the wolf controversy—environmentalists and animal activists on the one side, ranchers on the other. She wanted to know where Brad stood on the subject. He was well-known for his love of all things finned, feathered and furry—but that might have been part of his carefully constructed persona, like the notched bedpost and the trashed hotel rooms.

"You wouldn't just pick them off, would you? Wolves, I mean?"

"Of course not," Brad replied. "But wolves are predators, and Livie's not wrong to be concerned that they'll track Ransom and take him down if they catch the blood-scent from his wounds."

A chill trickled down Meg's spine, like a splash of cold water, setting her shivering. Like Brad, she came from a long line of cattle ranchers, and while she allowed that wolves had a place in the ecological scheme of things, like every other creature on earth, she didn't romanticize them. They were not misunderstood *dogs,* as so many people seemed to think, but hunters, savagely brutal and utterly ruthless, and no one who'd ever seen what they did to their prey would credit them with nobility.

"Sharks with legs," she mused aloud. "That's what Rance calls them."

Brad nodded, but didn't reply. They were gaining on Olivia now; she was still a ways ahead, and had dismounted to look at something on the ground.

Both Brad and Meg sped up to reach her.

By the time they arrived, Olivia's saddle bags were open beside her, and she was holding a syringe up to the light. Because of the darkness, and the movements of the horses, a few moments passed before Meg focused on the animal Olivia was treating.

A dog lay bloody and quivering on its side.

Brad was off his horse before Meg broke the spell of shock that had descended over her and dismounted, too. Her stomach rolled when she got a better look at the dog; the poor creature, surely a stray, had run afoul of either a wolf or coyote pack, and it was purely a miracle that he'd survived.

Meg's eyes burned.

Brad crouched next to the dog, opposite Olivia, and stroked the animal with a gentleness that altered something deep down inside Meg, causing a grinding sensation, like the shift of tectonic plates far beneath the earth.

"Can he make it?" he asked Olivia.

"I'm not sure," Olivia replied. "At the very least, he needs stitches." She injected the contents of the syringe into the animal's ruff. "I sedated him. Give the medicine a few minutes to work, and then we'll take him back to the clinic in Stone Creek."

"What about the horse?" Meg asked, feeling helpless, a bystander with no way to help. She wasn't used to it. "What about Ransom?"

Olivia's eyes were bleak with sorrow when she looked up at Meg. She was a veterinarian; she couldn't abandon the wounded dog, or put him to sleep because it would be more convenient than transporting him back to town, where he could be properly cared for. But worry for the stallion would prey on her mind, just the same.

"I'll look for him tomorrow," Olivia said. "In the daylight."

Brad reached across the dog, laid a hand on his sister's shoulder. "He's been surviving on his own for a long time, Liv," he assured her. "Ransom will be all right."

Olivia bit her lower lip, nodded. "Get one of the sleeping bags, will you?" she said.

Brad nodded and went to unfasten the bedroll from behind his saddle. They were miles from town, or any ranch house.

"How did a dog get all the way out here?" Meg asked, mostly because the silence was too painful.

"He's probably a stray," Olivia answered, between soothing murmurs to the dog. "Somebody might have dumped him, too, down on the highway. A lot of people think dogs and cats can survive on their own—hunt and all that nonsense."

Meg drew closer to the dog, crouched to touch his head. He appeared to be some kind of lab-retriever mix, though it was hard to tell, given that his coat was saturated with blood. He wore no collar, but that didn't mean he didn't have a microchip—and if he did, Olivia would be able to identify him immediately, once she got him to the clinic.

Though from the looks of him, he'd be lucky to make it that far.

Brad returned with the sleeping bag, unfurling it. "Okay to move him now?" he asked Olivia.

Olivia nodded, and she and Meg sort of helped each other to their feet. "You mount up," Olivia told Brad. "And we'll lift him."

Brad whistled softly for his horse, which trotted obediently to his side, gathered the dangling reins, and swung up into the saddle.

Meg and Olivia bundled the dog, now mercifully unconscious, in the sleeping bag and, together, hoisted him high enough so Brad could take him into his arms. They all rode slowly back down the trail, Brad holding that dog as tenderly as he would an injured child, and not a word was spoken the whole way.

When they got back to the ranch house, where Olivia's Suburban was parked, Brad loaded the dog into the rear of the vehicle.

"I'll stay and put the horses away," Meg told him. "You'd better go into town with Olivia and help her get him inside the clinic."

Brad nodded. "Thanks," he said gruffly.

Olivia gave Meg an appreciative glance before scrambling into the back of the Suburban to ride with the patient, ambulance-style. Brad got behind the wheel.

Once they'd driven off, Meg gathered the trio of horses and led them into the barn. There, in the breezeway, she removed their saddles and other tack and let the animals show her which stalls were their own. She checked their hooves for stones, made sure their automatic waterers were working, and gave them each a flake of hay. All the while, her thoughts were with Brad, and the stray dog lying in the back of Olivia's rig.

A part of her wanted to get into the Blazer and head straight for Stone Creek, and the veterinary clinic where Olivia worked, but she knew she'd just be in the way. Brad could provide muscle and moral support, if not medical skills, but Meg had nothing to offer.

With the O'Ballivans' horses attended to, she fired up the Blazer and headed back toward Indian Rock. She covered the miles between Stone Creek Ranch and the Triple M in a daze, and was a little startled to find herself at home when she pulled up in front of the garage door.

Leaving the Blazer in the driveway, Meg went into the barn to look in on Banshee and the four other horses who resided there. On the Triple M, horses were continually rotated between her place, Jesse's, Rance's and Keegan's, depending on what was best for the animals. Now they blinked at her, sleepily surprised by a late-night visit, and she paused to stroke each one of their long faces before starting for the house.

Angus fell into step with her as she crossed the side yard, headed for the back door.

"The stallion's all right," he informed her. "Holed up in one of the little canyons, nursing his wounds."

"I thought you said you couldn't help find him," Meg said, stopping to stare up at her ancestor in the moonlight.

"Turned out I was wrong," Angus drawled. His hat was gone; the bad weather he'd probably been expecting hadn't materialized.

"Mark the calendar," Meg teased. "I just heard a McKettrick admit to being wrong about something."

Angus grinned, waited on the small, open back porch while she unlocked the kitchen door. In his day, locks hadn't been necessary. Now the houses on the Triple M were no more immune to the rising crime rate than anyplace else.

"I've been wrong about plenty in my life," Angus said. "For one thing, I was wrong to leave Holt behind in Texas, after his mother died. He was just a baby, and God knows what I'd have done with him on the trail between there and the Arizona Territory, but I should have brought him, nonetheless. Raised him with Rafe and Kade and Jeb."

Intrigued, Meg opened the door, flipped on the kitchen lights and stepped inside. All of this was ancient family history to her, but to Angus, it was immediate stuff. "What else were you wrong about?" she asked, removing her coat and hanging it on the peg next to the door, then going to the sink to wash her hands.

Angus took a seat at the head of the table. In this house, it would have been Holt's place, but Angus was in the habit of taking the lead, even in small things.

"I ever tell you I had a brother?" he asked.

Meg, about to brew a pot of tea, stopped and stared at him, stunned out of her fatigue. "No," she said. "You didn't." The McKettricks were raised on legend and lore, cut their teeth on it; the brother came as news. "Are you telling me there could be a whole other branch of the family out there?"

"Josiah got on fine with the ladies," Angus reminisced. "It would be my guess his tribe is as big as mine."

Meg forgot all about the tea-brewing. She made her way to the table and sat down heavily on the bench, gaping at Angus.

"Don't fret about it," he said. "They'd have no claim on this ranch, or any of the take from that McKettrickCo outfit."

Meg blinked, still trying to assimilate the revelation. "No one has *ever* mentioned that you had a brother," she said. "In all the diaries, all the letters, all the photographs—"

"They wouldn't have said anything about Josiah," Angus

told her, evidently referring to his sons and their many descendents. "They never knew he existed."

"Why not?"

"Because he and I had a falling-out, and I didn't want anything to do with him after that. He felt the same way."

"Why bring it up now—after a century and a half?"

Angus shifted uncomfortably in his chair and, for a moment, his jawline hardened. "One of them's about to land on your doorstep," he said after a long, molar-grinding silence. "I figured you ought to be warned."

"*Warned?* Is this person a serial killer or a crook or something?"

"No," Angus said. "He's a lawyer. And that's damn near as bad."

"As a family, we haven't exactly kept a low profile for the last hundred or so years," Meg said slowly. "If Josiah has as many descendants as you do, why haven't any of them contacted us? It's not as if McKettrick is a common name, after all."

"Josiah took another name," Angus allowed, after more jaw-clamping. "That's what we got into it about, him and me."

"Why would he do that?" Meg asked.

Angus fixed her with a glare. Clearly, even after all the time that passed, he hadn't forgiven Josiah for changing his name and for whatever had prompted him to do that.

"He went to sea, when he was hardly more than a boy," Angus said. "When he came back home to Texas, years later, he was calling himself by another handle and running from the law. Hinted that he'd been a pirate."

"A *pirate?*"

"Left Ma and me to get by on our own, after Pa died," Angus recalled bitterly, looking through Meg to some long-ago reality. "Rode out before they'd finished shoveling dirt into Pa's grave. I ran down the road after him—he was riding a big buckskin horse—but he didn't even look back."

Tentatively, Meg reached out to touch Angus's arm. Clearly, Josiah had been the elder brother, and Angus a lot younger. He'd adored Josiah McKettrick—that much was plain—and his leaving had been a defining event in Angus's life. So defining, in fact, that he'd never acknowledged the other man's existence.

Angus bristled. "It was a long time ago," he said.

"What name did he go by?" Meg asked. She knew she wasn't going to sleep, for worrying about the injured dog and the stallion, and planned to spend the rest of the night at the computer, searching on Google for members of the heretofore unknown Josiah-side of the family.

"I don't rightly recall," Angus said glumly.

Meg knew he was lying. She also knew he wasn't going to tell her his brother's assumed name.

She got up again, went back to brewing tea.

Angus sat brooding in silence, and the phone rang just as Meg was pouring boiling water over the loose tea leaves in the bottom of Lorelei's pot.

Glancing at the caller ID panel, she saw no name, just an unfamiliar number with a 615 area code.

"Hello?"

"He's going to recover," Brad said.

Tears rushed to Meg's eyes, and her throat constricted. He was referring to the dog, of course. And using the cell phone he'd carried when he still lived in Tennessee. "Thank God," she managed to say. "Did Olivia operate?"

"No need," Brad answered. "Once she'd taken X-rays and run a scan, she knew there were no internal injuries. He's pretty torn up—looks like a baseball with all those stitches—but he'll be okay."

"Was there a microchip?"

"Yeah," Brad said after a charged silence. "But the phone number's no longer in service. Livie ran an internet search and found out the original owner died six months ago. Who knows where Willie's been in the meantime."

"Willie?"

"The dog," Brad explained. "That's his name. Willie."

"What's going to happen to Willie now?"

"He'll be at the clinic for a while," Brad said. "He's in pretty bad shape. Livie will try to find out if anybody adopted him after his owner died, but we're not holding out a lot of hope on that score."

"He'll go to the pound? When he's well enough to leave the clinic?"

"No," Brad answered. He sounded as tired as Meg felt. "If nobody has a prior claim on him, he'll come to live with me. I could use a friend—and so could he." He paused. "I hope I didn't wake you or anything."

"I was still up," Meg said, glancing in Angus's direction only to find that he'd disappeared again.

"Good," Brad replied.

A silence fell between them. Meg knew there was something else Brad wanted to say, and that she'd want to hear it. So she waited.

"I'm riding up into the high country again first thing in the morning," he finally said. "Looking for Ransom. I was wondering if—well—it's probably a stupid idea, but—"

Meg waited, resisting an urge to rush in and finish the sentence for him.

"Would you like to go along? Livie has a full schedule tomorrow—one of the other vets is out sick—and she wants to keep an eye on Willie, too. She's going to obsess about this horse until I can tell her he's fine, so I'm going to find him if I can."

"I'd like to go," Meg said. "What time are you leaving the ranch?"

"Soon as the sun's up," Brad answered. "You're sure? The country's pretty rough up there."

"If you can handle rough country, O'Ballivan, so can I."

He chuckled. "Okay, McKettrick," he said.

Meg found herself smiling. "I'll be there by 6:00 a.m., unless that's too early. Shall I bring my own horse?"

"Six is about right," Brad said. "Don't go to the trouble of trailering another horse—you can ride Cinnamon. Dress warm, though. And bring whatever gear you'd need if we had to spend the night for some reason."

Alone in her kitchen, Meg blushed. "See you in the morning," she said.

"'Night," Brad replied.

"Good night," Meg responded—long after Brad had hung up.

Giving up on the tea and, at least for that night, researching Josiah McKettrick, and having decided she needed to at least *try* to sleep, since tomorrow would be an eventful day, Meg locked up, shut off the lights and went upstairs to her room.

After getting out a pair of thermal pajamas, she took a long shower in the main bathroom across the hall, brushed her teeth, tamed her wet hair as best she could and went to bed.

Far from tossing and turning, as she'd half expected, she dropped into an immediate, consuming slumber, so deep she remembered none of her dreams.

Waking, she dressed quickly, in jeans and a sweatshirt, over a set of long underwear, made of some miraculous microfiber and bought for skiing, and finished off her ensemble with two pairs of socks and her sturdiest pair of boots. She shoved toothpaste, a brush and a small tube of moisturizer into a plastic storage bag, rolled up a blanket, tied it tightly with twine from the kitchen junk drawer and breakfasted on toast and coffee.

She called Jesse on her cell phone as she climbed into the Blazer, after feeding Banshee and the others. Cheyenne, Jesse's wife, answered on the second ring.

"Hi, it's Meg. Is Jesse around?"

"Sleeping," Cheyenne said, yawning audibly.

"I woke you up," Meg said, embarrassed.

"Jesse's the lay-abed in this family," Cheyenne responded warmly. "I've been up since four. Is anything wrong, Meg? Sierra and the baby—?"

"They're fine, as far as I know," Meg said, anxious to reassure Cheyenne and, at the same time, very glad she'd gotten Jesse's wife instead of Jesse himself. He'd look after her horses if she asked, but he'd want to know where she was going, and if she replied that she and Brad O'Ballivan were riding off into the sunrise together, he'd tease her unmercifully. "Look, Cheyenne, I need a favor. I'm going on a—on a trail ride with a friend, and I'll probably be back tonight, but—"

"Would this 'friend' be the famous Brad O'Ballivan?"

"Yes," Meg said, but reluctantly, backing out of the driveway and turning the Blazer around to head for Stone Creek. It was still dark, but the first pinkish gold rays of sunlight were rimming the eastern hills. "Cheyenne, will you ask Jesse to check on my horses if he doesn't hear from me by six or so tonight?"

"Of course," Cheyenne said. "So you're going riding with Brad, and it might turn into an overnight thing. Hmm—"

"It isn't anything romantic," Meg said. "I'm just helping him look for a stallion that might be hurt, that's all."

"I see," Cheyenne said sweetly.

"Just out of curiosity, what made you jump to the conclusion that the friend I mentioned was Brad?"

"It's all over town that you and country music's baddest bad boy met up at the Dixie Dog Drive-In the other day."

"Oh, great," Meg breathed. "I guess that means Jesse knows, then. And Rance and Keegan."

Cheyenne laughed softly, but when she spoke, her voice was full of concern. "Rance and Jesse are all for finding Brad and punching his lights out for hurting you so badly all those years ago, but Keegan is the voice of reason. He says give Brad a week to prove himself, *then* punch his lights out."

"The McKettrick way," Meg said. Her cousins were as protective as brothers would have been, and she loved them. But in terms of her social life, they weren't any more help than Angus had been.

"We'll talk later," Cheyenne said practically. "You're probably driving."

"Thanks, Chey," Meg answered.

When she got to Stone Creek Ranch, Brad came out of the house to greet her. He was dressed for the trail in jeans, boots, a work shirt and a medium-weight leather coat.

Meg's breath caught at the sight of him, and she was glad of the mechanics of parking and shutting off the Blazer, because it gave her a few moments to gather her composure.

Normally, she was unflappable.

She'd handled some of the toughest negotiations during her career with McKettrickCo, without so much as a flutter of nerves, but there was something about Brad that erased all the years she'd spent developing a thick skin and a poker face.

He opened the Blazer door before she was quite ready to face him.

"Hungry?" he asked.

"I had toast and coffee at home," Meg answered.

"That'll never hold you till lunch," he said. "Come on inside. I've got some *real* food on the stove."

"Okay," Meg said, because short of sitting stubbornly in the car, she couldn't think of a way to avoid accepting his invitation.

The O'Ballivan house, like the ones on the Triple M, was large and rustic, and it exuded a sense of rich history. The porch wrapped around the whole front of the structure, and the back door was on the side nearest the barn. Meg followed Brad up the porch steps in front and around to another entrance.

The kitchen was big, and except for the wooden floors, which looked venerable, the room showed no trace of the old days. The countertops were granite, the cupboards gleamed, and the appliances were ultramodern, as were the furnishings.

Meg felt strangely let down by the sheer glamour of the place. All the kitchens on the Triple M had been modernized, of course, but in all cases, the original wood-burning stoves had been incorporated, and the tables all dated back to Holt, Rafe, Kade and Jeb's time, if not Angus's.

If Brad noticed her reaction, he didn't mention it. He dished up an omelet for her, and poured her a cup of coffee.

"You cook?" Meg teased, washing her hands at the gleaming stainless steel sink.

"I'm a fair hand in a kitchen," Brad replied modestly. "Dig in. I'll go saddle the horses while you eat."

Meg nodded, sat down and tackled the omelet.

It was delicious, and so was the coffee, but she felt uncomfortable sitting alone in that kitchen, as fancy as it was. She kept wondering what Maddie O'Ballivan would think, if she could see it, or even Brad's mother. Surely if things had been as difficult financially as Brad had let on the night before, at Jolene's, the renovations were fairly recent.

Having eaten as much as she could, Meg rinsed her plate, stuck it into the dishwasher, along with her fork and coffee cup, and hurried to the back door. Brad was out in front of the barn, the big paint ready to ride, tightening the cinch on Cinnamon's saddle. He picked her rolled blanket up off the ground and tied it on behind.

"Not much gear," he said. "Do you know how cold it gets up there?"

"I'll be fine," Meg said.

Brad merely shook his head. His own horse was restless, and the rifle was in evidence, too, looking ominous in the worn scabbard.

"That's quite a kitchen," Meg said as Brad gave her a leg up onto Cinnamon's back.

"Big John said it was a waste of money," Brad recalled, smiling to himself as he mounted up. "That was my granddad."

Meg knew who Big John O'Ballivan was—everybody in the county did—but she didn't point that out. If Brad wanted to talk about his family, to pass the time, that was fine with Meg. She nudged Cinnamon to keep pace with Brad's horse as they crossed a pasture, headed for the hills beyond.

"He raised you and your sisters, didn't he?" she asked, though she knew that, too.

"Yes," Brad said, and the set of his jaw reminded her of the way Angus's had looked, when he told her about his estranged brother.

Meg's curiosity spiked, but she didn't indulge it. "I take it Willie's still on the mend?"

Brad's grin was as dazzling as the coming sunrise would

be. "Olivia called just before you showed up," he said with a nod. "Willie's going to be fine. In a week or two, I'll bring him home."

Remembering the way Brad had handled the dog, with such gentleness and such strength, Meg felt a pinch in the center of her heart. "You plan on staying, then?"

He tossed her a thoughtful look. "I plan on staying," he confirmed. "I told you that, didn't I?"

You also told me we'd get married and you'd love me forever.

"You told me," she said.

"Would this be a good time to tell you about my second wife?"

Meg considered, then shook her head, smiling a little. "Probably not."

"Okay," Brad said, "then how about my sisters?"

"Good idea." Meg had known Olivia slightly, but there was a set of twins in the family, too. She'd never met them.

"Olivia has a thing for animals, as you can see. She needs to get married and channel some of that energy into having a family of her own, but she's got a cussed streak and runs off every man who manages to get close to her. Ashley and Melissa—the twins—are fraternal. Ashley's pretty down-home—she runs a bed-and-breakfast in Stone Creek. Melissa's clerking in a law office in Flagstaff."

"You're close to them?"

"Yes," Brad said, expelling a long breath. "And, no. Olivia resents my leaving home— I can't seem to get it through her head that we wouldn't have *had* a home if I hadn't gone to Nashville. The twins are ten years younger than I am, and seem to see me more as a visiting celebrity than their big brother."

"When Olivia needed help," Meg reminded him, "she

came to you. So maybe she doesn't resent you as much as you think she does." There was something really different about Olivia O'Ballivan, Meg thought, looking back over the night before, but she couldn't quite figure out what it was.

"I hope you're right," Brad said. "It's fine to love animals—I'm real fond of them myself. But Olivia carries it to a whole new place. So much so that there's no room in her life for much of anything—or anybody—else."

"She's a veterinarian, Brad," Meg said reasonably. "It's natural that animals are her passion."

"To the exclusion of everything else?" Brad asked.

"She'll be fine," Meg said. "When Olivia meets the right man, she'll make room for him. Just wait and see."

Brad looked unconvinced. He raised his chin and said, "If we're going to find that horse, we'd better move a little faster."

Meg nodded in agreement and Cinnamon fell in behind Brad's gelding as they started the twisting, perilous climb up the mountainside.

CHAPTER FIVE

LOOKING FOR THAT WILD STALLION was a fool's errand, and Brad knew it. As he'd told Meg, his primary reason for undertaking the quest was to keep Olivia from doing it. Now he wondered how many times, during his long absence, his little sister had climbed this mountain alone, at all hours of the day and night, and in all seasons of the year.

The thought made him shudder.

The country above Stone Creek was as rugged as it had ever been. Wolves, coyotes and even javelinas were plentiful, as were rattlesnakes. There were deep crevices in the red earth, some of them hidden by brush, and they'd swallowed many a hapless hiker. But the worst threat was probably the weather—at that elevation, blizzards could strike literally without warning, even in July and August. It was October now, and that only increased the danger.

Meg, shivering in her too-light coat, rode along beside him without complaint. Being a McKettrick, he thought, with a sad smile turned entirely inward, she'd freeze to death before she'd admit she was cold.

Inviting her along had been a purely selfish act, and Brad regretted it. Too many things could happen, most of them bad.

They'd been traveling for an hour or so when he stopped alongside a creek to rest the horses. High banks on either side sheltered them from the wind, and Meg got a chance to warm up.

Brad opened his saddlebags and brought out a long-sleeved thermal shirt, extended it to Meg. She hesitated a moment—that damnable McKettrick pride again—then took the shirt and pulled it on, right over the top of her coat.

The effect was comically unglamorous.

"Where's a Starbucks when you need one?" she joked.

Brad grinned. "There's an old line shack up the trail a ways," he told her. "Big John always kept it stocked with supplies, in case a hiker got stranded and needed shelter. It's not Starbucks, but I'll probably be able to rustle up a pot of coffee and some lunch. If you don't mind the survivalist packaging."

Meg's relief was visible, though she wouldn't have expressed it verbally, Brad knew. "We didn't need to bring the blankets and other gear then," she reasoned. "If there's a line shack, I mean."

"You've been living in the five-star lane for too long," Brad replied, but the jibe was a gentle one. "A while back, some hunters were trespassing on this land—Big John posted No Hunting signs years ago—and a snowstorm came up. They were found, dead of exposure, about fifty feet from the shack."

She shivered. "I remember," she said, and for a moment, her blue eyes looked almost haunted. The story had been a gruesome one, and she obviously *did* remember—all too clearly.

"We're not all that far from the ranch," Brad said. "It would probably be best if I took you back."

Meg's gaze widened, and grew more serious. "And you'd turn right around and come back up here to look for Ransom?"

"Yes," Brad answered, resigned.

"Alone."

He nodded. Once, Big John would have made the journey with him. Now there was no one.

"I'm staying," Meg said and shifted slightly, as if planting her feet. "You *invited* me to come along, in case you've forgotten."

"I shouldn't have. If anything happened to you—"

"I'm a big girl, Brad," she interrupted.

He looked her over, and—as always—liked what he saw. Liked it so much that his throat tightened and he had a hard time swallowing so he could hold up his end of the conversation. "You probably weigh a hundred and thirty pounds wrapped in a blanket and dunked into a lake. And despite your illustrious heritage, you're no match for a pack of wolves, a sudden blizzard, or a chasm that reaches halfway to China."

"If you can do it," Meg said, "*I* can do it."

Brad shoved a hand through his hair, exasperated even though he knew it was his own fault that Meg was in danger. After all, he *had* asked her to come along, half hoping the two of them would end up sharing a sleeping bag.

What the hell had he been thinking?

The pertinent question, he decided, was what had he been thinking *with*—not his brain, certainly.

"We'd better get moving again," she told him, when he didn't speak. Before they'd left the ranch, he'd given her a pair of binoculars on a neck strap; now she pulled them out from under the donated undershirt, her coat, and whatever was beneath that. "We have a horse to find."

Brad nodded, cupped his hands to give her a leg up onto Cinnamon's back. She paused for a moment, deciding, before setting her left foot in the stirrup of his palms.

"This is a tall horse," she said, a little flushed.

"We should have named him Stilts instead of Cinnamon," Brad allowed, amused. Meg, like the rest of her cousins, had virtually grown up on horseback, as had he and Olivia and the twins. She'd interpret even the smallest courtesy—the offer of a boost, for instance—as an affront to her riding skills.

Forty-five minutes later, Meg, using the binoculars, spotted Ransom on the crest of a rocky rise.

"There he is!" she whispered, awed. "Wait till I tell Jesse he's real!"

After a few seconds, she lifted the binoculars off her neck by the strap and handed them across to Brad.

Brad drew in a breath, struck by the magnificence of the stallion, the defiance and barely restrained power. A moment or so passed before he thought to scan the horse for wounds. It was hard to tell, given the distance, even with binoculars, but Ransom wasn't limping, and Brad didn't see any blood. He could report to Olivia, in all honesty, that the object of her equine obsession was holding his own.

Before lowering the binoculars, Brad swept them across the top of that rise, and that was when he saw the two mares. He chuckled. Ransom had himself a harem, then.

He watched them a while, then gave the binoculars back to Meg, with a cheerful, "He has company."

Meg's face glowed. "They're beautiful," she whispered, as if afraid to startle the horses and send them fleeing, though they were well over a mile away, by Brad's estimation. "And Ransom. He knows we're here, Brad. It's almost as if he wanted to let us see that he's all right."

Brad raised his coat collar against a chilly breeze and wished he'd worn his hat. He'd considered it that morning, but it had seemed like an affectation, a way of asserting that he was still a cowboy, by his own standards if not those of the McKettricks. "He knows," he agreed finally, "but it's more likely that he's taunting us. Catch-me-if-you-can. That's what he'd say if he could talk."

Meg's entire face was glowing. In fact, Brad figured if he could strip all those clothes off her, that glow would come right through her skin and be enough to warm him until he died of old age.

"How about that coffee?" she said, grinning.

After seeing Brad's kitchen on Stone Creek Ranch, Meg had expected the "line shack" to be a fancy log A-frame with a Jacuzzi and internet service. It was an actual *shack,* though, made of weathered board. There was a lean-to on one side, to shelter the horses, but no barn, with hay stored inside. Brad gave the animals grain from a sealed metal bin, and filled two water buckets for them from a rusty old pump outside.

Meg might have gone inside and started the fire, so they could brew the promised coffee, but she was mesmerized, watching Brad. It was as though the two of them had somehow gone back in time, back to when all the earlier McKettricks and O'Ballivans were still in the prime of their lives.

Once, there had been several shacks like that one on the Triple M, far from the barns and bunkhouses. Ranch hands, riding the far-flung fence lines, or just traveling overland for some reason, used to spend the night in them, take refuge there when the weather was bad. Eventually, those tiny buildings had become hazards, rather than havens, and they'd been knocked down and burned.

"Pretty decrepit," Brad said, leading the way into the shack.

Things skittered inside, and the smell of the place was faintly musty, but Brad soon had a good fire going in the ancient potbellied stove. There was no furniture at all, but shelves, made of old wooden crates stacked on top of each other, held cups, food in airtight silver packets, cans of coffee.

The whole place was about the size of Meg's downstairs powder room on the Triple M.

"I'd offer you a chair," Brad said, grinning, "but obviously there aren't any. Make yourself at home while I rinse out these cups at the pump and fill the coffeepot."

Meg examined the plank floor, sat down cross-legged, and reveled in the warmth beginning to emanate from the wood-burning stove. The shack, inadequate as it was, offered a welcome respite from the cold wind outside. The hunters Brad had mentioned probably wouldn't have died if they'd been able to reach it. She remembered the news story; the facts had been bitter and brutal.

Like Stone Creek Ranch, the Triple M was posted, and hunting wasn't allowed. Still, people trespassed constantly, and Rance, Keegan and Jesse enforced the boundaries—mostly in a peaceful way. Just the winter before, though, Jesse had caught two men running deer with snowmobiles on the high meadow above his house, and he'd scared them off with a rifle shot aimed at the sky. Later, he'd tracked the pair to a tavern in Indian Rock—strangers to the area, they'd laughed at his warning—and put both of them in the hospital. He might have killed them, in fact, if Keegan hadn't gotten wind of the fight and come to break it up, and even with his help, it took the local marshal, Wyatt Terp, his deputy, and half the clientele in the bar to get Jesse off the second snowmobiler. He'd already pulverized the first one.

There was talk about filing assault charges against Jesse, and later it was rumored that there might be lawsuits, but nothing ever came of either. Meg, along with everybody else in Indian Rock, doubted the snowmobilers would ever set foot in town again, let alone on the Triple M.

But there was always, as Keegan liked to say, a fresh supply of idiots.

Brad came in with the cups and the full coffeepot, shoving the door closed behind him with one shoulder. Again, Meg had a sense of having stepped right out of the twenty-first century and into the nineteenth.

Despite cracks between the board walls, the shack was warm.

Brad set the coffeepot on the stove, measured ground beans into it from a can, and left it to boil, cowboy-style. No basket, no filter.

Then he emptied two of the crates being used as cupboards and dragged them over in front of the stove, so he and Meg could sit on them.

Overhead, thunder rolled across the sky, loud as a freight train.

Meg stiffened. "Rain?"

"Snow," Brad said. "I saw a few flakes drift past while I was outside. Soon as we've warmed up a little and fortified ourselves with caffeine and some grub, we'd better make for the low-country."

Had there been any windows, Meg would have gotten up to look out of one of them. She could open the door a crack, but the thought of being buffeted by the rising wind stopped her.

By reflex, she scrambled to extract her cell phone from her coat pocket, flipped it open.

"No service," she murmured.

"I know," Brad said, smiling a little as he rose off the crate he'd been sitting on to add wood to the stove. Fortunately, there seemed to be an adequate supply of that. "I tried to call Olivia and let her know Ransom was still king of the hill a few minutes ago. Nothing."

Another round of thunder rattled the roof, and out in the lean-to, the horses fussed in alarm.

"Be right back," Brad said, heading for the door.

When he returned, he had a bedroll and Meg's pitifully insufficient blanket with him. And the horses were quiet.

"Just in case," he said when Meg's gaze landed, alarmed, on the overnight gear. "It's snowing pretty hard."

Meg, feeling foolish for sitting on her backside while Brad had been tending to the horses and fetching their gear inside, stood to lift the lid off the coffeepot and peek inside. The water was about to boil, but it would be a few minutes before the grounds settled to the bottom and they could drink the stuff.

"Relax, Meg," Brad said quietly. "There's still a chance the snow will ease up before dark."

At once tantalized and full of dread at the prospect of spending the night alone in a line shack with Brad O'Ballivan, Meg paced back and forth in front of the stove.

She knew what would happen if they stayed.

She'd known when she accepted Brad's invitation. Known when she set out for Stone Creek Ranch before dawn.

And he probably had, too.

She shoved both hands into her hair and paced faster.

"Meg," Brad said, sitting leisurely on his upended crate, *"relax."*

"You knew," she accused, stopping to shake a finger at him. "You knew we'd be stuck here!"

"So did you," Brad replied, unruffled.

Meg went to the door, wrenched it open and looked out, oblivious to the cold. The snow was coming down so hard and so fast that she couldn't see the pine trees towering less than a hundred yards from where she stood.

Attempting to travel under those conditions would be suicide.

Brad came and helped her shut the door again.

On the other side of the wall, in the lean-to, the horses made no sound.

Meg was standing too close to Brad, no question about it. But when she tried to move, she couldn't.

They looked into each other's eyes.

The very atmosphere zinged around them.

If Brad had kissed her then, she wouldn't have had the will to do anything but kiss him right back, but he didn't. "I'd better get some drinking water," he said, turning away and reaching for a bucket. "While I can still find my way back from the pump."

He went out.

Meg, needing something to do, pushed the coffeepot to the back of the stove so it wouldn't boil over and then examined a few of the food packets, evidently designed for post-apocalyptic dinner parties. The expiration dates were fifty years in the future.

"Spaghetti à la the Starship Enterprise," she muttered. There was Beef Wellington, too, and even meat loaf. At least they wouldn't starve.

Not right away, anyhow.

They'd starve *slowly*.

If they didn't freeze to death first.

Meg tried her cell phone again.

Still no service.

It was just as well, she supposed. Cheyenne knew her approximate location. Jesse would feed her horses, and if her absence was protracted, he and Keegan and Rance were sure to come looking for her. In the meantime, though, there would be a lot of room for speculation about what might be going on up there in the high country. And Jesse wouldn't miss a chance to tease her about it.

She was still holding the phone when Brad came in again, carrying a bucket full of water. He looked so cold that Meg almost went to put her arms around him.

Instead, she poured him a cup of hot coffee, still chewy with grounds, and handed it to him as soon as he'd set the bucket down.

"I don't suppose there's a generator," she said because the shack was darkening, even though it wasn't noon yet, and by nightfall, she wouldn't be able to see the proverbial hand in front of her face.

He favored her with a tilted grin. "Just a couple of battery-operated lamps and a few candles. We'll want to conserve the batteries, of course."

"Of course," Meg said, and smiled determinedly, hoping that would distract Brad from the little quaver in her voice.

"We don't have to make love," Brad said, lingering by the stove and taking slow, appreciative sips from his coffee. "Just because we're alone in a remote line shack during what may be the snowstorm of the century."

"You are not making me feel better."

That grin again. It was saucy, but it had a wistful element. "Am I making you feel *something?*"

"Nothing discernible," Meg lied. In truth, all her nerves felt supercharged, and her body was remembering, against strict orders from her mind, the weight and warmth of Brad's hands, caressing her bare skin.

"I used to be pretty good at it. Making you feel things, that is."

"Brad," Meg said, "don't."

"Okay," he said.

Meg was relieved, but at the same time, she wished he hadn't given up quite so easily.

"You wanted coffee," Brad remarked. "Have some."

Meg filled a cup for herself. Scooted her crate an inch or two farther from Brad's and sat down.

The shadows deepened and the shack seemed to grow even smaller than it was, pressing her and Brad closer together. And then closer still.

"This," Meg said, inspired by desperation, "would be a good time to talk about your second wife. Since we've been putting it off for a while."

Brad chuckled, fished in his saddlebags, now lying on the floor at his feet, and brought out a deck of cards. "I was thinking more along the lines of gin rummy," he said.

"What was her name again?"

"What was whose name?"

"Your second wife."

"Oh, her."

"Yeah, her."

"Cynthia. Her name is Cynthia. And I don't want to talk about her right now. Either we reminisce, or we play gin rummy, or—"

Meg squirmed. "Gin rummy," she said decisively. "There is no reason at all to bring up the subject of sex."

"Did I?"

"Did you what?"

"Did I bring up the subject of sex?"

"Not exactly," Meg said, embarrassed.

Brad grinned. "We'll get to that," he said. "Sooner or later."

Meg swallowed so much coffee in the next gulp that she nearly choked.

"There are some things I've been wondering about,"

Brad said easily, watching her over the rim of his metal coffee mug. His eyes smoldered with lazy blue heat.

Outside, the snow-thunder crashed again, but the horses didn't react. They'd probably already settled down for the night, snug in their furry hides and their lean-to.

"I'm hungry," Meg said, reaching for one of the food packets.

Brad went on as though she hadn't spoken at all. "Do you still like to eat cereal with yogurt instead of milk?"

Meg swallowed. "Yes."

"Do you still laugh in your sleep?"

"I—I suppose."

"Do you still arch your back like a bucking horse when you climax?"

Meg's face felt hotter than the old stove, which rocked a little with the heat inside it, crimson blazes glowing through the cracks. "What kind of question is that?"

"A personal one, I admit," Brad said. He might have passed for a choirboy, so innocent was his expression, but his eyes gave him away. They had the old glint of easy confidence in them. He knew he could have her anyplace and anytime he wanted—he was just biding his time. "I'll know soon enough, I guess."

"No," she said.

"No?" He raised an eyebrow.

"No, I don't arch my back when I—I don't arch my back."

"Hmm," Brad said. "Why not?"

Because I don't have sex, Meg almost answered, but in the last, teetering fraction of a second, she realized she didn't want to admit that. Not to Brad, the man with all the notches on his bedpost.

"You haven't been sleeping with anybody?" he asked.

"I didn't say that," Meg replied, keeping her distance,

mainly because she wanted so much to take Brad's coffee from his hand, set it aside, straddle his thighs and let him work his slow, thorough magic. Peeling away her outer garments, kissing and caressing everything he uncovered.

"Nobody who could make you arch your back?"

Meg was suffused with aching, needy misery. She'd been in fairly close proximity to Brad all morning, and managed to keep her perspective, but now they were alone in a remote shack, and he'd already begun to seduce her. Without so much as a kiss, or a touch of his hand. With Brad O'Ballivan, even gin rummy would qualify as foreplay.

"Something like that," she said. It was a lame answer, and way too honest, but she'd figured if she tossed his ego a bone, the way she might have done to get past a junkyard dog, she'd get a chance to diffuse the invisible but almost palpable charge sparking between them.

"I came across one of Maddie's diaries a few years ago," Brad said, still stripping her with his eyes. Maddie, of course, was his ancestress—Sam O'Ballivan's wife. "She mentioned this line shack several times. She and Sam spent a night here, once, and conceived a child."

That statement should have quelled Meg's passion—unlike Sam and Maddie, she and Brad weren't married, weren't in love. She wasn't using any form of birth control, since there hadn't been a man in her life for nearly a year, and intuition told her that for all Brad's preparations, Brad hadn't brought any condoms along.

Yet, the mention of a baby opened a gash of yearning within Meg, a great, jagged tearing so deep and so dark and so raw that she nearly doubled over with the pain of it.

"Are you all right?" Brad asked, on his feet quickly, taking her elbows in his hands, looking down into her face.

She said nothing. She couldn't have spoken for anything, not in that precise moment.

"What?" Brad prompted, looking worried.

She couldn't tell him that she'd wanted a baby so badly she'd made arrangements with a fertility specialist on several occasions, always losing her courage at the last moment. That she'd almost reached the point of sleeping with strangers, hoping to get pregnant.

In the end, she hadn't been able to go through with that, either.

She'd never known her own father. Oh, she'd lacked for nothing, being a McKettrick. Nothing except the merest acquaintance with the man who'd sired her. He was so anonymous, in fact, that Eve had occasionally referred to him, not knowing Meg was listening, as "the sperm donor."

She wanted more for her own son or daughter. Granted, the baby's father didn't have to be involved in their day-to-day life, or pay child support, or much of anything else. But he had to have a face and a name, so Meg could show her child a photograph, at some point in time, and say, "This is your daddy."

"Meg?" Brad's hands tightened a little on her elbows.

"Panic attack," she managed to gasp.

He pressed her down onto one of the crates, ladled some water from the bucket he'd braved the elements to fill at the pump outside, and held it to her lips.

She sipped.

"Do you need to take a pill or something?"

Meg shook her head.

He dragged the second crate closer, and sat facing her, so their knees touched. "Since when do you get panic attacks?" he asked.

Tears stung Meg's eyes. She rocked a little, hugging

herself, and Brad steadied the ladle in her hands, raised it to her mouth again.

She sipped, more slowly this time, and Brad set it aside when she was finished.

"Meg," he repeated. "The panic attacks?"

It only happens when I suddenly realize I want to have a certain man's baby more than I want anything in the world. And when that certain man turns out to be you.

"It's a freak thing," she said. "I've never had one before."

Brad raised an eyebrow—he'd always been perceptive. It was one of the qualities that made him a good songwriter, for example. "I mentioned that Sam and Maddie conceived a child in this line shack, and you started hyperventilating." He leaned forward a little, took both Meg's hands gently in his. "I remember how much you wanted kids when we were together," he mused. "And now your sister is having a baby."

Meg's heart wedged itself into her windpipe. She'd wanted a baby, all right. And she'd conceived one, with Brad, and miscarried soon after he left for Nashville. Not even her mother had known.

She nodded.

Brad stroked the side of her cheek with the backs of his fingers, offering her comfort. She'd never told him about the pregnancy—she'd been saving the news for their wedding night—but now she knew she would have no choice, if they got involved again.

"I'm not jealous of Sierra," she said, anxious to make that clear. "I'm happy for her and Travis."

"I know," Brad said. He drew her from her crate onto his lap; she straddled his thighs. But beyond that, the gesture wasn't sexual. He simply held her, one hand gently pressing her head to his shoulder.

After a little deep breathing, in order to calm herself, Meg straightened and gazed into Brad's face.

"Suppose we had sex," she said softly. Tentatively. "And I conceived a child. How would you react?"

"Well," Brad said after pondering the idea with an expression of wistful amusement on his face, "I guess that would depend on a couple of things." He kissed her neck, lightly. Nibbled briefly at her earlobe.

A hot shudder went through Meg. "Like what?"

"Like whether we were going to raise the baby together or not," Brad replied, still nibbling. When Meg stiffened slightly, he drew back to look into her face again. "What?"

"I was sort of thinking I could just be a single mother," Meg said.

She was off Brad's thighs and plunked down on her crate again so quickly that it almost took her breath away.

"And my part would be what?" he demanded. "Keep my distance? Go on about my business? What, Meg?"

"You have your career—"

"I don't have my career. That part of my life is over. I've told you that."

"You're young, Brad. You're very talented. It's inevitable that you'll want to sing again."

"I don't have to be in a concert hall or a recording studio to sing," he said tersely. "I mean to live on Stone Creek Ranch for good, and any child of *mine* is going to grow up there."

Meg stood her ground. After all, she was a McKettrick. "Any child of *mine* is going to grow up on the Triple M."

"Then I guess we'd better not make a baby," Brad replied. He got up off the crate, went to the stove and refilled his coffee cup.

"Look," Meg said more gently, "we can just let the

subject drop. I'm sorry I brought it up at all—I just got a little emotional there for a moment and—"

Brad didn't answer.

They were stuck in a cabin together, at least overnight, and maybe longer. They had to get along, or they'd both go crazy.

She retrieved the pack of cards from the floor, where Brad had set them earlier. "Bet I can take you, O'Ballivan," she said, waggling the box from side to side. "Gin rummy, five-card stud, go fish—name your poison."

He laughed, and the tension was broken—the overt kind, anyway. There was an underground river of the stuff, coursing silently beneath their feet. "Go fish?"

"Lately, I've played a lot of cards—with my nephew, Liam. That's his favorite."

Brad chose rummy. Set a third crate between them for a table top. "You think you can take me, huh?" he challenged. And the look in his eyes, as he dealt the first hand, said *he* planned on doing the taking—and the cards didn't have a thing to do with it.

CHAPTER SIX

IT WAS A WONDER TO BRAD that he could sit there in the middle of that line shack, playing gin rummy with Meg McKettrick, when practically all he'd thought about since coming home to Stone Creek was bedding down with her. She'd practically invited him to father her baby, too.

Whatever his reservations might be where her insistence on raising the child alone was concerned, and on the Triple M to boot, he sure wouldn't have minded the *process* of conceiving it.

So why wasn't he on top of her at that very moment?

He studied his cards solemnly—Meg was going to win this hand, as she had the last half dozen—and pondered the situation. The wind howled around the shack like a million shrieking banshees determined to drive them both out into the freezing cold, making the walls shake. And the light was going, too, even though it wasn't noon yet.

"Play," Meg said impatiently, a spark of mischievous triumph—and something else—dancing in her eyes.

"If I didn't know better," Brad said ruefully, "I'd think you'd stacked the deck. You're going to lay down all your cards and set me again, aren't you?"

She grinned, looking at him coyly over the fan of cards. Even batting her eyelashes. "There's only one way to find out," she teased.

A cowboy's geisha, Brad thought. Later, when he was alone at the ranch, he'd tinker around with the idea, maybe make a song out of it. He might have retired from recording and life on the road, but he knew he'd always make music.

Resigned, he drew a card from the stack, couldn't use it, and tossed it away.

Meg's whole being seemed to twinkle as she took his discard, incorporated it into a grand-slam of a run and went out with a flourish, spreading the cards across the top of the crate.

"McKettrick luck," she said, beaming.

On impulse, Brad put down his cards, leaned across the crate between them and kissed Meg lightly on the mouth. She tensed at first, then responded, giving a little groan when he used his tongue.

Her arms slipped around his shoulders.

He wanted with everything in him to shove cards and crate aside, lay her down, then and there, and have her.

Whoa, he told himself. *Easy. Don't scare her off.*

There were tears in her eyes when she drew back from his kiss, sniffled once, and blinked, as though surprised to find herself alone with him, in the eye of the storm.

Like most men, Brad was always unsettled when a woman cried. He felt an urgent need to rectify whatever was wrong, and at the same time, knew he couldn't.

Meg swabbed at her cheeks with the back of one hand, straightened her proud McKettrick spine.

"What's the matter?" Brad asked.

"Nothing," Meg answered, averting her gaze.

"You're lying."

"Just hedging a little," she said, trying hard to smile and falling short. "It was like the old days, that's all. The kiss I mean. It brought up a lot of feelings."

"Would it help if I told you I felt the same way?"

"Not really," she said. A thoughtful look came into those fabulous, fathomless eyes of hers.

Brad slid the crate to one side and leaned in close, filled with peculiar suspense. He had to know what was going on in her head. "What?"

"Lots of people have sex," she told him, "without anybody getting pregnant."

"The reverse is also true," he felt honor-bound to say. "Far as I know, making love still causes babies."

"Making love," Meg said, "is not necessarily the same thing as having sex."

Brad cleared his throat, still walking on figurative eggshells. "True," he said very cautiously. Was she messing with him? Setting him up for a rebuff? Meg wasn't a particularly vengeful person, at least as far as he knew, but he'd hurt her badly all those busy years ago. Maybe she wanted to get back at him a little.

"What I have in mind," she told him decisively, "is *sex,* as opposed to making love." A pause. "Of course."

"Of course," he agreed. Hope fluttered in his chest, like a bird flexing its wings and rising, windborne, off a high tree branch. At the same time, he felt stung—Meg was making it clear that any intimacy they might enjoy during this brief time-out-of-time would be strictly for physical gratification. Frenetic coupling of bodies, an emotion-free zone.

Since beggars couldn't be choosers, he was willing to bargain, but the disturbing truth was, he wanted more from Meg than a noncommittal quickie. She wasn't, after all, a groupie to be groped and taken in the back of some tour bus, then forgotten.

She squinted at him, catching something in his expression. "This bothers you?" she asked.

He tried to smile. "If you want to have sex, McKettrick, I'm definitely game. It's just that—"

"What?"

"It might not be a good idea." Was he crazy? Here was the most beautiful woman he'd ever seen, essentially offering herself to him—and he was leaning on the brake lever?

"Okay," she said, and she looked hurt, uncomfortable, suddenly shy.

And that was his undoing. All his noble reluctance went right out the door.

He pulled her onto his lap again.

She hesitated, then wrapped both arms around his neck.

"Are you sure?" he asked her quietly, gruffly. "We're taking a chance here, Meg. We *could* conceive a child—"

The idea filled him with desperate jubilation, strangely mingled with sorrow.

"We could," she agreed, her eyes shining, dark with sultry heat, despite the chill seeping in between the cracks in the plain board walls.

He cupped her chin in his hand, made her look into his face. "Fair warning, McKettrick. If there's a baby, I'm not going to be an anonymous father, content to cut a check once a month and go on about my business as if it had never happened."

She studied him. "You're serious."

He nodded.

"I'll take that chance," she decided, after a few moments of deliberation.

He kissed her again, deeply this time, and when their mouths parted, she looked as dazed as he felt. Once, during a rehearsal before a concert, he'd gotten a shock from an electric guitar with a frayed chord. The jolt he'd taken, kissing Meg just now, made the first experience seem tame.

She was straddling him, and even through their jeans, the insides of her thighs, squeezing against his hips, seemed to sear his skin. She squirmed against his erection, making him groan.

Never in his life had Brad wanted a bed as badly as he did at that moment. It wasn't right to lay Meg down on a couple of sleeping bags, on that cold floor.

But even as he was thinking these disjointed thoughts, he was pulling her shirt up, slipping his hands beneath all that fabric, stroking her bare ribs.

She shivered deliciously, closed her eyes, threw her head back.

"Cold?" Brad asked, worried.

"Anything but," she murmured.

"You're sure?"

"Absolutely sure," Meg said.

He found the catch on her bra, opened it. Cupped both hands beneath her full, warm breasts.

She moaned as he chafed her nipples gently, using the sides of his thumbs.

And that was when they heard the deafening and unmistakable *thwup-thwup-thwup* of helicopter blades, directly above the roof of the line shack.

Meg looked up, disbelieving. Jesse, Rance, or Keegan—or all three. Who else would take a chopper up in weather like that?

Out in the lean-to, the horses whinnied in panic. The walls of the cabin shook as Meg jumped to her feet and righted her bra in almost the same motion. *"Damn!"* she sputtered furiously.

"That had better not be Phil," Brad said ominously.

He was standing, too, his gaze fixed on the trembling ceiling.

Meg smoothed her hair, straightened her clothes. "Phil?"

"My manager," Brad reminded her.

"We should be so lucky," Meg yelled, straining to be heard over the sound of the blades. "It's my cousins!"

They both went to the door and peered out, heedless of the blasting cold, made worse by the downdraft from the chopper, Meg ducking under Brad's left arm to see.

Sure enough, the McKettrickCo helicopter, a relic of the corporation days, was settling to the ground, bouncing on its runners in the deepening snow.

"I'll be damned," Brad said with a grin of what looked like rueful admiration, forcing the door shut against the icy wind. At the last second, Meg saw two figures moving toward them at a half crouch.

"I'll kill them," Meg said.

The door rattled on its hinges at the first knock.

Meg stood back while Brad opened it again.

Jesse came through first, followed by Keegan. They wore Western hats pulled low over their faces, leather coats thickly lined with sheep's wool, and attitudes.

"I tried to stop them," Angus said, appearing at Meg's elbow.

"Good job," Meg scoffed, under her breath, without moving her lips.

Angus spread his hands. "They're McKettricks," he reminded her, as though that explained every mystery in the universe, from spontaneous human combustion to the Bermuda Triangle.

"Are you crazy?" Meg demanded of her cousins, storming forward to stand toe-to-toe with Jesse, who was tight-jawed, casting suspicious glances at Brad. "You could have been killed, taking the copter up in a blizzard!"

Brad, by contrast, hoisted the coffeepot off the stove, grinning wryly, and not entirely in a friendly way. "Coffee?" he asked.

Jesse scowled at him.

"Don't mind if I do," Keegan said, pulling off his heavy leather gloves. He tossed Meg a sympathetic glance in the meantime, one that said, *Don't blame me. I'm just here to keep an eye on Jesse.*

Brad found another cup and, without bothering to wipe it out, filled it and handed it to Keegan. "It's good to see you again," he said with a sort of charged affability, but underlying his tone was an unspoken, *Not.*

"I'll just bet," Jesse said, whipping off his hat. His dark blond hair looked rumpled, as though he'd been shoving a hand through it at regular intervals.

"Jesse," Keegan warned quietly.

Meg stood nearly on tiptoe, her nose almost touching Jesse's, her eyes narrowed to slits. "What the *hell* are you doing here?"

Jesse wasn't about to back down, his stance made that clear, and neither was Meg. Classic McKettrick stand-off.

Keegan, used to the family dynamics, and the most diplomatic member of the current generation, eased an arm between them, holding his mug of hot coffee carefully in the other. "To your corners," he said easily, forcing them both to take a step back.

Jesse gave Brad a scathing look—once, they'd been friends—and turned to face Meg again. "I might ask you the same question," he countered. "What the hell are *you* doing here? With *him?*"

Brad cleared his throat, folded his arms. Waited. He

looked amused—the expression in his eyes notwith-standing.

"That, Jesse McKettrick," Meg seethed, "is my own business!"

"We came," Keegan interceded, still unruffled but, in his own way, as watchful as Jesse was, "because Cheyenne told us you were up here on horseback. When we got word of the blizzard, we were worried."

Meg threw her arms out, slapped them back against her sides. "Obviously, I'm all right," she said. "Safe and sound."

"I don't know about that," Jesse said, taking Brad's measure again.

A muscle bunched in Brad's jaw, but he didn't speak.

"Get your stuff, if you have any," Jesse told Meg. "We're leaving." He turned to Brad again, added reluctantly, "You'd better come with us. This storm is going to get a lot worse before it gets better."

"Can't leave the horses," Brad said.

Meg was annoyed. Her cousins had landed a helicopter in front of the line shack, in the middle of a blinding white-out, determined to carry her out bodily if they had to, and all he could think about was the horses?

"I'll stay and ride out with you," Jesse told Brad. Whatever his issues with Brad might be, he was a rancher, born and bred. And a rancher never left a horse stranded, whether it was his own or someone else's, if he had any choice in the matter. His blue eyes sliced to Meg's face. "Keegan will get you back to the Triple M."

"Suppose I don't want to go?"

"Better decide," Keegan put in. "This storm is picking up steam as we speak. Another fifteen or twenty minutes, and the four of us will be bunking in here until spring."

Meg searched Jesse's face, glanced at Brad.

He wasn't going to express an opinion one way or the other, apparently, and that galled her. She knew it wasn't cowardice—Brad had never been afraid of a brawl, with her rowdy cousins or anybody else. Which probably meant he was relieved to get out of a sticky situation.

Color flared in her cheeks.

"I'll get my coat," she said, glaring at Brad. Still hoping he'd stop her, send Jesse and Keegan packing.

But he didn't.

She scrambled into her coat with jamming motions of her fists, and got stuck in the lining of one sleeve.

"Call Olivia," Brad said, watching her struggle, one corner of his mouth tilted slightly upward in a bemused smile. "Let her know I'm okay."

Meg nodded once, angrily, and let Keegan shuffle her out into the impossible cold to the waiting helicopter.

"Smooth," Brad remarked, studying Jesse, shutting the door behind Meg and Keegan and offering a brief, silent prayer for their safety. Flying in this weather was a major risk, but if anybody was up to the job, it was Keegan. His father had been a pilot, and all three of the McKettrick boys were as skilled at the controls of a plane or a copter as they were on the back of a horse.

A little of the air went out of Jesse, but not much. "We'd better ride," he said, "if we're going to make it out of here before dark."

"What'd you think I was going to do, Jesse?" Brad asked evenly, reaching for the poker, opening the stove door to bank the fire. "Rape her?"

Jesse thrust a hand through his hair. "It wasn't that," he said, but grudgingly. "Until we spotted the smoke from the line shack chimney, we thought the two of you might still be out there someplace, in a whole lot of trouble."

"You couldn't have just turned the copter toward the Triple M and left well enough alone?" He hadn't shown it in front of Meg, but Brad was about an inch off Jesse. Meg wasn't a kid, and if she'd needed protection, he would have provided it.

Jesse's eyes shot blue fire. "Maybe Meg's ready to forget what you did to her, but I'm not," he said. "She put on a good show back then, but inside, she was a shipwreck. Especially after the miscarriage."

For Brad, the whole world came to a screeching, spark-throwing stop in the space of an instant.

"What miscarriage?"

"Uh-oh," Jesse said.

It was literally all Brad could do not to get Jesse by the lapels and drag an answer out of him. He even took a step toward the door, meaning to stop Meg from leaving, but the copter was already lifting off, shaking the shack, setting the horses to fretting again.

"There—was—a baby?"

"Let's go get those horses ready for a hard ride," Jesse said, averting his gaze. Clearly, he'd assumed Meg had told Brad about the child. Now Jesse was the picture of regret.

"Tell me," Brad pressed.

"You'll have to talk to Meg," Jesse answered, putting his hat on again and squaring his shoulders to go back out into the cold and around to the lean-to. "I've already said more than I should have."

"It was mine?"

Jesse reddened. Yanked up the collar of his heavy coat. *"Of course* it was yours," he said indignantly. "Meg's not the type to play that kind of game."

Brad put on his own coat and yanked on some gloves.

He felt strangely apart from himself, as though his spirit had somehow gotten out of step with his body.

Meg had been pregnant when he caught that bus to Nashville.

He knew in his bones it was true.

If he'd been anything but a stupid, ambitious kid, he'd have known it then. By the fragile light in her eyes. By the way she'd touched his arm, as if to get his attention so she could say something important, then drawn back, trembling a little.

He'd still have gone to Nashville—he'd had to, to save Stone Creek from the bankers and developers. But he'd have sent for Meg first thing, swallowed his pride whole if he had to, or thumbed it back to Arizona to be with her.

Tentatively, Jesse laid a hand on Brad's shoulder. Withdrew it again.

After securing the line shack as best they could, they left, made their way to the fitful horses, saddled them in silence.

The roar of the copter's engine and the whipping of the blades made conversation impossible, without a headset, and Meg refused to put hers on.

Keegan concentrated on working the controls, keeping a close watch on the instrument panel. The blizzard had intensified; they were literally flying blind.

Presently, though, visibility increased, and Meg relaxed a little.

Keegan must have been watching her out of the corner of his eye, because he reached over and patted her lightly on the arm. Picked up the second headset and nudged her until she took it, put on the earphones, adjusted the mic.

"I can't believe you did this," she said.

Keegan grinned. His voice echoed through the headset.

"Rule number one," he said. "Never leave another McKettrick stuck in a blizzard."

Meg huffed out a sigh. "I was perfectly all right!"

"Maybe," Keegan replied, banking to the northwest, in the direction of the Triple M. "But we didn't have any way of knowing that. Switch on your cell phone. You'll find we left at least half a dozen messages on your voice mail, trying to find out if you were okay."

"What if they don't make it out of that storm?" Meg fretted. Before, she'd just been furious. Now, with a little perspective, she was suddenly assailed by worries, on all sides. The fear was worse than the anger. "What if the horses get lost?"

"Brad knows the trail," Keegan assured her, "and Jesse could ride out of hell if he had to. If they don't show up in a few hours, I'll come back looking for them."

"You're not invincible, you know," Meg said tersely. "Even if you *are* a McKettrick."

"I'll do what I have to do," he told her. "Are you and Brad—well—back on?"

"That is patently none of your affair."

Keegan's grin was damnably endearing. "When has that ever stopped me?"

"No," Meg said, beaten. "We are *not* 'back on.' I was just helping him look for Ransom, that's all."

"Ransom? The stallion?"

"Yes."

"He's real?"

"I've seen him with my own eyes."

"You decided to go chasing a wild horse in the middle of a blizzard?"

"It wasn't snowing when we left Stone Creek Ranch," Meg said, feeling defensive.

"Know what I think?"

"No, but I'm afraid you're going to tell me."

Keegan's grin widened, took on a wicked aspect. "You wanted to sleep with Brad. He wanted to sleep with you. And I use the word *sleep* advisedly. Both of you knew snow's a real possibility in the high country, year 'round. And there's the old line shack, handy as hell."

"*So* none of your business. And who do you think you are, Dr. Phil?"

Keegan chuckled, shook his head once. "It probably won't help," he told her, "but if we'd known we were interrupting a tryst, we'd have stayed clear."

"We were *playing gin rummy.*"

"Whatever."

Meg folded her arms and wriggled deeper into the cold leather seat. "Keegan, I don't have to convince you. And I definitely don't have to explain."

"You're absolutely right. You don't."

By then, they were out of the snow, gliding through a golden autumn afternoon. They passed over the town of Stone Creek, continued in the direction of Indian Rock.

Meg didn't say another word until Keegan set the copter down in the pasture behind her barn, the downdraft making the long grass ripple like an ocean.

"Thanks for the ride," she said tersely, waiting for the blades to slow so she could get out without having her head cut off. "I'd invite you in, but right now, I am seriously pissed off, and the less I see of any of my male relatives, you included, the better."

Keegan cocked a thumb at her. "Got it," he said. "And for the record, I don't give a rat's ass if you're pissed off."

Meg reached across and slugged him in the upper arm, hard, but she laughed a little as she did it. Shook her head. "Goodbye!" she yelled, tossing the headset into his lap.

Keegan signaled her to keep her head down, and watched

as she pushed open the door of the copter and leaped to the ground.

Ducking, she headed for the house.

Angus was standing in the kitchen when she let herself in, looking apologetic.

"Thanks a heap for the help," Meg said.

"There's not much I can do with folks who can't see or hear me," Angus replied.

"I get all the luck," Meg answered, pulling off her coat and flinging it in the direction of the hook beside the door.

Angus looked solemn. "You've got trouble," he said.

Meg tensed, instantly alarmed. She'd ridden home from the mountaintop in relative comfort, but the trip would be dangerous on horseback, even for men who'd literally grown up in the saddle. "Jesse and Brad are okay, aren't they?"

"They'll be fine," Angus assured her. "A couple of shots of good whiskey'll fix 'em right up."

"Then what are you talking about?"

"You'll find out soon enough."

"Do you have to be so damned cryptic?"

Angus's grin was reminiscent of Keegan's. "I'm not cryptic," he said. "I can get around just fine."

"Very funny."

He chuckled.

Frazzled, Meg blurted, "First you tell me about your long-lost brother, and how some unknown McKettrick is about to show up. Then you say I've got trouble. Spill it, Angus!"

He sobered. "Jesse let the cat out of the bag. And that's all I'm going to say."

Meg froze. She had only one deep, dark secret, and

Jesse couldn't have let it slip because he didn't know what it was.

Did he?

She put one hand to her mouth.

Angus patted her shoulder. "You'd better go out to the barn and feed the horses early. You might be too busy later on."

Meg stared at her ancestor. "Angus McKettrick—"

He vanished.

Typical man.

Meg placed the promised call to Olivia O'Ballivan, got her voice mail and left a message. Next, she started a pot of coffee, then picked her coat up off the floor, put it back on and went out to tend to the livestock.

The work helped to ease her anxiety, but not all that much.

All the while, she was wondering if Jesse had found out about the baby somehow, if he'd told Brad.

You've got trouble, Angus had said, and the words echoed in her mind.

She finished her chores and returned to the house, shedding her coat again and washing her hands at the sink before pouring herself a mug of fresh coffee. She considered lacing it with a generous dollop of Jack Daniel's, to get the chill out of her bones, then shoved the bottle back in the cupboard, unopened.

If Jesse and Brad didn't get home, Keegan wouldn't be the only one to go out looking for them.

She reached for the telephone, dialed Cheyenne's cell number.

"I'm sorry," Cheyenne said immediately, not bothering with a hello. "When I passed your message on to Jesse, about checking on your horses if you didn't call before nightfall, he wanted to know where you'd gone." She paused. "And I told him."

Meg pressed the back of one hand to her forehead and closed her eyes for a moment. If a certain pair of stubborn cowboys got lost in that blizzard, or if Jesse had, as Angus put it, "let the cat out of the bag," the embarrassing scene at the line shack would be the least of her problems.

"There's a big storm in the high country," she said quietly, "and Jesse and Brad are on horseback. Let me know when Jesse gets back, will you?"

Cheyenne drew in an audible breath. "Oh, my God," she whispered. "They're riding in a *blizzard?*"

"Jesse can handle it," Meg said. "And so can Brad. Just the same, I'll rest easier when I know they're home."

Cheyenne didn't answer for a long time. "I'll call," she promised, but she sounded distracted. No doubt she was thinking the same thing Meg was, that it had been reckless enough, flying into a snowstorm in a helicopter. Taking a treacherous trail down off the mountain was even worse.

Meg spoke a few reassuring words, though they sounded hollow even to her, and she and Cheyenne said goodbye.

At loose ends, Meg took her coffee to the study at the front of the house and logged onto the computer. Ran a search on the name Josiah McKettrick, though her mind wasn't on genealogical detective work, and she started over a dozen times.

In the kitchen, she heated a can of soup and ate it mechanically, never tasting a bite. After that, she read for a couple of hours, then she took a long, hot bath, put on clean sweats and padded downstairs again, thinking she'd watch some television. She was trying to focus on a rerun of *Dog the Bounty Hunter* when she heard a car door slam outside.

Boot heels thundered up the front steps.

And then a fist hammered at the heavy wooden door.

"Meg!" Brad yelled. "Open up! *Now!*"

CHAPTER SEVEN

BRAD LOOKED CRAZED, standing there on Meg's doorstep. She moved to step out of his way, but before she could, he advanced on her, backing her into the entryway. Kicking the door shut behind him with a hard motion of one foot.

He hadn't stopped to change clothes after the long, cold ride down out of the hills, and he was soaked to the skin. He'd lost his gloves somewhere, and there was a faintly bluish cast to his taut lips.

"Why didn't you tell me about the baby?" he demanded, shaking an index finger under Meg's nose when she collided with the wall behind her, next to Holt and Lorelei's grandfather clock. The ponderous tick-tock seemed to reverberate throughout the known universe.

Meg's worst fears were confirmed in that moment. Jesse *had* known about her pregnancy and subsequent miscarriage—and he'd let it slip to Brad.

"Calm down," she said, recovering a little.

Brad gripped her shoulders. If he'd been anyone other than exactly who he was, Meg might have feared for her safety. But this was Brad O'Ballivan. Sure, he'd crushed her heart, but he wasn't going to hurt her physically, she knew that. It was one of the few absolutes.

"Was there a child?"

Meg bit her lower lip. She'd always known she'd have to tell him if they crossed paths again, but she hadn't wanted it to be like this. "Yes," she whispered, that one word scraping her throat raw.

"My baby?"

She felt a sting of indignation, hot as venom, but it passed quickly. "Yes."

"Why didn't you tell me?"

Meg straightened her spine, lifted her chin a notch. "You were in Nashville," she said. "You didn't write. You didn't call. I guess I didn't think you'd be interested."

The blue fury in Brad's eyes dulled visibly; he let go of her shoulders, but didn't step back. She felt cornered, overshadowed—but still not threatened. Oddly, it was more like being shielded, even protected.

He shoved a hand through his hair. "How could I not be interested, Meg?" he rasped bleakly. "You were carrying our baby."

Slowly, Meg put her palms to his cheeks. "I miscarried a few weeks after you left," she said gently. "It wasn't meant to be."

Moisture glinted in his eyes, and that familiar muscle bunched just above his jawline. "Still—"

"Go upstairs and take a hot shower," Meg told him. "I'll fix you something to eat, and we'll talk."

Brad tensed again, then relaxed, though only slightly. Nodded.

"Travis left some clothes behind when he and Sierra moved to town," she went on, when he didn't speak. "I'll get them for you."

With that, she led the way up the stairs, along the hallway to the main bathroom. After pushing the door open and waiting for Brad to enter, she went on to the master bedroom, pulled an old pair of jeans and a long-sleeved T-shirt from a bureau drawer.

Brad was already in the shower when she returned, naked behind the steamy glass door, but clearly visible.

Swallowing a rush of lust, Meg set the folded garments on the lid of the toilet seat, placed a folded towel on top of them and slipped out.

She was cooking scrambled eggs when Brad came down the back stairs fifteen minutes later, barefoot, his hair towel-rumpled, wearing Travis's clothes. Without comment, Meg poured a cup of fresh coffee and held it out to him.

He took it, after a moment's hesitation, and sipped cautiously.

Meg was relieved to see that the hot shower had restored his normal color. Before, he'd been ominously pale.

"Sit down," she said quietly.

He pulled out Holt's chair and sat, watching her as she turned to the stove again. Even with her back turned to him, she could feel his gaze boring into the space between her shoulder blades.

"What happened?" he asked, after a few moments.

She looked back at him briefly before scraping the eggs onto a waiting plate. Didn't speak.

"The miscarriage," he prompted grimly. "What made it happen?"

With a pang, Meg realized he thought it might have been his fault somehow, her losing their baby. Because he'd gone to Nashville, or because of the fight they'd had before he left.

She'd suffered her own share of guilt over the years, wondering if she could have done something differently, prevented the tragedy. She didn't want Brad to go through the same agony.

"There was no specific incident," she said softly. "I was pregnant, and then I wasn't. It happens, Brad. And it's not always possible to know why."

Brad absorbed that, took another sip of his coffee. "You should have told me."

"I didn't tell anyone," Meg said. "Not even my mother."

"Then how did Jesse know?"

Now that she'd had time to think, the answer was obvious. Jesse had been the one to take her to the hospital that long-ago night. She'd told him it was just a bad case of cramps, but he'd either put two and two together on his own or overheard the nurses and doctors talking.

"He was with me," she said.

"He was, and I *wasn't*," Brad answered.

She set the plate of scrambled eggs in front of him, along with two slices of buttered toast and some silverware. "It wouldn't have changed anything," she said. "Your being there, I mean. I'd still have lost the baby, Brad."

He closed his eyes briefly, like someone taking a hard punch to the solar plexus, determined not to fight back.

"You should have told me," he insisted.

She gave the plate a little push toward him and, reluctantly, he picked up his fork, began to eat. "We've been over that," she said, sitting down on the bench next to the table, angled to face Brad. "What good would it have done?"

"I could have—helped."

"How?"

He sighed. "You went through it alone. That isn't right."

"Lots of things aren't 'right' in this world," Meg reasoned quietly. "A person just has to—cope."

"The McKettrick way," Brad said without admiration. "Some people would call that being bullheaded, not coping."

She propped an elbow on the tabletop, cupped her chin in her hand, and watched as he continued to down the scrambled eggs. "I'd do the same thing all over again," she confessed. "It was hard, but I toughed it out."

"Alone."

"Alone," Meg agreed.

"It must have been a lot worse than 'hard.' You were only nineteen."

"So were you," she said.

"Why didn't you tell your mother?"

Meg didn't have to reflect on that one. From the day Hank Breslin had snatched Sierra and vanished, Eve had been hit by problem after problem—a serious accident, in which she'd been severely injured, subsequent addictions to painkillers and alcohol, all the challenges of steering McKettrickCo through a lot of corporate white water.

"She'd been through enough," she replied simply. Brad's question had been rhetorical—he'd known the McKettrick history all along.

"She'd have strung me up by my thumbs," Brad said. And though he tried to smile, he didn't quite make it. He was still in shock.

"Probably," Meg said.

He'd finished the food, shoved his plate away. "Where do we go from here?" he asked.

"I don't know," she said. "Maybe nowhere."

He moved to take her hand, but withdrew just short of touching her. Scraped back his chair to stand and carry the remains of his meal to the sink. Set the plate and silverware down with a thunk.

"Was our baby a boy or a girl?" he asked gruffly, standing with his back to her.

She saw the tension in his broad shoulders as he awaited her answer. "I didn't ask," she said. "I guess I didn't want to know. And it was probably too early to tell, anyway. I was only a few weeks into the pregnancy."

He turned, at last, to face her, but kept his distance, leaning back against the counter, folding his arms. "Do you ever think about what it would be like if he or she had survived?"

All the time, she thought.

"No," she lied.

"Right," he said, clearly not believing her.

"I'm—I'm sorry, Brad. That you had to find out from someone else, I mean."

"But not for deceiving me in the first place?"

Meg bristled. "I didn't deceive you."

"What do you call it?"

"You were *gone.* You had things to do. If I'd dragged you back here, you wouldn't have gotten your big chance. You would have hated me for that."

At last, he crossed to her, took her chin in his hand. "I couldn't hate you, Meg," he said gravely, choking a little on the words. "Not ever."

For a few moments, they just stared at each other in silence.

Brad was the first to speak again. "I'd better get back to the ranch." Another rueful attempt at a grin. "It's been a bitch of a day."

"Stay," Meg heard herself say. She wasn't thinking of leading Brad to her bed—not *exclusively* of that, anyhow. He'd just ridden miles through a blizzard on horseback, he'd taken a chill in the process, and the knowledge that he'd fathered a child was painfully new.

He was silent, perhaps at a loss.

"You shouldn't be alone," Meg said. *And neither should I.*

She knew what would happen if he stayed, of course. And she knew it was likely to be a mistake. They'd become strangers to each other over the years apart, living such different lives. It was too soon to run where angels feared to tread.

But she needed him that night, needed him to hold her, if nothing else.

And his need was just as great.

He grinned, though wanly. "How do we know your cousins won't land on the roof in a helicopter?" he asked.

"We don't," Meg said, and sighed. "They meant well, you know."

"Sure they did," he agreed wryly. "They were out to save your virtue."

Meg stood, went to Brad, slipped her arms around his middle. It seemed such a natural thing to do, and yet, at the same time, it was a breathtaking risk. "Stay," she said again.

He held her a little closer, propped his chin on top of her head. Stroked the length of her back with his hands. "Those who don't learn from history," he said, "are condemned to repeat it."

Meg rested her head against his shoulder, breathed in the scent of him. Felt herself softening against the hard heat of his body.

And the telephone rang.

"It might be important," Brad said, setting Meg away from him a little, when she didn't jump to answer.

She picked up without checking the ID panel. "Hello."

"Jesse's home," Cheyenne said, honoring her earlier promise to let Meg know when he returned. "He's half-frozen. I poured a hot toddy down him and put him to bed."

"Thanks for calling, Chey," Meg replied.

"You're all right?" Cheyenne asked shyly.

Wondering how much Jesse had told his wife when he got home, Meg replied that she was fine.

"He told me he and Keegan barged in on you and Brad, up in the mountains somewhere," Cheyenne went on. "I'm sorry, Meg. Maybe I should have kept my mouth shut, but I heard a report of the blizzard on the radio and I—well—I guess I panicked a little."

"Everything's all right, Cheyenne. Really."

"He's there, isn't he? Brad, I mean. He's with you, right now."

"Since I'd rather not have a midnight visit from my cousins," Meg said, "I'm admitting nothing."

Cheyenne giggled. "My lips are zipped. Want to have lunch tomorrow?"

"That sounds good," Meg answered, smiling. Brad was standing behind her by then, sliding his hands under the front of her sweatshirt, stopping just short of her bare breasts. She fought to keep her voice even, her breathing normal. "Good night, Cheyenne."

"I'll meet you in town, at Lucky's Bar and Grill at noon," Cheyenne said. "Call me if you're still in bed or anything like that, and we'll reschedule."

Brad tweaked lightly at Meg's nipples; she swallowed a gasp of pleasure. "See you there," she replied, and hung up quickly.

Brad turned Meg around, gave her a knee-melting kiss and then swept her up into his arms. Carried her to the back stairs.

She directed him to the very bed Holt and Lorelei had shared as man and wife.

He laid her down on the deep, cushy mattress, a shadow figure rimmed in light from the hallway behind him. She couldn't see his face, but she felt his gaze on her, gentle and hungry and so hot it seared her.

Afraid honor might get the better of him, Meg wriggled out of her sweatpants, pulled the top off over her head.

Planning to sleep in the well-worn favorites, she hadn't bothered to put on a bra and panties after her bath earlier. Now she was completely naked. Utterly vulnerable.

Brad made a low, barely audible sound, rested one knee on the mattress beside her.

"Hold me," she whispered, and traces of an old song ran through her mind.

Help me make it through the night...

He stripped, maneuvered Meg so she was under the covers and joined her. The feel of him against her, solid and warm and all man, sent an electric rush of dizziness through her, pervading every cell.

She wrapped her arms around his neck and clung—she who never allowed herself to cling to anyone or anything except her own fierce pride.

A long, delicious time passed, without words, without caresses—only the holding.

The decision that there would be no foreplay was a tacit one.

The wanting was too great.

Brad nudged Meg's legs apart gently, settled between them, his erection pressing against her lower belly like a length of steel, heated in a forge.

She moaned and arched her back slightly, seeking him.

He took her with a single long, slow, smooth stroke, nestling into her depths. Held himself still as she gasped in wordless welcome.

He kissed her eyelids.

She squirmed beneath him.

He kissed her cheekbones.

Craving friction, desperate for it, Meg tried to move her hips, but he had her pinned, heavily, delectably, to the bed.

She whimpered.

He nibbled at her earlobes, one and then the other.

She ran her hands urgently up and down his back.

He tasted her neck.

She pleaded.

He withdrew, thrust again, but slowly.

She said his name.

He plunged deep.

And Meg came apart in his arms, raising herself high. Clawing, now at his back, now at the bedclothes, surrendering with a long, continuous, keening moan.

The climax was ferocious, but it was only a prelude to what would follow, and knowing that only increased Meg's need. Her body merged with Brad's, fused to it at the most elemental level, and the instant he began to move upon her she was lost again.

Even as she exploded, like a shattering star, she was aware of his phenomenal self-control, but when she reached her peak, he gave in. She reveled in the flex of his powerful body, the ragged, half groan, half shout of his release. Felt the warmth of his seed spilling inside her—and prayed it would take root.

Finally, he collapsed beside her, his face buried between her neck and the curve of her shoulder, his arms and legs still clenched around her, loosening by small, nearly imperceptible shivers.

Instinctively, Meg tilted her pelvis slightly backward, cradling the warmth.

A long while later, when both their breathing had returned to normal, or some semblance of that, Brad lifted his head. Touched his nose to hers. Started to speak, then thrust out a sigh, instead.

Meg threaded her fingers through his hair. Turned her head so she could kiss his chin.

"Guess you just earned another notch for the bedpost," she said.

He chuckled. "Yeah," he said. "Except this is *your* bed, McKettrick. *You* seduced *me*. I want that on record. Either way, since it's obviously an antique, carving the thing up probably wouldn't be the best idea."

"We're going to regret this in the morning, you know," she told him.

"That's then," he murmured, nibbling at her neck again. "This is now."

"Umm-hmm," Meg said. She wanted *now* to last forever.

"I kept expecting a helicopter."

Meg laughed. "Me, too."

Brad lifted his head again, and in the moonlight she could see the smile in his eyes. "Know what?"

"What?"

"I'm glad it happened this way. In a real bed, and not the floor of some old line shack." He kissed her, very lightly. "Although I would have settled for anything I could get."

She pretended to slug him.

He laughed.

She felt him hardening against her, pressed against the outside of her right thigh. Stretching, he found the switch on the bedside lamp and turned it, spilling light over her. The glow of it seemed to seep into her skin, golden. Or was it the other way around? Was *she* the one shining, instead of the lamp?

"God," Brad whispered, "you *are* beautiful."

A tigress before, now Meg felt shy. Turned her head to one side, closed her eyes.

Brad caressed her breasts, her stomach and abdomen and the tops of her thighs; his touch so light, so gentle, that it made her breath catch in her throat.

"Look at me," he said.

She met his eyes. "The light," she protested weakly.

He slid his fingers between the moist curls at the juncture of her thighs. "So beautiful," he said.

She gasped as he made slow, sweet circles, deliberately exciting her. "Brad—"

"What?"

She was conscious of the softness of her belly; knew her breasts weren't as firm and high as he remembered. She wanted more of his lovemaking, and still more, but under the cover of darkness and finely woven sheets and the heirloom quilt Lorelei McKettrick had stitched with her own hands, so many years before. "The *light*."

He made no move to flip the switch off again, but continued to stroke her, watching her responses. When he slipped his fingers inside her, found her G-spot and plied it expertly, she stopped worrying about the light and became a part of it.

While Meg slept, Brad slipped out of bed, pulled his borrowed clothes back on and retrieved his own from the bathroom where he'd showered earlier. Sat on the edge of the big claw-foot bathtub to pull on his socks and boots, still damp from his ride down the mountainside with Jesse.

Downstairs, he found the old-fashioned thermostat and turned it up. Dusty heat whooshed from the vents. In the kitchen he switched on the lights, filled and set the coffeemaker. Maybe these small courtesies would make up for his leaving before Meg woke up.

He found a pencil and a memo pad over by the phone, planning to scribble a note, but nothing suitable came to mind, at least not right away.

"Thanks" would be inappropriate.

"Goodbye" sounded too blunt.

Only a jerk would write "See you around."

"I'll call you later"? Too cavalier.

Finally, he settled on "Horses to feed."

Four of his songs had won Grammies, and all he could come up with was "horses to feed"? He was slipping.

He paused, stood looking up at the ceiling for a few moments, wanting nothing so much as to go back upstairs, crawl in bed with Meg again and make love to her.

Again.

But she'd said they were going to have regrets in the morning, and he didn't want to see those regrets on her face. The two of them would make bumbling excuses, never quite meeting each other's eyes.

And Brad knew he couldn't handle that.

So he left.

Meg stood in her warm kitchen, bundled in a terry cloth bathrobe and surrounded by the aroma of freshly brewed coffee, peering at the note Brad had left.

Horses to feed.

"The man's a poet," she said out loud.

"Do you think it took?" Angus asked.

Meg whirled to find him standing just behind her, almost at her elbow. "You scared me!" she accused, one hand pressed to her heart, which felt as though it might scramble up her esophagus to the back of her throat.

"Sorry," Angus said, though there was nothing the least bit contrite about his tone or his expression.

"Do I think *what* took?" Meg had barely sputtered the words when the awful realization struck her: Angus was asking if she thought she'd gotten pregnant, which meant—

Oh, God.

"Tell me you weren't here!"

"What do you take me for?" Angus snapped. "Of *course* I wasn't!"

Meg swallowed. Flushed to the roots of her hair. "But you knew—"

"I saw that singing cowboy leave just before sunup," came the taciturn reply. Now Angus was blushing, too. "Wasn't too hard to guess the rest."

"Will you stop calling him 'that singing cowboy'? He has a name. It's Brad O'Ballivan."

"I know that," Angus said. "But he's a fair hand with a horse, and he croons a decent tune. To my way of thinking, that makes him a singing cowboy."

Meg gave him a look, padded to the refrigerator, jerked open the door and rummaged around for something that might constitute breakfast. She'd cooked the last of the eggs for Brad, and the remaining choices were severely limited. Three green olives floating in a jar, some withered cheese, the arthritic remains of last week's takeout pizza and a carton of baking soda.

"Food doesn't just appear in an icebox, you know," Angus announced. "In my day, you had to hunt it down, or grow it in a garden, or harvest it from a field."

"Yes, and you probably walked ten miles to and from school," Meg said irritably, "uphill both ways."

She was starving. She'd have to hit the drive-through in town, then pick up some groceries. All that before her lunch with Cheyenne.

"I never went to school," Angus replied seriously, not getting the joke. "My ma taught me to read from the Good Book. I learned the rest on my own."

Meg sighed as an answer, shoved the splayed fingers of one hand through her tangled hair. Although she'd been disappointed at first to wake up and find Brad gone, now she was glad he couldn't see her. She looked like—well—a woman who had been having howling, sweaty-sheet sex half the night.

She started for the stairs.

"Make yourself at home," she told Angus, wondering if he'd catch the irony in her tone. For him, "home" was the Great Beyond, or the main ranch house down by the creek.

When she came down again half an hour later, showered and dressed in jeans and a lightweight blue sweater, he was sitting in Holt's chair, waiting for her.

"You ever think about wearing a dress or a skirt?" he asked, frowning.

Meg let that pass. "I've got some errands to run. See you later."

The telephone rang.

Brad?

She checked the caller ID panel.

Her mother.

"Voice mail will pick up," she told Angus.

"Answer it," Angus said sternly.

Meg reached for the receiver. "Hello, Mom. I was just on my way out the door—"

"You'd better sit down," Eve told her.

The pit of Meg's stomach pitched. "Why? Mom, is Sierra all right? Nothing's happened to Liam—"

"Both of them are fine. It's nothing like that."

Meg let out her breath. Leaned against the kitchen counter for support. "What, then?"

"Your father contacted me this morning. He wants to see you."

Meg's knees almost gave out. She'd never met her father, never spoken to him on the telephone or received so much as a birthday or Christmas card from him. She wasn't even sure what his name was—he used so many aliases.

"Meg?"

"I'm here," Meg said. "I don't want to see him."

"I knew I should have talked to you in person," Eve sighed. "But I was so alarmed—"

"Mother, did you hear what I just said? I don't want to see my father."

"He claims he's dying."

"Well, I'm sincerely sorry to hear that, but I still don't want anything to do with him."

"Meg—"

"I mean it, Mother. He's been a nonentity in my life. What could he possibly have to say to me now, after all this time?"

"I don't know," Eve replied.

"And if he wanted to talk to me, why did he call you?" The moment the question left her mouth, Meg wished she hadn't asked it.

"I think he's afraid."

"But he wasn't afraid of you?"

"He's past that, I think," Eve said. She'd been downright secretive on the subject of Meg's father from the first. Now, suddenly, she seemed to be urging Meg to make contact with him. What was going on? "Listen, why don't you stop by the hotel, and I'll make you some breakfast. We'll talk."

"Mom—"

"Blueberry pancakes. Maple-cured bacon. Your favorites."

"All right," Meg said, because as shaken as she was, she could have eaten the proverbial horse. "I'll be there in twenty minutes."

"Good," Eve replied, a little smugly, Meg thought. She was used to getting her way. After all, for almost thirty years, when Eve McKettrick said "jump," everybody reached for a vaulting pole.

"Are you going to ride shotgun?" Meg asked Angus after she'd hung up.

"I wouldn't miss this for anything," Angus said with relish.

Less than half an hour later, Meg was knocking on the front door of her mother's hotel suite.

When it opened, a man stood looking down at her, his expression uncertain and at the same time hopeful. She saw her own features reflected in the shape of his face, the set of his shoulders, the curve of his mouth.

"Hello, Meg," said her long-lost father.

CHAPTER EIGHT

AFTER THE HORSES HAD BEEN FED, Brad turned them out
to pasture for the day and made his way not into the big,
lonely house, but to the copse of trees where Big John was
buried. The old man's simple marker looked painfully new,
amid the chipped and moss-covered stone crosses marking
the graves of other, earlier O'Ballivans and Blackstones.

Brad had meant to visit the small private cemetery first
thing, but between one thing and another, he hadn't managed it until now.

Standing there, in the shade of trees already shedding
gold and crimson and rust-colored leaves, he moved to
take off his hat, remembered that he wasn't wearing one
and crouched to brush a scattering of fallen foliage from
the now-sunken mound.

About time you showed up, he heard Big John O'Ballivan's booming voice observe, echoing through the channels
of his mind.

Brad gave a lopsided, rueful grin. His eyes smarted, so
he blinked a couple of times. "I'm here, old man," he answered hoarsely. "And I mean to stay. Look after the girls
and the place. That ought to make you happy."

There was no reply from his grandfather, not even in his
head.

But Brad felt like talking, so he did.

"I'm seeing Meg McKettrick again," he said. "Turns out

I got her pregnant, back when we were kids, and she lost the baby. I never knew about it until yesterday."

Had Big John been there in the flesh, there'd have been a lecture coming. Brad would have welcomed that, even though the old man could peel off a strip of hide when he was riled.

One more reason why you should have stayed here and attended to business, Big John would have said. And that would have been just the warm-up.

"You never understood," Brad went on, just as if the old man *had* spoken. "We were going to lose Stone Creek Ranch. Maybe you weren't able to face that, but I had to. Everything Sam and Maddie and the ones who came after did to hold on to this place would have been for nothing."

The McKettricks would have stepped in if he'd asked for help, Brad knew that. Meg herself, probably her mother, too. Contrary as that Triple M bunch was, they'd bailed more than one neighbor out of financial trouble, saved dozens of smaller farms and ranches when beef prices bottomed out and things got tough. Even after all this time, though, the thought of going to them with his hat in his hands made the back of Brad's throat scald.

Although the ground was hard, wet and cold, he sat, cross-legged, gazing upon his grandfather's grave through a misty haze. He'd paid a high price for his pride, big, fancy career notwithstanding.

He'd lost the years he might have spent with Meg, the other children that might have come along. He hadn't been around when Big John needed him, and his sisters, though they were all educated, independent women, had been mere girls when he left. Sure, Big John had loved and protected them, in his gruff way, but that didn't excuse *his* absence. He should have been their big brother.

Caught up in these thoughts, and all the emotions they

engendered, Brad heard the approaching rig, but didn't look around. Heard the engine shut off, the door slam.

"Hey," Olivia said softly from just behind him.

"Hey," he replied, not ready to look back and meet his sister's gaze.

"Willie's better. I've got him in the truck."

Brad blinked again. "That's good," he said. "Guess I'd better go to town and get him some dog food and stuff."

"I brought everything he needs," Livie said, her voice quiet. She came and sat down beside Brad. "Missing Big John?"

"Every day," Brad admitted. Their mother had hit the road when the twins were barely walking, and their dad had died a year later, herding spooked cattle in a lightning storm. Big John had stepped up to raise four young grandchildren without a word of complaint.

"Me, too," Livie replied softly. "You ever wonder where our mom ended up?"

Brad knew where Della O'Ballivan was—living in a trailer park outside of Independence, Missouri, with the latest in a long line of drunken boyfriends—but he'd never shared that information with his sisters. The story, brought to him by the private detective he'd hired on the proceeds from his first hit record, wasn't a pretty one.

"No," he said in all honesty. "I never wonder." He'd gone to see Della, once he'd learned her whereabouts. She'd been sloshed and more interested in his stardom, and how it might benefit her, than getting to know him. Ironically, she'd refused the help he *had* offered—immediate admission to one of the best treatment centers in the world—standing there in a tattered housecoat and scruffy slippers, with lipstick stains in the deep smoker's lines surrounding her mouth. She hadn't even asked about her daughters or the husband she'd left behind.

"She's probably dead," Livie said with a sigh.

Since Della's existence couldn't be called living, Brad agreed. "Probably," he replied. Except for periodic requests for a check, which were handled by his accountant, Brad never heard from their mother.

"It's why I don't want to get married, you know," Livie confided. "Because I might be like her. Just get on a bus one day and leave."

Just get on a bus one day and leave.

Like he'd done to Meg, Brad reflected, hurting. Maybe he was more like Della than he'd ever want to admit aloud.

"You'd never do that," he told his sister.

"I used to think she'd come home," Livie went on sadly. "To see me play Mary in the Christmas program at church, or when I got that award for my 4-H project, back in sixth grade."

Brad slipped an arm around Livie's shoulders, felt them trembling a little, squeezed. His reaction had been different from Livie's—if Della had come back, especially after their dad was killed, he'd have spit in her face.

"And you figure if you got married and had kids, you'd just up and leave them? Miss all the Christmas plays and the 4-H projects?"

"I remember her, Brad," Livie said. "Just the lilac smell of her, and that she was pretty, but I remember. She used to sing a lot, hanging clothes out on the line and things like that. She read me stories. And then she was—well—just *gone.* I could never make sense of it. I always figured I must have done something really bad—"

"The flaw was in her, Livie, not you."

"That's the thing about flaws like that. You never know where they're going to show up. Mom probably didn't expect to abandon us."

Brad didn't agree, but he couldn't say so without revealing way too much. The Della he knew was an unmedicated bipolar with a penchant for gin, light on the tonic water. She'd probably married Jim O'Ballivan on a manic high, and decided to hit the road on a low—or vice versa. It was a miracle, by Brad's calculations, that she'd stayed on Stone Creek Ranch as long as she had, far from the bright lights and big-town bars, where a practicing drunk might enjoy a degree of anonymity.

Coupled with things Big John had said about his daughter-in-law, "man to man" and in strictest confidence, that she'd hidden bottles around the place and slept with ranch hands when there were any around, Brad had few illusions about her morals.

Livie got to her feet, dusting off her jeans as she rose, and Brad immediately did the same.

"I'd better get Willie settled in," she said. "I've got a barn full of sick cows to see to, down the road at the Iversons' place."

"Anything serious?" Brad asked, as Livie headed for the Suburban parked next to his truck, and he kept pace. "The cows, I mean?"

"Some kind of a fever," Livie answered, looking worried. "I drew some random blood samples the last time I was there, and sent them to the university lab in Tempe for analysis. Nothing anybody's ever seen before."

"Contagious?"

Livie sighed. Her small shoulders slumped a little, under the weight of her life's calling, and not for the first time, Brad wished she'd gone into a less stressful occupation than veterinary medicine.

"Possibly," she said.

Brad waited politely until she'd climbed into the Suburban—Willie was curled comfortably in the backseat, in a nest of old blankets—then got behind the wheel of his truck to follow her to the house.

There, he was annoyed to see a black stretch limo waiting, motor purring.

Phil.

Muttering a curse, Brad did his best to ignore the obvious, got out of the truck and strode to Livie's Suburban to hoist Willie out of the backseat and carry him into the house. Livie was on his heels, arms full of rudimentary dog equipment, but she cast a few curious glances toward the stretch.

They entered through the kitchen door. Olivia set the dog bed down in a sunny corner, and Brad carefully lowered Willie onto it.

"Who's in the big car?" Livie asked.

"Probably Phil Meadowbrook," Brad said a little tersely.

"Your manager?" Livie's eyes were wary. She was probably thinking Phil would make an offer Brad couldn't refuse, and he'd leave again.

"*Former* manager."

Willie, his hide criss-crossed with pink shaved strips and stitches, looked up at Brad with luminous, trusting eyes.

Livie was watching him, too. There was something bruised about her expression. She knew him better than Willie did.

"We need you around, Brad," she said at great cost to her pride. "Not just the twins and me, but the whole community. If the Iversons have to put down all those cows, they'll go under. They're already in debt up to their eyeballs—last year, Mrs. Iverson had a bout with breast cancer, and they didn't have insurance."

Brad's jaw tightened, and so did the pit of his stomach. "I'll write a check," he said.

Livie caught hold of his forearm. *"No,"* she said with a vehemence that set him back on his heels a little. "That would make them feel like charity cases. They're good, decent people, Brad."

"Then what do you want me to do?" Half Brad's attention was on the conversation, the other half on the distant closing of the limo door, so he'd probably sounded abrupt.

"Put on a concert," Livie said. "There are half a dozen other families around Stone Creek in similar situations. Divvy up the proceeds, and that will spare everybody's dignity."

Brad frowned down at his sister. "How long has *that* plan been brewing in your busy little head, Dr. Livie?"

She smiled. "Ever since you raised all that money for the animals displaced during Hurricane Katrina," she said.

A knock sounded at the outside door.

Phil's big schnoz was pressed to the screen.

"Gotta go," Livie said. She squatted to give Willie a goodbye pat and ducked out of the kitchen, headed for the front.

"Can I come in?" Phil asked plaintively.

"Would it make a difference if I said no?" Brad shot back.

The screen door creaked open. "Of course not," Phil said, smiling broadly. "I came all the way from New Jersey to talk some sense into your head."

"I could have saved you the trip," Brad answered. "I'm not going to Vegas. I'm not going *anywhere*." He liked Phil, but after the events of the past twenty-four hours, he was something the worse for wear. With his chores done and the overdue visit to Big John's grave behind him, he'd planned to eat something, take a hot shower and fall face-first into his unmade bed.

"Who said anything about Vegas?" Phil asked, the picture of innocent affront. "Maybe I want to deliver a big fat royalty check or something like that."

"And maybe you're full of crap," Brad countered. "I just *got* a 'big, fat royalty check,' according to my accountant. He's fit to be tied because the recording company promised to parcel the money out over at least fifteen years, and it came in a lump sum instead. Says the taxes are going to eat me alive."

Phil sniffled, pretended to wipe tears from his eyes. "Cry me a river, Mr. Country Music," he said. "I belong to the you-can-never-be-too-rich school of thought. Until my niece suffered that bout with anorexia—thank God she recovered—I thought you could never be too thin, either, but that theory's down the swirler."

Brad said nothing.

"What happened to that dog?" Phil asked, after giving Willie the eyeball.

"He was attacked by coyotes—or maybe wolves."

Livie had lugged in a bag of kibble and a couple of bowls, along with the bed Willie was lounging on now, and she'd set two prescription bottles on the counter, too, though Brad hadn't noticed them until now. He busied himself with reading the labels.

"Why anybody'd want to live in a place where a thing like that is even remotely possible, even if he *is* a dog," Phil marveled, "is beyond me."

Willie was to have one of each pill—an antibiotic and a painkiller—morning and night. With food. "A lot of things are beyond you, Phil," Brad said, figuring Olivia must have dosed the dog that morning before leaving the clinic, which meant the medication could wait until suppertime.

"He's pretty torn up. Wouldn't have happened in Music City, to a dog *or* a man."

"Evidently," Brad said, still distracted, "you've repressed the gory memories of my second divorce."

Phil chuckled. "You could give all that extra royalty money you're so worried about to good ole Cynthia," he suggested. "Write it off as an extra settlement and let *her* worry about the taxes."

"You're just full of wisdom today. Something else, too."

Uninvited, Phil drew back a chair at the table and sank into it, one hand pressed dramatically to his heart. "Phew," he sighed. "The old ticker ain't what it used to be."

"Right," Brad said. "I was there for the celebration after your last cardiology workup, remember? You probably have a better heart than I do, so spare me the sympathy plays."

"You have a heart?" Phil countered, raising his bushy gray eyebrows almost to his thinning hairline. Even with plugs, the carpet looked pretty sparse. Phil's pate always reminded Brad of the dolls his sisters had had when they were little, sprouting shocks of hair out of holes in neat little rows. "Couldn't prove it by me."

"Whatever," Brad said, dipping one of Willie's bowls into the kibble bag, then setting it down, full, where the dog could reach it without getting off his bed. He followed up by filling the other bowl with tap water. Then, on second thought, he dumped that and poured the bottled kind, instead.

"This is something big," Phil said. "That's why I came in person."

"If I let you tell me, will you leave?" By then, Brad was plundering the fridge for the makings of breakfast.

"Got any kosher sausage in there?" the older man asked.

"Sorry," Brad answered. He'd come up with something

if Phil stayed, since he couldn't eat in front of the man, but he was still hoping for a speedy departure.

Next, he'd be hanging up a stocking on Christmas Eve, setting out an empty basket the night before Easter.

"Big opportunity," Phil continued. "Very, very big."

"I don't care."

"You don't care? This is a *movie*, Brad. The lead. A *feature*, too. A big Western with cattle and wagons and a cast of dozens. And you won't even have to sing."

"No."

"Two years ago, even a year ago, you would have *killed* for a chance like this!"

"That was then," Brad said, flashing back to the night before, when he'd said practically the same thing to Meg, "and this is now."

"I've got the script in the car. In my briefcase. Solid gold, Brad. It might even be Oscar material."

"Phil," Brad said, turning from the fridge with the makings of a serious omelet in his hands, "what part of 'no' is eluding you? Would it be the *N,* or the *O?*"

"But you'd get to play an *outlaw,* trying to go straight."

"Phil."

"You're really serious about this retirement thing, aren't you?" Phil sounded stunned. Aggrieved. And petulant. "In a year—hell, in *six months*—when you've got all this down-home stuff out of your system, you'll wish you'd listened to me!"

"I listened, Phil. Do you want an omelet?"

"Do I *want an omelet?* Hell, no! I want you to make a damned *movie!*"

"Not gonna happen, Phil."

Phil was suddenly super-alert, like a predator who's just spotted dinner on the hoof. "It's some woman, isn't it?"

Again, he flashed on Meg. The way she'd felt, silky and slick, against him. The way she'd scratched at his back and called his name...

"Maybe," he admitted.

"Do I need to remind you that your romantic history isn't exactly going to inspire a new line of Hallmark valentines?"

Brad sighed. Got out the skillet and set it on the stove. Willie gave him a sidelong look of commiseration from the dog bed.

"If you won't eat an omelet," Brad told Phil, "leave."

"That pretty little thing who sneaked out of here when I came to the door—was that her?"

"That was my sister," Brad said.

Phil raised himself laboriously to his feet, like he was ninety-seven instead of seventy-seven, and all that would save him from a painful and rapid descent into the grave all but yawning at the tips of his gleaming shoes was Brad's signature on a movie contract. "Well, whoever this woman is, I'd like her name. Maybe *she* can get you to see reason."

That made Brad smile. Meg made him see galaxies colliding. Once or twice, during the night, he'd almost seen God. But reason?

Nope.

He plopped a dollop of butter into the skillet.

Phil made a huffy exit, slamming the screen door behind him.

Willie gave a low whine.

"You're right," Brad told the dog. "He'll probably be back."

Meg stood as if frozen in the hallway of Indian Rock's only hotel, wanting to turn and run, but too stunned to move.

She'd just gathered the impetus to flee when her father stuck a hand out. "Ted Ledger," he said, by way of introduction. "Come in and meet your sister, Meg."

Her sister?

It was that, added to a desire to commit matricide, that brought Meg over the threshold and into her mother's simply furnished, elegantly rustic suite.

Eve was nowhere in sight, the coward. But a little girl, ten or twelve years old, sat stiffly on the couch, hands folded in her lap. She was blond and blue-eyed, clad in cheap discount-store jeans and a floral shirt with ruffles, and the look on her face was one of terrified defiance.

"Hello," Meg said, forcing the words past her heart, which was beating in her throat.

The marvelous blue eyes narrowed.

"Carly," said Ted Ledger, "say hello."

"Hello," Carly complied grudgingly.

Looking at the child, Meg couldn't help thinking that the baby she'd lost would have been about this same age, if it hadn't been for the miscarriage.

She straightened her spine. Turned to the father who hadn't cared enough to send her so much as an e-mail, let alone be part of her life. "Where is my mother?" she asked evenly.

"Hiding out," Ledger said with a wisp of a grin. In his youth, he'd probably been handsome. Now he was thin and gray-haired, with dark shadows under his pale blue eyes.

Carly looked Meg over again and jutted out her chin. "I don't want to live with her," she said. "She probably doesn't need a kid hanging around anyhow."

"Go in the kitchen," Ledger told the child.

To Meg's surprise, Carly obeyed.

"Live with me?" Meg echoed in a whisper.

"It's that or foster care," Ledger said. "Sit down."

Meg sat, not because her father had asked her to, but because all the starch had gone out of her knees. Questions battered at the back of her throat, like balls springing from a pitching machine.

Where have you been?

Why didn't you ever call?

If I kill my mother, could a dream-team get me off without prison time?

"I know this is sudden," Ted Ledger said, perching on the edge of the white velvet wingback chair Eve had had sent from her mansion in San Antonio, to make the place more "homey." "But the situation is desperate. *I'm* desperate."

Meg tried to swallow, but couldn't. Her mouth was too dry, and her esophagus had closed up. "I don't believe this," she croaked.

"Your mother and I agreed, long ago," Ledger went on, "that it would be best if I stayed out of your life. That's why she never brought you to visit me."

"Visit you?"

"I was in prison, Meg. For embezzlement."

"From McKettrickCo," Meg mused aloud, startled, but at the same time realizing that she'd known all along, on some half-conscious level.

"I told you he was a waste of hair and hide," Angus said. He stood over by the fake fireplace, one arm resting on the mantelpiece.

Meg took care to ignore him, not to so much as glance in his direction, though she could see him out of the corner of one eye. He was in old-man mode today, white-headed and wrinkled and John Wayne-tough, but dressed for the trail.

"Yes," Ledger replied. "Your mother saw that there was no scandal—easier to do in those days, before the media came into its own. I went to jail. She went on with her life."

"Where does Carly fit in?"

Ledger's smile was soft and sad. "While I was inside, I got religion, as they say. When I was released, I found a job, met a woman, got married. We had Carly. Then, three years ago, Sarah—my wife—was killed in a car accident. Things went downhill from there—I was diagnosed last month."

Tears burned in Meg's eyes, but they weren't for Ledger, or even for Sarah. They were for Carly. Although she'd grown up in a different financial situation, with all the stability that came with simply being a McKettrick, she knew what the child must be going through.

"You don't have any other family? Perhaps Sarah's people—"

Ledger shook his head. "There's no one. Your mother has generously agreed to pay my medical bills and arrange for a decent burial, but I'll be lucky if I live six weeks. And once I'm gone, Carly will be alone."

Meg pressed her fingertips to her temples and breathed slowly and deeply. "Maybe Mom could—"

"She's past the age to raise a twelve-year-old," Ledger interrupted.

He leaned forward slightly in his chair, rested his elbows on his knees, intertwined his fingers and let his hands dangle. "Meg, you don't owe me a damn thing. I was no kind of father, and I'm not pretending I was. But Carly is your half sister. She's got your blood in her veins. And she doesn't have anybody else."

Meg closed her eyes, trying to imagine herself raising a resentful, grieving preadolescent girl. As much as she'd longed for her own child, nothing had prepared her for this.

"She won't go to foster care," she said. "Mother would never allow it."

"Boarding school, then," Ledger replied. "Carly would hate that. Probably run away. She needs a real home. Love. Somebody young enough to steer her safely through her teens, at least."

"You heard her," Meg said. "She doesn't want to live with me."

"She doesn't know what she wants, except for me to have a miraculous recovery, and that isn't going to happen. I can't ask you to do this for me, Meg—I've got no right to ask anything of you—but I can ask you to do it for Carly."

The room seemed to tilt. From the kitchen, Meg heard her mother's voice, and Carly's. What were they talking about in there?

"Okay," Meg heard herself say.

Ledger's once-handsome face lit with a smile of relief and what looked like sincere gratitude. "You'll do it? You'll look after your sister?"

My sister.

"Yes," Meg said. On the outside, she probably looked calm. On the inside, she was shaking. "What happens now?"

"I go into the hospital for pain control. Carly goes home with you for a few days. When—and if—I get out, she'll come back to stay with me."

Meg nodded, her mind racing, groping, grasping for some handhold on an entirely new, entirely unexpected situation.

"We've got a room downstairs," Ledger said, rising painfully from the chair. "Carly and I will leave you alone with Eve for a little while."

Over by the fireplace, Angus scowled, powerful arms

folded across his chest. Fortunately, he didn't say anything, because Meg would have told him to shut up if he had.

Her father left, Carly trailing after him.

Eve stepped into the kitchen doorway the moment they'd gone.

Angus vanished.

"Nice work, Mom," Meg said, still too shaken to stand up. Since a murder would be hard to pull off sitting down, her mother was off the hook. Temporarily.

"She's about the same age as your baby would have been," Eve said. "It's fate."

Meg's mouth fell open.

"Of course I knew," Eve told her, venturing as far as the white velvet chair and perching gracefully on the edge of its cushion. "I'm your mother."

Meg closed her mouth. Tightly.

Eve's eyes were on the door through which Ted Ledger and Carly had just passed. "I loved him," she said. "But when he admitted stealing all that money, there was nothing I could do to keep him out of prison. We divorced after his conviction, and he asked me not to tell you where he was."

Meg sagged back in her own chair, still dizzy. Still speechless.

"She's a beautiful child," Eve said, referring, of course, to Carly. "You looked just like her, at that age. It's uncanny, really."

"She's bound to have a lot of problems," Meg managed.

"Of course she will. She lost her mother, and now her father is at death's door. But she has you, Meg. That makes her lucky, in spite of everything else."

"I haven't the faintest idea how to raise a child," Meg pointed out.

"Nobody does, when they start out," Eve reasoned. "Children don't come with a handbook, you know."

Suddenly, Meg remembered the lunch she had scheduled with Cheyenne, the groceries she'd intended to buy. Instantaneous motherhood hadn't been on her to-do list for the day.

She imagined making a call to Cheyenne. *Gotta postpone lunch. You see, I just gave birth to a twelve-year-old in my mother's living room.*

"I had plans," she said lamely.

"Didn't we all?" Eve countered.

"There's no food in my refrigerator."

"Supermarket's right down the road."

"Where have they been living? What kind of life has she had, up to now?"

"A hard one, I would imagine. Ted's something of a drifter—I suspect they've been living out of that old car he drives. He claims he homeschooled her, but knowing Ted, that probably means she knows how to read a racing form and calculate the odds of winning at Powerball."

"Great," Meg said, but something motherly was stirring inside her, something hopeful and brave and very, very fragile. "Can I count on you for help, or just the usual interference?"

Eve laughed. "Both," she said.

Meg found her purse, fumbled for her cell phone, dialed Cheyenne's number.

It was something of a relief that she got her friend's voice mail.

"This is Meg," she said. "I can't make it for lunch. How about a rain check?"

CHAPTER NINE

MEG MOVED THROUGH THE supermarket like a robot, pro-
grammed to take things off the shelves and drop them into
the cart. When she got home and started putting away her
groceries, she was surprised by some of the things she'd
bought. There were ingredients for actual meals, not just
things she could nuke in the microwave or eat right out of
the box or bag.

She was brewing coffee when a knock sounded at the
back door.

Glancing over, she saw her cousin Rance through the
little panes of glass and gestured for him to come in. Tall
and dark-haired, he looked as though he'd just come off a
nineteenth-century cattle drive, in his battered boots, old
jeans and Western-cut shirt. Favoring her with a lopsided
grin, he removed his hat and hung it on one of the pegs
next to the door.

"Heard you had a little shock this morning," he said.

Meg shook her head. She'd never gotten over how fast
word got around in a place like Indian Rock. Then again,
maybe Eve had called Rance, thinking Meg might need
emotional support. "You could say that," she replied. "Who
told you?"

Rance proceeded to the coffeemaker, which was still
doing its steaming and gurgling number, took a mug down
from the cupboard above and filled it, heedless of the brew

dripping, fragrant and sizzling, onto the base. Of course, being a man, he didn't bother to wipe up the overflow.

"Eve," he said, confirming her suspicions.

Meg, not usually a neatnik, made a big deal of paper-toweling up the spill around the bottom of the coffeemaker. "It's no emergency, Rance," she told him.

He looked ruefully amused. "Your dad walks into your life after something like thirty years and it's not an emergency?"

"I suppose Mom told you about Carly."

Rance nodded. Ushered Meg to a seat at the table, set down his coffee mug and went back to pour a cup for her, messing up the counter all over again. "Twelve years old, something of an attitude," he confirmed, giving her the cup and then sitting astride the bench. "And coming to live with you. Is that going to screw up your love life?"

"I don't *have* a love life," Meg said. Sure, she'd spent the night tangling sheets with Brad O'Ballivan but, one, primal sex didn't constitute a relationship and, two, it was none of Rance's business anyway.

"Whatever," Rance said. "The point is, you've got a kid to raise, and she's a handful, by all accounts. I'm no authority on bringing up kids, but I do have two daughters. I'll do what I can to help, Meg, and so will Emma."

Rance's girls, Maeve and Rianna, were like nieces to Meg, and so was Keegan's Devon. While they were all younger than Carly, they would be eager to include her in the family, and it was comforting to know that.

"Thanks," Meg said as her eyes misted over.

"You can do this," Rance told her.

"I don't seem to have a choice. Carly is my half sister, there's no one else, and blood is blood."

"If there's one concept a hardheaded McKettrick can comprehend right away, it's that."

"I don't know as we're all that hardheaded," Angus put in, after materializing behind Rance in the middle of the kitchen.

Meg didn't glance up, nor did she answer. She was close to Rance, Jesse and Keegan—always had been—but she'd never told them she saw Angus, dead since the early twentieth century, on a regular basis. Her mother knew, having overheard Meg talking to him, long after the age of entertaining imaginary playmates had passed, and for all the problems Eve had suffered after Sierra's kidnapping, she'd given her remaining daughter one inestimable gift. She'd believed her.

You're not the type to see things, Eve had said after Meg reluctantly explained. *If you say Angus McKettrick is here, then he is.*

Remembering, Meg felt a swell of love for her mother, despite an equal measure of annoyance.

"I'd better get back to punching cattle," Rance said, finishing his coffee and swinging a leg over the bench to stand. With winter coming on, he and his hired men were rounding up strays in the hills and driving the whole bunch down to the lower pastures. "If you need a hand over here, with the girl or anything else, you let me know."

Meg grinned up at him. He'd taken time out of a busy day to come over and check on her in person, and she appreciated that. "Once Carly's had a little time to settle in, we'll introduce her to Maeve and Rianna and Devon. I don't think she's got a clue what it's like to be part of a family like ours."

Rance laid a work-calloused hand on Meg's shoulder as he passed, carrying his empty coffee mug to the sink, then crossing to take his hat down from the peg. "Probably not," he agreed. "But she'll find out soon enough."

With that, Rance left.

Meg turned to acknowledge Angus. "We *are* hard-headed," she told him. "Every last one of us."

"I'd rather call it 'persistent,'" Angus imparted.

"Your decision," Meg responded, getting up to dispose of her own coffee cup then heading for the backstairs. She didn't know when Carly would be arriving, but it was time to get a room ready for her. That meant changing sheets, opening windows to air the place out and equipping the guest bathroom with necessities like clean towels, a tooth-brush and paste, shampoo and the like.

She'd barely finished, and returned to the kitchen to slap together a hasty lunch, when an old car rattled up along-side the house, backfired and shut down. As Meg watched from the window, Ted Ledger got out, keeping one hand to the car for balance as he rounded it, and leaned in on the opposite side, no doubt trying to persuade a reluctant Carly to alight.

Meg hurried outside.

By the time she reached the car, Carly was standing with a beat-up backpack dangling from one hand, staring at the barn.

"Do you have horses?" she asked.

Hallelujah, Meg thought. *Common ground.*

"Yes," she said, smiling.

"I hate horses," Carly said. "They smell and step on people."

Ted passed Meg a beleaguered look over the top of the old station wagon, his eyes pleading for patience.

"You do not," he said to Carly. Then, to Meg, "She's just being difficult."

Duh, Meg thought, but in spite of all her absent-father issues, she felt a pang of sympathy for the man. He was ter-minally ill, probably broke, and trying to find a place for his younger daughter to make the softest possible landing.

Meg figured it would be a fiery crash instead, complete with explosions, but she also knew she was up to the challenge. Mostly, that is. And with a lot of help from Rance, Keegan, Jesse and Sierra.

Oh, yeah. She'd be calling in her markers, all right.

Code-blue, calling all McKettricks.

"I'm not staying unless my dad can stay, too," Carly announced, standing her ground, there in the gravel of the upper driveway, knuckles white where she gripped the backpack.

Meg hadn't considered this development, though she supposed she should have. She forced herself to meet Ted's gaze, saw both resignation and hope in his eyes when she did.

"It's a big house," she heard herself say. "Plenty of room."

Rance's earlier question echoed in her mind. *Is that going to screw up your love life?*

There'd be no more overnight visits from Brad, at least not in the immediate future. To Meg, that was both a relief—things were moving too fast on that front—and a problem. Her body was still reverberating with the pleasure Brad had awakened in her, and already craving more.

"Okay," Carly said, moving a little closer to Ted. The two of them bumped shoulders in unspoken communication, and Meg felt a brief and unexpected stab of envy.

Meg tried to carry Ted's suitcase inside, but he wouldn't allow that. Manly pride, she supposed.

Angus watched from the back steps as the three of them trailed toward the house, Meg in the lead, Ted following and Carly straggling at the rear.

"She's a good kid," Angus said.

Meg gave him a look but said nothing.

Just walking into the house seemed to wear Ted out,

and as soon as Carly had been installed in her room, he expressed a need to lie down. Meg showed him to the space generations of McKettrick women—she being an exception—had done their sewing.

There was only a daybed, and Meg hadn't changed the sheets, but Ted waved away her offer to spruce up the room a little. She went out, closing the door behind her, and heard the bed-springs groan as if he'd collapsed onto them.

Carly's door was shut. Meg paused outside it, on her way to the rear stairway, considered knocking and decided to leave the poor kid alone, let her adjust to new and strange surroundings.

Downstairs, Meg went back to what she'd been doing when Ted and Carly arrived. She made a couple of extra sandwiches, just in case, wolfed one down with a glass of milk and eyeballed the phone.

Was Brad going to call, or was last night just another slam-bam to him? And if he *did* call, what exactly was she going to say?

Willie was surprisingly ambulatory, considering what he'd been through. When Brad came out of the upstairs bathroom, having showered and pulled on a pair of boxer-briefs and nothing else, the dog was waiting in the hall. Climbing the stairs must have been an ordeal, but he'd done it.

"You need to go outside, boy?" Brad asked. When Big John's health had started to decline, Brad had wanted to install an elevator, so the old man wouldn't have to manage a lot of steps, but he'd met with the usual response.

An elevator? Big John had scoffed. *Boy, all that fine Nashville livin' is goin' to your head.*

Now, with an injured dog on his hands, Brad wished he'd overridden his grandfather's protests.

He moved to lift Willie, intending to carry him downstairs and out the kitchen door to the grassy side yard, but a whimper from the dog foiled that idea. Carefully, the two of them made the descent, Willie stopping every few steps to rest, panting.

The whole process was painful to watch.

Reaching the kitchen at last, Brad opened the back door and waited as Willie labored outside, found a place in the grass after copious sniffing and did his business.

Once he was back inside, Brad decided another trip up the stairway was out of the question. He moved Willie's new dog bed into a small downstairs guest room, threw back the comforter on one of the twin-sized beds and fell onto it, face-first.

"Who's the old man?" Carly asked, startling Meg, who had been running more searches on Josiah McKettrick on the computer in the study, for more reasons than one.

"What old man?" Meg retorted pleasantly, turning in the chair to see her half sister standing in the big double doorway, looking much younger than twelve in a faded and somewhat frayed sleep shirt with a cartoon bear on the front.

"This house," Carly said implacably, "is haunted."

"It's been around a long time," Meg hedged, still smiling. "Lots of history here. Are you hungry?"

"Only if you've got the stuff to make grilled-cheese sandwiches," Carly said. She was in the gawky stage, but one day, she'd be gorgeous. Meg didn't see the resemblance Eve had commented on earlier, but if there was one, it was cause to feel flattered.

"I've got the stuff," Meg assured her, rising from her chair.

"I can do it myself," Carly said.

"Maybe we could talk a little," Meg replied.

"Or not," Carly answered, with a note of dismissal that sounded false.

Meg followed the woman-child to the kitchen, earning herself a few scathing backward glances in the process.

Efficiently, Carly opened the fridge, helped herself to a package of cheese and proceeded to the counter. Meg supplied bread and a butter dish and a skillet, but that was all the assistance Carly was willing to accept.

"Can you cook?" Meg asked, hoping to get some kind of dialogue going.

Carly shrugged one thin shoulder. Her feet were bare and a tiny tattoo of some kind of flower blossomed just above one ankle bone. "Dad's hopeless at it, so I learned."

"I see," Meg said, wondering what could have possessed her father to let a child get a tattoo, and if it had hurt much, getting poked with all those needles.

"You don't see," Carly said, skillfully preparing her sandwich, everything in her bearing warning Meg to keep her distance.

"What makes you say that?"

Another shrug.

"Carly?"

The girl's back, turned to Meg as she laid the sandwich in the skillet and adjusted the gas stove burner beneath, stiffened. "Don't ask me a bunch of questions, okay? Don't ask how it was, living on the road, or if I miss my mother, or what it's like knowing my dad is going to die. Just leave me be, and we'll get along all right."

"There's one question I have to ask," Meg said.

Carly tossed her another short, over-the-shoulder glower. "What?"

"Did it hurt a lot, getting that tattoo?"

Suddenly, a smile broke over Carly's face, and it changed everything about her. "Yes."

"Why did you do it?"

"That's *two* questions," Carly pointed out. "You said one."

"Was it because your friends got tattoos?"

Carly's smile faded, and she averted her attention again, spatula in hand, ready to turn her grilled-cheese sandwich when it was just right. "I don't have any friends," she said. "We moved around too much. And I didn't need them anyhow. Me and Dad—that was enough."

Meg's eyes burned.

"I got the tattoo," Carly said, catching Meg off-guard, "because my mom had one just like it, in the same place. It's a yellow rose—because Dad always called her his yellow rose of Texas."

Meg's throat went tight. How was she going to help this child face the loss of not one parent, but two? Sister or not, she was a stranger to Carly.

The phone rang.

Carly, being closest, picked up the receiver, peered at the caller ID panel, and went wide-eyed. *"Brad O'Ballivan?"* she whispered reverently, padding across the kitchen to give Meg the phone. *"The* Brad O'Ballivan?"

Meg choked out a laugh. Well, well, well. Carly was a fan. Just the opening Meg needed to establish some kind of bond, however tenuous, with her newly discovered kid sister. *"The* Brad O'Ballivan," she said before thumbing the talk button. "Hello?"

Brad's answer was an expansive yawn. Evidently, he'd either just awakened or he'd gone to bed early. Either way, the images playing in Meg's mind were scintillating ones, and they soon rippled into other parts of her anatomy, like tiny tsunamis boiling under her skin.

"Willie's home," he said finally.

Carly was staring at Meg. "I have all his CDs," she said.

"That's good," Meg answered.

"We ought to celebrate," Brad went on. "I grill a mean steak. Six-thirty, my place?"

"Only if you have a couple of spares," Meg said. "I have company."

The smell of scorching sandwich billowed from the stove.

Carly didn't move.

"Company?" Brad asked sleepily, with another yawn.

Meg pictured him scantily clothed, if he was wearing anything at all, with an attractive case of bed head. And she blushed to catch herself thinking lascivious thoughts with a twelve-year-old in the same room. "It's a lot to explain over the phone," she said diplomatically, gesturing to Carly to rescue the sandwich, which she finally did.

"The more the merrier," Brad said. "Whoever they are, bring them."

"We'll be there," Meg said.

Carly pushed the skillet off the burner and waved ineffectually at the smoke.

Meg said goodbye to Brad and hung up the phone.

"We're going to *Brad O'Ballivan's house?*" Carly blurted. *"For real?"*

"For real," Meg said. "If your dad feels up to it."

"He's your dad, too," Carly allowed. "And he likes Brad's music. We listen to it in the car all the time."

Meg let the part about Ted Ledger being her dad pass. He'd been her sire, not her father. "Let's let him rest," she said, taking over the grilled cheese operation and feeling glad when Carly didn't protest, or try to elbow her aside.

"How long have you known him?" Carly demanded, almost breathless.

It was a moment before Meg realized the girl was talking about Brad, not Ted, so muddled were her thoughts. "Since junior high," she said.

"What's he like?"

"He's nice," Meg said carefully, slicing cheese, reaching for the butter dish and then the bread bag.

"'Nice'?" Carly looked not only skeptical, but a little disappointed. "He trashes hotel rooms. He pushed a famous actress into a swimming pool at a big Hollywood party—"

"I think that's mostly hype," Meg said, hoping the kid hadn't heard the notches-in-the-bedpost stuff. She started the new sandwich in a fresh skillet and carried the first one to the sink. When she glanced Carly's way, she was surprised and touched to see she'd taken a seat on the bench next to the table.

"Do you think he'd autograph my CDs?"

"I'd say there was a fairly good chance he will, yes." She turned the sandwich, got out a china plate, poured a glass of milk.

Carly glowed with anticipation. "If I had any friends," she said, "I'd call them all and tell them I get to meet Brad O'Ballivan *in the flesh*."

And what flesh it was, Meg thought, and blushed again. "Once you start school," she said, "you'll have all kinds of friends. Plus, there are some kids in the family around your age."

"It's not my family," Carly said, stiffening again.

"Of course it is," Meg argued, but cautiously, scooping a letter-perfect grilled-cheese sandwich onto a plate and presenting it to Carly with a flourish, along with the milk. She wished Angus had been there, to see her cooking. "You and I are sisters. I'm a McKettrick. So that means you're related to them, too, if only by association."

"I hate milk," Carly said.

"Brad drinks it," Meg replied lightly.

Carly reached for the glass, took a sip. Pondered the taste, and then took another. "You see him, too," the child observed. "The old man, I mean."

Before Meg could come up with an answer, Angus reappeared.

"I'm not that old," he protested.

"Yes, you are," Carly argued, looking right at him. "You must be a hundred, and that's *old*."

Meg's mouth fell open.

"I *told* you I could see him," Carly said with a touch of smugness.

Angus laughed. "I'll be damned," he marveled.

Carly's brow furrowed. "Are you a ghost?"

"Not really," Angus said.

"What are you, then?"

"Just a person, like you. I'm from another time, that's all."

No big deal. I just step from one century to another at will. Anybody could do it.

Meg watched the exchange in amazement, speechless. Ever since she'd started seeing Angus, way back in her nursery days, she'd wished for one other person—just one—who could see him, too. Being different from other people was a lonely thing.

"When my dad dies, will he still be around?"

Angus approached the table, drew back Holt's chair, and sat down. His manner was gruff and gentle, at the same time, and Meg's throat tightened again, recalling all the times he'd comforted her, in his grave, deep-voiced way. "That's a question I can't rightly answer," he said solemnly.

"But I can tell you that folks don't really die, in the way you probably think of it. They're just in another place, that's all."

Carly blinked, obviously trying hard not to cry. "I'm going to miss him something awful," she said very softly.

Angus covered the child's small hand with one of his big, work-worn paws. There was such a rough tenderness in the gesture that Meg's throat closed up even more, and her eyes scalded.

"It's a fact of life, missing folks when they go away," Angus said. "You've got Meg, here, though." He nodded his head slightly, in her direction, but didn't look away from Carly's face. "She'll do right by you. It's the McKettrick way, taking care of your own."

"But I'm not a McKettrick," Carly said.

"You could be if you wanted to," Angus reasoned. "You're not a Ledger, either, are you?"

"We've changed our name so many times," the child admitted, her eyes round and sad and a little hungry as she studied Angus, "I don't remember who I am."

"Then you might as well be a McKettrick as not," Angus said.

Carly's gaze slid to Meg, swung away again. "I'm not going to forget my dad," she said.

"Nobody expects you to do that," Angus replied. "Thing is, you've got a long life ahead of you, and it'll be a lot easier with a family to take your part when the trail gets rugged."

Upstairs, a door opened, then closed again.

"Your pa," Angus told Carly, lowering his voice a little, "is real worried about you being all right, once he's gone. You could put his mind at ease a bit, if you'd give Meg a chance to act like a big sister."

Carly bit her lower lip, then nodded. "I wish you

wouldn't go away," she said. "But I know you're going to."
She paused, and Meg grappled with the sudden knowledge
that it was true—one day soon, Angus would vanish, for
good. "If you see my mom—her name is Rose—will you
tell her I've got a tattoo just like hers?"

"I surely will," Angus promised.

"And you'll look out for my dad, too?"

Angus nodded, his eyes misty. It was a phenomenon
Meg had never seen before, even at family funerals. Then
he ruffled Carly's hair and vanished just as Ted came down
the stairs, moving slowly, holding tightly to the rail.

It was all Meg could do not to rush to his aid.

"Hungry?" she asked moderately.

"I could eat," Ted volunteered, looking at Carly. His
whole face softened as he gazed at his younger child.

It made Meg wonder if he'd ever missed *her,* during all
those years away.

As if he'd heard her thoughts, her father turned to her.
"You turned out real well," he said after clearing his throat.
"Your mom did a good job, raising you. But, then, Eve was
always competent."

"We're going to meet Brad O'Ballivan," Carly said.

"Get out," Ted teased, a faint twinkle shining in his eyes.
"We're not, either."

"Yes, we are," Carly insisted. "Meg knows him. He just
called here. Meg says he might autograph my CDs."

Ted grinned, made his way to the table and sank into the
chair Angus had occupied until moments before. Spent a
few moments recovering from the exertion of descending
the stairs and crossing the room.

Meg served up the extra sandwiches she'd made earlier,
struggling all the while with a lot of tangled emotions. Carly
could see Angus. Ted Ledger might be a total stranger, but
he was Meg's father, and he was dying.

Last but certainly not least, Brad was back in her life, and there were bound to be complications.

A strange combination of grief, joy and anticipation pushed at the inside walls of Meg's heart.

They arrived right on time, Meg and a young girl and a man who put Brad in mind of a faster-aging Paul Newman. Willie, who'd been resting on the soft grass bordering the flagstone patio off the kitchen, keeping an eye on his new master while he prepared the barbecue grill for action, gave a soft little woof.

Brad watched as Meg approached, thinking how delicious she looked in her jeans and lightweight, close-fitting sweater. She hadn't explained who her company was, but looking at them, Brad saw the girl's resemblance to Meg, and guessed the man to be the father she hadn't seen since she was a toddler.

He smiled.

The girl blushed and stared at him.

"Hey," he said, putting out a hand. "My name's Brad O'Ballivan."

"I know," the girl said.

"My sister, Carly," Meg told him. "And this is my—this is Ted Ledger."

Shyly, Carly slipped off her backpack, reached inside, took out a couple of beat-up CDs. "Meg said I could maybe get your autograph."

"No maybe about it," Brad answered. "I don't happen to have a pen on me at the moment, though."

Carly swallowed visibly. "That's okay," she said, her gaze straying to Willie, who was thumping his tail against the ground and grinning a goofy dog grin at her, hoping for friendship. "What happened to him?"

"He had a run-in with a pack of coyotes," Brad said.

"He'll be all right, though. Just needs a little time to mend."

The girl crouched next to the dog, stroked him gently. "Hi," she said.

Meanwhile, Meg's father took a seat at the patio table. He looked bushed.

"I had to have stitches once," Carly told Willie. "Not as many as you've got, though."

"Brad's sister is a veterinarian," Meg said, finally finding her voice. "She fixed him right up."

"I'd like to be a veterinarian," Carly said.

"No reason you can't," Brad replied, turning his attention to Ted Ledger. "Can I get you a drink, Mr. Ledger?"

Ledger shook his head. "No, thanks," he said quietly. His gaze moved fondly between Meg and Carly, resting on one, then the other. "Good of you to have us over. I appreciate it. And I'd rather you called me Ted."

"Is there anything I can do to help?" Meg asked.

"I've got it under control," Brad told her. "Just relax."

Great advice, O'Ballivan, he thought. *Maybe you ought to take it.*

Meg went to greet Willie, who gave a whine of greeting and tried to lick her face. She laughed, and Brad felt something open up inside him, at the sound. When he'd conceived the supper idea, he'd intended to ply her with good wine and a thick steak, then take her to bed. The extra guests precluded that plan, of course, but he didn't regret it. When it finally registered that his and Meg's child might have looked a lot like Carly, though, he felt bruised all over again.

"Any news about Ransom?" Meg asked, stepping up beside him when he turned his back to lay steaks on the grill, along with foil-wrapped baked potatoes that had been cooking for a while.

Brad shook his head, suddenly unable to look at her. If he did, she'd see all the things he felt, and he wasn't ready for that.

"According to the radio," Meg persisted, "the blizzard's passed, and the snow's melted."

Brad sighed. "I guess that means I'd better ride up and look for that stallion before Livie decides to do it by herself."

"I'd like to go with you," Meg said, sounding almost shy.

Brad thought about the baby who'd never had a chance to grow up. The baby Meg hadn't seen fit to tell him about. "We'll see," he answered noncommittally. "How do you like your steak?"

CHAPTER TEN

AFTER THE MEAL HAD BEEN served and enjoyed, with
Willie getting the occasional scrap, Brad signed the as-
tounding succession of CDs Carly fished out of her backpack. Ted, who had eaten little, seemed content to watch
the scene from a patio chair, and Meg insisted on clean-
ing up; since she'd had no part in the preparations, it only
seemed fair.

As she carried in plates and glasses and silverware,
rinsed them and put them into the oversize dishwasher,
she reflected on Brad's mood change. He'd been warm
to Ted, and chatted and joked with Carly, but when she'd
mentioned that she'd like to accompany him when he went
looking for Ransom again, it was as if a wall had slammed
down between them.

She was just shutting the dishwasher and looking for the
appropriate button to push when the screen door creaked
open behind her. She turned, saw Brad hesitating on the
threshold. It was past dusk—outside, the patio lights were
burning brightly—but Meg hadn't bothered to flip a switch
when she came in, so the kitchen was almost dark.

"Kid wants a T-shirt," he said, his face in shadow so she
couldn't read his expression. "I think I have a few around
here someplace."

Meg nodded, oddly stricken.

Brad didn't move right away, but simply stood there for

a few long moments; she knew by the tilt of his head that he was watching her.

"You've gone out of your way to be kind to Carly," Meg managed, because the silence was unbearable. "Thank you."

He still didn't speak, or move.

Meg swallowed hard. "Well, it's getting late," she said awkwardly. "I guess we'd better be heading for home soon."

Brad reached out for a switch, and the overhead lights came on, seeming harsh after the previous cozy twilight in the room. His face looked bleak to Meg, his broad shoulders seemed to stoop a little.

"Seeing her—Carly, I mean—"

"I know," Meg said very softly. Of course Brad saw what she had, when he looked at Carly—the child who might have been.

"She's her own person," Brad said with an almost inaudible sigh. "It wouldn't be right to think of her in any other way. But it gave me a start, seeing her. She looks so much like you. So much like—"

"Yes."

"What's going on, Meg? You said you couldn't explain over the phone, and I figured out that Ledger had to be your dad. But there's more to this, isn't there?"

Meg bit her lower lip. "Ted is dying," she said. "And it turns out that Carly has no one else in the world except me."

Brad processed that, nodded. "Be careful," he told her quietly. "Carly is Carly. It would be all too easy—and completely unfair—to superimpose—"

"I wouldn't do that, Brad," Meg broke in, bristling. "I'm not pretending she's—she's our daughter."

"Guess I'll go rustle up that T-shirt," Brad said.

Meg didn't respond. For the time being, the conversation—at least as far as their lost child was concerned—was over.

Carly wore the T-shirt home—Brad's guitar-wielding profile was silhouetted on the front, along with the year of a recent tour and an impressive list of cities—practically bouncing in the car seat as she examined the showy signature on the face of each of her CDs.

"I bet he never trashed a single hotel room," she enthused, from the backseat of Meg's Blazer. "He's way too nice to do that."

Meg and Ted exchanged a look of weary amusement up front.

"It was quite an evening," Ted said. "Thanks, Meg."

"Brad did all the work," she replied.

"I like his dog, too," Carly bubbled. She seemed to have forgotten her situation, for the time being, and Meg could see that was a relief to Ted. "Brad said he'd change his name to Stitches, if he didn't already answer to Willie."

Meg smiled.

All the way home, it was Brad said this, Brad said that.

Once they'd reached the ranch house, Ted went inside, exhausted, while Carly and Meg headed for the barn to feed the horses. Despite her earlier condemnation of the entire equine species, Carly proved a fair hand with hay and grain.

"Is he your boyfriend?" Carly asked, keeping pace with Meg as they returned to the house.

"Is who my boyfriend?" Meg parried.

"You *know* I mean Brad," Carly said. "Is he?"

"He's a *friend*," Meg said. But a voice in her mind chided, *Right. And last night, you were rolling around on a mattress with him.*

"I may be twelve, but I'm not stupid," Carly remarked, as they reached the back door. "I saw the way he looked at you. Like he wanted to put his hands on you all the time."

Yeah, Meg thought wearily. *Specifically, around my throat.*

"You're imagining things."

"I'm very sophisticated for twelve," Carly argued.

"Maybe *too* sophisticated."

"If you think I'm going to act like some *kid,* just because I'm twelve, think again."

"That's exactly what I think. A twelve-year-old *is* a kid." Meg pushed open the kitchen door; Ted had turned on the lights as he entered, and the place glowed with homey warmth. "Go to bed."

"There's no TV in my room," Carly protested. "And I'm not sleepy."

"Tough it out," Meg replied. Crossing to the china cabinet on the far side of the room, she opened a drawer, found a notebook and a pen, and handed them to her little sister. "Here," she said. "Keep a journal. It's a tradition in the McKettrick family."

Carly hesitated, then accepted the offering. "I guess I could write about Brad O'Ballivan," she said. She held the notebook to her chest for a moment. "Are you going to read it?"

"No," Meg said, softening a little. "You can write anything you want to. Sometimes it helps to get feelings out of your head and onto paper. Then you can get some perspective."

Carly considered. "Okay," she said and started for the stairs, taking the notebook with her.

Meg, knowing she wouldn't sleep, tired as she was, headed for the study as soon as Carly disappeared, logged on to the internet and resumed her research.

"You won't find him on that contraption," Angus told her.

She looked up to see him sitting in the big leather wing-back chair by the fireplace. Like many other things in the house, the chair was a holdover from the Holt and Lorelei days.

"Josiah, I mean," Angus added, jawline hard again as he remembered the brother who had so disappointed him. "I told you he didn't use the McKettrick name." He gave a snort. "Sounded too Irish for him."

"Help me out, here," Meg said.

Angus remained silent.

Meg sighed and turned back to the screen. She'd been scrolling through names, intermittently, for days. And now, suddenly, she had a hit, more an instinct than anything specific.

"Creed, Josiah *McKettrick,*" she said excitedly, clicking on the link. "I must have passed right over him dozens of times."

Angus materialized at her elbow, stooping and staring at the screen, his heavy eyebrows pulled together in consternation and curiosity.

"Captain in the United States Army," Meg read aloud, and with a note of triumph in her voice. "Founder of 'the legendary Stillwater Springs Ranch,' in western Montana. Owner of the Stillwater Springs *Courier,* the first newspaper in that part of the territory. On the town council, two terms as mayor. Wife, four sons, active member of the Methodist Church." She stopped, looked up at Angus. "Doesn't sound like an anti-Irish pirate to me." She tapped at Josiah's solemn photograph on the home page. Bewhiskered, with a thick head of white hair, he looked dour and prosperous in his dark suit, the coat fastened with one button at his breastbone, in that curious nineteenth-century way. "There he is, Angus," she said. "Your brother, Josiah McKettrick Creed."

"I'll be hornswoggled," Angus said.

"Whatever that is," Meg replied, busily copying information onto a notepad. The website was obviously the work of a skillful amateur, probably a family member with a genealogical bent, and there was no "contact us" link, but the name of the town, and the ranch if it still existed, was information enough.

"Looks like you missed something," Angus said.

Meg peered at the screen, trying to see past Angus's big index finger, scattering a ring of pixels around its end.

She pushed his hand gently aside.

And saw a tiny link at the bottom of the page, printed in blue letters.

A press of a mouse button and she and Angus were looking at the masthead of Josiah's newspaper, the *Courier*.

The headline was printed in heavy type. *MURDER AND SCANDAL BESET STILLWATER SPRINGS RANCH.*

Something quivered in the pit of Meg's stomach, a peculiar combination of dread and fascination. The byline was Josiah's own, and the brief obituary beneath it still pulsed with the staunch grief of an old man, bitterly determined to tell the unflinching truth.

Dawson James Creed, 21, youngest son of Josiah McKettrick Creed and Cora Dawson Creed, perished yesterday at the hand of his first cousin, Benjamin A. Dawson, who shot him dead over a game of cards and a woman. Both the shootist and the woman have since fled these parts. Services tomorrow at 2:00 p.m., at the First Street Methodist Church. Viewing this evening at the Creed home. Our boy will be sorely missed.

"Creed," Angus repeated, musing. "That was my mother's name, before she and my pa hitched up."

"So maybe Josiah *wasn't* a McKettrick," Meg ventured. "Maybe your mother was married before, or—"

Angus stiffened. "Or nothing," he said pointedly. "Back in those days, women didn't go around having babies out of wedlock. Pa must have been her second husband."

Meg, feeling a little stung, didn't comment. Nor did she argue the point, which would have been easy to back up, that premarital pregnancies weren't as uncommon in "his day" as Angus liked to think.

"Where's that old Bible Georgia set such store by?" he asked now.

Georgia, his second wife, mother of Rafe, Kade and Jeb, had evidently been her generation's record-keeper and family historian. "I suppose Keegan has it," she answered, "since he lives in the main ranch house."

"Ma wrote all the begats in that book," Angus recalled. "I never thought to look at it."

"She never mentioned being married before?"

"No," Angus admitted. "But folks didn't talk about things like that much. It was a private matter and besides, they had their hands full just surviving from day to day. No time to sit around jawing about the past."

"I'll drop in on Keegan and Molly in the morning," Meg said. "Ask if I can borrow the Bible."

"I want to look at it *now*."

"Angus, it's late—"

He vanished.

Meg sighed. There were no more articles on the website—just that short, sad obituary notice—so she logged off the computer. She was brewing a cup of herbal tea in the microwave, hoping it would help her sleep, when Ted came down the backstairs, wearing an old plaid flannel bathrobe and scruffy slippers.

Lord, he wanted to talk.

Now, from the look on his face.

She wasn't ready, and that didn't matter.

The time had come.

Dragging back a chair at the table, Ted crumpled into it.

"Tea?" Meg asked, and immediately felt stupid.

"Sit down, Meg," Ted said gently.

She took the mug from the microwave, grateful for its citrusy steamy scent, and joined him, perching on the end of one of the benches.

"There's no money," Ted said.

"I gathered that," Meg replied, though not flippantly. And the dizzying thought came to her that maybe this was all some kind of con—a *Paper Moon* kind of thing, Ted playing the Ryan O'Neal part, while Carly handled Tatum's role. But the idea fizzled almost as quickly as it had flared up in her mind—a scam would have been so much easier to take than the grim reality.

Ted ran a tremulous hand through his thinning hair. "I wish things had happened differently, Meg," he said. "I wanted to come back a hundred times, say I was sorry for everything that happened. I convinced myself I was being noble—you were a McKettrick, and you didn't need an ex-yardbird complicating your life. The truth gets harder to deny when you're toeing up to the pearly gates, though. I was a coward, that's all. I tried to make up for it by being the best father I could to Carly." He paused, chuckled ruefully. "I won't take any prizes for that, either. After Rose died, it was as if somebody had greased the bottom of my feet. I just couldn't stay put, and it was mostly downhill, a slippery slope, all the way. The worst part is, I dragged

Carly right along with me. Last job I had, I stocked shelves in a discount store."

"You don't have to do this," Meg said, blinking back tears she didn't want him to see.

"Yes," Ted said, "I do. I loved your mother and she loved me. You need to know how happy we were when you were born—that you were welcome in this big old crazy world."

"Okay," Meg allowed. "You were happy." She swallowed. "Then you embezzled a lot of money and went to prison."

"Like most embezzlers," Ted answered, "I thought I could put it back before it was missed. It didn't happen that way. Your mother tried to cover for me at first, but there were other McKettricks on the board, and they weren't going to tolerate a thief."

"Why did you do it?" The question, more breathed than spoken, hovered in the otherwise silent room.

"Before I met Eve, I gambled. A lot. I still owed some people. I was ashamed to tell Eve—and I knew she'd divorce me—so I 'borrowed' what I needed and left as few tracks as possible. That got my creditors off my back—they were knee-breakers, Meg, and they wouldn't have stopped at hurting me. They'd have gone after you and Eve, too."

"So you stole the money to protect Mom and me?" Meg asked, not bothering to hide her skepticism.

"Partly. I was young and I was scared."

"You should have told Mom. She would have helped you."

"I know. But by the time I realized that, it was too late." He sighed. "Now it's too late for a lot of things."

"It's not too late for Carly," Meg said.

"Exactly my point. She's going to give you some trouble, Meg. She won't want to go to school, and she's used to being a loner. I'm all the family she's had since her mother was killed. Like I said before, I've got no right to ask you for anything. I don't expect sympathy. I know you won't grieve when I'm gone. But Carly *will,* and I'm hoping you're McKettrick enough to stand by her till she finds her balance. My worst fear is that she'll go down the same road I did, drifting from place to place, living by her wits, always on the outside looking in."

"I won't let that happen," Meg promised. "Not because of you, but because Carly is my sister. And because she's a child."

They'd been over this before, but Ted seemed to need a lot of reassurance. "I guess there is one other favor I could ask," he said.

Meg raised an eyebrow. Waited.

"Will you forgive me, Meg?"

"I stopped hating you a long time ago."

"That isn't the same as forgiving me," Ted replied.

She opened her mouth, closed it again. A glib, "Okay, I forgive you" died on her tongue.

Ted smiled sadly. "While you're at it, forgive your mother, too. We were both wrong, Eve and I, not to tell you the whole truth from the beginning. But she was trying to protect you, Meg. And it says a lot about the other McKettricks, that none of them ever let it slip that I was a thief doing time in a Texas prison while you were growing up. A lot of people would have found that secret too juicy to keep to themselves."

Meg wondered if Jesse, Rance and Keegan had known, and decided they hadn't. Their parents had, though, surely. All three of their fathers had been on the company board with Eve, back in those days. Meg thought of them as uncles—and they'd looked after her like a daughter, taken her under their powerful wings when she summered on the

Triple M, and so had her "aunts." Stirred her right into the boisterous mix of loud cousins, remembered her birthdays and bought gifts at Christmas. All the while, they'd been conspiring to keep her in the dark about Ted Ledger, of course, but she couldn't resent them for it. Their intentions, like Eve's, had been good.

"Who are you, really?" Meg asked, remembering Carly's remark about changing last names so many times she was no longer sure what the real one was. And underlying the surface question was another.

Who am I?

Ted smiled, patted her hand. "When I married your mother, I was Ted Sullivan. I was born in Chicago, to Alice and Carl Sullivan. Alice was a homemaker, Carl was a finance manager at a used car dealership."

"No brothers or sisters?"

"I had a sister, Sarah. She died of meningitis when she was fifteen. I was nineteen at the time. Mom never recovered from Sarah's death—she was the promising child. I was the problem."

"How did you meet Mom?" She hadn't thought she needed, or even wanted, to know such things. But, suddenly, she did.

Ted grinned at the memory, and for just a moment, he looked young again, and well. "After I left home, I took college courses and worked nights as a hotel desk clerk. I moved around the country, and by the time I wound up in San Antonio, I was a manager. McKettrickCo owned the chain I worked for, and one of your uncles decided I was a bright young man with a future. Hired me to work in the home office. Where, of course, I saw Eve every day."

Meg imagined how it must have been, both Ted and Eve still young, and relatively mistake-free. "And you fell in love."

"Yes," Ted said. "The family accepted me, which was decent of them, considering they were rich and I had an old car and a couple of thousand dollars squirreled away in a low-interest savings account. The McKettricks are a lot of things, but they're not snobs."

Having money doesn't make us better than other people, Eve had often said as Meg was growing up. *It just makes us luckier.*

"No," she agreed. "They're not snobs." She tried to smile and failed. "So I would have been Meg Sullivan, not Meg McKettrick—if things hadn't gone the way they did?"

Ted chuckled. "Not in a million years. You know the McKettrick women don't change their names when they marry. According to Eve, the custom goes all the way back to old Angus's only daughter."

"Katie," Meg said. Her mind did a time-warp thing— for about fifteen seconds, she was nineteen and pregnant, having her last argument with Brad before he got into his old truck and drove away. Late that night, he would board a bus for Nashville.

We'll get married when I get back, Brad had said. *I promise.*

You're not coming *back,* Meg had replied, in tears.

Yes, I am. You'll see—you'll be Meg O'Ballivan before you know it.

I'll never be Meg O'Ballivan. I'm not taking your name.

Have it your way, Ms. McKettrick. *You always do.*

"Meg?" Ted's voice brought her back to the kitchen on the Triple M. Her tea had grown cold, sitting on the tabletop in its heavy mug.

"You're not the first person who ever made a mistake," she told her father. "I hereby confer upon you my complete forgiveness."

He laughed, but his eyes were glossy with tears.

"You're tired," Meg said. "Get some rest."

"I want to hear your story, Meg. Eve sent me a few pictures, the occasional copy of a report card, when I was on the inside. But there are a lot of gaps."

"Another time," Meg answered. But even as Ted stood to make his way back upstairs, and she disposed of her cold tea and put the mug into the dishwasher, she wondered if there would *be* another time.

Phil was back.

Brad, accompanied to the barn by an adoring Willie, tossed the last flake of hay into the last feeder when he heard the distinctive purr of a limo engine and swore under his breath.

"This is getting old," he told Willie.

Willie whined in agreement and wagged his tail.

Phil was walking toward Brad, the stretch gleaming in the early morning light, when he and Willie stepped outside.

"Good news!" Phil cried, beaming. "I spoke to the Hollywood people, and they're willing to make the movie right here at Stone Creek!"

Brad stopped, facing off with Phil like a gunfighter on a windswept Western street. "No," he said.

Phil, being Phil, was undaunted. "Now, don't be too hasty," he counseled. "It would really give this town a boost. Why, the jobs alone—"

"Phil—"

Just then, Livie's ancient Suburban topped the hill, started down, dust billowing behind. Brad took a certain satisfaction in the sight when the rig screeched to a halt alongside Phil's limo, covering it in fine red dirt.

Livie sprang from the Suburban, smiling. "Good news,"

she called, unknowingly echoing Phil's opening line. "The Iversons' cattle aren't infected."

Phil nudged Brad in the ribs and said in a stage whisper, "She could be an extra. Bet your sister would like to be in a movie."

"In a what?" Livie asked, frowning. She crouched to examine Willie briefly, and accept a few face licks, before straightening and putting out a hand to Phil Meadowbrook. "Olivia O'Ballivan," she said. "You must be my brother's manager."

"*Former* manager," Brad said.

"But still with his best interests at heart," Phil added, placing splayed fingers over his avaricious little ticker and looking woebegone, long-suffering and misunderstood. "I'm offering him a chance to make a *feature film,* right here on the ranch. Just *look* at this place! It's perfect! John Ford would salivate—"

"Who's John Ford?" Livie asked.

"He made some John Wayne movies," Brad explained, beginning to feel cornered.

Livie's dusty face lit up. She had hay dust in her hair—probably acquired during an early morning visit to the Iversons' dairy barn. "Wait till I tell the twins," she burst out.

"Hold it," Brad said, raising both hands, palms out. "There isn't going to *be* any movie."

"Why not?" Livie asked, suddenly crestfallen.

"Because I'm retired," Brad reminded her patiently.

Phil huffed out a disgusted sigh.

"I don't see the problem if they made the movie right here," Livie said.

"At last," Phil interjected. "Another voice of reason, besides my own."

"Shut up, Phil," Brad said.

"You always talked about making a movie," Livie went on, watching Brad with a mischievous light dancing in her eyes. "You even started a production company once."

"Cynthia got it in the divorce," Phil confided, as though Brad wasn't standing there. "The production company, I mean. I think that soured him."

"Will you stop acting as if I'm not here?" Brad snapped.

Willie whimpered, worried.

"See?" Phil was quick to say. "You're upsetting the dog." Another patented Phil Meadowbrook grin flashed. "Hey! He could be in the movie, too. People eat that animal stuff up. We might even be able to get Disney in on the project—"

"*No,*" Brad said, exasperated. "No Disney. No dog. No petite veterinarian with hay in her hair. *I don't want to make a movie.*"

"You could build a library or a youth center or something with the money," Phil said, trailing after Brad as he broke from the group and strode toward the house, fully intending to slam the door on his way in.

"We could use an animal shelter," Livie said, scrambling along at his other side.

"Fine," Brad snapped, slowing down a little because he realized Willie was having trouble keeping up. "I'll have my accountant cut a check."

The limo driver gave the horn a discreet honk, then got out and tapped at his watch.

"Plane to catch," Phil said. "Big Hollywood meeting. I'll fax you the contract."

"Don't bother," Brad warned.

Livie caught at his arm, sounding a little breathless. "What is the *matter* with you?" she whispered. "That movie would be the biggest thing to happen in Stone Creek since that pack of outlaws robbed the bank in 1907!"

Brad stopped. Thrust his nose right up to Livie's. "I. Am. *Retired*."

Livie set her hands on her skinny hips. She really needed to put some meat on those fragile little bones of hers. "I think you're chicken," she said.

Willie gave a cheery little yip.

"You stay out of this, Stitches," Brad told him.

"Chicken," Livie repeated, as the now-dusty limo made a wide turn and started swallowing up dirt road.

"Not," Brad argued.

"Then what?"

Brad shoved a hand through his hair as the answer to Livie's question settled over him, like the red dust that had showered the limo. He was making some headway with Meg, slowly but surely, but Meg and show business mixed about as well as oil and water. Deep down, she probably believed, as Livie had until this morning, that he'd go back to being that other Brad O'Ballivan, the one whose name was always written in capital letters, if the offer was good enough.

Too, if he agreed to do the movie, Phil would never get off his back. He'd be back, before the cameras stopped rolling, with another offer, another contract, another big idea.

"I used to be a performer," Brad said finally. "Now I'm a rancher. I can't keep going back and forth between the two."

"It's one movie, Brad, not a world concert tour. And you wanted to do a movie for so long. What happened? *Was* it losing the production company to Cynthia, like your manager said?"

"No," Brad said. "This is a Pandora's box, Livie. It's

the proverbial can of worms. One thing will lead to another—"

"And you'll leave again? For good, this time?"

He shook his head. "No."

"Then just think about it," Livie reasoned. "Making the movie, I mean. Think about the money it would bring into Stone Creek, and how excited the local people would be."

"And the animal shelter," Brad said, sighing.

"Small as Stone Creek is, there are a lot of strays," Livie said.

"Did you come out here for a reason?"

"Yes, to see my big brother and check up on Willie."

"Well, here I am, and Willie's fine. Go or stay, but I don't want to talk about that damn movie anymore, understood?"

Livie smirked. "Understood," she said sweetly.

At four-thirty that afternoon, the movie contract sputtered out of the fax machine in Brad's study.

He read it, signed it and faxed it back.

CHAPTER ELEVEN

CARLY SAT HUNCHED IN the front passenger seat of the Blazer, arms folded, glowering as kids converged on Indian Rock Middle School, colorful clothes and backpacks still new, since class had only been in session for a little over a month. It was Monday morning and Ted was scheduled to enter the hospital in Flagstaff for "treatment" the following day. Meg's solemn promise to take Carly to visit him every afternoon, admittedly small comfort, was nonetheless all she had to offer.

"I don't want to go in there," Carly said. "They're going to give me some stupid test and put me with the little kids. I just know it."

Ted had homeschooled Carly, for the most part, and though she was obviously a very bright child, there was no telling what kind of curriculum he'd used, or if the process had involved books at all. Her scores would determine her placement, and she was understandably worried.

"Everything will be all right," Meg said.

"You keep saying that," Carly protested. "Everybody says that. *My dad is going to die*. How is that 'all right'?"

"It isn't. It totally bites."

"You could homeschool me."

Meg shook her head. "I'm not a teacher, Carly."

"Neither is my dad, and he did fine!"

That, Meg thought, *remains to be seen.* "More than

anything in the world, your dad wants you to have a good life. And that means getting an education."

Tears brimmed in Carly's eyes. "*My* dad? He's *your* dad, too."

"Okay," Meg said.

"You hate him. You don't care if he dies!"

"I *don't* hate him, and if there was any way to keep him alive, I'd do it."

Carly's right hand went to the door handle; with her left, she gathered up the neon pink backpack Meg had bought for her over the weekend, along with some new clothes. "Well, not hating somebody isn't the same as *loving* them."

With that, she shoved open the car door, unfastened her seat belt and got out to stand on the sidewalk, facing the long brick schoolhouse, her small shoulders squared under more burdens than any child ought to have to carry.

Meg waited, her eyes scalding, until Carly disappeared into the building. Then she drove to Sierra's house, where she found her other sister on the front porch, deadheading the flowers in a large clay pot.

The bright October sunshine gilded Sierra's chestnut hair; she looked like Mother Nature herself in her floral print maternity dress.

Meg parked the Blazer in the driveway and approached, slinging her bag over her shoulder as she walked.

Sierra beamed, delighted, and straightened, one hand resting protectively on her enormous belly, the other shading her eyes. "I just made a fresh pot of coffee," she called. "Come in, and we'll catch up."

Meg smiled. She'd lived her life as an only child; now she had two sisters. She and Sierra had had time to bond, but establishing a relationship with Carly was going to be a major challenge.

"I suppose Mom told you the latest," Meg said, referring to Ted and Carly's arrival.

"Some of it. The gossip lasted about twenty minutes, though—you got beat out by the news that Brad O'Ballivan is making a movie over at Stone Creek. Everybody in the county wants to be an extra."

Meg stopped in the middle of the sidewalk. Brad hadn't called since the barbecue, and she hadn't heard about the movie. That hurt, and though she regained her composure quickly, Sierra was quicker.

"You didn't know?" she asked, holding the front door open and urging Meg through it.

Meg sighed, shook her head.

Sierra patted her shoulder. "Let's have that coffee," she said softly.

For the next hour, she and Meg sat in the sunny kitchen, catching up. Meg told her sister what she knew about Ted's condition, Carly, and *most* of what had happened between her and Brad.

Sierra chuckled at the account of Jesse and Keegan's helicopter rescue the day of the blizzard. Got tears in her eyes when Meg related Willie's story.

Although Sierra was one of the most grounded people Meg knew, her emotions had been mercurial since the beginning of her last trimester.

"So when is this baby going to show up, anyhow?" Meg inquired cheerfully when she was through with the briefing. It was definitely time to change the subject.

"I was due a week ago," Sierra answered. "The nursery is all ready, and so am I. Apparently, the baby isn't."

Meg touched her sister's hand. "Are you scared?"

Sierra shook her head. "I'm past that. Mostly, I feel like a bowling-ball smuggler."

"You know," Meg teased, "if you'd spilled the beans

about whether this kid is a boy or a girl, you wouldn't have gotten so many yellow layettes at your baby shower."

Sierra laughed, crying a little at the same time. "The sonogram was inconclusive," she said. "The little dickens drew one leg up and hid the evidence."

Meg sobered, looked away briefly. "Would you hate me if I admitted I'm a little envious? Because the baby's coming, I mean, and because you already have Liam, and Travis loves you so much?"

"You know I couldn't hate you," Sierra answered gently, but there was a worried expression in her blue eyes. Long ago, Meg and Travis had dated briefly, and they were still very good friends. While Sierra surely knew neither of them would deceive her, ever, she might think she'd stolen Travis's affections and broken Meg's heart in the process. "Truth time. Do you still have feelings for Travis?"

"The same kind of feelings I have for Jesse and Keegan and Rance," Meg replied honestly. She drew a deep breath and puffed it out. "Truth time? Here's the whole enchilada. I fell hard for Brad O'Ballivan when I was in high school, and I don't think I'm over it."

"Is that a bad thing?"

Meg remembered the way Brad had looked as they stood in his kitchen, after the steak dinner on the patio. She'd seen sorrow, disappointment and a sense of betrayal in his eyes, and the set of his face and shoulders. "I'm not sure," she said. Then she stood, carried her empty cup and Sierra's to the sink. "I'd better get home. Ted's there alone, and he wasn't feeling well when I left to take Carly to school."

Sierra nodded, remaining in her chair, squirming a little and looking anxious.

"You're okay, right?" Meg asked, alarmed.

"Just a few twinges," Sierra said. "It's probably nothing."

Meg was glad she'd already set the cups down, because she'd have dropped them to the floor if she hadn't. *"Just a few twinges?"*

"Would you mind calling Travis?" Sierra asked. "And Mom?"

"Oh, my God," Meg said, grabbing her bag, scrabbling through it for her cell phone. "You've been sitting there listening to my tales of woe and all the time you've been *in labor?*"

"Not the whole time," Sierra said lamely. "I thought it was indigestion."

Meg speed-dialed Travis. "Come home," she said before he'd finished his hello. "Sierra's having the baby!"

"On my way," he replied, and hung up in her ear.

Next, she called Eve. "It's happening!" she blurted. "The baby—"

"For heaven's sake," Sierra protested good-naturedly, "you make it sound as though I'm giving birth on the kitchen floor."

"Margaret McKettrick," Eve instructed sternly, "calm yourself. We have a plan. Travis will take Sierra to the hospital, and I will pick Liam up after school. I assume you're with Sierra right now?"

"I'm with her," Meg said, wondering if she'd have to deliver her niece or nephew before help arrived. She'd watched calves, puppies and colts coming into the world, but *this* was definitely in another league.

"Did you call Travis?" Eve wanted to know.

"Yes," Meg watched Sierra anxiously as she spoke.

"My water just broke," Sierra said.

"Oh, my God," Meg ranted. "Her water just broke!"

"Margaret," Eve said, "get a grip—and a towel. I'll be there in five minutes."

Travis showed up in four flat. He paused to bend and

kiss Sierra soundly on the mouth, then dashed off, return-
ing momentarily with a suitcase, presumably packed with
things his wife would need at the hospital.

Meg sat at the table, with her head between her knees,
feeling woozy.

"I think she's hyperventilating," Sierra told Travis. "Do
we have any paper bags?"

Just then, Eve breezed in through the back door. She tsk-
tsked Meg, but naturally, Sierra was her main concern. As
her younger daughter stood, with some help from Travis,
Eve cupped Sierra's face between her hands and kissed her
on the forehead.

"Don't worry about a thing," she ordered. "I'll see to
Liam."

Sierra nodded, gave Meg one last worried glance and
allowed Travis to steer her out the back door.

"Shouldn't we have called an ambulance or something?"
Meg fretted.

"Oh, for heaven's sake," Eve replied. "You don't need
an ambulance!"

"Not for *me,* Mother. For Sierra."

Eve soaked a cloth at the sink, wrung it out and slapped
it onto the back of Meg's neck. "Breathe," she said.

Brad watched from a front window as Livie parked the
Suburban, got out and headed for the barn. "Here we go,"
he told Willie, resigned. "She's on the hunt for Ransom
again, and that means I'll have to go. You're going to have
to stay behind, buddy."

Willie, curled up on a hooked rug in front of the living
room fireplace, simply sighed and closed his eyes for a
snooze, clearly unconcerned. Some of the advance people
from the movie studio had already arrived in an RV, to
scout the location, and the kid with the backward baseball

cap was a dog-lover. If necessary, Brad would press him into service.

Brad had been up half the night going over the script, faxed by Phil, penning in the occasional dialogue change. For all his reluctance to get involved in the project, he liked the story, tentatively titled *The Showdown,* and he was looking forward to trying his hand at a little acting.

The truth was, though, he'd had to read and reread because his mind kept straying to Meg. He'd been so sure, right along, that they could make things work. But seeing Carly—a younger version of Meg, and most likely of the daughter they might have had—brought up a lot of conflicting feelings, ones he wasn't sure how to deal with.

It wasn't rational; he knew that. Meg's explanation was believable, even if it stung, and her reasons for keeping the secret from him made sense. Still, a part of him was deeply resentful, even enraged.

Livie was saddling Cinnamon when he reached the barn.

"Where do you think you're going?" he asked.

She gave him a look. "Three guesses, genius," she said pleasantly. "And the first two don't count."

"I guess you didn't hear about the blizzard that blew up in about five minutes when Meg and I were up in the hills trying to find that damn horse?"

"I heard about it," Livie said. She put her shoulder to Cinnamon's belly and pulled hard to tighten the cinch. "I just want to check on him, that's all. Just take a look."

Brad leaned one shoulder against the door frame, arms folded, letting his body language say he wasn't above blocking the door.

Livie's expression said *she* wasn't above riding right over him.

"I'll see if I can talk one of Meg's cousins into taking you up in the helicopter," Brad said.

"Oh, right," Livie mocked. "And scare Ransom to death with the noise."

"Livie, will you listen to reason? That horse has survived all this time without a lick of help from you. What's different now?"

"Will you stop calling him 'that horse'? His name is Ransom and he's a *legend*, thank you very much."

"Being a legend," Brad drawled, "isn't all it's cracked up to be."

Livie led Cinnamon toward him; he moved into the center of the doorway and stood his ground.

"What's different, Livie?" he repeated.

She sighed, seemed even smaller and more fragile than usual. "You wouldn't believe me if I told you."

"Give it a shot," Brad said.

"Dreams," Livie said. "I have these dreams—"

"Dreams."

"I knew you wouldn't—"

"Hold it," Brad interrupted. "I'm listening."

"Just get out of my way, please."

Brad shook his head, shifted so his feet were a little farther apart, kept his arms folded. "Not gonna happen."

"He talks to me," Livie said, her voice small and exasperated and full of the O'Ballivan grit that was so much a part of her nature.

"A horse talks to you." He tried not to sound skeptical, but didn't quite succeed.

"In dreams," Livie said, flushing.

"Like Mr. Ed, in that old TV show?"

Livie's temper flared in her eyes, then her cheekbones. "No," she said. "Not 'like Mr. Ed in that old TV show'!"

"How, then?"

"I just hear him, that's all. He doesn't move his lips, for pity's sake!"

"Okay."

"You believe me?"

"I believe that you believe it, Liv. You have a lot of deep feelings where animals are concerned—sometimes I wish you liked people half as much—and you've been worried about that—about Ransom for a long time. It makes sense that he'd show up in your dreams."

Livie let Cinnamon's reins dangle and set her hands on her hips. "What did you do, take an online shrink course or something? Jungian analysis in ten easy lessons? Next, you'll be saying Ransom is a symbol with unconscious sexual connotations!"

Brad suppressed an urge to roll his eyes. "Is that really so far beyond the realm of possibility?"

"Yes!"

"Why?"

"Because Ransom isn't the only animal I dream about, that's why. And it isn't a recent phenomenon—it's been happening since I was little! Remember Simon, that old sheepdog we had when we were kids? He told me he was leaving—and three days later, he was hit by a car. I could go on, because there are a whole lot of other stories, but frankly, I don't have time. Ransom is in trouble."

Surprise was too mild a word for what Brad felt. Livie had always been crazy about animals, but she was stone practical, with a scientific turn of mind, not given to spooky stuff. And she'd never once confided that she got dream messages from four-legged friends.

"Why didn't you tell me? Did Big John know?"

"You'd have packed me off to a therapist. Big John had enough to worry about without Dr. Doolittle for a grand-daughter. Now—will you please move?"

"No," Brad said. "I won't move, please or otherwise. Not until you tell me what's so urgent about tracking down a wild stallion on top of a damn mountain!"

Tears glistened in Livie's eyes, and Brad felt a stab to his conscience.

Livie's struggle was visible, and painful to see, but she finally answered. "He's in pain. There's something wrong with his right foreleg."

"And you plan to do what when—and if—you find him? Shoot him with a tranquilizer gun? Livie, this is Stone Creek, Arizona, not the *Wild Kingdom*. And dream or no dream, that horse—" He raised both hands to forestall the impatience brewing in her face. "*Ransom* is not a character in a Disney movie. He's not going to let you walk up to him, examine his foreleg and give him a nice little shot. If you *did* get close, he'd probably stomp you down to bone fragments and a bloodstain!"

"He wouldn't," Livie said. "He knows I want to help him."

"Livie, suppose—just *suppose,* damn it—that you're wrong."

"I'm not wrong."

"Of *course* you're not wrong. You're a freaking O'Ballivan!" He paused, shoved a hand through his hair. Tried another tack. "There aren't that many hours of daylight left. You're not going up that mountain alone, little sister—not if I have to hog-tie you to keep you here."

"Then you can come with me."

"Oh, that's noble of you. I'd *love* to risk freezing to death in a freaking blizzard. Hell, I've got nothing *better* to do, besides nurse a wounded dog that *you* brought to me, and make a freaking *movie*—also your idea—"

Livie's mouth twitched at one corner. She fought the grin, but it came anyway. "Do you realize you've used the word 'freaking' three times in the last minute and a half? Have you considered switching to decaf?"

"Very funny," Brad said, but he couldn't help grinning back. He rested his hands on Livie's shoulders, squeezed lightly. "You're my little sister. I love you. If you insist on tracking a wild stallion all over the mountain, at least wait until morning. We'll saddle up at dawn."

Livie looked serious again. "You promise?"

"I promise."

"Okay," she said.

"Okay? That's it? You're giving up without a fight?"

"Don't be so suspicious. I said I'd wait until dawn, and I will."

Brad raised one eyebrow. "Shake on it?"

Livie put out a hand. "Shake," she said.

He had to be satisfied with that. In the O'Ballivan family, shaking hands on an agreement was like taking a blood oath—Big John had drilled that into them from childhood. "Since we're leaving so early, maybe you'd better spend the night here."

"I can do that," Livie said, turning to lead Cinnamon back to his stall. "But since I'm not going tonight, I might as well make my normal rounds first. I conned Dr. Summers into covering for me, but he wasn't too happy about it." Her eyes took on a mischievous twinkle as he approached, took over the process of unsaddling the horse. "How are things going with Meg?"

Brad didn't look at her. "Not all that well, actually."

"What's wrong?"

"I'm not sure I could put it into words."

Livie nudged him before pushing open the stall door to leave. "It's a long ride up the mountain," she said. "Plenty of time to talk."

"I might take you up on that," he answered.

"I'll just look in on Willie, then go make my rounds. See you later, alligator."

Brad's eyes burned. Like the handshake, "See you later, alligator" was a holdover from Big John. "In a while, crocodile," he answered on cue.

By the time he got back to the house, Livie had already examined Willie, climbed into the Suburban and driven off. A note stuck to the refrigerator door read, *Are you making supper, Mr. Movie Star? Or should I pick up a pizza?*

Brad chuckled and took a package of chicken out of the freezer.

The phone rang.

"Yea or nay on the double Hawaiian deluxe with extra ham, cheese and pineapple?" Livie asked.

"Forget the pizza," Brad replied. "I'm not eating anything you've handled. You stick your arm up cows' butts for a living, after all."

She laughed, said goodbye and hung up.

He started to replace the receiver, but Meg was still on his mind, so he punched in the digits. Funny, he reflected, how he remembered her number at the Triple M after all this time. He couldn't have recited the one he'd had in Nashville to save his life.

Voice mail picked up. "You've reached 555-7682," Meg said cheerily. "Leave a message and, if it's appropriate, I'll call you back."

Brad moved to disconnect, then put the receiver back to his ear. "It's Brad. I was just—a—calling to see how things are going with your dad and Carly—"

She came on the line, sounding a little breathless. "Brad?"

His heart did a slow backflip. "Yeah, it's me," he said.

"I hear you're making a movie in Stone Creek."

He closed his eyes. He'd blown it again—Meg should

have heard the news from him, not via the local grapevine. "I thought maybe Carly could be an extra," he said.

"She'd love that, I'm sure," Meg said with crisp formality.

"Meg? The movie thing—"

"It's all right, Brad. I'm happy for you. Really."

"You sound thrilled."

"You could have mentioned it. Not exactly an everyday occurrence, especially in the wilds of northern Arizona."

"I wanted to talk about it in person, Meg."

"You know where I live, and clearly, you know my telephone number."

"I know where your G-spot is, too," he said.

He heard her draw in a breath. "Dirty pool, O'Ballivan."

"All's fair in lust and war, McKettrick."

"Is that what this is? Lust?"

"You tell me."

"I'm not the one who took a step back," she reminded him.

He knew what she was talking about, of course. He'd been pretty cool to her the night of the steak dinner. "Livie and I are riding up the mountain again tomorrow, to look for Ransom. Do you still want to go?"

She sighed. He hoped she was thawing out, but with Meg, it could go either way. Ice or fire. "I wish I could. Ted's being admitted to the hospital tomorrow morning, and I promised to take Carly to visit him as soon as school lets out for the day."

"She's having a pretty rough time," he said. "If there's anything I can do to help—"

"The T-shirt was a hit. So is having your autograph on all those CDs. Your kindness means a lot to her, Brad." A pause. "On a happier note, Sierra went into labor today. I'm expecting to be an aunt again at any moment."

"That is good news," Brad said, but he put one hand to his middle, as though he'd taken a fist to the stomach.

"Yeah," Meg said, and he knew by the catch in her voice that, somehow, she'd picked up on his reaction. "Well, anyway, congratulations on the movie, and thanks for getting in touch. Oh, and be careful on the mountain tomorrow."

The invisible fist moved from his solar plexus to his throat, squeezing hard. *Congratulations on the movie... thanks for getting in touch...so long, see you around.*

She'd hung up before he could get out a goodbye.

He thumbed the off button, leaned forward and rested his head against a cupboard door, eyes closed tight.

Willie nuzzled him in the thigh and gave a soft whine.

Two hours later, Livie returned, freshly showered and wearing a dress.

"Got a hot date?" Brad asked, trying to remember the last time he'd seen his sister in anything besides boots, ragbag jeans and one of Big John's old shirts.

She ignored the question and, with a flourish, pulled a bottle of wine from her tote bag and set it on the counter, sniffing the air appreciatively. "Fried chicken? Is there no end to your talents?"

"Not as far as I know," he joked.

Livie elbowed him. "We should have invited the twins to join us. It would be like old times, all of us sitting down together in this kitchen."

Not quite like old times, Brad thought, missing Big John with a sudden, piercing ache, as fresh as if he'd just gotten the call announcing his grandfather's death.

Livie was way too good at reading him. She snatched a cucumber slice from the salad and nibbled at it, leaning back against the counter and studying his face. "You really miss Big John, don't you?"

He nodded, not quite trusting himself to speak.

"He was so proud of you, Brad."

He swallowed. Averted his eyes. "Keep your fingers out of the salad," he said.

Livie laid a hand on his arm. "I know you think you disappointed him at practically every turn. That you should have been here, instead of in Nashville or on the road or wherever, and maybe all of that's true, but he *was* proud. And he was grateful, too, for everything you did."

"He'd raise hell about this movie," Brad said hoarsely.

"He'd brag to everybody who would let him bend their ear," Livie replied.

"Do you know what I'd give to be able to talk to Big John just one more time? To say I'm sorry I didn't visit—call more often?"

"A lot, I guess. But you can still talk to him. He'll hear you." She stood on tiptoe, kissed Brad lightly on the cheek. "Tell me you've already fed the horses, because I'd hate to have to swap out this getup for barn gear."

Brad laughed. "I've fed them," he said. He turned, smiled down into her upturned face. "I never would have taken you for a mystic, Doc. Do you talk to Big John? Or just wild stallions and sheepdogs?"

"All the time," Livie said, plundering a drawer for a corkscrew, which Brad immediately took from her. "I don't think he's really gone. Most of the time, it feels as if he's in the next room, not some far-off heaven—sometimes, I even catch the scent of his pipe tobacco."

Since Brad had taken over opening the cabernet, Livie got out a couple of wineglasses. Willie poked his nose at her knee, angling for attention.

"Yes," she told the dog. "I know you're there."

"Does he talk to you, too?" Brad asked, only half kidding.

"Sure," Livie replied airily. "He likes you. You're a little awkward, but Willie thinks you have real potential as a dog owner."

Grinning, Brad sloshed wine into Livie's glass, then his. Raised it in a toast. "To Big John," he said, "and King's Ransom, and Stone Creek's own Dr. Doolittle. And Willie."

"To the movie and Meg McKettrick," Livie added, and clinked her glass against Brad's.

Brad hesitated before he drank. "To Meg," he said finally.

During supper, they chatted about Livie's preliminary plans for the promised animal shelter—it would be state of the art, offering free spaying and neutering, inoculations, etc.

They cleaned up the kitchen together afterward, as they had done when they were kids, then took Willie out for a brief walk. He was still sore, though the pain medication helped, and couldn't make it far, but he managed.

Since he hadn't slept much the night before, Brad crashed in the downstairs guest room early, leaving Livie sitting at the kitchen table, absorbed in his copy of the script.

Hours later, sleep-grogged and blinking in the harsh light of the bedside lamp, he awakened to find Livie standing over him, fully dressed—this time in the customary jeans—and practically vibrating with anxiety.

He yawned and dragged himself upright against the headboard, "Liv, it's the middle of the night."

"Ransom's cornered," Livie blurted. "We have to get to him, and quick. Call a McKettrick and borrow that helicopter!"

CHAPTER TWELVE

THE WHOLE THING WAS CRAZY.

It was two in the morning.

He'd have to swallow his pride to roust Jesse or Keegan at that hour, and ask for a monumental favor in the bargain. *My sister had this dream, involving a talking horse,* he imagined himself saying.

But the look of desperation in Livie's eyes made the difference.

"Here's a number," she said, shoving a bit of paper at him and handing him the cordless phone from the kitchen.

"Where did you get this?" Brad asked as Willie, curled at the foot of his bed, stood, made a tight circle and laid himself down again.

Livie answered from the doorway, plainly exasperated. "Jesse and I used to go out once in a while," she said. "Make the call and get dressed!"

She didn't give him a chance to suggest that *she* make the request, since she and Jesse had evidently been an item at one time, but hurried out.

As soon as the door shut behind her, Brad sat up, reached for his jeans, which had been in a heap on the floor, and got into them while he thumbed Jesse's number.

McKettrick answered on the second ring, growling, "This had better be good."

Brad closed his eyes for a moment, used one hand to button his fly while keeping the receiver propped between his ear and his right shoulder. "It's Brad O'Ballivan," he said. "Sorry to wake you up, but there's an emergency and—" He paused only briefly, for the last words had to be forced out. "I need some help."

Barely forty-five minutes later, the McKettrickCo helicopter landed, running lights glaring like something out of *Close Encounters of the Third Kind,* in the field directly behind the ranch house. Jesse was at the controls.

"Hey, Liv," he said with a Jesse-grin once she'd scrambled into the small rear seat and put on a pair of earphones.

"Hey," Livie replied. There was no stiffness about either of them—the dating scenario must have ended affably, or not been serious in the first place.

Brad sat up front, next to Jesse, with a rifle between his knees, dreading the moment when he'd have to explain what this moonlight odyssey was all about.

But Jesse didn't ask for an explanation. All he said was, "Where to?"

"Horse Thief Canyon," Livie answered. "On the eastern rim."

Jesse nodded, cast one sidelong glance at Brad's rifle, and lifted the copter off the ground.

I might have to get one of these things, Brad thought, still sleep-jangled.

Within fifteen minutes, they were high over the mountain, spot-lighting the canyon, so named for being the place where Sam O'Ballivan and some of his Arizona Rangers had once cornered a band of horse rustlers.

"There he is!" Livie shouted, fairly blowing out Brad's eardrums. He leaned for a look and what he saw made his heart swoop to his boot heels.

Ransom gleamed in the glare of the searchlight, rearing and pawing the ground with his powerful forelegs. Behind him, against a rock face, were his mares—Brad counted three, but it was hard to tell how many others might be in the shadows—and before him, a pack of nearly a dozen wolves was closing in. They were hungry, focused on their cornered prey, and they paid no attention whatsoever to the copter roaring above their heads.

"Set this thing down!" Livie ordered. "Fast!"

Jesse worked the controls with one hand and hauled a second rifle out from under the pilot's seat with the other. Clearly, he'd spotted the wolves, too.

He landed the copter on what looked like a ledge, too narrow for Brad's comfort. The wait for the blades to slow seemed endless.

"Showtime," Jesse said, shoving open his door, rifle in hand. "Keep your heads down. The updraft will be pretty strong."

Brad nodded and pushed open the door, willing Livie to stay behind, knowing she wouldn't.

Just fifty yards away, Ransom and the wolf pack were still facing off. The mares screamed and snorted, frantic with fear, their rolling eyes shining white in the darkness.

With only the moon for light now, the scene was eerie.

The small hairs rose on the back of Brad's neck and one of the wolves turned and studied him with implacable amber eyes. His gray-white ruff shimmered in the silvery glow of cold, distant stars.

Some kind of weird connection sparked between man and beast. Brad was only vaguely aware of Jesse coming up behind him, of Livie already fiddling with her veterinary kit.

I'm a predator, the wolf told Brad. *This is what I do.*

Brad cocked the rifle. *I'm a predator, too,* he replied silently. *And you can't have these horses.*

The wolf pondered a moment, took a single stealthy step toward Ransom, the stallion bloody-legged and exhausted from holding off the pack.

Brad took aim. *Don't do it, Brother Wolf. This isn't a bluff.*

Tilting his massive head back, the wolf gave a chilling howl.

Ransom was stumbling a little by then, looking as though he'd go down. That, of course, was exactly what the pack was waiting for. Once the great steed was on the ground, they'd have him—and the mares. And the resultant carnage didn't bear considering.

Jesse stood at Brad's side, his own rifle ready. "I wouldn't have believed he was real," McKettrick said in a whisper, though whether he was referring to Ransom or the old wolf was anybody's guess, "if I hadn't seen him with my own eyes."

The wolf yowled again, the sound raising something primitive in Brad.

And then it was over.

The leader turned, moving back through the pack at a trot, and they rounded, one by one, with a lethal and hesitant grace, to follow.

Brad let out his breath, lowered his rifle. Jesse relaxed, too.

Livie, carrying her kit in one hand, headed straight for Ransom.

Brad moved to stop her, but Jesse put out his arm.

"Easy," he said. "This is no time to spook that horse."

It would be the supreme irony, Brad reflected grimly, if they had to shoot Ransom in the end, after going to all this trouble to save his hide. If the stallion made one aggressive move toward Livie, though, he'd do it.

"It's me, Olivia," Livie told the legendary wild stallion in a companionable tone. "I came as soon as I could."

Brad brought his rifle up quickly when Ransom butted Livie with his massive head, but Jesse forced the barrel down, murmuring, "Wait."

Ransom stood, lathered and shining with sweat and fresh blood, and allowed Livie to stroke his long neck, ruffle his mane. When she squatted to run her hands over his forelegs, he allowed that, too.

"I'll be damned," Jesse muttered.

The vision was surreal—Brad wasn't entirely convinced he wasn't dreaming at home in his bed.

"You're going to have to come in," Livie told the horse, "at least long enough for that leg to heal."

Unbelievably, Ransom nickered and tossed his head as though he were nodding in agreement.

"How the hell does she expect to drive a band of wild horses all the way down the mountain to Stone Creek Ranch?" Brad asked. He wasn't looking for an answer from Jesse—he was just thinking out loud.

Jesse whacked him on the shoulder. "You've been in the big city too long, O'Ballivan," he said. "You stay here, in case the wolves come back, and I'll go gather a roundup crew. It'll be a few hours before we get here, though—keep your eye out for the pack and pray for good weather. About the last thing we need is another of those blizzards."

By that time, Livie had produced a syringe from her kit, and was preparing to poke it through the hide on Ransom's neck.

Brad moved a step closer.

"Stay back," Livie said. "Ransom's calm enough, but these mares are stressed out. I'd rather not find myself at the center of an impromptu rodeo, if it's all the same to you."

Jesse chuckled, handed Brad his rifle, and turned to sprint back to the copter. Moments later, it was lifting off again, veering southwest.

Brad stood unmoving for a long time, still not sure he wasn't caught up in the aftermath of a nightmare, then leaned his and Jesse's rifles against the trunk of a nearby tree.

Ransom stood with his head down, dazed by the drug Livie had administered minutes before. The mares, still fitful but evidently aware that the worst danger had passed, fanned out to graze on the dry grass.

In the distance, the old wolf howled with piteous fury.

Pinkish-gold light rimmed the eastern hills as Meg returned to the house, after feeding the horses, and the phone was ringing.

She dived for it, in case it was Travis calling to say Sierra had had the baby.

In case it was Brad.

It was Eve.

"You're an aunt again," Meg's mother announced, with brisk pride. "Sierra had a healthy baby boy at four-thirty this morning. I think they're going to call him Brody, for Travis's brother."

Joy fluttered inside Meg's heart, like something trying delicate wings, and tears smarted in her eyes. "She's okay? Sierra, I mean?"

"She's fine, by all reports," Eve answered. "Liam and I are heading for Flagstaff right after breakfast. He's beside himself."

After washing her hands at the kitchen sink, Meg poured herself a cup of hot coffee. By habit, she'd set it brewing before going out to the barn. Upstairs, she heard Ted's slow step as he moved along the corridor.

"Ted's checking in today," she said, keeping her voice down. "I'll stop by to see Sierra and the baby after I get him settled." She drew a breath, let it out softly. "Mother, Carly is not handling this well."

Eve sighed sadly. "I'm sure she isn't, the poor child," she said. "Why don't you keep her out of school for the day and let her come along with you and Ted?"

"I suggested that," Meg replied, as her father appeared on the back stairs, dressed, with a shaving kit in one hand.

Their gazes met.

"And?" Eve prompted.

"And Ted said he wants her to attend class and visit later, when school's out for the day."

Ted nodded. "Is that Eve?"

"Yes," Meg said.

He gestured for the phone, and Meg handed it to him.

"This is Ted," he told Meg's mother. While he explained that Carly needed to settle into as normal a life as possible, as soon as possible, Carly herself appeared on the stairs, looking glum and stubborn.

She wore jeans and the souvenir T-shirt Brad had given her, in spite of the fact that it reached almost to her knees. The expression in her eyes dared Meg to object to the outfit—or anything else in the known universe.

"Hungry?" Meg asked.

"No," Carly said.

"Too bad. In this house, we eat breakfast."

"I might puke."

"You might."

Ted cupped a hand over one end of the phone. "Carly," he said sternly, "you *will* eat."

Scowling, Carly swung a leg over the bench next to the table and plunked down, angrily bereft. Meg poured orange juice, carried the glass to the table, set it down in front of her sister.

It was a wonder the stuff didn't come to an instant boil, considering the heat of Carly's glare as she stared at it.

"This bites," she said.

"Okay, I'll pass the word," Ted told Eve. "See you later."

He hung up. "Eve's hoping you can have lunch with her and Liam after you visit Sierra and the baby."

Meg nodded, distracted.

"It bites," Carly repeated, watching Ted with thunderous eyes. "You're going to the *hospital*, and I have to go to that stupid school, where they'll probably put me in *kindergarten* or something. I'm *supposed* to be in seventh grade."

Meg had no idea how Carly had fared on the tests she'd taken the day before, but it seemed safe to say things probably wouldn't go as badly as all that.

She got a frown for her trouble.

"This time next week," Ted told his younger daughter, "you'll probably be a sophomore at Harvard. Drink your orange juice."

Carly took a reluctant sip and eyeballed Meg's jeans, which were covered with bits of hay. "Don't you have like a *job* or something?"

"Yeah," Meg said, putting a pan on the stove to boil water for oatmeal. "I'm a ranch hand. The work's hard, the pay is lousy, there's no retirement plan and you have to shovel a lot of manure, but I love it."

Breakfast was a dismal affair, one Carly did her best to drag out, but, finally, the time came to leave.

Meg remained in the house for a few extra minutes while Ted and Carly got into the Blazer, giving them time to talk privately.

When she joined them, Carly was in tears, and Ted looked weary to the center of his soul.

Meg gave him a sympathetic look, pushed the button to roll up the garage door and backed out.

When they reached the school, Ted climbed laboriously out of the Blazer and stood on the sidewalk with Carly. They spoke earnestly, though Meg couldn't hear what they said, and Carly dashed at her cheeks with the back of one hand before turning to march staunchly through the colorful herd of kids toward the entrance.

Ted had trouble getting back into the car, but when Meg moved to get out and come around to help him, he shook his head.

"Don't," he said.

She nodded, thick-throated and close to tears herself.

When they reached the hospital in Flagstaff, Eve was waiting in the admittance office.

"I'll take over from here," she told Meg, standing up extra-straight as she watched a nurse ease Ted into a waiting wheelchair. "You go upstairs and see your sister and your new nephew. Room 502."

Meg hesitated, nodded. Then, surprising even herself, she bent and kissed Ted on top of the head before walking purposefully toward the nearest elevator.

Sierra glowed from the inside, as though she'd distilled sunlight to a golden potion and swallowed it down. The room was bedecked in flowers, splashes of watercolor pink, blue and yellow shimmered all around.

"Aunt Meg!" Liam cried delightedly, zooming out of the teary blur. "I've got a brand-new brother and his name is Brody Travis Reid!"

With a choked laugh, Meg hugged the little boy, almost displacing his Harry Potter glasses in the process. "Where *is* this Brody yahoo, anyhow?" she teased. "His legend looms large in this here town, but so far, I haven't seen hide nor hair of him."

"Silly," Liam said. "He's in the *nursery,* with all the other babies!"

Meg ruffled his hair. Went to give Sierra a kiss on the forehead.

"Congratulations, little sister," she said.

"He's so beautiful," Sierra whispered.

"Boys are supposed to be *handsome,* not beautiful," Liam protested, dragging a chair up on the other side of Sierra's bed and standing in the seat so he could be eye to eye with his mother. "Was I handsome?"

Sierra smiled, squeezed his small hand. "You're *still* handsome," she said gently. "And Dad and I are counting on you to be a really good big brother to Brody."

Liam turned to Meg, beaming. "Travis is going to adopt me. I'll be Liam McKettrick Reid, and Mom's changing her name, too."

Meg lifted her eyebrows slightly.

"Somebody had to break the tradition," Sierra said. "I've already told Eve."

Sierra would be the first McKettrick woman to take her husband's last name in generations.

"Mom's okay with that?" Meg asked.

Sierra grinned. "Timing is everything," she said. "If you want to break disturbing news to her, be sure to give birth first."

Meg chuckled. "You are a brave woman," she told Sierra. Then, turning to her nephew, she held out a hand. "How about showing me that brother of yours, Liam McKettrick Reid?"

Jesse returned at midmorning, as promised, with a dozen mounted cowboys. To Brad, the bunch looked as though they'd ridden straight out of an old black-and-white movie, their clothes, gear and horses only taking on color as they drew within hailing distance.

Brad was bone-tired, and Livie, her doctoring completed for the time being, had fallen asleep under a tree, bundled in his coat as well as her own. He'd built a fire an hour or so before dawn, but he craved coffee something fierce, and he was chilled to his core.

Before bedding down in the wee small hours, Livie had cheerfully informed her brother that while he ought to keep watch for the wolf pack, he didn't need to worry that Ransom and the mares would run off. They knew, she assured him, that they were among friends.

He'd kept watch through what remained of the night, pondering the undeniable proof that his sister *had* received an SOS from Ransom.

Now, with riders approaching, Livie wakened and got up off the ground, smiling and dusting dried pine needles and dirt off her jeans.

Jesse, Keegan and Rance were in the lead, ropes coiled around the horns of their saddles, rifles in their scabbards.

Rance nodded to Brad, dismounted and walked over to Ransom. He checked the animal's legs as deftly as Livie had.

"Think he can make it down the mountain to the ranch?" Rance asked.

Livie nodded. "If we take it slowly," she said. Her smile took in the three McKettricks and the men they'd rallied to help. "Thanks, everybody."

Most of the cowboys stared at Ransom as though they expected him to sprout wings, like Pegasus, and take to the blue-gold morning sky. One rode forward, leading mounts for Livie and Brad.

Livie took off Brad's coat and handed it to him, then swung up into the saddle with an ease he couldn't hope to emulate. He kicked dirt over the last embers of the campfire while Rance handed up Livie's veterinary kit.

The ride down the mountain would be long and hard, though thank God the weather had held. The sky was blue as Meg's eyes.

Brad took a deep breath, jabbed a foot into the stirrup and hauled himself onto the back of a pinto gelding. He was still pretty sore from the *last* trip up and down this mountain.

The cowboys went to work, starting Ransom and his mares along the trail with low whistles to urge them along.

Livie rode up beside Brad and grinned. "You look like hell," she said.

"Gosh, thanks," Brad grimaced, shifting in the saddle in a vain attempt to get comfortable.

She chuckled. "Think of it as getting into character for the movie."

Seeing Brody for the first time was the high point of Meg's day, but from there, it was all downhill.

Ted's tests were invasive, and he was drugged.

Liam was hyper with excitement, and didn't sit still for a second during lunch, despite Eve's grandmotherly reprimands. The food in the cafeteria tasted like wood shavings, and she got a call from the police in Indian Rock on her way home.

Carly had ditched school, and Wyatt Terp, the town marshal, had picked her up along Highway 17. She'd been trying to hitchhike to Flagstaff.

Meg sped to the police station, screeched to a stop in the parking lot and stormed inside.

Carly sat forlornly in a chair near Wyatt's desk, looking even younger than twelve.

"I just wanted to see my dad," she said in a small voice, taking all the bluster out of Meg's sails.

Meg pulled up a chair alongside Carly's and sat down, taking a few deep breaths to center herself. Wyatt smiled and busied himself in another part of the station house.

"You could have been kidnapped, or hit by a car, or a thousand other things," Meg said carefully.

"Dad and I thumbed it lots of times," Carly said defensively, "when our car broke down."

Meg closed her eyes for a moment. Waited for a sensible reply to occur to her. When that didn't happen, she opened them again.

"Will you take me to see him now?" Carly asked.

Meg sighed. "Depends," she said. "Are you under arrest, or just being held for questioning?"

Carly relaxed a little. "I'm not busted," she answered seriously. "But Marshal Terp says if he catches me hitchhiking again, I'll probably do hard time."

"You pull any more stupid tricks like this one, kiddo," Meg said, "and *I'll* give you all the 'hard time' you can handle."

Wyatt approached, doing his best to look like a stern lawman, but the effect was more Andy-of-Mayberry. "You can go, young lady," he told Carly, "but I'd better not see you in this office again unless you're selling Girl Scout cookies or 4-H raffle tickets or something. Got it?"

"Got it," Carly said meekly, ducking her head slightly.

Meg stood, motioned for her sister to head for the door.

Carly didn't move until the lawman raised an eyebrow at her.

"Is it the badge that makes her mind?" she whispered to Wyatt, once Carly was out of earshot. "And if so, do you happen to have a spare?"

He needed to see Meg.

It was seven-thirty that night before Ransom and his band were corralled at Stone Creek Ranch, and the McKettricks and their helpers had unsaddled all their horses, loaded them into trailers and driven off. Livie had greeted Willie, taken a hot shower and, bundled in one of Big John's ugly Indian-blanket bathrobes, gobbled down a bologna sandwich before climbing the stairs to her old room to sleep.

Brad was tired.

He was cold and he was hungry and he was saddle sore.

The only sensible thing to do was shower, eat and sleep like a dead man.

But he still needed to see Meg.

He settled for the shower and clean clothes.

Calling first would have been the polite thing to do, but he was past that. So he scrawled a note to Livie—*Feed the dog and the horses if I'm not back by morning*—and left.

The truck knew its way to the Triple M, which was a good thing, since he was in a daze.

Lights glowed warm and golden from Meg's windows, and his heart lifted at the sight, at the prospect of seeing her. The McKettricks, he recalled, tended to gather in kitchens. He parked the truck in the drive and walked around to the back of the house, knocked at the door.

Carly answered. She looked wan, as worn-out and used-up as Brad felt, but her face lit up when she saw him.

"I get to stay in seventh grade," she said. "According to my test scores, I'm gifted."

Brad rustled up a grin and resisted the urge to look past her, searching for Meg. "I could have told you that," he said as she stepped back to let him in.

"Meg's upstairs," Carly told him. "She has a sick headache and I'm supposed to leave her alone unless I'm bleeding or there's a national emergency."

Brad hid his disappointment. "Oh," he said, because nothing better came to him.

"I heard you were making a movie," Carly said. Clearly she was lonesome, needed somebody to talk to.

Brad could certainly identify. "Yeah," he answered, and this time the grin was a little easier to find.

"Can I be in it? I wouldn't have to have lines or anything. Just a costume."

"I'll see what I can do," Brad said. "My people will call your people."

Carly laughed, and the sound was good to hear.

He was about to excuse himself and leave when Meg appeared on the stairs wearing a cotton nightgown, with her hair all rumpled and shadows under her eyes.

"Rough day?" he asked, a feeling of bruised tenderness stealing up from his middle to his throat, like thick smoke from a smudge fire.

She tried to smile, pausing a moment on the stairs.

"Time for me to get lost," Carly said. "Can I use your computer, Meg?"

Meg nodded.

Carly left the room and Brad stood still, watching Meg.

"I guess I should have called first," he said.

"Sit down," Meg told him. "I'll make some coffee."

"I'll make the coffee," Brad replied. "*You* sit down."

For once, she didn't give him any back talk. She just

padded over to the table and plunked into the big chair at the head of it.

"Did you find Ransom?" she asked, while Brad opened cupboard doors, scouting for a can of coffee.

"Yes," he said, pleased that she'd remembered, given everything else that was going on in her life. "He and the mares have the run of my best pasture." He told Meg the rest of the story, or most of it, leaving out the part about Livie's dreams, not because he was afraid of what she might think of his sister's strange talent, but because the tale was Livie's to tell or keep to herself.

Meg grinned as she listened, shaking her head. "Rance and Keegan and Jesse must have been in their element, driving wild horses down the mountain like they were back in the old West."

"Maybe," Brad agreed, leaning back against the counter as he waited for the coffee to brew. "As for me—if I never have to do that again, it'll be too soon."

Meg laughed, but her eyes misted over in the next moment. She'd looked away too late to keep him from seeing. "Sierra—my other sister—had a baby this morning. A boy. His name is Brody."

Brad ached inside. It had been hard for Meg to share that news, and it shouldn't have been. Given the way he'd shut her out after meeting Carly, he couldn't blame her for being wary.

He went to her, crouched beside her chair, took one of her hands in both of his. "I'm sorry about the other night, Meg. I was just—I don't know—a little rattled by Carly's age, and her resemblance to you."

"It's okay," Meg said, but a tear slipped down her cheek.

Brad brushed it away with the side of one thumb. "It isn't okay. I acted like a jerk."

She sniffled. Nodded. "A *major* jerk."

He chuckled, blinked a couple of times because his eyes burned. Rose to his full height again. "I was hoping to spend the night," he said. "Until I remembered Carly's living here now."

Meg bit her lip. "I have guest rooms," she told him.

She didn't want him to leave, then.

Brad's spirits rose a notch.

"But what about Willie, and your horses?"

"Livie's at the house," he said, moving away from her, getting mugs down out of a cupboard. If he'd stayed close, he'd have hauled her to her feet and laid a big sloppy one on her, complete with tongue, and with a twelve-year-old in practically the next room, that was out. "She'll take care of the livestock."

After that, they sat quietly at the venerable old McKettrick table and talked about ordinary things. It made him surprisingly happy, just being there with Meg, doing nothing in particular.

In fact, life seemed downright perfect to him.

Which just went to show what *he* knew.

CHAPTER THIRTEEN

BRAD BLINKED AWAKE, sprawled on his back on the big leather couch in Meg's study, fully dressed and covered with an old quilt.

Carly stood looking down at him, a curious expression on her face, probably surprised that he hadn't slept with Meg.

"What time is it?" he asked, yawning.

"Six-thirty," Carly answered. She was wearing jeans and the T-shirt he'd given her, and it looked a little the worse for wear. "Have you decided if I get to be in your movie?"

Brad chuckled, yawned again. "I haven't heard from your agent," he teased.

She frowned. "I don't have an agent," she replied. "Is that a problem?"

"No," he relented, smiling. "I can promise you a walk-on. Beyond that, it's out of my hands. Deal?"

"Deal!" Carly beamed. But then her face fell. "I hope my dad makes it long enough to see me on the big screen," she said.

Brad's heart slipped, caught itself with a lurch that was almost painful. "We could show him the rushes," he said after swallowing once. "Right in his hospital room."

"What are rushes?"

"Film clips. They're not edited, and there's no music— not even sound, sometimes. But he'd see you."

Meg appeared in the doorway of the study, clad in chore clothes.

"I get to be in the movie," Carly informed her excitedly. "Even though I don't have an agent."

"That's great," Meg said softly, her gaze resting with tender gratitude on Brad. "Coffee's on, if anybody's interested."

Brad threw back the quilt, sat upright, pulled on his boots. "Somebody's interested, all right," he said. "I'll feed the horses if you'll make breakfast."

"Sounds fair," Meg answered, turning her attention back to Carly. "Nix on the T-shirt, Ms. Streep. You've worn it for three days in a row now—it goes in the laundry."

On her way to certain stardom, Carly apparently figured she could give ground on the T-shirt edict. "Okay," she said, and headed out of the room, ostensibly to go upstairs and change clothes.

"Carly got arrested yesterday," Meg announced, looking wan.

Brad stood, surprised. And not surprised. "What happened?"

"She decided to cut school and hitchhike to Flagstaff to see Ted in the hospital. Thank God, Wyatt happened to be heading up Highway 17 and spotted her from his squad car."

Brad approached Meg, took her elbows gently into his hands. "Having doubts about being an instant mother, McKettrick?" he asked quietly. She seemed uncommonly fragile, and knowing she'd been flattened by a headache the night before worried him.

"Yes," she said after gnawing at her lower lip for a couple of seconds. "I've always wanted a child, more than anything, but I didn't expect it to happen this way."

He drew her close, held her, buried his face in her hair

and breathed in the flower-and-summer-grass scent of it. "I know you don't think of Ted as a father," he said close to her ear, "but a reunion with him this late in the game, especially with a terminal diagnosis hanging over his head, has to be a serious blow. Maybe you need to acknowledge that Carly isn't the only one with some grieving to do."

She tilted her head back, her blue eyes shining with tears. "Damn him," she whispered. "Damn him for coming back here to die! Where was he when I took my first steps—lost my front teeth—broke my leg at horseback riding camp—graduated from high school and college? Where was he when you—"

"When I broke your heart?" Brad finished for her.

"Well—" Meg paused to sniffle once. "Yeah."

"I'd do anything to make that up to you, Meg. Anything for a do over. But the world doesn't work that way. Maybe besides finding a place for Carly, where he knows she'll be loved and she'll be safe, Ted's looking for the same thing I am. A second chance with you."

She looked taken aback. "Maybe," she agreed. "But he sure took his sweet time putting in an appearance, and so did you."

Brad gave her another hug. They were on tricky ground, and he knew it. Carly could be heard clattering down the stairs at the back of the house, into the kitchen.

They needed privacy to carry the conversation any further.

"I'll go feed the horses," he reiterated. "You make breakfast." He kissed her forehead, not wanting to let her go. "Once you've dropped Carly off at school, you could drop in at my place."

He held his breath, awaiting her answer. Both of them knew what would happen if he and Meg were alone at Stone Creek Ranch.

"I'll let you know," she said at long last.

He hesitated, nodded once and left her to feed the horses.

Breakfast turned out to be toaster waffles and microwave bacon.

"Next time," Brad told Meg, after they'd exchanged a light kiss next to her Blazer, with Carly watching avidly from the passenger seat, "I'll cook and *you* feed the horses."

He sang old Johnny Cash favorites all the way home, at the top of his lungs, with the truck windows rolled down.

But the song died in his throat when he topped the rise and saw a sleek white limo waiting in the driveway. Some gut instinct, as primitive as what he'd felt facing down the leader of the wolf pack up at Horse Thief Canyon, told him this wasn't Phil, or even a bunch of movie executives on an outing.

The chauffer got out, opened the rear right-hand door of the limo as Brad pulled to a stop next to it, buzzing up the truck windows and frowning.

A pair of long, shapely legs swung into view.

Brad swore and slammed out of the truck to stand like a gunfighter, his hands on his hips.

"I'd be perfect for the female lead in this movie," Cynthia Donnigan said, tottering toward him on spiked heels that sank into the dirt. Her short, stretchy skirt rode up on her gym-toned thighs, and she didn't bother to adjust it.

He stared at her in amazement and disbelief, literally speechless.

Cynthia lowered her expensive sunglasses and batted her lashes—as fake as her breasts—and her collagen-enhanced lips puckered into a pout. "Aren't you glad to see me?"

Her hair, black as Ransom's coat, was arranged in artfully careless tufts stiff enough to do damage if she decided to head butt somebody.

"What do you think?" he growled.

Luck, Big John had often said, was never so bad that it couldn't get worse. At that moment, Meg's Blazer came over the rise, dust spiraling behind it.

"I think you're not very forgiving," Cynthia said, following his gaze and then zeroing in on his face with a smug little twist of her mouth. "Bygones are bygones, baby. I'm ideal for the part and you know it."

Brad took a step back as she teetered a step forward. "Not a chance," he said, aware of Meg coming to a stop behind him, but not getting out of the Blazer.

Cynthia smiled and did a waggle-fingered wave in Meg's direction. "I've checked into a resort in Sedona," she said sweetly. "I can wait until you come to your senses and agree that the part of the lawman's widow was written for me."

Brad turned, approached the Blazer and met Meg's wide eyes through the glass of the driver's-side window. He opened the door and offered a hand to help her down.

"The second wife?" Meg asked, more mouthing the words than saying them.

Brad nodded shortly.

Meg peered around him as she got out of the Blazer. Then, with a big smile, she walked right up to Cynthia with her hand out. "I think I've seen you in several feminine hygiene product commercials," she said.

That made Brad chuckle to himself.

Cynthia simmered. "Hello," she responded, in a dangerous purr. "You must be the girl Brad left behind."

Meg had grown up rough-and-tumble, with a bunch of mischievous boy cousins, and served on the executive staff of a multinational corporation. She wasn't easy to intimidate. To Brad's relief—and amusement—she hooked an arm through his, smiled winningly and said, "It's sort of an on-again, off-again kind of thing with Brad and me. Right now, it's definitely on."

Cynthia blinked. She was strictly a B-grade celebrity, but as Brad's ex-wife and sole owner of an up-and-coming production company, she was used to deference of the Beverly Hills variety.

But this was Stone Creek, Arizona, not Beverly Hills.

And the word *deference* wasn't in Meg's vocabulary.

Temporarily stymied, Cynthia pushed her sunglasses back up her nose, minced back toward the waiting limo. The driver stood waiting, still holding her door open and staring off into space as though oblivious to everything going on in what was essentially the barnyard.

Brad followed. "If you manage to wangle your way into this movie," he said, "I'm out."

Cynthia plopped her scantily clad butt onto the leather seat, but didn't draw her killer legs inside. "Read your contract, Brad," she said. "You signed with Starglow Productions. *My* company."

The shock that made his stomach go into a free fall must have shown in his face, because his ex-wife smiled.

"Didn't I tell you I changed the name of the company?" she asked. "No me, no movie, cowboy."

"No movie," Brad said, feeling sick. The whole county was excited about the project—they'd have talked about it for years to come. Carly and a lot of other people would be disappointed—not least of all, himself.

"Back to Sedona," Cynthia told the driver, with a lofty gesture of one manicured hand.

"Yes, ma'am," he replied. But he gave Brad a sympathetic glance before getting behind the wheel.

Brad stood still, furious not only with Cynthia, and with Phil, who had to have known who owned Starglow Productions, but with himself. He'd been too quick to sign on the dotted line, swayed by his own desire to play big-screen cowboy, and by Livie's suggestion that he build an animal shelter with the proceeds. If he tried to back out of the deal now, Cynthia's lawyers would be all over him like fleas on an old hound dog, and he didn't even want to think of the potential publicity.

"So that's the second wife," Meg said, stepping up beside him and watching as the sleek car zipped away.

"That's her," he replied gloomily. "And I am royally, totally screwed."

She moved to stand in front of him, looking up into his face. "I was trying hard not to eavesdrop," she said, "but I couldn't help gathering that she wants to be in the movie."

"She *owns* the movie," Brad said.

"And this is so awful because—?"

"Because she's a first-class, card-carrying bitch. And because I can hardly stand to be in the same room with her, let alone on a movie set for three or four months."

Meg took his hand, gave him a gentle tug in the direction of the house. "Can't you break the contract?"

"Not without getting sued for everything I have, including this ranch, and bringing so many tabloid stringers to Stone Creek that they'll be swinging from the telephone poles."

"Then maybe you should just bite the proverbial bullet and make the movie."

"You haven't read the script," Brad said. "I have to kiss her. And there's a love scene—"

Meg's eyes twinkled. "You sound like a little boy, balking at being in the school play with a *girl*." She tugged him up the back steps, toward the kitchen door.

Willie met them on the other side, wagging cheerfully.

Brad let him out, scowling, and he and Meg waited on the porch while the dog attended to his duties.

"You have no idea what she's like," Brad said.

Meg gave him a light poke with her elbow. "I know you must have loved her once. After all, you married her."

"The truth is a lot less flattering than that," he replied, unable, for a long moment, to meet Meg's eyes. What he had to say was going to upset her, for several reasons, and there was no way to avoid it. "We hooked up after a party. Six weeks later, she called and told me she was pregnant, and the baby was mine. I married her, because she said she was going to get an abortion if I didn't. I went on tour—she wanted to go along and I refused. Frankly, I wasn't ready to present Cynthia to the world as my adored bride. She called the press in, gave them pictures of the 'wedding.' And then, just to make sure I knew what it meant to cross her, she had the abortion anyway."

The pain was there in Meg's face—she had to be thinking that, had she told him about *their* baby, he'd have married her with the same singular lack of enthusiasm—but her words took him by surprise. "I'm sorry, Brad," she said softly. "You must have really wanted to be a dad."

He whistled for Willie, since speaking was beyond him for the moment, and the dog, obviously on the mend, made it up the porch steps with no help. "Yeah," he said.

"I have an idea," Meg said.

He glanced at her. "What?"

"We could rehearse your love scene. Just to be sure you get it right."

In spite of everything, he chuckled. The sound was raw and hurt his throat, but it was genuine. "Aren't you the least bit jealous?" he asked.

She looked honestly puzzled. "Of what?"

"I'm going to have to kiss Cynthia. Get naked with her on the silver screen. This doesn't bother you?"

"I'll cover my eyes during that part of the movie," she joked, with a little what-the-hell motion of her shoulders. Then her expression turned serious. "Of course, there's a fine line between hatred and passion. If you care for Cynthia, you need to tell me—now."

He laid his hands on her shoulders, remembered the satiny smoothness of her bare skin. "I care for *you*, Meg McKettrick," he said. "I tried hard—with Valerie, even with Cynthia—but it never worked. I was always thinking about you—reading about you in the business pages of newspapers, getting what news I could through my sisters, checking the McKettrickCo website. Whenever I read or heard your name, I got this sour ache in the pit of my stomach, because I was scared a wedding announcement would follow."

Meg stiffened slightly. "What would you have done if one had?"

"Stopped the wedding," he said. "Made a scene Indian Rock and Stone Creek would never forget." He smiled crookedly. "Kind of a sticky proposition, given that I could have been married at the time."

"Not to mention that my cousins would have thrown you bodily out of the church," Meg huffed, but there was a smile beginning in her eyes, already tugging at the corners of her mouth.

"I said it would have been an unforgettable scene," he reminded her, grinning. "I would have fought back, you see, and yelled your name, like Stanley yelling for Stella in *A Streetcar Named Desire*."

She pretended to punch him in the stomach. "You're impossible."

"I'm also horny. And a lot more—though I'm not sure you're ready to hear that part."

"Try me."

"Okay. I love you, Meg McKettrick. I always have. I always will."

"You're right. I wasn't ready."

"Then I guess rehearsing the love scene is out?"

She smiled, stood on tiptoe and kissed the cleft in his chin. "I didn't say that. Hardworking actors should know their scenes cold."

He bent his head, nibbled at her delectable mouth. "Oh, I'll know the scene," he breathed. "But there won't be anything 'cold' about it."

Meg hauled herself up onto her elbows, out of a sated sleep, glanced at the clock on the table next to Brad's bed and screamed.

"What?" Brad asked, bolting awake.

"Look at the time!" Meg wailed. "Carly will be out of school in fifteen minutes!"

Calmly, Brad reached for the telephone receiver, handed it to her. "Call the school and tell them you've been detained and you'll be there soon."

"Detained?"

"Would you rather say you've been in bed with me all afternoon?"

"No," she admitted, and dialed 411, asking to be connected to Indian Rock Middle School.

When she arrived at the school forty-five minutes later, Carly was waiting glumly in the principal's office. Her expression softened, though, when she saw that Brad had come along.

"Oh, great," she said. "Brad O'Ballivan shows up at my

school, *in person,* and nobody's around to see but the geek-wads in detention. Who'd believe a word *they* said?"

Brad laughed. "Did I ever tell you I was one of those 'geek-wads' once upon a time, always in detention?"

"Get out," Carly said, intrigued.

"Don't get the idea that being in detention is cool," Meg warned.

Carly rolled her eyes.

The three of them made the drive to Flagstaff in Brad's truck. Carly chattered nonstop for the first few miles, pointing out the place where she'd been "busted" for trying to hitch a ride, but as they drew nearer to their destination, she grew more and more subdued.

It didn't help that Ted was worse than he'd been the day before. He looked shrunken, lying there in his bed with tubes and monitors attached to every part of his body.

Looking at her father, it seemed to Meg that he'd used up the last of his personal resources to fling himself over an invisible finish line—getting Carly to her for safekeeping. For the first time it was actually real to Meg: he *was* dying.

Brad gave her a nudge toward the bed, an unspoken reminder of what he'd said about her having grieving to do, just as Carly did.

"How about a milk shake in the cafeteria?" Meg heard Brad say to Carly.

In the next moment, the two of them were gone, and Meg was alone with the man who had abandoned her so long ago that she didn't even remember him.

"That young man," Ted said, "is in love with you."

"He left me, too," Meg said without meaning to expose the rawest nerve in her psyche. "It's a pattern. First you, then Brad."

"Do yourself a favor and don't superimpose your old

man over him," Ted struggled to say. "And when Carly gets old enough, don't let her make that mistake, either. I don't have time to make it up to you, what I did and didn't do, but he does. You give him the chance."

Tears welled in Meg's eyes, thickened her throat. "I hate it that you're dying," she said.

Ted put out his left hand, an IV tube dangling from it. "Me, too," he ground out. "Come here, kid."

Meg let him pull her closer, lowered her forehead to rest against his.

She felt moisture in the gray stubble on his cheeks and didn't know if the tears were hers or her father's. Or both.

"If I could stay around a little longer, I'd find a way to prove that you're still my little girl and I've always loved you. Since I'm not going to get that chance, you'll have to take my word for it."

"It isn't fair," Meg protested, knowing the remark was childish.

"Not much is, in this life," Ted answered, as Meg raised her head so she could look into his face. "Know what I'd tell you if I'd been around all this time like a regular father, and had the right to say what's on my mind?"

Meg couldn't answer.

"I'd tell you not to let Brad O'Ballivan get away. Don't let your damnable McKettrick pride get in the way of what he's offering, Meg."

"He told me he loves me," she said.

"Do you believe him?"

"I don't know."

"All right, then, do you love him?"

Meg bit her lower lip, nodded.

"Have you told him?"

"Sort of," Meg said.

"Take it from me, kid," Ted countered, trying to smile. "'Sort of' ain't good enough." His faded eyes seemed to memorize Meg, take her in. "Get the nurse for me, will you? This pain medication isn't working."

Meg immediately rang for the nurse, and when help came, rushed to the elevators and punched the button for the cafeteria. By the time she got back with Carly and Brad, the room was full of people in scrubs.

Carly broke free and rushed to her dad's bedside, squirming through until she caught hold of his hand.

The medical team, in the midst of an emergency, would have pushed Carly aside if Brad hadn't spoken in a voice of calm but unmistakable authority.

"Let her stay," he said.

"Dad?" Carly whispered desperately. "Dad, don't go, okay? Don't go!"

A nurse eased Carly back from the bedside, and the work continued, but it was too late, and everyone knew it.

The heartbeat monitor blipped, then flatlined.

Carly turned, sobbing, not into Meg's arms, but into Brad's.

He held her and drew Meg close against his side at the same time.

After that, there were papers to sign. Meg would have to call her mother later, but at the moment, she simply couldn't say the words.

Carly seemed dazed, allowing herself to be led out of the hospital, back to Brad's truck. She'd been inconsolable in Ted's hospital room, but now she was dry-eyed and the only sound she made was the occasional hiccup.

Brad didn't take them back to the Triple M, but to his own ranch. There, he called Eve, then Jesse. Vaguely, as if from a great distance, Meg heard him ask her cousin to make sure her horses got fed.

There were other calls, too, but Meg wasn't tracking. She simply sat at the kitchen table, watching numbly while Carly knelt on the floor, both arms around a sympathetic Willie, her face buried in his fur.

Olivia arrived—Brad must have summoned her—and brought a stack of pizza boxes with her. She set the boxes on the counter, washed her hands at the sink and immediately started setting out plates and silverware.

"I'm not hungry," Carly said.

"Me, either," Meg echoed.

"Humor me," Olivia said.

The pizza tasted like cardboard, but it filled a hole, if only a physical one, and Meg was grateful. Following her example, Carly ate, too.

"Are we staying here tonight?" Carly asked Brad, her eyes enormous and hollow.

Olivia answered for him. "Yes," she said.

"Who are you?"

"I'm Livie—Brad's sister."

"The veterinarian?"

Olivia nodded.

"My dad died today."

Olivia's expressive eyes filled with tears. "I know."

Meg swallowed, but didn't speak. Next to her, Brad took her hand briefly, gave it a squeeze.

"Do you like being an animal doctor?" Carly asked. She'd said hardly a word to Meg or even Brad since they'd left the hospital, but for some reason, she was reaching out to Olivia O'Ballivan.

"I love it," Olivia said. "It's hard sometimes, though. When I try really hard to help an animal, and they don't get better."

"I kept thinking my dad would get well, but he didn't."

"Our dad died, too," Olivia said after a glance in Brad's direction. "He was struck by lightning during a roundup. I kept thinking there must have been a mistake—that he was just down in Phoenix at a cattle auction, or looking for strays up on the mountain."

Meg felt a quick tension in Brad, a singular alertness, gone again as soon as it came. Her guess was he hadn't known his sister, a child when the accident happened, had secretly believed their father would come home.

"Does it ever stop hurting?" Carly asked, her voice small and fragile.

Meg squeezed her eyes shut. Does *it ever stop hurting?* she wondered.

"You'll never forget your dad, if that's what you mean," Olivia said. "But it gets easier. Brad and our sisters and I, we were lucky. We had our grandfather, Big John. Like you've got Meg."

Brad pushed his chair back, left the table. Stood with his back to them all, as if gazing out the darkened window over the sink.

"Big John passed away, too," Olivia explained quietly. "But we were all grown up by then. He was there when it counted, and now we've got each other."

Carly turned imploring eyes on Meg. "You won't die, too? You won't die and leave me all alone?"

Meg got up, went to Carly, gathered her into her arms. "I'll be here," she promised. *"I'll be here."*

Carly clung to her for a long time, then, typically, pulled away. "Where am I going to sleep?" she asked.

"I thought maybe you'd like to stay in my room," Olivia said. "It has twin beds. You can have the one by the window, if you'd like."

"You're going to stay, too?"

"For tonight," Olivia answered.

Carly looked relieved. Maybe, for a child, it was a matter of safety in numbers—herself, Meg, Brad, Olivia and Willie, all huddled in the same house, somehow keeping the uncertain darkness at bay. "I think I'd like to sleep now," she said. "Can Willie come, too?"

"He'll need to go outside first, I think," Olivia said.

Brad took Willie out, without a word, returned and watched as the old dog climbed the stairs, Carly leading the way, Olivia bringing up the rear.

"Thanks," Meg said when she and Brad were alone. "You've been wonderful."

Brad began clearing the table, disposing of pizza boxes.

Meg caught his arm. "Brad, what—?"

"My grandfather," he said. "I just got to missing him. Regretting a lot of things."

She nodded. Waited.

"I'm sorry, Meg," he told her. "That your dad's gone, and you didn't get a chance to know him. That you've got a rough time ahead with Carly. And most of all, I'm sorry there's nothing I can do to make this better."

"You could hold me," Meg said.

He pulled her into an easy, gentle embrace. Kissed her forehead. "I could hold you," he confirmed.

She wanted to ask if he'd meant it, when—was it only a few hours ago?—he'd said he loved her. The problem was, she knew if he took the words back, or qualified them somehow, she wouldn't be able to bear it. Not now, while she was mourning the father she'd lost years ago.

They stood like that for a while, then, by tacit agreement, finished tidying up the kitchen. Before they started up the backstairs, Brad switched out the lights, and Meg stood waiting for him, blinded, not knowing her way around the house, but unafraid. As long as Brad was there, no gloom would have been deep enough to swallow her.

In his room upstairs, they undressed, got into bed together, lay enfolded in each other's arms.

I love you, Meg thought with stark clarity.

They didn't make love.

They didn't talk.

But Meg felt a bittersweet gratification just the same, a deep shift somewhere inside herself, where spirit and body met.

On the edge of sleep, just before she tumbled helplessly over the precipice, Angus crossed her mind, along with a whisper-thin wondering.

Where had he gone?

CHAPTER FOURTEEN

THE SNOWS CAME EARLY THAT YEAR, to the annoyance of the movie people, and Brad was away from the ranch a lot, filming scenes in a studio in Flagstaff. He'd grudgingly admitted that Cynthia had been right—she *was* perfect for the part of Sarah Jane Stone—and while Meg visited the set once or twice, she stayed away when the love scenes were on the schedule.

She had a lot of other things on her mind, as it happened. She and Carly were bonding, slowly but surely, but the process was rocky. With the help of a counselor, they felt their way toward each other—backed off—tried again.

When the day came for Carly's promised scene—she played a nameless character in calico and a bonnet who brought Brad a glass of punch at a party and solemnly offered it. She'd endlessly practiced her single line—a "you're welcome, mister" to his "thank you"—telling Meg very seriously that there were no small parts, only small actors.

The movie part gave Carly something to hold on to in the dark days after Ted's passing, and Meg was eternally grateful for that. Both she and Carly spent a lot of time at Brad's house, even when he wasn't around, looking after Willie and gradually becoming a part of the place itself.

Ransom and his mares occupied the main pasture at Stone Creek Ranch, and the job of driving hay out to them usually fell to Olivia and Meg, with Carly riding in the back of the truck, seated on the bales. During that time, Meg and Olivia became good friends.

In the spring, when there would be fresh grass in the high country, and no snow to impede their mobility, Ransom and the mares would be turned loose.

"You'll miss him," Meg said once, watching Olivia as she stood in the pickup bed, tossing bales of grass hay to the ground after Carly cut the twine that held them together.

Olivia swallowed visibly and nodded, admiring the stallion as he stood, head turned toward the mountain, sniffing the air for the scents of spring and freedom. On warmer days, he was especially restless, prancing back and forth along the farthest fence, tail high, mane flying in the breeze.

Meg knew there had been many opportunities to sell Ransom for staggering amounts of money, but neither Olivia nor Brad had even considered the idea. In their minds, Ransom wasn't theirs to sell—he belonged to himself, to the high country, to legend. With his wounds healed, he'd have been able to soar over any fence, but he seemed to know the time wasn't right. There in the O'Ballivans' pasture, he had plenty of feed and easily accessible water, hard to find in winter, especially up in the red peaks and canyons, and he'd be at a disadvantage with the wolves. Still, there was a palpable, restless air of yearning about him that bruised Meg's heart.

It would be a sad and wonderful day when the far gate was opened.

Olivia cheered herself, along with Meg and Carly, with the fact that Brad had decided to make the ranch a haven for displaced mules, donkeys and horses, including unwanted Thoroughbreds who hadn't made the grade as racers, studs or broodmares. At the first sign of spring, the adoptees would begin arriving, courtesy of the Bureau of Land Management and various animal-rescue groups.

In the meantime, the ranch, like the larger world, seemed to Meg to be hibernating, practically in suspended animation. Like Ransom, she longed for spring.

It was after one of their visits to Brad's, while they were attending to their own horses on the Triple M, that Carly brought up a subject Meg had been troubled by, but hadn't wanted to raise.

"Where do you suppose Angus is?" the child asked. "I haven't seen him around in a couple of months."

"Hard to know," Meg said carefully.

"Maybe he's busy on the other side," Carly suggested. "You know, showing my dad around and stuff."

"Could be," Meg allowed. Until his last visit—the night he'd been so anxious for a look at the McKettrick family Bible—Meg had seen and spoken to her illustrious ancestor almost every day of her life. She hadn't had so much as a glimpse of him since then, and while there had been countless times she'd wished Angus would stay where he belonged, so she could be a normal person, she missed him.

Surely he wouldn't have simply stopped visiting her without even saying goodbye. It appeared, though, that that was exactly what he'd done.

"I wish he'd come," Carly said somewhat wistfully. "I want to ask him if he's seen my dad."

Meg slipped an arm around her sister, held her close against her side for a second or two. "I'm sure your—our—dad is fine," she said softly.

Carly smiled, but sadness lingered in her eyes. "For a while, I hoped Dad would come back, the way Angus did. But I guess he's busy or something."

"Probably," Meg agreed. It went without saying that the

Angus phenomenon was rare, but there were times when she wondered if that was really true. How many children, prattling about their imaginary playmates, were actually seeing someone real?

They started back toward the house, two sisters, walking close.

Inside, they both washed up—Meg at the kitchen sink, Carly in the downstairs powder room—and began preparing supper. After the meal, salad and a tamale pie from a recently acquired cookbook geared to the culinarily challenged, Meg cleared the table and loaded the dishwasher while Carly settled down to her homework.

Like most kids, she had a way of asking penetrating questions with no preamble. "Are you going to marry Brad O'Ballivan?" she inquired now, looking up from her math text. "We spend a lot of time at his place, and I know you sleep over when I'm visiting Eve. Or he comes here."

Things were good between Brad and Meg, probably because he was so busy with the movie that they rarely saw each other. When they *were* together, they took every opportunity to make love.

"He hasn't asked," Meg said lightly. "And you're in some pretty personal territory, here. Have I mentioned lately that you're twelve?"

"I might be twelve," Carly replied, "but I'm not stupid."

"You're definitely not stupid," Meg agreed good-naturedly, but on the inside, she was dancing to a different tune. Her period, always as regular as the orbit of the moon, was two weeks late. She'd bought a home pregnancy test at a drugstore in Flagstaff, not wanting word of the purchase to get around Indian Rock as it would have if she'd made the purchase locally, but she hadn't worked up the nerve to use it yet.

As much as she'd wanted a child, she almost hoped the results would be negative. She knew what would happen if the plus sign came up, instead of the minus. She'd tell Brad, he'd insist on marrying her, just as he'd done with both Valerie and Cynthia, and for the rest of her days, she'd wonder if he'd proposed out of honor, or because he actually loved her.

On the other hand, she wouldn't dare keep the knowledge from him, not after what had happened before, when they were teenagers. He'd never forgive her if something went wrong; even the truest, deepest kind of love between a man and a woman couldn't survive if there was no trust.

All of which left Meg in a state of suspecting she was carrying Brad's child, not knowing for sure, and being afraid to find out.

Carly, whose intuition seemed uncanny at times, blindsided her again. "I saw the pregnancy-test kit," she announced.

Meg, in the process of wiping out the sink, froze.

"I didn't mean to snoop," Carly said quickly. By turns, she was rebellious and paranoid, convinced on some level that living on the Triple M as a part of the McKettrick family was an interval of sorts, not a permanent arrangement. In her experience, everything was temporary. "I ran out of toothpaste, and I went into your bathroom to borrow some, and I saw the kit."

Sighing, Meg went to the table and sat down next to Carly, searching for words.

"Are you mad at me?" Carly asked.

"No," Meg said. "And I wouldn't send you away even if I was, Carly. You need to get clear on that."

"Okay," Carly said, but she didn't sound convinced. Meg guessed it would take time, maybe a very long time, for her little sister to feel secure. Her face brightened. "It would be so cool if you had a baby!" she spouted.

"Yes," Meg agreed, smiling. "It would."

"So what's the problem with finding out for sure?"

"Brad's really busy right now. I guess I'm looking for a chance to tell him."

Just then, as if by the hand of Providence, a rig drove up outside, a door slammed.

Carly rushed to the window, gave a yip of excitement. "He's here!" she crowed. "And Willie's with him!"

Meg closed her eyes. So much for procrastination.

Carly hurried to open the back door, and Brad and the dog blew in with a chilly wind.

"Here," Brad said, handing Carly a DVD case. "It's your big scene, complete with dialogue and music."

Carly grabbed the DVD and fled to the study, which contained the only TV set in the house, fairly skipping and Willie, now almost wholly recovered from his injuries, dashed after her, barking happily.

Meg was conscious, in those moments, of everything that was at stake. The child and even the dog would suffer if the conversation she and Brad were about to have went sour.

"Sit down," she said, turning to watch Brad as he shed his heavy coat and hung it from one of the pegs next to the door.

"Sounds serious," Brad mused. "Carly get into trouble at school again?"

"No," Meg answered, after swallowing hard.

Brad frowned and joined her at the table, sitting astraddle the bench while she occupied the chair at the end. "Meg, what's the trouble?" he asked worriedly.

"I bought a kit—" she began, immediately faltering.

His forehead crinkled. "A kit?" The light went on. "A *kit!*"

"I think I might be pregnant, Brad."

A smile spread across his face, shone in his eyes, giving her hope. But then he went solemn again. "You don't sound very happy about it," he said, looking wary. "When did you do the test?"

"That's just it. I haven't done it yet. Because I'm afraid."

"Afraid? Why?"

"Things have been so good between us, and—"

Gently, he took her hand. Turned it over to trace patterns on her palm with the pad of his thumb. "Go on," he said, his voice hoarse, obviously steeling himself against who knew what.

"I know you'll marry me," Meg forced herself to say. "If the test is positive, I mean. And I'll always wonder if you feel trapped, the way you did with Cynthia."

Brad considered her words, still caressing her palm. "All right," he said presently. "Then I guess we ought to get married *before* you take the pregnancy test. Because either way, Meg, I want you to be my wife. Baby or no baby."

She studied him. "Maybe we should live together for a while. See how it goes."

"No way, McKettrick," Brad replied instantly. "I know lots of good people share a house without benefit of a wedding these days, but when it comes down to it, I'm an old-fashioned guy."

"You'd really do that? Marry me without knowing the results of the test? What if it's negative?"

"Then we'd keep working on it." Brad grinned.

Meg bit her lower lip, thinking hard.

Finally, she stood and said, "Wait here."

But she only got as far as the middle of the back stairway before she returned.

"The McKettrick women don't change their names when they get married," she reminded him, though they both knew Sierra had already broken that tradition, and happily so.

"Call yourself whatever you want," Brad replied. "For a year. At the end of that time, if you're convinced we can make it, then you'll go by O'Ballivan. Deal?"

Meg pondered the question. "Deal," she said at long last.

She went upstairs, slipped into her bathroom and leaned against the closed door, her heart pounding. Her reflection in the long mirror over the double sink stared back at her.

"Pee on the stick, McKettrick," she told herself, "and get it over with."

Five minutes later, she was staring at the little plastic stick, filled with mixed emotion. There was happiness, but trepidation, too. *What-ifs* hammered at her from every side.

A light knock sounded at the door, and Brad came in.

"The suspense," he said, "is killing me."

Meg showed him the stick.

And his whoop of joy echoed off every wall in that venerable old house.

"I think I have a future in show business," Carly confided to Brad later that night when she came into the kitchen to say good-night. She'd watched her scene on the study TV at least fourteen times.

"I think you have a future in the eighth grade," Meg responded, smiling.

"What if I end up on the cutting-room floor?" Carly

fretted. Clearly, she'd been doing some online research into the movie-making process.

"I'll see that you don't," Brad promised. "Go to bed, Carly. A movie star needs her beauty sleep."

Carly nodded, then went upstairs, DVD in hand. Willie, who had been following her all evening, sighed despondently and lay down at Brad's feet, muzzle resting on his forepaws.

Brad leaned down to stroke the dog's smooth, graying back. "Looks like Carly's already got one devoted fan," he remarked.

Meg chuckled. "More than one," she said. "I certainly qualify, and so do you. Eve spoils her, and Rance's and Keegan's girls think of her as the family celebrity."

Brad grinned. "Carly's a pro," he said. "But you're wise to steer her away from show business, at least for the time being. It's hard enough for adults to handle, and kids have it even worse."

The topics of the baby and marriage pulsed in the air between them, but they skirted them, went on talking about other things. Brad was comfortable with that—there would be time enough to make plans.

"According to her teachers," Meg said, "Carly has a near-genius affinity for computers, or anything technical. Last week she actually got the clock on the DVD player to stop blinking twelves. This, I might add, is a skill that has eluded presidents."

"Lots of things elude presidents," Brad replied, finishing his coffee. "We're wrapping up the movie next week," he added. "The indoor scenes, at least. We'll have to do the stagecoach robbery and all the rest next spring. Think you could pencil a wedding into your schedule?"

Meg's cheeks colored attractively, causing Brad to wonder what *other* parts of her were turning pink. She hesitated, then nodded, but as she looked at him, her gaze switched to something just beyond his left shoulder.

Brad turned to look, but there was nothing there.

"I hate leaving you," he said, turning back, frowning a little. "But I've got an early call in the morning." Neither of them were comfortable sleeping together with Carly around, but that would change after they were married.

"I understand," Meg said.

"Do you, Meg?" he asked very quietly. "I love you. I want to marry you, and I would have, even if the test had been negative."

She said them then, the words he'd been waiting for. Before that, she'd spoken them only in the throes of passion.

"I love you right back, Brad O'Ballivan."

He stood, drew her to her feet and kissed her. It was a lingering kiss, gentle but thorough.

"But there's still one thing I haven't told you," she choked out, when their mouths parted.

Brad braced himself. Waited, his mind scrambling over possibilities—there was another man out there somewhere after all, one with some emotional claim on her, or more she hadn't told him about the first pregnancy, or the miscarriage...

"Ever since I was a little girl," she said, "I've been seeing Angus McKettrick. In fact, he's here right now."

Brad recalled the glance she'd thrown over his shoulder a few minutes before, the odd expression in her eyes. First Livie, with her Dr. Doolittle act—now Meg claimed she could see the family patriarch, who had been dead for over a century.

He thrust out a sigh.

She waited, gnawing at her lip, her eyes wide and hopeful.

"If you say so," he said at last, "I believe you."

Joy suffused her face. "Really?"

"Really," he said, though the truth was more like: *I'm trying to believe you.* As with Livie, he would believe if it killed him, despite all the rational arguments crowding his mind.

She stood on tiptoe and kissed him. "I'd insist that you stay, since we're engaged," she whispered, "but Angus is even more old-fashioned than you are."

He laughed, said good-night and looked down at Willie.

The dog was standing, wagging his tail and grinning, looking up at someone who wasn't there.

There were indeed, Brad thought, as he and Willie made the lonely drive back to Stone Creek Ranch in his truck, more things in heaven and earth than this world dreams of.

"Where have you been?" Meg demanded, torn between relief at seeing Angus again, and complete exasperation.

"You always knew I wouldn't be around forever," Angus said. He looked older than he had the last time she'd seen him, even careworn, but somehow serene, too. "Things are winding down, girl. I figured you needed to start getting used to my being gone."

Meg blinked, surprised by the stab of pain she felt at the prospect of Angus's leaving for good. On the other hand, she *had* always known the last parting would come.

"I'm going to have a baby," she said, struggling not to cry. "I'll need you. The baby and Carly will need you."

Angus seldom touched her, but now he cupped one hand under her chin. His skin felt warm, not cold, and solid, not ethereal. "No," he said gruffly. "You only need yourselves and each other. Things are going to be fine from here on out, Meg. You'll see."

She swallowed, wanting to cling to him, knowing it wouldn't be right. He had a life to live, somewhere else, beyond some unseen border. There were others there, waiting for him.

"Why did you come?" she asked. "In first place, I mean?"

"You needed me," he said simply.

"I did," she confirmed. For all the nannies and "aunts and uncles," she'd been a lost soul as a child, especially after Sierra was kidnapped and Eve fell apart in so many ways. She'd never blamed her mother, never harbored any resentment for the inevitable neglect she'd suffered, but she knew now that, without Angus, she would have been bereft.

He was carrying a hat in his left hand, and now he put it on, the gesture somehow final. "You say goodbye to Carly for me," he said. "And tell her that her pa's just fine where he is."

Meg nodded, unable to speak.

Angus leaned in, planted a light, awkward kiss on Meg's forehead. "When you get to the end of the trail," he said, "and that's a long ways off, I promise, I'll be there to say welcome."

Still, no words would come. Not even ones of farewell. So Meg merely nodded again.

Angus turned his back and, in the blink of an eye, he was gone.

She cried that night, for sorrow, for joy and for a thousand other reasons, but when the morning came, she knew Angus had been right.

She didn't need him anymore.

* * *

The wedding was small and simple, with only family and a few friends present. Meg still considered the marriage provisional, and went on calling herself Meg McKettrick, although she and Carly moved in at Stone Creek Ranch right away. All the horses came with them, but Meg still paid regular visits to the Triple M, always hoping, on some level, for just one more glimpse of Angus.

It didn't happen, of course.

So she sorted old photos and journals when she was there, and with some help from Sierra, catalogued them into something resembling archives. Eve, tired of hotel living, planned on moving back in. A grandmother, she maintained, with Eve-logic, ought to live in the country. She ought to bake pies and cookies and shelter the children of the family under broad, sturdy branches, like an old oak tree.

Meg smiled every time she pictured her rich, sophisticated, well-traveled mother in an apron and sensible shoes, but she had to admit Eve had pulled off a spectacular country-style Christmas. There had been a massive tree, covered in lights and heirloom ornaments, bulging stockings for Carly and Liam and little Brody, and a complete turkey dinner, only partly catered.

She'd already taken over the master bedroom, and she'd brought her two champion jumpers from the stables in San Antonio, and installed them in the barn. She rode every chance she got, often with Brad and Carly and sometimes with Jesse, Rance and Keegan.

Meg, being pregnant and out of practice when it came to horseback riding, usually watched from a perch on the pasture fence. She didn't believe in being overly cautious— it wasn't the McKettrick way—but this baby was precious to her, and to Brad. She wasn't taking any chances.

Dusting off an old photograph of Holt and Lorelei, Meg

stepped back to admire the way it looked on the study mantle. She heard her mother at the back of the house.

"Meg? Are you here?"

"In the study," Meg called back.

Eve tracked her down. "Feeling nostalgic?" she asked, eyeing the picture.

Meg sighed, sat down in a high-backed leather chair, facing the fireplace. "Maybe it's part of the pregnancy. Hormones, or something."

Eve, always practical, threw off her coat, draping it over the back of the sofa, marched to the fireplace and started a crackling, cheerful blaze. She let Meg's words hang, all that time, finally turning to study her daughter.

"Are you happy, Meg? With Brad, I mean?"

When it came to happiness, she and Brad were constantly charting fresh territory. Learning new things about each other, stumbling over surprises both profound and prosaic. For all of that, there was a sense of fragility to the relationship.

"I'm happy," she said.

"But?" Eve prompted. She stood with her back to the fireplace, looking very ungrandmotherly in her tailored slacks and silk sweater.

"It feels—well—too good to be true," Meg admitted.

Eve crossed to drag a chair closer to Meg's and sit beside her. "You're holding back a part of yourself, aren't you? From Brad, from the marriage?"

"I suppose I am," Meg said. "It's sort of like the first day we were allowed to swim in the pond, late in the spring, when Jesse and Rance and Keegan and I were kids. The water was always freezing. I'd stick a toe in and stand shivering on the bank while the boys cannonballed into the water, howling and whooping and trying to splash me. Finally, more out of shame than courage, I'd jump in."

She shuddered. "I still remember that icy shock—it always knocked the wind out of me for a few minutes."

Eve smiled, probably remembering similar swimming fests from her own childhood, with another set of McKettrick cousins. "But then you got used to the temperature and had as much fun as the boys did."

Meg nodded.

"It's not smart to hold yourself apart from the shocks of life, Meg—the good ones or the bad. They're all part of the mix, and paradoxically, shying away from them only makes things harder."

Meg was quiet for a long time. Then she said quietly, "Angus is gone."

Eve waited.

"I miss him," Meg confessed. "When I was a teenager, especially, I used to wish he'd leave me alone. Now that he's gone—well—every day, the memories seem less and less real."

Eve took her hand, squeezed. "Sometimes," she said very softly, "just at twilight, I think I see them—Angus and his four sturdy, handsome sons—riding single-file along the creek bank. Just a glimpse, a heartbeat really, and then they're gone. It's odd, because they don't look like ghosts. Just men on horseback, going about their ordinary business. I could almost convince myself that, for a fraction of a moment, a curtain had opened between their time and ours."

"Rance told me the same thing once," Meg said. "He used different words, but he saw the riders, traveling one behind the other beside the creek, and he knew who they were."

The two women sat in thoughtful silence for a while.

"It's a strange thing, being a McKettrick," Meg finally said.

"You're an O'Ballivan now," Eve surprised her by saying. "And your baby will be an O'Ballivan, too."

Meg looked hard at her mother, startled. Eve had been miffed when Sierra took Travis's last name, and made a few remarks about tradition not being what it once was.

"What about the McKettrick way?" she asked.

"The McKettrick way," Eve said, giving Meg's hand another squeeze, "is living at full throttle, holding nothing back. It's taking life—and change—as they come. Anyway, lots of women keep their last names these days—taking their husbands' is the novelty now." She paused, studying Meg with loving, intelligent eyes. "It's what's standing in your way," she said decisively. "You're afraid that if you're not Meg McKettrick anymore, you'll lose some part of your identity, and have to get to know yourself as a new person."

Meg realized that she *was* a new person—though of course still herself in the most fundamental ways. She was a wife now, a mother-figure as well as a sister to Carly. When the baby came, there would be yet another new level to who she was.

"I've been hiding behind the McKettrick name," she mused, more to herself than Eve.

"It's a fine name," Eve said. "We take a lot of pride in it—maybe too much, sometimes."

"Would *you* take your husband's name, if you remarried?" Meg ventured.

Eve thought about her answer before shaking her head from side to side. "No," she said. "I don't think so. I've been a McKettrick for so long, I wouldn't know how to be anything else."

Meg smiled. "And you don't want me to follow in your footsteps?"

"I want you to be *happy*. Don't stand on the bank shivering, Meg. *Jump in. Get wet.*"

"Were *you* happy, Mom?" The reply to that question seemed terribly important; Meg held her breath to hear it.

"Most of the time, yes," Eve said. "When Hank took Sierra and vanished, I was shattered. I don't think I could have gone on if it hadn't been for you. Though I realize it probably didn't seem that way to you, that you were my main reason for living, you and the hope of getting Sierra back. I'm so sorry, Meg, for coming apart at the seams the way I did. For not being there for you."

"I've never resented that, Mom. As young as I was, I knew you loved me, and that the things that were happening didn't change that for a moment. Besides, I had Angus."

The clock on the mantelpiece ticked ponderously, marking off the hours, the minutes, the seconds, as it had been doing for over a hundred years. It had ticked and tocked through the lives of Holt and Lorelei and their children, and the generations to follow.

The sound reminded Meg of something she'd always known, at least unconsciously. Life seemed long, but it was finite, too. One day, some future McKettrick would sit listening to that same clock, and Meg herself would be a memory. An ancestor in a photo.

"Gotta go pick Carly up at school," she said, standing up.

Time to find Brad, she added silently, *and introduce him to his wife.*

"Hello," I'll say, *as if we're meeting for the first time. "My name is Meg O'Ballivan."*

CHAPTER FIFTEEN

THAT LATE MARCH DAY WAS blustery and cold, but there was a fresh, piney tinge to the air. Brad, Meg and Carly stood watching from a short distance as Olivia squared her shoulders, walked to the far gate, sprung the latch and opened the way for Ransom to go.

A part of Meg hoped he'd choose to stay, but it wasn't to be.

Ransom approached the path to freedom cautiously at first, the mares straggling behind him, still shaggy with their winter coats.

When the great stallion drew abreast of Olivia, he paused, nickered and tossed his magnificent head once, as if to bid her goodbye. Tears slipped down Olivia's cheeks, and she made no attempt to wipe them away. She'd arrived during breakfast that morning and said Ransom had told her it was time.

Meg, who had after all seen a ghost from childhood, didn't question her sister-in-law's ability to communicate with animals. Even Brad, quietly skeptical about such things, couldn't write it all off to coincidence.

Carly, her own face wet, leaned into Brad a little. Meg sniffled, trying to be brave and philosophical.

He put one arm around her shoulders and one around Carly's. Glancing up at him, Meg didn't see the sorrow she and Carly and Olivia were feeling, but an expression of almost transported wonder and awe.

Ransom walked through the gate, turned a little way beyond and reared onto his hind legs, a startlingly beautiful sight against the early-spring sky, summoning his mares with a loud whinny.

"I guess being in a couple of movie scenes went to his head," Brad joked, a rasp in his voice. "He thinks he's Flicka." The filming was over now, and things were settling down on the ranch, and around town. Local attention had turned to the new animal shelter, now under construction just off Main Street.

Meg's throat was so clogged with emotion, she couldn't speak. She rested her head against Brad's shoulder and watched, riveted, as Ransom shot off across the meadow, headed back up the mountain.

The mares followed, tails high.

Olivia watched them out of sight. Then, with a visible sigh and another squaring of her shoulders, she slowly closed the gate.

Meg started toward her, but Brad caught hold of her hand and held her back.

Olivia passed them by as if they were invisible, climbed agilely over the inside fence, and moved toward her perennially dusty Suburban.

"She'll be all right," Brad assured Meg quietly, watching his sister go.

Together, Brad, Carly and Meg returned to the house, saying little.

Life went on. Willie needed to go out. The phone was ringing. The fax machine in Brad's study was spewing paper.

Business as usual, Meg thought, quietly happy, despite her sadness over the departure of Ransom and the mares. She knew, as Brad did, and certainly Olivia, that they might never see those horses again.

"I don't suppose I could stay home from school, just for today?" Carly ventured, as Brad answered the phone and Meg started a fresh pot of coffee.

Outside, the toot of a horn announced the arrival of the school bus, and Brad cocked a thumb in that direction and gave Carly a mock stern look.

She sighed dramatically, still angling for an Oscar, as Brad had once observed, but grabbed up her backpack and left the house.

"No, Phil," Brad said into the telephone receiver, "I'm *still* not doing that gig in Vegas. I don't *care* how good the buzz is about the movie—"

Meg smiled.

Brad rolled his eyes, listening. "I am so not over the way you stuck me with Cynthia for a leading lady," he went on. "You owe me for that one, big-time."

When the call was over, though, Brad found his guitar and settled into a chair in the living room, looking out over the land, playing soft thoughtful chords.

Meg knew, without being told, that he was writing a new song. She loved listening to him, loved being his wife. While he was still adamant about not doing concert tours, they'd been drawing up plans for weeks for a recording studio to be constructed out behind the house. Brad O'Ballivan was filled with music, and he had to have some outlet for it.

He didn't seem to long for the old life, though. First and foremost, he was a family man. He and Meg had legally adopted Carly, though he was still Brad to her, and Ted would always be Dad. He looked forward to the baby's birth as much as Meg did, and had even gone so far as to have the first sonogram framed.

Their son, McKettrick "Mac" O'Ballivan, was strong

and sturdy within Meg's womb. He was due on the Fourth of July.

Meg paused by Brad's chair, bent to kiss the top of his head.

He looked up at her, grinned and went on strumming and murmuring lyrics.

When a knock came at the front door, Willie growled halfheartedly but didn't get up from his favorite lounging place, the thick rug in front of the fire.

Meg went to answer, and felt a strange shock of recognition as she gazed into the face of a stranger, somewhere in his midthirties.

His hair was dark, and so were his eyes, and yet he bore a striking resemblance to Jesse. Dressed casually in clean, good-quality Western clothes, he took off his hat and smiled, and only then did Meg remember Angus's prediction.

One of them's about to land on your doorstep, he'd said.

"Meg McKettrick?" the man asked, showing white teeth as he smiled.

"Meg O'Ballivan," she clarified. Brad was standing behind her now, clearly curious.

"My name is Logan Creed," said the cowboy. "And I believe you and I are kissin' cousins."

* * * * *

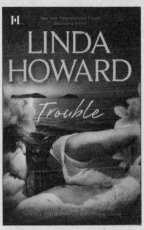

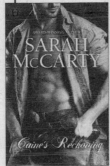

REQUEST YOUR
FREE BOOKS!

2 FREE NOVELS
FROM THE ROMANCE COLLECTION
PLUS 2 FREE GIFTS!

YES! Please send me 2 FREE novels from the Romance Collection and my 2 FREE gifts (gifts are worth about $10). After receiving them, if I don't wish to receive any more books, I can return the shipping statement marked "cancel." If I don't cancel, I will receive 4 brand-new novels every month and be billed just $5.74 per book in the U.S. or $6.24 per book in Canada. That's a saving of at least 28% off the cover price. It's quite a bargain! Shipping and handling is just 50¢ per book in the U.S. and 75¢ per book in Canada.* I understand that accepting the 2 free books and gifts places me under no obligation to buy anything. I can always return a shipment and cancel at any time. Even if I never buy another book, the two free books and gifts are mine to keep forever.

194/394 MDN FDC5

Name	(PLEASE PRINT)
Address	Apt. #
City	State/Prov.	Zip/Postal Code

Signature (if under 18, a parent or guardian must sign)

Mail to the **Reader Service:**
IN U.S.A.: P.O. Box 1867, Buffalo, NY 14240-1867
IN CANADA: P.O. Box 609, Fort Erie, Ontario L2A 5X3

Not valid for current subscribers to the Romance Collection
or the Romance/Suspense Collection.

**Want to try two free books from another line?
Call 1-800-873-8635 or visit www.ReaderService.com.**

* Terms and prices subject to change without notice. Prices do not include applicable taxes. Sales tax applicable in N.Y. Canadian residents will be charged applicable taxes. Offer not valid in Quebec. This offer is limited to one order per household. All orders subject to credit approval. Credit or debit balances in a customer's account(s) may be offset by any other outstanding balance owed by or to the customer. Please allow 4 to 6 weeks for delivery. Offer available while quantities last.

Your Privacy—The Reader Service is committed to protecting your privacy. Our Privacy Policy is available online at www.ReaderService.com or upon request from the Reader Service.

We make a portion of our mailing list available to reputable third parties that offer products we believe may interest you. If you prefer that we not exchange your name with third parties, or if you wish to clarify or modify your communication preferences, please visit us at www.ReaderService.com/consumerschoice or write to us at Reader Service Preference Service, P.O. Box 9062, Buffalo, NY 14269. Include your complete name and address.

MROM11

  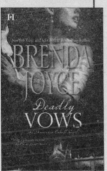

LINDA LAEL MILLER

77446	McKETTRICKS OF TEXAS: AUSTIN	___ $7.99 U.S.	___ $9.99 CAN.
77441	McKETTRICKS OF TEXAS: GARRETT	___ $7.99 U.S.	___ $9.99 CAN.
77436	McKETTRICKS OF TEXAS: TATE	___ $7.99 U.S.	___ $9.99 CAN.
77364	MONTANA CREEDS: TYLER	___ $7.99 U.S.	___ $7.99 CAN.
77358	MONTANA CREEDS: DYLAN	___ $7.99 U.S.	___ $7.99 CAN.
77561	MONTANA CREEDS: LOGAN	___ $7.99 U.S.	___ $9.99 CAN.
77388	THE BRIDEGROOM	___ $7.99 U.S.	___ $8.99 CAN.
77330	THE RUSTLER	___ $7.99 U.S.	___ $7.99 CAN.
77296	A WANTED MAN	___ $7.99 U.S.	___ $7.99 CAN.
77198	THE MAN FROM STONE CREEK	___ $7.99 U.S.	___ $9.50 CAN.
77256	DEADLY DECEPTIONS	___ $7.99 U.S.	___ $9.50 CAN.
77200	DEADLY GAMBLE	___ $7.99 U.S.	___ $9.50 CAN.
77194	McKETTRICK'S HEART	___ $7.99 U.S.	___ $9.50 CAN.
77563	McKETTRICK'S PRIDE	___ $7.99 U.S.	___ $9.99 CAN.
77562	McKETTRICK'S LUCK	___ $7.99 U.S.	___ $9.99 CAN.

(limited quantities available)

TOTAL AMOUNT	$ _____
POSTAGE & HANDLING	$ _____
($1.00 FOR 1 BOOK, 50¢ for each additional)	
APPLICABLE TAXES*	$ _____
TOTAL PAYABLE	$ _____

(check or money order—please do not send cash)

To order, complete this form and send it, along with a check or money order for the total above, payable to HQN Books, to: **In the U.S.:** 3010 Walden Avenue, P.O. Box 9077, Buffalo, NY 14269-9077; **In Canada:** P.O. Box 636, Fort Erie, Ontario, L2A 5X3.

Name: _____

Address: _____ City: _____

State/Prov.: _____ Zip/Postal Code: _____

Account Number (if applicable): _____

075 CSAS

*New York residents remit applicable sales taxes.
*Canadian residents remit applicable GST and provincial taxes.

HQN™

We *are* romance™

www.HQNBooks.com

PHLLM1110BL